ACROSS A VAST AND CHALLENGING CONTINENT—A NOVEL OF COURAGEOUS LOVE!

Lovely, eighteen-year-old Emerald Regan was brought up in the finest Southern finishing schools, perfectly groomed for life on her family's Baton Rouge plantation. Then her slave heritage was exposed and she faced the unbridled lust of a man who would take her body, but never give her his name.

Forced to flee west, in St. Louis she joined a wagon train and met an undreamed of lover, the mysterious mountain guide, Mace Bridgeman. Theirs was a great love, until she met Wolf Dreamer . . .

Wolf Dreamer, Sioux medicine man, who initiated her into his sensual world of drugs and magic—but whose passions could never keep her from the love that tore at her heart, and the triumphant destiny that awaited her in the beautiful Sierra Mountains.

EMERALD FIRE

JULIA GRICE

AVON
PUBLISHERS OF BARD, CAMELOT AND DISCUS BOOKS

EMERALD FIRE is an original publication of Avon Books.
This work has never before appeared in book form.

AVON BOOKS
A division of
The Hearst Corporation
959 Eighth Avenue
New York, New York 10019

Copyright © 1978 by Julia Grice
Published by arrangement with the author.
Library of Congress Catalog Card Number: 78-57624
ISBN: 0-380-38596-1

For Michael and Andy. For my parents, Jean and Will Haughey, and for all the others I love.

They must travel two thousand miles, and they must do this within the limits of a single summer and fall. They could not carry sufficient supplies of food to last over till spring and they would have little chance of surviving through the winter on any local supplies of game.

—George R. Stewart, in *The California Trail*

Prologue

THE afternoon sun was hot and yellow; the smell of the dried grasses and dust was pungent.

Wolf Dreamer pulled his horse up at the top of a low rise and sat looking off to the east. It was the Moon of Strawberries. Soon, he thought, the plains would freshen and turn green with millions of blades of new grass. There would be plenty of grazing for the horses and for the buffalo. More grass than any of his people could use, or ever hope to use.

A breeze touched the folds of his tanned-hide robe, decorated with painted designs and horizontal bands of quilling. It rippled across his shoulder-length black hair, its warmth a promise of hot weather to come. Squinting against the sun, Wolf Dreamer stared to the east, where a cloud of dust gathered at the base of a rise.

His lean body tensed. Like a chimera, a mirage, a wagon train emerged over the curve of land. It was a long, dusty line of eight wagons, pulled by slowly plodding oxen. The white men's wagons. Another dust cloud rose behind them on the horizon—a herd of spare oxen and horses.

A small boy galloped on a pony, his seat as easy and light as that of any Sioux youth. A man rode ahead of the train. He was tall, his body well made, his back straight, proud. His mouth smiled slightly, and something about him made Wolf Dreamer imagine a war club, stout and sturdy.

A girl walked beside one of the wagons, her blue skirt swaying like a flower. Without seeing them, Wolf Dreamer knew that her eyes were green, like grasses in spring.

He knew, too, that Iya, god of all evil, rode with this wagon train, with these white men. And, somehow, his own destiny lay with the wagon train as well.

Death waited for the girl, for himself, too. Iya would slay him; of the girl he was not sure.

This was Wolf Dreamer's vision.

Chapter One

❦ ❧

Baton Rouge, Louisiana, 1847

WELL, and what pretty little sweeting do we have here?"

The male voice—deep, lazy, and filled with arrogance—floated toward Emerald Regan, almost as if it were part of her thoughts.

It was April in Baton Rouge, and the air was heavy with the smell of flowers and grasses and wet earth. Emerald sat on the wooden slatted swing on the upper veranda of her uncle's big plantation house at Hundred Oaks. She had fled here to escape the dull chatter of the guests who had come to attend funeral services for her Uncle Calvin.

Her cold and businesslike uncle had been her guardian since she had been orphaned at nine. Emerald knew she was expected to mourn—and of course she did, she assured herself hastily. She was very grateful for the home she had enjoyed all of these years, and would miss her uncle.

Still . . . today was an azure spring day, with a clear, sunny sky that made your heart ache. Today was a day for life, for living and doing, not for a death.

"Don't you have a voice? Or do you ignore me deliberately?" The male voice prodded her again, a note of unpleasantness creeping into it.

Emerald jumped and turned. A tall man stood at the end of the veranda, near the delicately carved white railing. His face was in shadow.

"Oh! I didn't know anyone was . . ." Hurriedly she composed herself into a more ladylike position. She felt a flush of embarrassment that a man could catch her lounging, her legs apart and her back arched against the swing.

The man, whoever he was, didn't introduce himself. He stepped closer, and she could see that he was solidly built, with broad, formidable shoulders under his black coat. His face was heavy, with a full, thrusting jaw. His eyes were fixed on her curiously.

"Who are you?" he said. "Are you one of my sisters' friends? And why aren't you with the others? We're almost ready to leave for the church."

She flushed. "I—I wanted to be alone for a bit. And it's so hot in the drawing room. Aunt Anna said I could—"

"Aunt Anna? Don't tell me that you're Emerald! Emerald Regan! Why, of course." He eyed her speculatively. "Those green eyes and that black, black hair —who else could you be? My God, I'd never have recognized you now, though."

She stared at him, wondering why she felt a faint prickle of unease. Who was he? Surely she had never before seen this man, with his thick-built body. Or— had she?

Then, suddenly, she remembered. In the flurry of her uncle's last illness, there had been something said about locating his older son, Anton. Anton deLane had run away North nine years ago, six months after the little girl Emerald had arrived at Hundred Oaks.

"Oh—you're Anton, aren't you?" she said. "Aunt said they were trying to locate you. They even hired a detective agency to try to find you."

The man grimaced unpleasantly. "Well, they found me. I got here about an hour ago. And just in time, I'd say. The plantation looks as if it's done well. Although it's no thanks to me, is it?"

"I'm glad you did manage to get here in time for the funeral," Emerald said politely.

Anton! She remembered Anton as a boy of sixteen, tall, gangly, sullen, with eruptions of acne on his cheeks. Once, wandering out to see a litter of kittens that had been born in the stables, she had been startled to see movements back in the shadows. There were low cries, heavy breathing. Then Anton's voice, telling her to get away, little prying bitch, if she knew what was good for her. . . .

Hadn't there been a slave girl, the beautiful Lucinda, later sold off the plantation? And there had been things whispered in the slave quarters and in the nursery. Strange, dark things, the meaning of which the child Emerald could not guess.

For one of these crimes, his father had whipped Anton one windy February night. And the next day he was gone.

Now, abruptly, she became conscious that Anton was looking at her slowly, up and down, seeing her full breasts, her narrowly curved waist, her rounded hips beneath the black silk.

"Yes," Anton said. "You've changed a bit since last I saw you, Emerald. You were a little girl when I left, all skinny and wild and putting your nose into places where you shouldn't. And now look at you. Your hair up and your—" He drew in his breath quickly. "Emerald. God, but that name is appropriate

5

for you. Your eyes are exactly like two green gem stones. Proud and flashing and full of fire."

She felt the color flood to her cheeks. She jumped off the swing, wanting only to get away from this man and his too-feverish words.

He took her arm. He held her lightly, but through the cloth of her sleeve she could feel his strength.

"We have a few minutes," he said. "Sit down again, Emerald. We can get to know each other. After all, I haven't seen you in nine years, is it? In that time, you've become a woman, Emerald. A ripe woman."

She lifted her chin. *Ripe.* She'd never heard any man talk like this before. So bold and sure of himself, and yet contemptuous, too. As if underneath the compliments he really despised her.

"Why, what's wrong, Emerald?" he was asking. "You have a stubborn little jaw, don't you? Don't you like me?"

"I don't know you well enough to like you," she said hurriedly. "I'm upset about Uncle's death, of course. He'd been ill for months with consumption. But we didn't think he was going to die as suddenly as he did. He and Aunt Anna have been extremely kind to me."

"Kind?" Anton's lips twisted slightly. "Yes, they certainly have been. I remember the day you arrived here. A little orphan from the territories, both your parents killed by cholera. Big green eyes, a mop of curly black hair, wearing your ragged linsey-woolsey dress and clutching a dirty doll in one hand and a box of paints in the other. Even then you had your paints and pencils, didn't you? Drawing pictures of everyone on the plantation, always making people look worse than they really were . . ."

Yes, painting had always been her talent, a skill as natural as breathing. With a few quick pencil strokes,

6

she could recreate a face or a figure. She could capture Aunt Anna as she bent over her embroidery, or, with a few more artful lines, her cousin Charmaine would suddenly appear on paper, lively and almost real.

One day she had drawn Anton, had pictured him pouting and scowling as usual. But Anton, seeing the sketch, had turned pale. He had taken the sketch, balled it up, and thrown it in her face. Then he had slapped her on the cheek.

"Never draw me again, ever," he had hissed at her. "You ugly creature. You're ugly, Emerald. Do you hear that? Ugly!"

She had grown up remembering that. *Ugly*. And now, nine years later, Anton was back.

She pulled herself back to reality, hearing Anton telling her about Chicago, where he had lived. He had taken a job on the docks there, he said, loading lumber schooners. Then he had left that work and become a dentist's apprentice. He could pull teeth very quickly, he told her, and without much pain. He had had many customers among the dock workers. Then he was approached by the detective, who told him that his father was trying to trace him.

"I didn't want to come back. But I figured there might be some money in it. Was I ever surprised to find out that the old man was dead."

He talked quickly, explosively, his accent almost Northern. Emerald watched him, trying to see in the heavy, sensual face any trace of the boy she had once sketched.

The eyes, she thought. They were still sullen, and yet shrewd. He kept glancing at her breasts. She shivered, edging away from him to the end of the swing.

Tensely she answered his questions. Yes, she was

7

eighteen now, and had completed Miss Frannie Wyland's Finishing School, where she had learned to speak
French, do mathematics, dance, play the harp, and do
needlework, both embroidery and petit point. She
could paint on china and weave locks of hair into
brooches. Her sketching, however, had surpassed the
teaching abilities of Miss Frannie, who didn't quite
approve of the bold lines of her drawings. Yes, she
had had suitors. She had traveled, too, once as far
away as Biloxi, Mississippi.

"You are very accomplished, aren't you?" he asked
mockingly. "All those very useful skills! Painting!
Petit point! Won't you make someone a wonderful
wife!"

She was angry. He was a disconcerting, rude man,
who filled her mind with bad memories. And she simply didn't want to be near him anymore. She stood up.

"I was very lucky to have been given any education
at all," she told him coldly. "And now I think I will
go back to the drawing room. Aunt Anna needs me."

She slipped past Anton and into the house.

That evening, after the funeral guests had left, the
family gathered in the library for the reading of the
will. The library always smelled of books and old cigar
smoke. Aunt Anna, very thin now, but with a remnant
of red-haired beauty, sat rigidly in a chair. The four
deLane daughters, ranging in age from Cora, six, to
Charmaine, seventeen, sat in a row on the yellow
brocade couch. They all had the deLane look—the
blue eyes and narrow faces, the blood surging beneath
the fair, transparent skin.

Only Anton was different. Tall, thick, heavy, he
lounged near the big pecan-wood desk, his legs in their

black boots crossed jauntily. Periodically he glanced at Emerald, as if he could not stop looking at her.

She shifted in her chair, flushing. But no one seemed to notice.

Jeremy Judson, the family lawyer, a bony man with a bald skull fringed by wispy brown hair, sat at Uncle Calvin's desk. In his hand he held a sheaf of papers. He glanced at his watch and cleared his throat.

"Is everyone here? Are we ready to begin?"

Before Anna could reply, Anton said, "Yes, yes, let's get on with it."

The lawyer looked coldly at Anton. "Very well, then. If you're all ready." He looked down at the papers, shifted them, and began to read aloud in a flat monotone.

"Whereas I declare myself to be of sound mind and judgment . . ."

The words, dry as dead leaves, seemed to rustle past Emerald's ears. She stared out of the window at Aunt Anna's ordered garden, with its twin weeping willows, their branches carefully trimmed to exactly three feet above the ground.

There would be nothing for her, of course. She was only a poor relation, a girl dutifully provided with a home and a ladylike upbringing. She couldn't reasonably expect more.

"I hereby devise and bequeath to my wife, Anna Robeland deLane, one-half of my plantation, Hundred Oaks, and all of the properties and chattels thereof."

The girls stirred, looked at each other. Anna stared straight ahead, her features pale. Anton's face flushed red. "But my share!" he protested. "What about me? I thought—"

"I'm coming to that," the lawyer said. "Be patient,

9

please, Mr. deLane. I assure you, you haven't been neglected."

He read on. The other half of Hundred Oaks was to be split equally among the four girls and Anton. Anton's share, however, was contingent upon his remaining to manage the plantation.

"What!" Anton, who had been half-leaning against the desk, jumped to his feet. "He— There must be a mistake! Why, I'll have to stay here. I'll have to run this place like—like any common overseer! I—"

"It was his express wish, Mr. deLane, that you stay home with your mother and do some honorable work for a change," the lawyer said dryly. "If you do not choose to act as manager, you will lose all rights to your share of the estate."

Anton's fists were clenched, and for an instant Emerald thought he was going to punch the lawyer. Slowly his hands relaxed, although the redness of his face did not subside.

"There is more, if you don't mind," Judson said over the buzz of talk that had risen. "I would like to read *all* of the will, if you don't mind. Then we can discuss the ramifications."

There was other property, Emerald learned. A half-share in a cotton-ginning mill. Some jewels that had belonged to Uncle Calvin's mother. Most of these went to the sisters, save for a small emerald pendant that was to go to "Emerald Regan, daughter of my brother Robert deLane and the woman Ophelia, both deceased."

A pendant for herself! And made of the stone after which she was named. For a moment Emerald felt overwhelmed, as if a hand had reached out from the grave and touched her benevolently.

Then she frowned in puzzlement. Odd—he had called her father Robert deLane instead of Robert Regan. And he had referred to her mother as *the woman Ophelia,* when her mother's name had been Mary.

A mistake, of course, she decided quickly. But she noticed that Aunt Anna was avoiding her glance. And Anton was looking at her strangely.

Within an hour, their business was done. Anna, her eyes red, went upstairs, speaking to no one. Emerald, her thoughts in a turmoil, went directly to the room she shared with Charmaine. Thankfully, she saw that her cousin was elsewhere. She sank down on a small walnut chair and, without thinking, reached for her pencil and her sketchbook.

Balancing the pad across her knees, she began to draw. Almost within seconds, Anton's face appeared on the paper, distorted, as she had seen it in the study, his mouth twisted with rage.

So, she thought. Anton would be living at Hundred Oaks. She remembered the way his eyes had raked over her. He would be master here. Master of two hundred slaves and his four sisters and his mother. Master of herself as well.

She shuddered, and crumpled the sheet of paper in her hands.

That night, Emerald had uneasy, turbulent dreams. Dreams in which Anton deLane chased her beneath the weeping willow trees, his face congested with rage and desire. Dreams in which her mother, Mary Regan, appeared, her face blurred. And in the dream her mother was weeping, weeping. . . .

She awoke covered with perspiration, feeling very

11

frightened and alone. That odd mix-up of names at the reading of the will—surely it had been only a mistake, a clerical error. But she went downstairs for breakfast with a tight feeling in her throat.

To her relief, Anton was not in the paneled dining room, and Anna explained that he had spent a late night going through his father's papers, and would breakfast in his room. Anna herself looked pale and unwell this morning, her skin waxy against the dull black of her mourning costume. Even the deLane girls were subdued.

"Aunt," Emerald began, after the meal was over and the cousins had left. "Aunt, there is something I wanted to ask you about the reading of the will. My—my mother's name was not read correctly. Surely a mistake must have been made?"

"Mistake?" Anna put a hand wearily to her forehead. "Oh, Emerald, I can't talk about it now, my head aches so. Perhaps later . . . when I feel better, when I've had a chance to rest. . . ." Again her eyes avoided her niece's.

"Very well, Aunt," Emerald said slowly. "As you wish. We'll talk later, then."

The day stretched ahead of her, long and empty. She decided to take her sketchbook and walk about the plantation, drawing the slaves at their work. It was a pleasure of hers to catch the image of a wiry, muscular body bending to the hoe or straining over the bellows in the blacksmith shed.

But she no longer showed these sketches to anybody. Uncle Calvin had grown curiously angry when he had seen one, and Anna had looked uncomfortable. As for the girls, they only giggled and asked her why she didn't want to draw flowers or birds. Those were far prettier, weren't they?

She approached the neat row of log slave cabins, each with its little kitchen garden, overhung by huge live oaks draped with gray Spanish moss. At the end of the row was the nursery cabin, presided over by old Audrey. Two toddlers were playing with cornhusk dolls beside the door.

"Emerald! Emerald! I want to talk to you!"

The voice came from behind her. She turned to see Anton, dressed in a brown broadcloth suit, defiantly out of mourning. He strode toward her, his arms swinging easily. He's almost good-looking, she thought. It's the sullen look that spoils his face.

"Yes?" She stopped, shifting the sketchbook under her arm.

"What are you doing out here?" he demanded. "The slave cabins are no place for a woman."

"I came out here to sketch."

"To draw slaves?" He threw back his head and laughed. "What would you want to draw them for?"

She didn't answer.

"I said I wanted to talk to you," Anton repeated after a moment. His full mouth twisted. Unwillingly, she followed him to a big live oak that shaded the slaves' well.

"Oh, go ahead, then. Talk if you must," she said. Anger made her stare directly back at him.

"I never liked you, you know," he began abruptly.

"I realize that."

"I think my mother loved you more than the rest of us put together. We had to be nice to you, she said. Let you use our things and live in our house. Let you go around with your dirty little sketch pads . . ."

He looked at the book she held, and she instinctively stepped back. "We had to let you spy on us, and creep around, and tattle on us. . . ."

"I never tattled on you, Anton deLane!"

"Never? Ha, I don't believe you. I often wondered about that time my father whipped me. . . ."

"That wasn't my fault—" she began.

"Yes, you were always the center of things, weren't you? But you didn't know they fought over you. Oh, yes, I heard them one night—quarreling and shouting they were. She wanted to keep you. He didn't."

"Oh. I—" She faltered.

She felt the hot blood in her face as she remembered. Anna clasping her close and stroking her travel-matted hair. Uncle Calvin had been watching coldly. *Someday, Anna, you'll regret doing this,* he had said. *News will get out. It'll come back to haunt you.* She hadn't understood at the time, and hadn't wanted to.

"Yes, there's so much you don't know, my little Miss Emerald. You've grown up, haven't you? Filled out like a woman. . . ."

"Of course I've grown up," she told him quickly. "I was eighteen last month. One of these days, if anyone asks me, I'll probably be marrying."

"Marry! I doubt it." Again Anton laughed. It was an unpleasant sound. "Not after what I found in Father's papers last night. Since you like drawing black faces so much, I suggest that you take that sketchbook back to the house. Go and stand in front of a mirror. See what kind of a nigger you'll find there."

He looked at her, his expression curiously like that of the malevolent boy she remembered. Then he turned with a scrape of his boot heel and strode away toward the house.

Stand in front of a mirror. See what kind of a nigger you'll find there.

Emerald stood, stunned, the warm, scented day whirling about her.

No. She drew in a sharp breath. No. He couldn't possibly have meant. . . .

"Anton!" she screamed. "Come back here! What do you mean? What are you saying?" She chased after him, the full flounces of her mourning dress nearly tripping her.

"I found it in my father's papers last night," he told her, turning. "The truth about you. And your mother."

Daughter of my brother Robert deLane and the woman Ophelia.

"But my mother wasn't named Ophelia!" she burst out. "I'm sure of it. Her name was Mary."

"Whatever name she went by, it doesn't matter. She belonged to the plantation. You're nothing but a little nigger gal. You've got white skin and green eyes, but that doesn't make any difference. You're still the child of a Hundred Oaks slave. *My* slave."

She ran into the house, her slippers skidding, the folds of her black dress flying, until she reached her own bedroom and the oval mirror over the bureau.

Stand in front of a mirror. . . .

It was all a mistake, she told herself wildly. It had to be! Anton had hated her ever since she had first come to Hundred Oaks, had always been jealous of her.

But the words, the ugly words, beat at her like fists.

She looked carefully in the mirror. Oval face with a firm chin and full, curved lips. A pretty nose, uptilted and saucy. Black, curly hair. And wide, changeable

15

green eyes, sometimes emerald-green, at other times the gray-green of cane fields on a misty day.

She leaned closer, inspecting herself savagely. Her skin was fresh and clear, her cheeks flushed from the exertion of running on a warm day. She couldn't see any trace of a dark tint. Even her black hair, thick with tumbled curls, seemed uniquely her own. Not like anyone else at all, and certainly not like the hair of the black women on the plantation.

Abruptly she turned away from the glass. She didn't understand. She was as white as Anton was. Her mother, too, had been white. Her childhood memories were dim, but she was sure of that.

And yet her cousin had spoken with the certainty of truth. There had been something in Uncle Calvin's papers, he said. What? She thought of the odd wording of the will. *The woman Ophelia*. That was the way slaves were referred to. The man Ajax, the wench Dicey.

She walked frantically to the window and looked down on the front lawn of the house. Calvary, the gardener, was walking across the lawn, a hoe in his hand, his black face shining with sweat. She had always liked Calvary. Was it possible?

No. Of course it wasn't true. It just wasn't! Surely Aunt Anna would be able to explain this. She would have done so this morning at breakfast if she had not had a headache.

Emerald drew a quick breath and hurried down the corridor to the door of Anna's bedroom, which was located at the far end of the long bedroom wing. She hesitated, then rapped at the door.

"Who is it?" her aunt called.

"It's me, Emerald. Please . . . I have to talk. . . ."

There was a tiny pause. "Come in, then."

Emerald opened the door. Anna was lying on her bed with only a light-blue muslin wrapper about her thin body, her hair down around her shoulders.

Her aunt had been a beauty in her girlhood, a belle who had many admirers, some of them riding many miles to court her. But now, five children and three miscarriages later, the firm flesh had begun to shrink from her bones. There were hollows beneath her cheeks, and her arms seemed almost pitifully fragile. Her fine red hair was streaked with white at the temples.

"I didn't mean to disturb your rest, but I—I had to see you." Now that she was here, in her aunt's perfumed and precise bedroom, Emerald didn't know what to say. Am I black? Am I a slave? The words seemed too horrible to say.

"You're upset, aren't you, Emerald," Anna said at last, her voice low. "Is it about the will?"

"Yes. I—" Suddenly the words came in a rush. "Oh, Aunt, Anton has just said the most terrible things to me. The most terrible things! He said he was going through Uncle's papers and he found something about me. Something—well, something saying that my mother was a slave."

She stepped closer to Anna's bed. "It's not true, is it?" she said beseechingly. "Anton was lying, wasn't he? Why would he say such a thing to me, Aunt Anna?"

There was a long silence. Anna's eyes remained fixed on her long white fingers, covered with rings. Emerald began to feel her heart constrict.

"It *isn't* true, is it?"

Anna lifted her eyes. There was pity in them.

17

"Emerald," she said at last. "There are so many things I should tell you. I—I did something with your life that perhaps I should not have done. Perhaps I was wrong to—to love you as I did, to protect you against all reason and all better sense. But you were such a vulnerable little girl. You'd been so hurt. You needed a mother."

, Completely unaware of what she was doing, Emerald sank down on a low gros point footstool.

"You see, Emerald, I loved your father. He was— Calvin's brother. He lived here, at Hundred Oaks. He was tall and high-spirited, twelve years older than I was, full of life. But, of course, I wasn't free, I was married to Calvin." The pale hands fluttered.

"One day your father—found someone. Someone else."

"My mother," Emerald said through dry lips.

"Yes. She was a slave here at Hundred Oaks, and she was beautiful, Emerald. Really lovely. She was an octoroon woman bought at a fantastically high price to serve as a skilled lady's maid to Calvin's mother."

"But *my* mother—surely she wasn't—" Frantically Emerald tried to remember. Yes, her mother's hair had been black. But weren't her eyes blue?

"Your father was a good man, and he fell in love with her," Anna went on. "And when she was going to have his child, he couldn't bear the thought that his child—who, of course, would look white—would be born a slave. So one night the two of them just disappeared. Went away to the territories, it was said. To the West. We never saw them again."

"Oh." Emerald thought of the woman who had been her mother. Of the soft, lilting, warm voice. The arms that could hold and soothe. *Mary Carstairs!* she thought suddenly. That was her mother's maiden name!

But her aunt put up a slim, restraining hand.

"Then one day, Emerald, the *Mississippi Queen* docked, and there was a little girl aboard. She was you. Incredibly dirty, you were. I don't think you'd bathed in all the days of your journey. But you had a bit of luggage—a few clothes and your doll and some paints. And you carried a letter with you, written by a settler who found you hiding under the wagon bed after your parents had died. He knew you had relatives here in Baton Rouge named deLane, no more."

"So you took me, and you reared me," Emerald said shakily.

"Yes. I didn't tell anyone who you really were. Your parents had taken the name of Regan, so I used that. I told them you were the child of distant relatives of mine, from Ohio. That part, at least, was true enough. But Calvin said it wouldn't work. He said one day the truth would come out."

Emerald remembered the arguments heard in her childhood, and not understood. "But I'm sure my mother's name was Mary Carstairs, not Ophelia. And she was white. I'm sure she was. Oh, Aunt, I *know* she was white."

But Anna seemed not to hear her. She was openly weeping now, her face buried in her hands. "I'm sorry, Emerald. I shouldn't have done what I did. Shouldn't have given you this sort of life. But I—I wanted you. I—I loved you from the minute I saw you."

Emerald flung herself into her aunt's arms.

Chapter Two

✖⊱⊰✖

EMERALD went down to supper that night feeling as if she were moving in a trance. Anna, making an obvious effort, had come downstairs to preside at the table. Her firm, light voice guided the talk away from funerals and into more pleasant topics. Baby Cora told them about a frog she had found. Cynthia, who was twelve, talked about her new pony. The long table seemed almost as usual.

Only Emerald and Anton were quiet. Anton ate sullenly, his glance alternately avoiding Emerald's and raking over her, so that she flushed crimson. What was going to happen to her with Anton in charge of the plantation?

"Against my will and against my advice," Anna had told her earlier, "Calvin placed Anton in charge of Hundred Oaks. I told him the boy probably hadn't changed, but he insisted. He wanted a male heir."

"And now he has one," Emerald said bitterly.

"Yes." Anna was thoughtful. "But I'll talk to him, Emerald. I'll try to make him see what an injustice he's done you."

But Emerald didn't know if her aunt had talked to Anton yet. She sat at her place, pretending to eat, her stomach balled into a hard knot of tension.

You've got white skin and green eyes, but that doesn't make any difference. You're still the child of a Hundred Oaks slave. My slave.

Slave.

With just one word, Anton could wreck her life at Hundred Oaks. Here in the South there was a high iron fence separating the two races, black and white. Anyone with a drop of black blood was considered all black.

If Anton spoke, she could never marry any of the young planters' sons who came courting. Anton could bar her even from the love and company of her young cousins.

She had been reared as a gentle, well-bred Southern girl, educated as well as any other woman of quality in Baton Rouge. She didn't belong with the slaves.

But now, according to Anton, she didn't belong with the white people, either.

Slave . . . slave . . .

It was all a nightmare.

"Come into the library," Anton ordered her after supper. He spoke sharply, as if he were issuing orders to a servant. Except that no one at Hundred Oaks ever spoke to the servants in quite that hard, Northern tone of voice.

Emerald hesitated. She could see her cousin Charmaine gesturing to her. There was a book, *The Murders in the Rue Morgue,* by a wonderful man named Edgar Allan Poe, that she and Charmaine were reading aloud to each other.

She shook her head reluctantly.

"Come on, Emerald," Anton said. "What are you waiting for? I said I wanted to talk with you."

"Very well."

Anton closed the library door behind them and settled himself behind his father's big desk. He did not ask her to sit down, but opened a box decorated with shells and took out a long, thick Havana cigar. With ostentatious ceremony, he trimmed the cigar, lit it, and blew smoke in her direction.

"Good cigar," he said. "My father had hundreds left—too bad he didn't live to smoke them. Well. As I said, Emerald, you've grown up, haven't you?"

He surprised her. She had expected, oh, anything, but not this casual remark about something so obvious.

"I suppose so," she said.

"You're beautiful now."

"I—"

"In fact, very beautiful. Girls like you often are. They say the high-yellow women of New Orleans and Natchez are among the loveliest women in the world. And you, Emerald, have an advantage over them. Your green eyes give you a very unusual look—for your kind."

"For my kind? What 'kind' do you mean?" she exploded.

"Why, I'm referring to your black blood, of course," Anton replied lazily.

"My blood isn't black! And my skin isn't high-yellow, either. I—I'm myself. How dare you speak to me like this?"

"I dare because I'm the master of Hundred Oaks now. I've been forced back to this godforsaken place, but I intend to get some pleasure out of it. I deserve something for staying here and working like a dog in the hot sun."

Again he looked over her body, savoring it, his eyes lingering at the neckline of her gown.

"I don't care if you have to work like a dog!" she blurted. "I just wish you would go back North where you came from, and leave us alone. None of us want you here, Anton. You'll cause my aunt nothing but grief and sorrow—"

"I'm going to take care of her plantation for her," Anton said sharply. "And shut up, will you? I've got Hundred Oaks, and I want you, too. You, as my own personal slave. And you can't deny me, not now, not with what I found out about you. I have every right to you."

"No!" she shouted. "You don't have any right at all! Why—this is insane!"

"Is it? I don't think so. I think it's very sensible. You'll be my—my mistress, shall we say? If you cooperate, I'll keep quiet about you and your tainted blood, and all can go on as before. If you refuse—"

"If I refuse, then what?"

"Why, if you don't cooperate, I'll have you chained in the slave quarters. I have that power. You'll come around fast enough then, I'll wager."

"You wouldn't!" She stared at him in horror.

"Why not?" He shrugged. "You're the child of one of Hundred Oaks' runaway slaves, aren't you? Ophelia's daughter? That makes you a slave, too, no matter who your father was."

Before she could stop herself, she had slapped him, and the smack was loud in the room. Anton's eyes glistened with rage.

"Damn you, you little slave slut! No woman slaps me and gets away with it. Now I *will* have you!"

Emerald backed away from the dangerous fury in his eyes, clinging to one straw of hope. "Aunt Anna," she said. "She'll never permit you to do this, Anton. You know she won't. She—"

"My mother won't know about this."

"She will! I'll tell her myself! You can't keep me chained up like a—an animal without her knowing."

"My mother isn't to be disturbed about this, Emerald. She's in poor health, didn't you know that? Her doctor says she has a bad heart. Any excitement, any exertion . . ."

"I don't believe you."

"She told me herself, last night in the library. She gets pains when she climbs stairs or walks too far. Do you want to run to her with your little news and kill her, Emerald?"

What Anton said was true. In her heart, Emerald knew it. Anna did look ill, and had for months. Several times Emerald had discovered her breathless and swaying upon the staircase. Now Anton's eyes were fixed upon her, filled with triumph.

She edged away from him, moving toward the study door. "I love my aunt, and I won't hurt her," she whispered through stiff lips. "But I'm not a slave, I'm not *anyone's* slave, and I never will be, no matter what you might think. And now please let me leave this room. Charmaine is expecting me to come and read a book with her. If I don't arrive, she'll start asking questions. And you don't want *that,* do you, cousin? Remember your mother's health!"

His face flamed, but he permitted her to open the door. She fled down the corridor and up the back staircase, the tears and terror and fury raging inside her.

In her room, Emerald flung herself on her bed, choking back sobs. Cora's room was next door, Uncle Calvin's old room on the other side. She couldn't let anyone hear her. They would ask questions. And what on earth could she tell them?

A slave! Anton's slave!

She couldn't even imagine what horrors that might mean. Her mind groped for understanding. Anton, in the barn with the slave girl. Whispers she had overheard among the slaves. *Lucinda, she beat up. Lucinda, she have raw, red sores around her wrists and ankles. . . .*

Emerald knew that she was ignorant about the act that took place between men and women—but then unmarried girls were. Once, after the lamps were out, she and Charmaine had whispered about it. Charmaine was of the opinion that a man put a baby in a woman's stomach. But how, neither of them knew. They did know that on the night before each girl's wedding day, Aunt Anna would tell her "what she needed to know."

But raw, red sores around Lucinda's wrists and ankles? It was hideous, all the more so because she didn't understand what it meant. Something terrible, she was sure.

She lay on the bed, her thoughts beating about in her skull like the wings of a terrified bird. At last she slept, only to be awakened when Charmaine came in, demanding to know where she had been. Charmaine had been looking everywhere for her, had Emerald completely forgotten that they had been going to read Mr. Poe's novel aloud?

Later that night, Aunt Anna came and told Emerald that she had discussed the matter of Emerald's parentage with Anton, and he had agreed not to mention the matter to anyone.

"He—he did?" Emerald said, dazed. She couldn't believe it.

"My son is a man of honor after all," her aunt said happily. "I was mistaken about him, Emerald. He knows how much I love you, and he is willing to let you live here just as before."

"But Aunt—"

"Yes, darling? Is there anything more you'd like to talk about? If not, I'd like to go to my room now. My migraine has gotten so much worse today, and I think I have a slight congestion in my chest. . . ."

"Oh, of course, Aunt. I know this has been very hard on you, with Uncle's death and all." Emerald swallowed dryly, and let her aunt go. Her husband's death had sapped most of Anna's remaining strength, and now she seemed more fragile than ever. Even without Anton's statement, Emerald would have known she was ill. No, she couldn't do anything to hurt her, ever.

Another day passed, breathless, slow, uneasy. Anton spent most of his time in the plantation office and in the fields. He had decided to retain Biggs, the white overseer, and the two of them went over accounts and inspected every portion of outbuildings, scullery, kitchens, laundry, shops, slave quarters, and fields. Anton had a fierce understanding of business, and it was possible that Hundred Oaks would prosper under him. Aunt Anna seemed to relax a bit, and told Emerald one night that she was now sure Calvin had done the right thing in bringing Anton back.

On the fourth day, at supper, Anton announced

that he was making some changes inside the house. He would move into Calvin's big bedroom, and he would put a door through to the adjoining bedroom to use as his sitting room.

Anna agreed, obviously pleased by Anton's recent behavior. She would help him select carpet and furnishings. Emerald—for it was she and Charmaine who were being displaced—would be very comfortable in the large extra bedroom over the kitchen wing. And Charmaine would have her own room, too, next to her mother's.

"No," Emerald said abruptly. "No, I don't want to change bedrooms."

She felt suddenly uneasy. Her room would be separated from the other sleeping quarters by the staircase and the linen and storage areas. She would, in effect, be sleeping in an isolated section of the house.

"But why not, darling?" Anna asked, smiling. "We'll put in new Brussels carpeting, of course. It's really a lovely room, with two big windows, and you'll have a view of the garden. And a room of your own for the first time. I don't know why we didn't do this years ago."

"We're doing it now because *I* need a sitting room," Anton said authoritatively. "And I mean to have it. Surely it won't hurt you to move your sleeping room?"

"And I've always wanted a room of my own, too!" bubbled Chairmaine. "Oh, I can't wait!"

Emerald sighed. She had been outmaneuvered as, she supposed, Anton had known she would be.

"Very well," she said shortly, concealing her dismay. "If it will make you all happy."

By the next day, all had been arranged. The new carpet had been laid in Emerald's room, the elegant

Chippendale furniture polished with beeswax until it shone. Aunt Anna had even given Emerald a beautiful embroidered coverlet for her bed, one that had been in the family for two generations.

But that night, when Emerald put away her sketchbook and climbed the stairs for bed, she noticed that the bolt lock on her door had been tampered with. It would be impossible to lock the door properly.

Outdoors, it was raining, a cozy whisper of water against the windowpanes. But neither the comforting sound of the rain nor the lovely, warm bedroom could calm her panic. The house was old, she told herself. Maybe the lock had never worked well. Perhaps—

And perhaps Anton had sent a slave up here during the day to be sure that the lock wouldn't work, a tough, realistic voice told her. This room was separated from the rest of the sleeping quarters. It would be a perfect place for a man to come to the woman he considered his private slave. . . .

Feverishly Emerald looked about the room, lit by one flickering lamp and full of the pungent smell of wick and oil. She must leave Hundred Oaks, leave this house and everything in it. Go somewhere, anywhere she would be safe from Anton and his twisted ideas.

She would pack tonight, she decided with sudden energy. Clothes, luggage, money—those would be all she would need. She would sell her emerald pendant and buy passage on a riverboat North. She would travel as far away from Hundred Oaks as paddlewheels could take her.

She crossed to the heavy wardrobe and began flinging dresses onto the bed. She would take a small trunk from the attic, pack a few clothes, and then go and say good-bye to Aunt Anna.

Anna. Emerald's hands paused on the stack of underclothing and gowns, her eyes misting with tears. A wave of homesickness flooded through her, sharp and piercing. Her aunt had been so kind, so loving. She had been all the mother a homeless girl could ever wish. How Emerald would miss her! And her young cousins, Charmaine, Cora, and the others.

But it had to be done. She couldn't stay here anymore.

Then, as she was brushing away her tears, Emerald heard a creak in the corridor.

She froze, still clutching a froth of lace-trimmed petticoats. It was only the house settling, she told herself frantically. The house was old, and its timbers were adjusting themselves to the dampness of the rain.

She heard another creak, and the sound of footsteps.

The petticoats fell from her hands, making a limp heap on the bed.

The door opened.

"Anton!" Anger and fear hardened her voice. "You have no right to enter my room!"

"On the contrary, I have every right. This is my house, and I am master here. As a matter of fact, you're mine, too. As much mine as any other slave here."

She backed away from him, her mouth too dry to scream. As he stepped closer to her, she saw that he was wearing a dark silk dressing gown and carried something twisted in his hands. Something long, like a silk muffler. Or a rope.

With an ache of fear, she remembered the slave Lucinda, and the red, raw sores around the girl's wrists and ankles. As if Lucinda had been tied up and had hurt herself fighting to be free . . .

Anton's voice was harsh, and seemed to come from very far away. "Take off your clothes, dear Emerald. I believe it's customary, isn't it, to inspect the goods at a slave auction? Well, this is going to be our own private auction, just you and me. And I want to see what I'm getting."

"No!" She forced the word from between stiff, dry lips. "No, Anton. I won't be a part of your insane fantasies!"

She backed away from him, toward the bed, and now stood beside the bedside table. Under her hand, she found a book, Mr. Poe's novel, which she had brought up here earlier in the day, when she had still been innocent, untouched by ugliness.

She threw the heavy, gold-embossed book at Anton, and it struck him heavily on the temple. He staggered, and blood trickled from a cut.

"Damn you! Damn you, you little slut!" he shouted. "I'll make you sorry for this, I'll make you very, very sorry."

He started toward her, breathing heavily. And Emerald screamed.

Chapter Three

꧁ ꧂

"DARLING Emerald. Oh, child, how could I have let this happen? How could Anton have done such a monstrous thing?"

"I know, Aunt Anna. But fortunately no harm was done. He—he was stopped in time."

Emerald felt heavy and weak with shock. And she felt terrible about disturbing Anna. But there had been little else to do but come to her aunt. One of the slaves had heard her screams and come running upstairs, and Charmaine must have heard her, too, because she had come soon after. At last Anton had stalked off, muttering something about female hysteria and a bat trapped in Emerald's bedroom.

"See to the bat, Chuffey," he had ordered one of the frightened slaves. "Find it and kill it or I'll have you whipped."

Then Anton had gone off to his own quarters, anger in every line of his body. This, Emerald knew with a sick feeling, would not be their last encounter if she stayed here. It would be only the first of many. For Anton, true to his word, would not forget. . . .

Now, five minutes later, Emerald was in the haven

of her aunt's bedroom, which was warm and glowing with oil lamps.

"Emerald?" Anna's voice was weary. "Emerald, what are we going to do about this? I'll have to speak to my son, of course. Rebuke him, theaten him that if he ever approaches you again—"

"He *will* approach me again," Emerald said grimly. "He'll make promises, but then he'll do exactly what he wishes to do."

"But—he must stop. Surely—Oh, Emerald, surely after I've spoken to him, he'll begin to see his obligations. After all, he had a good upbringing. . . ." Anna's voice faltered, and one fluttering hand flew to her breast.

"Aunt, I'm afraid Anton's promises are worthless. He intended to rape me. And he will rape me if I stay here. No, I must leave, as soon as possible. I'll go somewhere far away where they don't know me. Where I won't be considered a—a slave."

"But Emerald! This is your home; this is where people love you! Where would you go? What would you do?"

"I don't know," Emerald said grimly. "After tonight, I only know I have to get away. Besides," she added, "I know I'm not a slave, I just know it. There must be some reasonable explanation for all of this. Suppose—suppose my father did run away with Ophelia, but—but she and her baby died? And then later my father married my mother and they had me?"

Anna looked pityingly at her. "Emerald, if that had happened, your father would have returned home."

"But what if he didn't want to come back? What if there was some reason he couldn't?"

"Then he would have written."

Letters can get lost, Emerald wanted to say, but something about Anna's face made her keep still.

"Perhaps if I talked to Anton, Emerald," Anna began again. "Made him see. . . ."

How innocent Aunt Anna was, Emerald thought slowly. She must have known little evil or ugliness in her life. Or perhaps she just refused to recognize it, as she had refused to see the evil in her son for so many years.

"Aunt Anna," she said. "You know it's useless to talk to Anton. And . . ." She hesitated. "I would be very watchful around Cora and Charmaine and the other girls."

There was a tight little silence.

"Oh!" Anna sat down on a delicately carved chair, her face abruptly white. She pressed her hands together in her lap. "I see."

Emerald threw herself into Anna's arms. "Oh, Aunt, I'm sorry, so sorry this has happened. If it hadn't been for me—"

"No, this isn't your fault." Anna straightened her spine. "Well, Emerald," she said briskly. "You are fortunate enough to have the pendant Calvin left to you. You must take it with you and sell it if you have to. I'll give you all the money I have. And Calvin's pearls. I'll give you anything I can. You must sew your jewels and money into a linen sack and wear them next to your body. That way, you can't lose them or have them stolen."

Emerald drew a deep breath, admiring her aunt's courage. "But I couldn't take those things, the jewels Uncle left you—"

"How is he to know about it?" Anna stood up, smoothing her dark skirts. Her cheeks were ash-white, save for two red patches. "I have distant relatives in

Ohio, cousins. You can go to them. On a riverboat, and then overland. I will give you a letter of introduction. They are respectable farmers, and I am sure they will give you a home, or—or at least help you find decent employment."

Ohio was so far away. A pain squeezed in Emerald's chest.

As if reading her thoughts, Anna continued, "Emerald, darling, you must go to the North, somewhere where slavery isn't allowed. You look white, and as far as I'm concerned, you are white. But in the North, you'll be safe. From Calvin, from—from any taint to your name. You can forget all this, forget us, and lead a normal life."

"I'll never forget you, Aunt Anna," Emerald choked.

"Nor I you, darling."

The next morning, Calvary drove her into Baton Rouge and she boarded a riverboat heading North.

Emerald sat on the bed in her hotel room in Saint Louis, thinking dully about going down to the dining room and eating something. The past five days had been lonely and frightening. Her long journey as an orphaned nine-year-old had been made under the wing of the captain's wife, but now she was totally alone.

On Anna's advice, she had decided to travel in full mourning, with a heavy veil over her face. It would give her a valid reason for traveling, Anna said, and it would protect her from the attentions of men.

"Whatever you do, dear Emerald, *don't* speak to any strange men, not even to ask directions," Anna had advised. "If they engage you in conversation, I'm afraid they can only wish you harm. A young girl traveling alone is extremely vulnerable. I would suggest that you attach yourself to some nice, older, respectable woman. You'll be safe with her. Oh, I do wish we had time to find some friends who are traveling up the river. . . ."

But there hadn't been time. As it was, they had spent nearly all night packing and planning so that Emerald could catch her boat at dawn.

The trip upriver had offered endless vistas of flat brown water, edged with lush, tangled forest, plantations, levees, and occasional high bluffs. Now she was waiting in Saint Louis, a booming river town, to take passage on a shallow-bottomed boat for the trip farther up the river.

Ohio, she thought dully. A wave of homesickness flooded through her as she thought of Hundred Oaks. Cora, Charmaine, Aunt Anna—all of those she had loved so dearly. What was happening to them now? Had Anton turned his attentions to—to his sisters? Was Aunt Anna managing to cope with him?

Emerald took her letter of introduction out of her black reticule and reread it.

Dear Cousin Franklin,

I am writing this letter as an introduction for my niece, Emerald Regan, who is coming to Ohio to seek news of her father, whom she believes to have died near the town of Toledo. I have tried to dissuade her, but she insists upon coming, which, I suppose, is to her credit, since she is a very fine and moral girl, a graduate of Miss Frannie Wyland's Finishing School in Baton Rouge. I hope that you can find it in your hearts to offer her your hospitality or to assist her in finding suitable employment while she makes her search.

Yours very truly,

Anna Robelard deLane

Emerald did not think the story very convincing, and she was sure that Cousin Franklin would feel the same. No respectable girl would cross half the country by herself, except in extreme desperation. But it was the best that she and Anna could do in such haste.

She tried to push away the nagging worry that they wouldn't want her, that they'd refuse even to let her cross their doorstep, and concentrated on her immediate problem, which was food.

She was hungry. Yet, in a strange and uncomfortable way, she had been unable to eat since leaving Baton Rouge. It was only homesickness, but she was beginning to feel weak and shaky from lack of food. Even her face seemed to have a new, hollow boniness. If she didn't begin to eat soon, she would lose her looks.

Well, she thought, tossing her head with sudden courage, if she had been homely, Anton might have left her alone. But, pretty or ugly, it didn't matter now. She had been banished from her home and loved ones, and given in exchange only the most tenuous link with the future.

She refolded the letter and stuffed it back into her reticule, checking beneath her petticoats to be sure that the small bag of jewels was safely dangling from her waist.

Then she adjusted the black veil over her face, tugged at the skirts of her black silk, trying to smooth out the travel wrinkles, and walked into the corridor.

The Planters' Hotel was a plain, bare building with long, drafty passages. It had skylights above each doorway, intended, she supposed, for the free circulation of air. It also had a room clerk with a piercing stare, a young boy who continuously pushed a filthy mop down the halls, and a mustached baggage porter who had thrown her trunk down with such force that it must have broken every object within, including her precious pencils, crayons, and paint tins. Further, the bed in her room had sheets that were definitely not clean.

But she had survived this far, and she would survive to the end of her journey. Drawing a deep breath of stale hotel air, Emerald decided that she had starved long enough. She would force herself to eat, no matter how tasteless the food, no matter how her stomach churned, or how the waiter looked at her. If she didn't eat, she would get sick. Then what would happen to her?

As she was walking down the corridor toward the stairs, she heard voices from an adjoining passage, a child's wail, rather high-pitched and fretful, then a woman's lower-pitched, warm voice.

Emerald passed the open mouth of the adjoining corridor, and saw a woman, tall, auburn-haired, rather pale, and obviously expecting a baby. With her was a little girl of about four years. The child clung to her mother's skirts, her head buried in her waist.

A little girl very much like Cora. Sweet, bubbly, appealing little Cora, whom Emerald would never see again.

"Susannah, darling, you mustn't carry on so—I'll have a bread crust for you as soon as we get into the room." The woman's voice had a musical warmth to it rather like Anna's, although it was also full of weariness.

"No! Don't want a bread crust—want candy! Candy, Mama!"

Emerald stepped forward on impulse, digging into her reticule. There was a small packet of paper-wrapped candies that Anna had given her at the last moment.

"Please," she said. "Please let the little girl take these. I haven't been able to touch them, and they'll surely go to waste."

The woman looked at Emerald and smiled. "Oh— oh, thank you so much. You're very kind. We haven't had much money for candy; we've had to spend it all on food and supplies for the trip. We're going West, you know. To California."

Again that note of warmth in the woman's voice, the tone so like Anna's, whom she would never see again.

"It—it's quite all right," Emerald said.

Then, shamefully, she burst into tears.

Chapter Four

❧❧

W HEN the girl in black burst into sobbing, Margaret Wylie felt utterly taken aback. She herself had spent two days in this musty hotel, pacing up and down their small room and wondering if she and Orrin were doing the right thing, and she felt like sobbing, too. The strange men in the corridors, her weak, aching legs, the nausea that was still with her after all these months . . .

But tears weren't for a woman about to embark on miles of featureless prairie, unknown mountains, Indians, God knew what other terrors. Once she started crying, she might not be able to stop.

How had Orrin gotten this incredible idea into his head? Perhaps it was the letter they had received from her brother last winter, a letter full of incoherent enthusiasm and vagueness.

California. Her baby would be born somewhere in the wilderness.

And now this woman was weeping, giving voice to the very uncertainties that Margaret had been trying to quell in herself ever since they had left New Orleans.

"Please, ma'am. Are you all right? Would you like

41

to come into our room for a minute? It's rather untidy, I'm afraid."

She turned the key and ushered the woman into their room. She hadn't exaggerated when she said it was untidy. Susannah's toys—her cornhusk dolls and pinewood horses and her carved letter blocks—were scattered all over the floor. Two opened trunks stood near the window, filled with a haphazard assortment of clothes, bedding, and household goods.

"Wouldn't you like to sit down?" Margaret swept one of Susannah's dresses off the room's one chair, and gestured toward it.

The young woman took the candy out of her reticule and gave it to Susannah. Greedily, Susie began to suck.

"I'm sorry," the woman said in a voice surprisingly young. "I didn't mean to blubber like a baby. I don't usually cry. It's just that—I haven't been eating properly, and I've been away from home five days now. And your little girl made me think of home. . . ."

Hadn't had anything to eat? For an instant Margaret forgot her own worries and looked sharply at the other woman. Anyone who could afford a room in this hotel could afford to buy food. But of course, she told herself, the woman was in mourning. She had lost someone, probably her husband, and that would be enough to take anyone's appetite.

"Dear, would you like to lie down for a minute or two?" Margaret offered. "The bed's clean—well, almost."

"Lie down? No, I couldn't. Really, I'm all right." With a surprisingly quick gesture, the woman pulled the black veil away from her face.

Margaret couldn't help staring. Why, this wasn't a woman at all, but a young girl. She couldn't have been more than eighteen at the most. She had an oval, pretty face, with enormous smudged green eyes, as deep and clear as spring grass. Margaret could see black, glossy curls peeking from beneath the ugly bonnet.

"Why, honey, I had no idea you were so young!" Margaret burst out.

"I'm eighteen."

"Don't tell me you're traveling alone!"

"Yes, I—I'm going to Ohio," the girl explained.

"Ohio? Do you have family there?"

"Well—no, not really. Some distant cousins. I have a letter of introduction, and they are going to take me in—if they like me, that is."

"Take you in *if they like you?* But what if they don't? And what's your name, anyway? Mine is Margaret Wylie. But you can call me Margaret."

"Emerald Regan." The clear green eyes regarded her bleakly. "And as far as that goes, I don't think they *will* like me. It's a bit odd, isn't it, if a strange girl arrives on your doorstep with a letter saying you have to take her in?"

"If they're not going to like you, then you shouldn't go there, that's all."

The girl lifted her chin and laughed for the first time, revealing white, even teeth. The laughter seemed to transform her face, giving it an eager, warm look.

"Oh, but I have to go somewhere. I—I couldn't stay where I was anymore. So if Cousin Franklin doesn't like me, I'll just get a job somewhere."

"A job?" Margaret looked at the soft white hands that had clearly never done any work. Not like her own, reddened from years of scrubbing with lye soap. "What could you do?"

"Not much, I guess," Emerald admitted. "I can

sketch—perhaps I could do portraits or teach art in a girls' school. Or I—I could manage a household, I suppose. Aunt Anna was teaching me how to do that, how to keep accounts and count the linens and order dinner and so forth. She was showing me how to make herbal potions to doctor the slaves when they become ill. . . ."

So she had lived on a plantation. As a lady of quality. That would explain the good quality of her dress, the soft hands. The ringless hands, Margaret now observed.

"I'm not sure how much chance there will be for you to make herbal potions," Margaret said gently. "Do you know how to cook? Or to scrub, or take care of children?"

The green eyes looked down. "Not really," the girl admitted. "There were slaves to do all of that. But I did have younger cousins," she added eagerly. "I did mind them sometimes and help them with their letters. And I do think I could learn almost anything if I tried. I'm very quick, Miss Frannie said. I learned French faster than any other girl she'd ever taught."

"I'm sure you did." Margaret smiled. She had an idea. But first she would have to find out more about the girl. And she would have to persuade Orrin. She would be doing this completely on impulse, of course. But she had a feeling about this girl.

They had had to leave New Orleans because Orrin, who had been the white overseer at Denton, one of the more prosperous sugar plantations, had stolen eight hundred dollars from the books.

Orrin wasn't a criminal, of course. Margaret insisted this to herself, even though he had been dishonest. But the Dentons had not been nice people to work for.

They regarded their overseer as being miles below them in the social scale, scarcely a cut above the slaves. Mrs. Denton barely spoke to Margaret and wouldn't permit Timmie to share the tutor they had engaged for their own sons, although Timmie, nine, was nearly the same age as the Denton boys, and smarter. If Margaret had not once been a teacher herself, Timmie would be illiterate, a thought that still had power to hurt her.

The Wylies had lived in the overseer's cottage, a dismal, four-room log dwelling nearly buried under honeysuckle vines. It was situated at the bottom of a dip and was always damp, the dooryard usually filled with black mud.

Margaret had struggled to keep the mud out. It had become a crusade for her. If she could just keep the bare wood floors clean and shining, it would mean that they were more than just trash, more than just hirelings.

With this latest pregnancy she had been very sick. The varicose veins in her legs pained her from sunup, when she rose to start the cooking and washing, to sundown, when she finally sank exhausted onto the cornhusk mattress beside Orrin.

Orrin had wanted to buy her a fancy soft upholstered chair with a footstool, like Mrs. Denton's, to rest her legs. And he had wanted to buy Timmie a pony. Timmie had learned to ride with the Denton boys and was a good, natural rider. Her son deserved good things, she told herself fiercely. He would be a good, strong, intelligent man someday.

The letter had come in December from her brother, Adam, the runaway, the wanderer, whom she hadn't seen in ten years. It had been badly spelled but full of enthusiasm. *The clymit here is like the Gardn of Eden frut anythin will grow. . . .*

At first, Orrin hadn't told her. He'd just said he was quitting the job and moving on, moving up the river to see if he could find something better. Then, the night before they were to leave, he had shown her the money.

"Orrin!" she had gasped.

"Don't worry none, Margaret. It'll be months before old Denton discovers this—if he ever does. He's such a drinker he couldn't find his toes if they weren't attached to his feet."

"But Orrin," she'd whispered, clutching him in her fright. "You know that's wrong! Why it—it's dishonest! What about God? The Commandments! And what if they find out what you did and come searching up the river for you?"

Her husband had looked at her, this rather short, broad man with a wide face, rumpled brownish hair, and stiff, proud chin.

"They won't find us if they do. As for God, He showed me how to do it, and He didn't stand in my way. He must of wanted me to do it. And He must of wanted us to go to California."

"California!" She stared at him. She had been married to him for ten years, and suddenly felt as if she didn't know him.

"It's like another world out there, Margaret, I hear tell. Adam wrote us, didn't he? Maybe not the land of milk and honey, but damned close to it. It's always sunny, they say, and they've got no fever like we do here. And the soil is so fertile it'll grow anything. And the fish and the salmon, they are just lying in the rivers waiting for some man to scoop them into his hands. A man could be a king there, Margaret! And no one to tell him what to do, to look down on him because he's only an overseer and doesn't own any slaves of his own."

"But—you must be crazy, Orrin, just crazy! How could we do that? Why, I've never even heard of anybody ever going there—only Adam, and he's half-wild. I don't even know where it *is!*"

"They've been, though, folks have."

"Who?"

"Why, mountain men and trappers and missionaries, and wagon trains, too. A man named Walker, people called the Bartelsons, the Stevens . . . You can get there, Margaret, with wagons and oxen. The Indians might bother you, and the way is rough, but it can be done. Maybe sometime lots of folks will go, thousands of 'em. But we'll be among the first."

Orrin looked at her, firming up his chin. "And God wants me to do this. I know it. Otherwise, why would He have shown me the way to get that money? Because we have to buy oxen, at least two yoke and some spares, and we have to get a wagon, and some seed, and food. . . . Just because a man hasn't got slaves doesn't mean he's dirt."

Slaves. It was almost a sickness in him, she had thought to herself, the way Orrin would lord it over those black people. As if to reassure himself he was not like them . . .

But in California there wouldn't be any slaves. They would make a farm, and live off the land, and they would be free, free as they had never been. If God had showed Orrin the way, then it was fated to happen and she could not fight it. And God, too, knew that she was pregnant and might have a rough time on the trail, so he had sent her this girl to help.

"I happen to know of a job you could get," Margaret said slowly to the girl in black. "It would be hard work, but I think you could do it. Only thing is, you couldn't go on to Ohio as you'd planned. But I don't think you really want to do that anyway, do you?"

Margaret and the girl talked for a long time. Margaret heard the rather odd little story of Emerald's father having died near Toledo and the girl's mission to go and look for him. The green eyes avoided Margaret's as this story unfolded.

"You aren't pregnant, are you?" Margaret asked sharply. "That isn't why you left home, is it?"

"Pregnant? Why, no!" Emerald looked stunned and horrified at the very thought.

"Well, whatever the reason you're here, it's good enough for me. Why don't I take you down to the dining room, and we'll get some food. You said you hadn't eaten in days."

"I—haven't been hungry."

"Well, you'll have to eat up if you're going to be my hired girl. And you'll have to get out of those mourning clothes, too. You do have something else to wear, don't you? Not that you don't look very nice and pretty, but it kind of depresses me to look at all that black."

By the time Orrin and Timmie were back, they had eaten and the girl was in her own room again. Quickly Margaret told Orrin the news, seeing Timmie's sun-freckled face turn up to hear it, too, eyes wide.

"Nope," Orrin said with finality. "I don't want no extra female along to eat up my food and clutter up my wagon and probably get married out from under our noses. What in God's name were you thinking of, Margaret?"

"Exactly that! I was thinking of God!" she cried. "If God told you to take us to California, then He told me to bring this girl along! Orrin, what do you think I'm going to do along the trail? Big as I am, like a haybarn, how do you think I'm going to cook and wash and take care of Susannah? And what do I do when the baby comes, with maybe not even another woman to help me? What about that, Orrin? You never stopped to think about me when you got this grand idea to go to California. Well, if we go, we take the girl. I need some help. And that's the way it's going to be."

When Orrin finally agreed, Margaret felt a flare of triumph. She had done the right thing, she was sure of it.

Chapter Five

E MERALD, draw me, draw me!"

As soon as the Wylie children had seen Emerald's quick fingers moving over the pages of her sketchbook, they were entranced. They crowded about her with awe as their own faces appeared on the paper.

When Emerald gave Susannah some paper, she sat down on the floor and tried to draw, too, her blond curls mussed, her tongue between her teeth.

"A pony," she announced, holding up the stick figure. "Timmie's new pony." They had bought the pony only hours before.

"Very good," praised Emerald.

"I'm calling him Windy," Timmie burst out. "Because he can go like the wind! He's the best horse I've ever seen, and he's going to be all mine—Pa said so! I'm going to ride him all the way to California!"

In only two days, Emerald's life had changed totally. With relief, she had discarded the mourning clothes and put on her favorite blue-chintz day dress.

The Wylie children had taken to her at once. And she liked them, too. Susannah was tiny and blond and fragile, but Timmie was all boisterous boy, jubilant over his new pony, proud to be going on errands with his father, begging every day to know when they would finally be leaving.

She had volunteered to help Margaret with the packing, and the two of them had been sorting the contents of the two trunks. Emerald's trunk, too, would have to be repacked, and some of her more ornate dresses sold. But both agreed about the books. Between them, their supply now totaled ten, and these would be used along the trail to help Timmie with his reading. Susannah, too, could begin her letters under Emerald's charge.

It was odd, Emerald thought, how happy she was. Thoughts of Anna and the deLane cousins had retreated to a dull ache. As for Anton, she had totally blanked him from her daytime thoughts. It was only at night that he returned in nightmares that gripped her in icy claws of fear. Anton's heavy body moving toward her . . . demanding. . . .

Orrin Wylie made daily forays into the cluttered, damp streets of Saint Louis, with its grogshops, dry-goods stores, wheelwrights, and harness makers, its endless bustle and confusion. He had already bought oxen, four yoke of them, and had his eye on a good milch cow. He had found a good, used wagon, big enough to hold hundreds of pounds of supplies, including the seeds and farm equipment he said they needed.

There was so *much* to buy, Emerald learned. Tents for sleeping, blankets, rifles, sturdy clothes, enormous quantities of food. Flour. Dried fruit. Coffee, salt, yeast, vinegar, pickles.

Emerald and Margaret spent hours shopping, until it seemed as if they were stocking a small general store of their own. Awls, nails, tacks, oil for lamps, soap, candles, a liniment called opoldedoc, herbs, tin drinking cups, a washbowl, campstool, scissors, knitting yarn, needles, shoe leather and pegs, knife, twine, a Dutch oven, cotton cloth . . . They always needed something more.

It seemed incredible to Emerald that she should really be going along on this wonderful and crazy journey. California! It was another world, a foreign land. Of course, her father and mother had gone to the territories. But she'd never known anyone who had gone so far West. Why, California was Mexican land, not American, and no one knew very much about it.

But they were really going. They had rented a keelboat and would transport their belongings up the Missouri River as far as Council Bluffs.

It was only Orrin Wylie who made Emerald feel uneasy, less than accepted. His small blue eyes seemed to regard her suspiciously. But she tried to be friendly. No one here knew her full story, and she didn't plan to tell it. She was free now, free and on her own. She would never have to think about Anton deLane again.

They arrived at the Council Bluffs campsite, after an uneventful passage up the river, late at night. Emerald was excited to see that other wagons were camped there already, as well as a big herd of oxen and horses. Most of the people seemed to be asleep, but Orrin spoke to one group still sitting about a campfire, and came back jubilant. All were going to California! They were only waiting here until the grass grew thick enough to support the oxen.

To Emerald the river encampment, simple and bare as it was, seemed full of excitement. Soon she would join these people, camp with them, travel with them!

At Hundred Oaks, she had never dreamed of such a thing.

The Wylie party pitched sleeping tents and went to bed right away, for they were all tired. But Emerald had never slept out-of-doors before, and as the hours of darkness passed, she tossed and turned on the crude mattress she had fashioned out of folded quilts. She longed for a featherbed mattress, but there was no room in the wagon for such luxuries.

Each time she turned, her hipbone seemed to find a harder place, and the ground was peppered with stones. But when she finally slept, it was the first dreamless sleep she had experienced since leaving Baton Rouge.

Her first encounter with the other settlers came the next morning, when she was seeking a place to empty the chamber pot. She had found a clump of low bushes on the far side of the camp nearest the river, and—flushed with embarrassment—was dumping out the pot when a girl emerged from the clump of bushes, adjusting her skirts around her. Her mission there was so plain that Emerald did not know in which direction to look. At Hundred Oaks, bathroom needs were taken care of in privacy, certainly not like this, where anyone could—

But the girl seemed unaware of Emerald's confusion.

"Oh, hello! You must be with the Wylies, aren't you? My pa was talking with your pa last night." She was a pretty girl of about Emerald's own age, with blond, almost white hair and pale eyelashes. Her face was round, her cheeks glowed with the sun, and her body was full, with large, voluptuous breasts.

"I—I'm with them, yes, but he's not my pa. I'm their hired girl," Emerald explained uncomfortably.

"My parents are both dead, and I have to earn my own living."

"Oh? You're getting paid to go to California, is that it?" But as if respecting Emerald's privacy, the girl did not ask any more questions, although her blue eyes were curious enough.

"Well," she added, "My name's Trude VandeBusch. Trude is short for Geertrud. I'm named after my ma. We've been here three weeks now; we were the first ones to get here. We come from Kalamazoo, Michigan," she said proudly. "We've got a thousand tulip bulbs in the wagon, and we're going to plant them in California as soon as we can. I love flowers, don't you? Are you going to ride in the wagon, or are you going to ride a horse? I'm going to ride. My pa has bought horses for all four of us, my two brothers and my sister as well. The boys are going to help out with the herd. I think having a horse will be much more fun than riding in the wagon, don't you?"

Trude was full of bubbling talk, flitting so rapidly from subject to subject that Emerald could barely follow her. But she gathered that the VandeBusches numbered six. Katje, the other girl, was fifteen.

Pieert was nineteen, according to Trude, "a big farm boy who'll be right at home with all the wonderful fertile soil we're going to." And Jan, twelve, was "rather a pest, but I suppose he'll be useful enough when we get to buffalo country. Jan loves to hunt."

"What do you think of all this?" Trude demanded, fixing Emerald with her blue eyes. "I mean, we're going to be on the trail, just a few women—six, counting you—and all those men. . . ."

"I—I've never thought about it."

"*I* think about it," Trude announced with relish. "My pa has the idea that he's going to tie Katje and me down and make married ladies of us when we get to California. Ha! Who wants to be old and washed out from having babies by the time you're thirty?"

"I—I suppose. . . ." Emerald did not know what to say. She had never heard a girl talk quite so boldly before. Trude's whole face, when she said the word *men,* actually sparkled with pleasure. Emerald supposed that Aunt Anna would disapprove of Trude. Still, there was something about Trude that she liked, something irrepressible, open, and natural.

Well, if Orrin was right, they would see a good deal of Trude in the days to come. For all of the campers were going to travel West in one wagon train.

At breakfast, Margaret showed Emerald how to bake biscuits. She mixed flour, warm water, soda, and salt in a tin basin, trying to keep out as much blowing sand as she could. She kneaded the dough and then flattened it until it was about an inch thick. She put this into a liberally greased skillet and heaped hot coals on the lid. The trick, Margaret said, was to cook the inside of the bread through without turning the top and bottom crusts to charcoal.

"Not bad," Orrin commented, breaking off a piece of the fragrant bread and taking a bite. He washed it down with a huge swallow of the coffee Margaret had brewed.

Emerald felt herself turning pink with pleasure. She had helped to make those biscuits. She had helped to gather wood for the fire, and had fried the bacon. She felt a little thrill of pride. She was learning fast, and would soon be a real help to Margaret.

After washing the tin dishes and spoons, Emerald and Margaret took Susannah and went to meet the other emigrants, leaving Timmie to make friends with the other boys on his own.

Besides the VandeBusches, there was only one other family wagon. These were the Rigneys, farmers who had come from near Saint Louis. Saul Rigney, a short, wiry man, was also a cabinet maker. He had brought along the tools of his trade, as well as his two sons, Bob and Martin, and his wife, Martha.

They all looked at Emerald curiously. Quickly Margaret explained, "Emerald is here to help us out. I haven't been feeling well lately, and I wanted another woman to be with me." With Margaret's taut belly bulging out her skirt, no further explanation was necessary.

"She looks too young to be much help. And she's probably flighty, too," Martha Rigney said. She was a rawboned farm woman with wide shoulders and big red hands, who looked as if she could do the work of two men.

"She'll do," Margaret said. "She's a good, strong girl."

"She'd better be, out there on that prairie with them wild, Godless savages."

Martha went on to express more of her opinions about the Indians, most of them in the same vein, and after a few moments Margaret and Emerald said their good-byes and moved on. As they left, Emerald stifled a giggle. She, Emerald Regan, gently reared, being called a "good, strong girl." Her Aunt Anna would have died!

The rest of the emigrants were men. They seemed to pass before Emerald's eyes in a blur of deerskin pants and shirts, blue twilled cotton and linsey-woolsey, red flannel, and stout white hats. Zelig York was a squat, barrel-chested man. Billie Colfax, a preacher, was tall, long-nosed, and stoop-shouldered, with cold gray eyes.

Old Red Arbuthnot was by twenty years the oldest man she met. At least sixty-five, he was freckled and vital, his pinkish-red hair now grizzled into white.

"Me, I get itchy feet," he told Emerald, his smile revealing two missing front teeth. "Well, my wife, she died this winter, and I figured it was time to move on. I got my two boys with me, Matt and Pete. Matt, he's a widower, too; and Pete, he didn't want to stay behind."

Matt and Pete, the "boys," were grown men in their thirties, both of them red-haired and freckled.

Charles Morris was a jaunty-looking man of twenty-five, whose eyes lingered on Emerald's bodice until she felt herself blushing furiously.

"You'll have to watch your step in camp, I can see that," Margaret commented dryly. "The way that Charles Morris has been staring at you—and that Zelig York, too. . . ."

On their way back to their own wagon, they met a man kneeling on the ground bandaging an ox's leg. Lean, with dark, unruly hair and a scowling expression, he nodded curtly at them.

But Margaret walked up to him smiling. "Martha Rigney told me that you're a doctor," she said. "Dr. Ben Coult, she said your name was." She glanced down at the bulge of her belly. "I'm glad you're coming to California, Dr. Coult. I'm so relieved to know there will be a doctor along when my time comes."

Ben Coult looked away. "I don't practice medicine anymore except on animals."

Margaret flushed. "But—I thought—"

"You thought wrong. I've given up doctoring."

Margaret looked bewildered. And Emerald was about to burst out with an angry comment—how dare anyone hurt Margaret's feelings like this?—when they heard footsteps behind them.

They turned to see a man clad in well-worn buckskins. A leather folder, carefully tied with thongs, was slung under his arm.

He was about thirty, Emerald supposed, and more than six feet tall. His body was rangy, with wide, powerful shoulders. His face was square and strong, his chin deeply clefted, his mouth humorous.

Or, Emerald thought, his mouth would have been humorous save for the fury that twisted it now.

"I heard that, Ben Coult," he said harshly. "So you're refusing to doctor this good woman?"

The taciturn doctor looked away from the hard gray eyes. "I—" he began.

"You're a useless sod, aren't you, Ben Coult?" the man in buckskin went on grimly. "Oh, yes, I heard your talk around the campfire last night—all about the futility of medicine, as if everything were hopeless. A fine attitude to take into the wilderness with a group of folks who are going to need prayers and a hell of a lot of human help if they are going to make it to California safely."

Ben Coult tossed his head, obviously uncomfortable.

"Well, let me warn you of something, Coult. On this journey we'll all have to give everything we have, and you're no exception. You'll practice medicine, damn you, or I personally will hold a pistol to your head. And use it, too, if I must."

Ben Coult hesitated, then finally stalked off in the direction of a nearby wagon. The man in buckskins snorted bitterly. Then he turned to look at Emerald and Margaret as if seeing them for the first time.

"Pardon my language, ladies." His voice had softened. "And pardon the things I said. I didn't wish to

59

scare you. It's just that people like him—" He drew a sharp breath. "Well, I just wanted you to know, ma'am, that there will be help for you when your time comes. You can count on it."

"I—I'm very grateful," Margaret murmured.

"And I am, too," Emerald said.

The man bowed, his gray eyes coming to rest on Emerald. There was a curious light in them. "I suppose I should—" he began.

But before he could introduce himself to them, someone shouted from the other side of the campsite. The man in the buckskins waved to him, and said, "Pardon me, ladies, I think my counsel is wanted elsewhere. Formal introductions will have to wait. But I'm sure we'll be seeing much more of each other in the future—we won't be able to avoid it, will we?"

He tipped his hat, gave Emerald another disturbing look, and was gone.

The two women glanced at each other.

"Who was that?" Emerald asked.

"Why, I suppose he must be our guide. Martha Rigney told me about him. His name is Mace Bridgeman, and they hired him in Saint Louis to take us across the plains. He'll guide us on the trail and help find water for us. It's an important job, Orrin says, for without someone who knows the area we could all get lost and die out there." Margaret shivered. "This won't be like traveling a turnpike, Emerald. We'll need a man like him."

"Yes . . ." Emerald wasn't thinking of the potential dangers, but rather of Mace Bridgeman's face, the broad bone structure, the tantalizing cleft in the chin, the gray eyes that could blaze with fury.

Margaret gave her a sharp look. "Martha says he's as wild as a mountain antelope—and just about as

60

eccentric, too. The only reason he guides at all is to get money for his painting. He's a naturalist, Emerald —an artist. He wanders all over the wilderness painting the animals he sees."

"An artist?"

Emerald remembered the way he had looked at her, and felt her heart begin to beat faster.

The caravan's three young girls, Emerald, Trude, and her sister, Katje, were down at the river's edge, wondering if the water would be warm enough to bathe in. Supper was over. People had gathered about the campfires in sociable groups. Red Arbuthnot was playing the fiddle in a high, plaintive wail. Distantly, someone laughed. An ox bellowed.

"*I* think the water's going to be too cold," Katje said. "And besides, there might be snakes or quicksand or something. We'd better not."

Although Katje was as pretty as Trude, she was entirely different otherwise. Almost every word Katje uttered was a complaint. She didn't like Missouri, she didn't like the black flies that seemed to be everywhere, she didn't like camp food, and she didn't want to go to California. In fact, in an obscure way, she seemed to blame Trude for the fact that they were here at all.

"Oh, the water's going to be just right," Trude scoffed. "Don't you agree, Emerald? After all, we've been camped here weeks. I feel as if I'm walking around with an extra skin of dirt. You just can't get clean with a bucket of water in a tent. So I'm going to bathe. And what's more, I'm going to get *really* clean."

Katje's mouth fell open. "Trude! You can't— Pa said—"

61

"Pa didn't say a thing about me not getting clean. Not a thing, Katje!"

"But not *that* way!"

To Emerald's amazement, Trude was unfastening her dress and peeling it off. "Bare is the only way to bathe, dear sister," she said. "You should try it, too."

"Bare? Oh, no, I couldn't— Someone might—"

"Nonsense," Trude said. "They're all up at camp listening to the fiddle. Anyway, I'll be under the water where no one will see me. Come on, Emerald. Join me. I promise you'll like it. There's no feeling quite like it in the world!"

Trude was now down to petticoats and corset cover. She stripped them off, revealing full, round, soft breasts with pink nipples, a rounded belly, and a pale blond fuzz of pubic hair. "Come on," she urged. "No one will see us."

"I—I can't." Emerald could feel a flush spreading crimson over her neck and face.

Trude laughed. "Are you shy like my sister? Well, come in with your petticoats on, then. At least you'll get wet and clean, and, believe me, you'll appreciate that once we get on the trail. Pa says we're practically going to eat dust and dirt!"

Trude plunged into the waist-high water and squatted down so that only her face showed, white in the last rays of sun.

Emerald hesitated. She hadn't had a real bath since she'd left home. Her skin felt sticky and grimy. Finally she took off her shoes and slipped out of her blue gown, leaving it on a bush next to Trude's. She felt shivery and naked with only the skimpy petticoat and corset cover. If Aunt Anna could see her now—

But Anna wasn't here, she reminded herself. She,

Emerald, was. And she wanted a bath. She hadn't realized how desperately until now.

Leaving Katje on the bank, she cautiously waded out to where Trude floated.

Water extended cool fingers all over her skin, cleansing, soothing, wonderful. Imitating Trude, Emerald squatted, too, until the water lapped close to her mouth.

"Can you swim?" Trude called. She was splashing happily.

"Not a bit. Can you?"

"A few strokes," Trude admitted. "But not very well. My brothers Pieert and Jan used to go to the swimming hole, but I'd get whipped if I tried to follow them."

"Whipped?"

"Pa said swimming was for boys, not girls. He was afraid I might see them swimming bare, I guess."

They continued to splash and talk. Katje had disappeared, evidently having gone back to camp, so there were just the two of them to enjoy the last red streaks of the sunset.

Then they heard a noise along the riverbank.

Emerald stiffened. "What was that?"

"Oh, I'm sure it was nothing. Probably just an animal."

"I think it's a person!" Emerald gasped. "Someone coming down to the water!"

But Trude only giggled and splashed harder.

"I think we'd better get dressed. I'm going to!" Emerald waded toward shore. What a situation they were in! Trude naked in the water and herself next to naked, with the wet cambric undergarments clinging to every line of her body. Now she was angry at herself for having consented to join such foolishness.

"Well, and who have we here?" Mace Bridgeman

was leading a roan horse down to the water to drink. His head was bare, and she could see the windblown light hair, the broad, humorous face, the strong, clefted chin. And the eyes, dancing at her with amusement.

"Oh!" Emerald uttered a little shriek and stepped backward, both hands covering her chest, where the fabric was pasted to the outline of her breasts. Miserably, she was aware that the thin material revealed everything—from the pointed tips of her nipples to the curve of her belly with its faint shadow of body hair. If only it were darker! If only she hadn't come here!

"Taking a little dip, I see." He was smiling, and his eyes roved boldly over her body.

"If you were a real gentleman, you'd turn your back and leave this place, so that Trude and I could—"

Mace Bridgeman grinned. "But I'm not a gentleman. Far from it. I'm a guide and a mountain man. And a naturalist, when I can find the time." He was teasing her. "And I think I should stay here and guard the two of you so that no unfriendly Indians or other varmints can sneak over here and steal your clothes. Or worse, steal you."

"But you can't stay here!" Emerald was close to tears. "Trude is—"

"Trude most certainly is." Amused, Mace glanced toward the water, where Trude still splashed.

"But you can't be here when she comes out!"

For the first time, he grew serious. "Maybe I'd better be, my foolish little girl. What's your name, anyway?"

"E-Emerald," she faltered. She plucked her dress off the low bush where she and Trude had left their gowns and held it nervously in front of her. "Emerald Regan."

"Well, Emerald Regan, I hope you realize that this isn't a sedate Southern drawing room, where pretty women play charming parlor games. This is the wilderness—or near enough. And women are a rarity here, especially women as lovely as yourself. You should have posted a guard before you bathed. There are footloose men in this wagon train—men accustomed to taking what they want when they want it. Do you want to get raped?"

"I—I didn't know—" She was flushing furiously, torn between the desire to have him smile at her, and the wish to have him gone so that she could settle her wits and put on her dress.

"Well, now you do know. And I'm going to stay here until you and your friend are safely out of the water—whether you like it or not."

"But—But— You'll have to turn your back!"

A grin flashed across his face, revealing white, square teeth and the flicker of a dimple in one cheek.

"Oh, I'll turn my back," he said lightly. "I do know enough about gentlemanly behavior to do that."

"Good," she said. "Then please do so."

He grinned again, and then slowly, deliberately, he turned a broad expanse of buckskinned back to her.

"Oh, Emerald, are you getting my clothes?" Trude called from the waters of the river.

"Y-yes, right away."

"Please fetch my dress! I'm getting cold!"

All too conscious of Mace waiting patiently, Emerald snatched up Trude's dress. She waded back into the water and thrust the other girl's garments at her. "Hurry! Mace Bridgeman is here. Put these on before he sees you."

"I don't care if he does see me; I can't get dressed here in the water." Trude stood up luxuriously, her breasts bare and white in the gathering dusk. "He's quite a man, Emerald. Or hadn't you noticed?"

Chapter Six

❧❧

ZELIG York, crouched in the thick, shadowed underbrush, stared openmouthed at the two girls coming out of the river, one of them naked, her breasts gleaming in the pearly evening light. He was unpleasantly aware of Mace Bridgeman standing vigil only twenty feet away from where he himself crouched. Uneasily he wiped one hand across the stubble of his chin.

Damn! he thought. If they wasn't pretty. Jest like two flowers.

But it was the dark-haired one with the green eyes whom he liked best, though she was not naked as the blond one was. Emerald Regan—was that her name? She was more delicate than the blond, her breasts smaller and more pointed, tilting upward under the damp gown, their nipples plainly, excitingly revealed. Wouldn't he like to get her down on the ground somewhere!

He could almost feel what she would be like beneath him, her skin as soft as velvet, and as strokable. Yet there was fire in the girl, too, he felt sure. Fire that would smolder at first, then light to quick burning.

He wanted to kindle that fire.

And he would, too, he thought. He moistened his lips and stared at her, thinking that they had two thousand miles to go, just the few wagons and the people who were in them. He would have many chances to get her alone and show her what a real man was like.

He watched as Emerald finished buttoning her own clothes, and handed a heap of garments to Trude. He swallowed and again wiped a hand across his chin, wondering what Emerald Regan would think if she knew that he and Billie had nine bars of gold bullion hidden under the false floor of their wagon.

Nine bars. Even now, Zelig could not believe their good fortune. In his mind he could still see the man in the bank, on State Street near the *Daily Tribune* buildings. The man had turned and started to speak to Billie, then been mowed down with a blast from Billie's "pepperbox" pistol.

The man had died in a gush of blood and protruding entrails, splattering everywhere. Even Zelig had been queasy, but the sight hadn't affected Billie Colfax in the slightest. He was after the gold, his eyes cold and blank.

Zelig had trained his own pistol on the frightened bank employees and the five customers who had been in the bank at the time. One of these had been a woman with two small children. About twenty she had been, small and fair. She had clutched the youngest to her breast, nearly weeping in her terror. Zelig had shoved the baby aside, pushed the girl into the vault, and raped her, thrusting himself into her moistness over and over again, until he was spent.

He still remembered that. It had not been much of

a pleasure, for the woman had lain as still as a rag doll, mindlessly letting him do whatever he wished. No, it had not been as exciting as if she had fought back. That was what he liked best. When the woman fought back.

Now Zelig narrowed his eyes as Emerald finished dressing. He would wager that Miss Emerald Regan would fight back. Fight hard, she would. But he would have her, anyway. He always did.

Of course, he added mentally, he might figure a way to have the other girl, too, the blond with the voluptuous, full breasts. He would have them both, he decided.

The overland trip to California had been Billie's idea. After the robbery, the newspapers had been full of angry articles crying for vengeance. But he and Billie, traveling as a preacher and his cousin, had disappeared West, leaving no trace. Once in California, they could establish themselves in the West Coast shipping, or the lumber business. This was what Billie wanted to do. And, respecting the coldness in those pale eyes, Zelig did Billie's bidding.

But Billie couldn't tell him what to do with women, Zelig thought now. No, he couldn't.

It was going to be a nice trip.

It was two weeks into May, and the wagon train was ready to start. Orrin Wylie had been elected captain of the party, and they had been joined at the last minute by a short, bandy-legged man named Wyatt Thatcher. Wyatt had a snub nose, small, button-sharp eyes, and announced to everyone that he sold patent medicines. His wares included Mrs. Thatcher's Soothing Catarrh Syrup, Mrs. Thatcher's Cough Cure, and Mrs. Thatcher's Aphroditine.

"A-course, this ain't my only source of income, but it helps," he told them, winking. "Lots of folks got the ache or the cough and are wantin' a bit of relief. Which I can provide at a very reasonable price."

There was no Mrs. Thatcher and never had been, Wyatt admitted cheerfully. But anyone in the wagon train who wished to buy his cures was welcome to do so. They had better hurry, though, because the settlers in the newly named city of San Francisco were sure to snap them up, just as the folks in Chicago had, and parts farther East.

Privately Emerald thought Wyatt Thatcher rather funny. With his quick, rabbitlike movements and deep voice, he added a note of life and zest to the group. And, he told Timmie and Susannah solemnly, he had a supply of medicine-show costumes in his wagon, and one of these nights they would stage a program.

The days of waiting in camp had slipped by. Each time Emerald saw Mace Bridgeman he grinned at her as if he were remembering the way she had looked soaking wet.

One morning, engaged in the dull but necessary chore of hauling water from the river, she had encountered him sitting on a rock by the water, the big, worn leather folder spread out before him. He was frowning at something, his expression curiously concentrated and intense. It was as if he were aware of nothing else—not herself or the loveliness of the morning—but only his work.

Emerald felt oddly piqued that he hadn't even noticed her. And she wanted to see his drawings for herself.

"Hello," she said loudly.

He looked up, at last grinning at her, his eyes crinkled from sun and the outdoors.

"Well, so it's Emerald Regan again," he drawled. "And this time more fully clad, I see.'" He surveyed her sturdy gray-striped seersucker gown, long-sleeved, buttoned in front, and covered by a cotton apron.

She felt sudden, irrational anger. Was he laughing at her again? "Yes," she burst out furiously. "And I see that you are very busy this morning being our guide. I'm sure that drawing pictures is going to be a very great help to us on our trip West!"

The full lips pressed together tightly. "Emerald, I was hired as a guide and I'll do that job. But my painting is a part of my life, and I'm not going to change it for anyone. Not even for you, lovely as you are. Besides, I understand that you yourself draw, and I can't understand why you would mock someone who is an artist."

The words were a rebuke, and Emerald felt the hot color flood up to her cheeks.

"I didn't mean—I only meant—"

The dimple in Mace's cheek flashed. "I know what you meant. I got you mad, didn't I? Well, I'm sorry, Emerald. Here," he added. "Would you like to see my picture?"

Involuntarily she took a step closer, to look at the square of precious canvas.

It was a painting of a group of deerlike animals, spindly-legged, delicate, with white body markings and long, curved, hooking horns. There were four of them, three adults and a baby. Each brush stroke was delicate, yet sure, capturing the grace and beauty of the large-eyed animals.

"Why—why, they're lovely!" Emerald breathed, her anger lost in her interest and admiration. "What sort of animals are they?"

"Pronghorn antelope," he told her, smiling. "I

71

sketched these near the North Platte River. We're sure to see some on our trip—they're beautiful, elusive beasts that can hit enormous bursts of speed when they are being pursued by a predator—up to thirty miles an hour."

"But they don't look strong enough to do that."

"They are. Their long legs are built for speed. They can outdistance most enemies easily. The only thing that can kill them is snowdrifts that bog them down so they can't move, wolves or coyotes that attack them in groups, and—of course—man."

Emerald hesitated. "Yes, your brush seems to capture that in them. You make them seem to have a—a kind of nobility. As if they are too proud ever to be conquered."

Mace gave her a long look. "You caught that? Would you like to see more of my work? Eventually I plan to take these back to New York and have them published, as my friend Audubon is doing."

"Audubon?"

"Yes," Mace said. "An old friend and teacher of mine. Someday, I'll tell you about him." He took other canvases from the folder and showed her artfully sketched animal portraits. Some were fully rendered, others still only sketches. There were woolly sheep-like animals with enormous horns, and other creatures unfamiliar to Emerald.

"Why—why, they are all wonderful!" she exclaimed. "But they look so very strange. That one, for instance. What is it?"

"That? That, my girl, is a buffalo. We'll see plenty of those later. And that one is a wapiti, or elk. They live in the Rocky Mountains, and every autumn you can hear them 'bugling' as the bull elks battle each other for mastery of their harems. It's an awesome sight, I'll tell you that. Sometimes they spar until one of them is actually killed—quite a bit to go through for a female, wouldn't you say?"

He flipped through other drawings, pointing out grizzy bears, timber wolves, gray and red foxes, beavers, and jackrabbits.

"Your paintings," Emerald breathed at last. "Even the sketches, the ones that aren't finished, seem to give these animals a kind of—dignity. You paint them as if they *belong*."

Again Mace gave her that long look of respect. "They do belong, Emerald. This vast land is really theirs, not ours. Any man who has roamed the wilderness as much as I have is aware of that."

For a moment they were silent, Mace's face calm and distant, his mouth curved thoughtfully.

"Well, Emerald?" Carefully he began to wrap up the paintings again in the portfolio. "Then I take it that we are going to be friends? We might as well, don't you think, since we are going to be traveling two thousand miles together?"

"Friends—" Abruptly reality came flooding back to her. She remembered how amused he'd been at her discomfiture at the bathing hole, how he had enjoyed seeing her half-revealed body. But she couldn't help being intrigued by what he said. "Two thousand miles, did you say?"

"Give or take a few hundred. What with all the windings and turnings and climbings and detours, no one really knows how far it is."

"I can hardly imagine such distances. It makes a person feel very small and insignificant, doesn't it?"

He got to his feet and looked at her. "Exactly. When we get out there under those Western stars, Emerald, glowing down at us as big as frying pans, millions of them—then you'll know just how small we really are."

"We?" Some reckless urge made her say. "We'll watch the stars?"

"Yes, *we*. Why not?" For a second he stood looking at her, a quizzical expression in his eyes. Then, before she could move or turn, he scooped her into his arms.

His mouth was soft, yet mobile, seeking, demanding. Back in Baton Rouge, a few of the planters' sons had stolen kisses—and she hadn't struggled very hard to get away. But never had Emerald been kissed like this. There was something that crackled and leaped from him to her, sending a melting quiver into the very core of her.

She felt as if she could stay in his arms all day, all night, forever.

"No— Please—" Desperately, afraid of her own tumultuous feelings, she managed to pull away from him. She could feel her knees wobbling.

"What's wrong, little Emerald? Haven't you ever been kissed before?" But he spoke gently, his voice laughing at her.

"Yes, of course I have! I— Oh—"

She felt confused and self-conscious, all too aware of her heart hammering inside her, of the odd, melting weakness that consumed her.

Mace gave her a light swat on her bottom. "Well, go along with you, Emerald. Go and get the water you came for, and go back to camp."

"Water?" she repeated foolishly.

"Yes, water." Again his gray eyes were filled with a gentle laughter. "That *is* what brought you here to the river, isn't it?"

Hurriedly she finished her chores and lugged the heavy buckets back to the Wylie wagon, angry at herself for the pink blush that still blazed in her cheeks. And for the thoughts that kept disturbing her. Mace Bridgeman . . . his paintings, his gray eyes, the way he had held her . . .

During these long days, while they had waited for the grass on the prairie to grow long enough to feed the animals, Emerald's sketchbook was with her nearly all of her free moments. She drew Timmie on his chestnut pony, Windy, the mane and tail of the animal blowing in the wind as freely as the shaggy, sun-lightened hair of the boy who rode him.

"Look, Emerald! Windy's the best!" Timmie would scream at her as he wheeled by. He rode as if he had been born in the saddle. "Watch me! Watch me go!"

And go he would, circling the camp and along the river with such enthusiasm that Orrin told him if he weren't more careful, he would wear Windy out and ruin him before they even got started.

Margaret Wylie, with the benefit of added rest, was beginning to look less tired. Each day she took time to instruct Emerald in some new aspect of camp life, from making butter to starting a fire.

Emerald had taken over the job of teaching Timmie and Susannah, and held lessons after each noon meal. She invited Jan VandeBusch and Bob Rigney, who were twelve and thirteen and the only other children in camp, to join them as well. But both boys refused.

"We're not going to need book learning where we're going," the blond Jan VandeBusch protested. And Bob Rigney said he couldn't read at all, and didn't plan to start now.

Timmie, however, could read through any of the

books she had brought with ease, and especially liked Mr. Poe.

Susannah, too, who would celebrate her fifth birthday on the trail, was very quick and picked up her letters almost instantly. Emerald was making a little book for the children, illustrated with her own sketches and captions.

Somewhere in Council Bluffs, Orrin acquired a small black terrier puppy. Timmie named the dog Edgar, for reasons of his own, and the boy spent hours playing with him. Edgar, too, became an illustration in the little book Emerald was making.

One afternoon Mace Bridgeman came upon her as she was sketching Timmie and Susannah at their play.

"I see you're at work, Emerald."

"Yes. I'm not an accomplished painter like you, I've never had the training. But I do love to draw, I always have."

"Do you mind if I look?"

"Go ahead, if you'd like."

Slowly Mace turned the pages of her sketchbook, inspecting the drawings she had done—Orrin at work, Margaret cooking, Red Arbuthnot playing his fiddle, Timmie's horse, Windy. There were even some of the sketches she had done at Hundred Oaks—the muscular slaves at their work, the old gardener, Calvary, pushing his wheelbarrow with tired dignity.

Tensely Emerald waited for his verdict. Yet he turned page after page, saying nothing.

"You're very good," he told her at last. "Your eye is very accurate, Emerald, and what's more, you draw with a sense of humor. Somehow you manage to show not only the physical forms of these people but also the unconscious humor of them, the courage and the pathos, too."

"I—I do?"

She was not used to being taken so seriously. The people at Hundred Oaks had laughed at her efforts, or else treated her sketching only as a harmless hobby. Mace was the first person who had ever acted as if she were an artist to be respected.

"Your drawings are going to be an invaluable record of this journey," he went on slowly. "Someday, perhaps, even an historical record. You must take very good care of your sketchbook. Waterproof it in oilcloth, as I do my portfolio. Perhaps when you reach California, you can see to its publication."

"Publication?" She stared at him.

"Why not?" His eyes smiled at her, their gray depths burning with a light that seemed to catch and hold the afternoon sun. "You're an artist, Emerald, as much so in your way as I am in mine. And that is one thing I've learned from working with Audubon—it isn't enough to keep our talent to ourselves. No, the world needs everyone who has something to give, no matter how large or small. It needs our talent and our caring."

Heady words—joyous words. After Mace left, Emerald sat for a long time, staring down at the half-finished drawing in her lap. She was an artist—Mace said so. Somehow the thought filled her with a strong and soaring warmth.

But the lazy days in the campground were over, and on a Tuesday morning in mid-May, they left.

It was not an auspicious morning for beginning such a journey, for the sky was cloudy, filled with clouds of a gun-metal gray heaped upon each other like sullen whipped cream. Rain, Orrin said, was coming. But Emerald didn't mind—her heart was filled with a wild excitement. They were really leaving for a land few had seen or knew anything about.

Their first problem came almost immediately, for the oxen did not want to swim across the Missouri River. Frightened by the swirling water, they began to swim in a confused circle, each animal trying to climb on the back of the one in front of it.

"Giddap, you goddamned black-hearted bastards!" Emerald heard Orrin bellow above the general hubbub. She had to smile. A Bible was prominent in the Wylies' book box, but evidently the strictures of that Book didn't apply toward stubborn oxen.

The solution was found when Mace suggested they cross the river in a borrowed canoe, pulling behind one of the most tractable of the oxen with a rope tied around its horns. This worked; the others, driven forward, followed the lead of the first and swam safely over.

The wagons with the women and children were ferried across, and Emerald clutched Susannah as she looked at the brown, swirling water beneath them.

"Oh, well," Trude said. "If we tip in, at least I get another bath. I don't mind getting wet for that."

"That's fortunate!" gasped Emerald, certain they would get their dunking very soon indeed.

To her relief, the crossing was relatively dry, but they made only a few miles that first day because it began to rain—cold, wet torrents of water. They set up camp quickly, but could light no fires in all the rain, and they had to eat cold biscuits and leftover beef, washed down with fresh milk from the little milch cow, Bossie, who, happily, didn't seem to mind the water at all. Then, miserable, wet and cold, they huddled in the cramped confines of the wagon, all five of them plus the dog, Edgar. They made, as Margaret tried to joke, a mighty tight fit.

The wagon was like one that Emerald vaguely remembered from her childhood, a good, sturdy farm wagon that could carry as much as a ton of goods. Its floor, or bed, was a wooden box about nine feet long and four feet wide, with two-foot-high sides. Orrin had caulked the bed for river crossings, and had a false floor built into it so that supplies and tools could be stored in the lower level.

The top was made of canvas, waterproofed with linseed oil, and supported by six curved bows made of hickory. There were flaps at the front and a "puckering string" at the back to allow opening and closing. Inside was formed a tiny room with sides of wood and canvas, and an arching canvas roof. A man could stand upright in the center, but had to crouch near the edges. And if he searched carefully, he could spot the secret pockets that Margaret had sewn into the canvas to hold valuables and keepsakes.

Rain. Never had Emerald seen so much of it or disliked it so much. Nearly every day it showered for at least an hour, until every garment they owned was cold and clammy, and their spirits were bleak. Even Timmie, trotting alongside the wagon on his pony, bundled up in sweaters, seemed subdued.

Slowly, awkwardly, they established their routines. Orrin's job was to drive the oxen, which he did by walking alongside them and shouting out commands. "Giddap! Gee! Haw! Whoa!" He carried a long-handled and long-lashed whip, and used it when necessary.

Margaret and Susannah rode in the wagon, but Emerald, already tired of the slow, monotonous jouncing of the wagon bed, walked alongside. Timmie, exulting in his freedom, rode his pony. Often he joined Trude, Katje, and Jan VandeBusch as they galloped by.

Sometimes, watching Trude ride, Emerald felt a pang of envy. But after Trude let her spend a day on her mare, Golden, Emerald changed her mind. Prolonged riding made her sore, and was awkward in a long dress. Walking was more fun.

One evening Mace Bridgeman rode back to camp after scouting ahead, and stopped to talk to Emerald. The rain had cleared away to reveal gray, low skies. Red Arbuthnot had once more brought out his fiddle, to be joined by Wyatt Thatcher with a banjo.

"I heard some of the men talking about using mules," Emerald said, trying to quell the excited leap in her throat she felt whenever Mace was near. "They said it would be faster and better than this."

"Mules are faster, sure. And some use 'em. But you'd end up sitting on your mule roasting in the sun all day," he told her. "If you wanted to stop and rest, you'd have to lead your animal. And you'd have to unpack everything at night and load up again the next morning."

"But—"

"Look, you'd better not wish for pack mules if you fall and break a leg," Mace said. "The trouble with mules is that if a man is hurt, there's no way to carry him along. You just have to leave him beside the trail and hope that another party comes along. Or put a bullet through his head, if he begs you."

"What?" Emerald was horrified. "You can't mean that!"

"Sorry, but that's how it is. I've heard of it happening myself. The men who take mule trains know what the risks are."

Emerald thought of Margaret, big with child. "Well, I'm glad we're not like that," she said. "I'd hate to leave someone I knew beside the trail."

"Odds are you'll have to, whether you like it or not," Mace said. But he did not explain what he had meant, and something made Emerald afraid to ask.

Chapter Seven

❦ ❧

T HEY had gone about a hundred miles, Mace estimated. They had crossed the Kansas River—ferried across by Shawnee and Delaware Indians on precarious hide-covered bull boats—when Emerald became uncomfortably aware that she was about to begin her monthly flux.

Usually this event did not bother her overmuch, and she had often scoffed at Aunt Anna's calling this female function a sickness. But the unaccustomed work and food, and the worry of the past few months had sapped her strength, and today she had to admit that she felt very sick indeed.

They pulled up for their customary noon rest, the wagons strung out in a long line. People moved about, stretching their legs, starting fires, or collecting wood for fuel. Martha Rigney scolded her son Bob for something, her voice shrill.

Emerald dragged herself over to sit down under the shade of a large, dull-green bush. The sun was hot today, a glaring ball overhead, hurting her eyes. At any other time, she would have basked in its warmth after the days of rain. But now she could only sit and suffer from the grinding cramps that clawed at her.

"Emerald?" Margaret called from the wagon.

"What? I'm here," she managed to reply.

Margaret climbed down from the wagon, her brown merino dress crumpled from hours of sitting. She held up the half-finished sleeve of a blue sweater she was knitting for Orrin.

"Emerald, would you come and help me wind some more yarn? I—" Her voice abruptly stopped when she saw Emerald. "Why, what's wrong, Emerald? Your face is as white as biscuit dough."

"I—I'm fine."

"You most certainly are not. You're wet with perspiration." Margaret stepped closer and peered down at the younger girl. Then she drew in her breath sharply. "Why, Emerald, I think you'd better come in the wagon."

Weakly Emerald allowed herself to be helped to the shelter of the Wylie wagon. Her knees felt rubbery beneath her, her forehead clammy. She collapsed on the crude padding of blankets that Margaret had fashioned on the floor of the wagon, in front of the stacks of foods, trunks, and boxes.

"Good heavens, Emerald, is it your monthlies? I had no idea you felt them so hard."

"I don't usually," Emerald whispered.

There was a long pause. Emerald could hear Margaret's breathing. Then she spoke, almost as if to herself.

"Forgive me, honey. I—I thought—" Margaret's rough hand touched hers. "I've wronged you, Emerald. I guess I thought—your coming away with us as sudden as you did—I still thought you might be pregnant, even though you said you weren't."

"I could have been," something made Emerald say. She went on in a muffled voice, telling Margaret about Anton deLane, the confused story about herself being a "slave," Anton forcing himself into her room, the headlong flight from Hundred Oaks.

"Honey. Oh, honey." Margaret's hand patted her. "The good Lord must have been watching over you to get you away as He did. Well, you can rest assured I'll never tell anyone. And don't you speak of it again, either, especially not in front of the other women. That Martha Rigney—I've a feeling about her. She can be hard and unforgiving when she chooses to be."

Margaret knelt awkwardly and put a blanket over Emerald. "You just rest now," she said. "You'll feel better after a while."

That afternoon and the next day, Emerald rode in the wagon. Evidently Margaret had given a satisfactory explanation to Orrin, for he said nothing.

Geertrud VandeBusch and Martha Rigney stopped by the wagon the next evening, ostensibly to talk to Margaret. Geertrud, a thin, pale woman of about forty-five, had brought a batch of raisin cakes.

"For the young'uns to try," she explained. "For all that Herman's such a hearty eater, we did have some left. I made a double batch."

As Margaret thanked her, Martha Rigney, twisting her big hands in the folds of her apron, looked sharply at Emerald, who was sitting beside the fire.

"If you ask me, Margaret, that hired girl of yours is not as strong as you let on. In fact, she looks downright peaked."

"Oh, she's fine," Margaret said. "It's her monthlies, that's all."

"Sickly once a month means a sickly woman,"

Martha said. The three women moved away from the wagon, but Emerald could still hear them.

"But you don't know anything about her, do you?" Martha commented. "Other than that she's an orphan and comes from some plantation near Baton Rouge?"

"I know enough to know she's a good worker. She's been a good deal of help to me."

"She'll be no help to you when she gets herself pregnant," Martha said. "That's what happens to these little baggages when they find themselves footloose and fancy-free. With all these men about camp lookin' at her the way they are—"

"I haven't noticed anyone looking at her."

"Then you're not watching. I've seen 'em, all right. That Charles Morris, he can't take his eyes off'n her. And Zelig York, for all he's travelin' with a preacher, don't appear to be no better than he should be. Mark my words, you'd better keep that girl close to the wagon. Or there's going to be some fornicating."

Emerald flushed angrily as she heard this last word. Then, surprisingly, Geertrud VandeBusch sprang to her defense. "If I were you, I'd watch my tongue, Martha Rigney. Just because a girl is pretty doesn't mean she's loose." Geertrud pushed at a pale strand of hair that had escaped her sunbonnet, looking tired.

"You've got two girls of your own, Geertrud. Did I hit a wee bit close to home?" Martha's rawboned face looked triumphant. "Well, so long as I'm along, there'll be no hanky-panky around here. I don't stand for it. And God is watching everything we do. I do know that."

"I'm sure you do," Margaret said dryly.

Later, as Emerald helped to wash up the supper dishes, Margaret gave an irritated shrug of the shoulders. "Never you mind about that Martha Rigney," she consoled Emerald. "She's led a hard life, working on the farm like a man and all. She takes God's word a bit much to heart."

Emerald smiled. She wished there was some way she could thank Margaret for all she had done. Taking her along on this Western trip, defending her to the other women of the camp, showing such sympathy and warmth when she heard the real reason that Emerald had had to leave Hundred Oaks.

That night, Emerald had a strange and disturbing dream. In it, she struggled to climb a barren, rocky hillside, her feet scraping on loose stones and boulders. There was some need, some urgent, dreamlike need for her to reach the top of that hill. Yet her limbs felt leaden, so that it was an effort to take each step.

But the strange part of the dream was that three men waited at the top of the hill. One of them was Mace Bridgeman, his light-brown hair wind-tossed, his face jaunty and confident. Next to him was the doctor, Ben Coult, his thin lips twisted bitterly. But the third man she had never seen before. He was dark-skinned, his face wild, exotic, fierce. He had amber eyes, eyes that seemed to pierce through her very body, to mesmerize her. They made her think of a wolf. . . .

She awoke perspiring. Faint light had crept into her tent; it was nearly dawn. What a thing to dream! she told herself. What could it have meant?

They were really on the prairie now. That morning they crossed a stream bed with a steep bank on one side, swirling, spring-flooded water, and an equally steep bank on the other side. Saul Rigney had snapped an axle, delaying them for several hours while he made repairs.

Everyone took advantage of the delay, and after the noon meal, eaten in the shade of the cottonwoods that grew along the river, Emerald got out the books and set Timmie to copying a page. As the children worked, she sat making quick sketches of the camp's activity.

To her right, groups of cattle, oxen, and horses grazed. Trude VandeBusch wandered about, her bonnet off, her yellow-white hair shining in the sun as she picked wild flowers. To Emerald's left, Red Arbuthnot and his sons were carving up an antelope they had shot, a process so grisly that Emerald decided *not* to draw it. They would all have fresh meat for supper, Red had boasted. But, seeing the red-and-white, mottled carcass, already swarming with flies, Emerald was not sure if she would enjoy that treat or not.

How beautiful this country was, she thought, averting her eyes from the butchering. She wished she could capture the brilliance of its colors. The grass was like a rolling green sea, set into undulating waves by the gentle prairie wind. In places it grew as tall as she herself, and everywhere were wild flowers, goldenrod, wild indigo, and others she could not name.

In places, cutting the sea of grass like islands, were streams and scattered groves, or marshes where frogs bellowed and croaked. They had found bleached elk antlers, buffalo skulls, had heard wolves and coyotes howling in the night. Five times they had seen antelope, graceful, quicksilver animals it seemed a shame to kill and eat.

But as yet, other than at the Kansas River, they had seen no Indians, although Mace said there had been rumors of raiding Pawnees from the north.

"But I don't think they're dangerous now," he had added. "They were hard hit by smallpox about ten years ago. They don't give much trouble these days."

Indians! Emerald had shivered. Nighttime talk about the campfires often touched on this topic. Wyatt Thatcher told of a family he knew that had been waylaid by Indians, the adults scalped and killed, and one eight-year-old boy taken captive and never heard from again. "Them Indian men do nothing but lust for white women," Martha Rigney had said in a deep whisper. "That's all they want."

Mace, hearing this, had laughed uproariously. "I think they've enough to keep them busy with their own women. Their women outnumber the men, anyway," he had added. But Martha had been angry. And she had stubbornly stuck to her own ideas.

It was midafternoon before the repairs were made and the wagon train got under way again. And it was immediately after the wheels started rolling that Emerald had her encounter with Zelig York.

Zelig was a bulky, barrel-chested man in his early forties, with a rolling gait and untidy, stained clothing. His arms were slightly longer than usual, and his shoulders were hunched. Even his jaw was forward-thrusting, his mouth set with large yellowish teeth that gapped in front where several were missing. Yet Zelig was a dextrous whittler, and spent his time in camp carving out odd, gnomelike animals and birds that he put away in his wagon afterward.

Emerald did not like him. She wasn't sure why; the man had been polite enough to her, although his eyes had stared at her boldly. But most of the men had given her appraising looks, she reminded herself. And, as Margaret had pointed out, Zelig was traveling with a man of God, which must make him all right.

The Reverend Billie Colfax, however, also made her uneasy. He spoke little, and the pair generally kept to themselves, close to their own wagon. They were carrying sawmill equipment, Billie said. It would be well received in California, where goods of all kinds, especially machinery, were scarce. This was why their wagon was so heavy that it took four yoke of oxen to pull it.

But it didn't seem right to Emerald that a preacher should be quite so concerned with business and saw-mills. And why would he be so quiet, so distant from other people?

But she was not thinking of this now, for there was a more immediate problem to concern her. When the wagons had started up again, Timmie couldn't find his dog.

"Please, Emerald, help me look for Ed, will you?" the boy begged. "He's only a pup, and I'm afraid he might get lost and not be able to find us agin. That grass is taller than he is."

Emerald laughed. "Dogs have pretty good noses, Timmie. He'll be able to smell us, I'm sure."

"But maybe his nose hasn't grown up enough yet!" Timmie wailed. "He's still only a puppy. Please, you have to help me. Susie's too little, and Ma's in the wagon, and Jan and Bob are both helping with the herd. Oh, please, Em!"

"All right, we'll look."

Obediently, Emerald began searching. She had covered an area about a quarter of a mile on either side of the wagons, wading through the tall grass where the grasshoppers jumped, when suddenly she remembered Billie Colfax's dog, Blackie. She recalled hearing barking and yipping coming from the rear of the wagon train. And Blackie was a mean-tempered beast, she thought uneasily. Surely he wouldn't—

Leaving Timmie, she walked toward the rear of the wagon train. Here she found Billie's wagon, today the last in line. He was cracking his whip over the heads of his oxen, and lash marks on their backs told that the whip had been used often.

"Is it really necessary to whip your animals so hard?" she demanded indignantly.

Cold blue eyes regarded her. "I've a lot of equipment to haul, and I've no intention of abandoning it here on the prairie. These beasts had better pull, or I'll know the reason why."

"But—"

"Be careful there, miss, of the dog. You don't want him to bite you, do you?"

The animal, moving silently, had come to crouch at Emerald's side. He was a part-mongrel shepherd, and his ears were flattened, his neck hackles raised. Emerald edged away.

"Don't worry, he won't hurt you none if you just leave," came another voice. "We got him trained so he don't like intruders. Nope, he don't like 'em one bit."

Emerald whirled about to see Zelig York approaching, his gait rolling slightly. He wore dark pants, a linsey-woolsey shirt, and a broad white felt hat. His cheeks were covered with stubbly beard.

"I'm looking for Timmie's dog," she explained. "I thought I heard barking coming from back here. You haven't seen Edgar, have you?"

Somehow she found that Zelig had taken her arm and was leading her away from the wagon. A sour body smell emanated from him, and she was aware of the food and grease stains on his clothes. Didn't he ever bathe?

"You thought maybe Blackie there might have eaten him up?" Zelig's grin revealed the gap in his front teeth.

"Oh, no, I'm sure your dog wouldn't do such a thing," she said hastily. "I just thought—"

"Blackie don't eat little dogs," Zelig observed with another grin. "But maybe I did see him run by here an hour or so back. Maybe he got caught in a prairie dog hole. There's a big town of 'em near here —a hundred acres at least. Them animals dig tunnels under the grass. Can break a horse's leg. Maybe even a dog's."

"Oh, do you think so? Timmie's so worried!"

They were still walking, and were almost out of sight of the wagon train, which had moved into a slight dip in the undulating land.

"Why do you keep such a savage dog?" she asked.

"Blackie isn't savage. He's ornery, that's all. Billie has got him trained to guard the wagon. We got some valuable equipment in there. This way we can be sure it won't be stolen."

"But who would want to steal your equipment? And even if they did, where could they possibly take it?"

"Jest a precaution, that's all. You don't get to be a preacher without being a cautious man." Zelig laughed.

"Perhaps."

They reached the prairie dog town. The grass was shorter here, revealing the prairie dog holes, each one a little raised mound of earth guarded by a funny, squirrellike little rodent that watched their passage alertly.

Although they passed several of the mounds, there was no sign of Edgar.

"Unless he's burrowed down in one," Zelig said. "And can't get back out."

"Oh, I'm sure Edgar wouldn't do anything as foolish as that! He's been such a good dog."

"Dogs is dogs. Now, why don't we jest stop here and look for signs of digging and scratching? If'n he's gone and done a thing like that, that's what we'll probably find."

Bending anxiously to the next little hole, thinking of Edgar trapped in the dark earth, Emerald suddenly felt Zelig's hand closing about her right breast. She tried to move away, but he embraced her from behind, both hands cupping her flesh. She screamed, and he clamped one hand over her mouth.

"Now, now, Miss Emerald. You don't want no one to hear you, do you? Not that they would. The train's mebbe half a mile ahead by this time. And them oxen will be makin' so much noise that they won't hear you yell out at all."

Furiously, she tried to pull the large, sweaty palm away from her face.

"Hey, keep still, will you?" His free hand was all over her, runnning down her belly and into the apex of her thighs. "This won't take long, little book-readin' girl. And then you'll know what a real man is like."

Trude VandeBusch galloped ahead of the wagon train, feeling the powerful movements of her mare, Golden, between her thighs. It was a delicious, sensual feeling, curiously exciting.

She rode astride, her bonnet hanging by its string, her hair flying, her breasts bobbing. She wore a pair of her brother Pieert's pants underneath her skirt.

Shameless, Martha Rigney had declared, but Trude didn't care. Who would see her here? And what did it matter, anyway? Pa had finally given his consent for this type of costume—she could twist him around her little finger. And she didn't care what others thought of her. No matter what ugly names they had for her, it just wasn't important.

What a shame it all was, she thought rebelliously. Boys could gallop about as they pleased. They could go swimming nude if they wished, with no questions asked, and no whipping to face when they got back. Girls, however, were hemmed in on every side, by fathers, by mothers, by family and neighbors and convention. By women like Martha Rigney who were secretly jealous of young females.

Well, she, Trude, didn't plan to be hemmed in, no matter what Pa thought he had planned for her. As if to give emphasis to this thought, Trude spurred Golden to a full gallop, dodging a prairie dog hole just in time. Those little entrances could cost a horse a leg, she knew. But not Golden, she thought. Golden was like Trude herself, too free-spirited to be brought down, by marriage or by any man.

They had left Michigan because of her, her and the Klaus twins from down the road. They had lain in the Klaus barn for hours, it seemed, all three of them twined together, arm upon thigh, breast against belly, lip upon flesh.

Never, if she lived to be a hundred, could she forget *that* experience. She could have lived the rest of her life there in that barn, giving herself to the unthinking delights of the body.

Then, like an avenging apparition, Pa stood in the doorway. Herman VandeBusch, all three hundred and ten pounds of him, back unexpectedly from church, pitchfork in hand.

Ordinarily she considered Pa a rather humorous person, with his indecisive ways, his rambling discourses, his hearty appetite for food that kept mother busy in the kitchen for hours. But now his anger was anything but humorous.

"What in God's name do you think you're doing? Going to produce a long line of bastards to help me with the farming?"

"Ah, no, Pa. No." She would never have a bastard, for she was sure she was barren. She scrambled for her clothes, all three of them stumbling over each other in their haste. But it was not funny, not funny at all. That pitchfork had long tines. Once she had seen Pa spear a rat with it.

"Well, get your clothes on and get yourself back to the house. I'll take care of you there. As for you, young men, you can settle among yourselves which one of you is going to marry my daughter. I expect to hear the answer in half an hour." His voice sank low, as if talking to himself. "My God—two of 'em . . ."

Back at the VandeBusch farmhouse, in half an hour's time, came a sheepish Rolf Klaus, to inform her father that neither he nor Jan could oblige, since they were not the only ones to have taken advantage of Trude's body. It seemed that a number of others had also done so, some of them married and some of them not.

It had been going on for years, Rolf said, since Trude was twelve. She was well known in the area, for twenty miles about. Laughed at. And sought.

Pa had locked Trude in her room for two days, with only her mother to bring her food. Angry as he was, it was physically impossible for Pa VandeBusch to deny anyone food.

"He's thinking," was all that Geertrud would tell her, looking at her daughter with mixed amazement, revulsion, and grief. "He's still thinking."

They hadn't known, Trude could tell. They really hadn't known. A big lump seemed to stick in her throat. Well, she had lived from day to day, not thinking ahead. The men had promised to keep it quiet, but they had betrayed her.

Trude knew that as much as the men and boys needed her, she needed them more. There was a hunger in her, a desire as powerful as the urge for food or water. Men, she knew, satisfied *their* hunger as best they could, and with whom they could. But women were supposed to keep themselves pure. Whether they wanted to stay pure or not, and no matter what their sexual needs were. It just was not fair.

At the end of the second day, Pa unlocked Trude's door and told her—to her utter astonishment—that the entire family was going to California. There no one would know them, or laugh at them. There Trude could find a man to marry her. Katje, too, could find a husband along the trail or after they arrived. The boys, Pieert and Jan, would eventually get farms of their own. The soil was incredibly rich, he explained, the climate fabulous. They would grow grapes for wine. They would raise lettuce, cucumbers, cherries, apricots, oranges. They would fish for trout in the rivers, and hunt wild animals, which would practically fall in front of their rifles.

Trude could only stare at him. Pa had wanted to go to California all the time, she began to realize, and was seizing upon her as an excuse. Under these circumstances, Geertrud could hardly object to leaving her home. They *had* to leave.

Trude felt a wild impulse to laugh. She, by serving

her own needs, was serving her father's needs as well.

He laid down strict rules for her behavior. "Now, the damage is done, but I don't expect to see any more foolin' out of you. If you openly become a whore, that's what you're going to have to *be,* you understand? Best place for you is marriage to a good, strong man who doesn't know you. Be lots of them in California. So you mind yourself until we get there, hear? I haven't told the others what you did. Maybe they don't know. But don't you tell 'em. Give yourself half a chance. Or, believe me, folks won't give you none at all."

Trude listened, then put this speech out of her mind. She was eighteen now, a grown woman by anyone's standards. She would do as she pleased. But since she loved her family and thought that they loved her, she would go with them. Whatever happened after they reached California, would happen.

Now, having galloped half a mile ahead of the wagon train and its ever-present dust cloud, she decided to circle back. As she rode, she began to think idly of Emerald Regan. She wished that Emerald, too, had a horse of her own to ride. Emerald would have been more fun to ride with than Katje, who could only whine and complain of the heat.

Five minutes later, Trude heard a high, furious scream.

She urged Golden forward, and saw Emerald and Zelig York struggling together. Emcrald's fists pounded at Zelig's York's face. Emerald screamed again, and in spite of herself Trude had to admire the girl's courage. Didn't she know that she was no physical match for those powerful arms of Zelig's? He was only playing with her, as a barnyard cat might toy with a sparrow.

And soon, when Zelig tired of the game, he would get down to the real business, Trude knew. And no one from the train would be able to hear Emerald's screams. With iron wheels squealing, men shouting, dogs barking, and hooves clopping the earth, those in the wagons could hear nothing but their own noises.

She wheeled up on Golden and jumped out of the saddle. Zelig paused and looked up at her, his pupils widening.

"Hello, Zelig," Trude said.

As the man's mouth fell open, Emerald twisted away from him.

"Emerald, take my horse and ride back to the wagons," Trude ordered quickly. "Zelig and I will take care of this little problem. And do promise Zelig you won't talk, will you? I'm sure he didn't mean to go so far. He just lost control of himself, that's all."

Emerald tossed her head, two angry red spots outlined on her cheeks. "I'll think about it," she said. "But Trude—shouldn't you come, too? We'll ride pillion. I don't want to leave you alone here."

"No."

"But—"

"I said no, Emerald. You go along."

For an instant, the two girls stared at each other. Then Emerald swung herself onto Golden's back and was gone in a clatter of hoofbeats.

Trude looked at Zelig. His lips were twisted in a half-smile.

"I saw you in the river," he said hoarsely.

"Did you? Well, I'm waiting."

Then he was upon her, growling low in his throat and pulling off her clothes. She sank into the grass and let it happen, watching over his shoulder at the deep blue bowl of sky above her.

Chapter Eight

❧ ❧

THEY reached the Platte River, and traveled along its south bank, beside the broad, meandering brown water, its shores dotted with cottonwood and oak. In places, the river divided around islands of trees or sandbars, bare and gleaming in the sun. The banks were rich, soft, yellow mud, the water so brown that in a cup it looked like chocolate.

Everywhere were signs of the buffalo—their skulls and whitening bones, their tracks to the water, the circular indentations where they had wallowed in the mud. Edgar—for he had been found after all, yapping at a prairie dog—chased back and forth, exhilarated by the strange new scents.

"They're immense beasts, Emerald," Mace told her with relish. "A bull might weigh more than two thousand pounds—that's a heck of a lot of buffalo. And this is their miserable time of year—in the warm weather they shed their coats until their hindquarters are practically bare. This makes them tempting targets for flies and mosquitoes. That's why we're seeing the wallows. They love to roll around and plaster themselves with wet mud—anything to get away from the torment of being bitten." He swatted at a fly, making a wry face. "And there are times when I'm tempted to see if mud doesn't work just as well for humans!"

One afternoon Emerald received an unexpected chance to write a letter. They met a covey of bullboats —she counted eleven—navigating precariously down the Platte. The boats sagged with their burden of furs and shaggy, bearded, wild-looking men in buckskins. The two groups hailed each other, and the men from the bullboats joined them for the noon meal. They were from the Rocky Mountain Fur Company, they explained, and planned to market their furs in Saint Louis.

One of them was younger than the others, a pimply boy with a beard only poorly begun. He kept staring at Emerald until she did not know whether to laugh or be irritated. As they sat around the noon fire, eating fried beefsteaks and dried apple pie, he confided to her that his name was Bill, and if she wished to send a letter, he would mail it in Saint Louis for her.

A letter! Emerald's heart gave an enormous jump. Abruptly a wave of homesickness swept over her. Aunt Anna, Cora, Charmaine . . . the lovely columned house at Hundred Oaks, with its gracious verandas . . .

Did they ever think of her? Did they miss her as she did them? Were they—all right? Emerald had to blink hard to keep from crying.

Although she had already posted Aunt Anna one letter in Council Bluffs, she managed to compose another one: *I am fine, and I am working my way to California with a respectable family. We are traveling by wagon. We have not had bad going thus far, and I am finding this mode of travel very interesting. . . .*

She could imagine the shock and excitement when

Aunt Anna opened it, the bubbling, eager questions of Cora and the other girls. Would she ever see little Cora again? She supposed not. This country was too sweepingly enormous for that. There would be no reason for any of the deLanes to leave Baton Rouge. The girls would marry, would become planters' wives themselves. Anna would live the circumspect life of a widow. Anton would—

But Emerald could not think about him. She felt her lips trembling as she sealed the letter.

She was cheered, however, when she handed the letter to the pimpled Bill, for he stuttered and blushed, nearly dropping the letter before tucking it into his filthy buckskin shirt.

He would probably wear it next to his heart for the entire trip, she thought in amusement. She only hoped that the bullboat wouldn't capsize. If it did, and the letter got wet, Aunt Anna might never learn what had happened to her.

Several of the other emigrants also sent letters. Trude pressed several into the hands of one of the men, smiling at him boldly. But Orrin and Margaret did not send any, Emerald noticed. Nor did Zelig York or Billie Colfax.

A preacher not having anyone to send a letter to? But perhaps it was so. As Wyatt Thatcher said wistfully, "Guess I passed through too many towns, gamblin' a bit and sellin' my medicine, to pick up any dust."

During these days she learned something more of Mace Bridgeman. One dusk they made a late camp, and night was falling as she started the fire and began to cut up beef for supper. Mace, who as guide alternated taking his meals among the various wagons, was at the Wylie wagon this night. After the meal was over, he lingered on, talking to Emerald as she cleared away the dishes they had used.

"What would make a girl like you start on a trip like this, anyway?" he asked. "You should be back wherever you came from, getting ready to marry some good-looking man and have a dozen babies."

She flushed, scraping food scraps off a tin plate and not looking at him. "I—I had to leave the plantation when my uncle died and I had a—disagreement with my cousin," she finished miserably.

Mace's eyes were thoughtful. "Well, if the truth were known, there are many men who've traveled West with a secret or two under their belts. Not to mention a woman or two."

Emerald flushed. "Perhaps. And *your* secret, Mace? Why are *you* here with the rest of us?"

Mace gave her a quick grin. Then he began to tell her about his life as a boy on a large rice plantation near Charleston, as the son of an impoverished schoolmaster.

"Dad was a tutor at Kingdom Come—that was the rather fancy name of the plantation." Mace laughed ruefully. "There were seven boys in the King family, and they were kind enough to allow me to share their lessons. We learned Latin, Greek, mathematics—all the subjects a boy might need if he planned to go to Harvard College. But I also studied drawing and painting whenever I had a free moment."

"But however did you get *here?*" Emerald wondered. "Here on the prairie, of all places?"

The gray eyes smiled at her. "There were times, Emerald, when my father and I disagreed—rather violently. He was a determined man. And I suppose I was a headstrong boy. He thought I was a fool to be so absorbed in my painting. And his job required him to

102

give a lot of attention to boys stupider than myself. Boys who had the money to go to college, but not the brains. He had hopes for me, and instead I dreamed of going away to Paris to study painting—and knew I'd never be able to. The best I could ever hope for was to be a white overseer on one of the plantations or a tutor like my father.

"One day in 1831, though, that changed. A man came to dinner at Kingdom Come, and I was lucky enough to meet him. He had sad eyes and a long nose and long, flowing hair, and white sideburns, and his name was John James Audubon. He was a naturalist and an extraordinary artist. He painted birds and small animals in their own natural settings, Emerald— not just sketches, but exquisite paintings of birds among leaves and branches and berries. He had won great fame in Europe with his *Ornithological Biography,* and he was at our own dinner table, showing us some of his best work.

"And when he announced that he was looking for a new assistant artist, that he planned to leave Charleston and head South to the Floridas—and then the Red River, the Arkansas, and even the Pacific Ocean— well, I couldn't stop myself. I volunteered."

"And then you traveled with him?"

"Yes, at age fourteen I left with him and a bird-skinner to become his assistant, and—"

"A bird-skinner?"

"Yes. I'm afraid that Audubon did all his drawings of stuffed birds. He would shoot them and then stuff and draw them posed so they would seem lifelike. That was the one area where we disagreed. I could never see killing a beautiful creature just to do a painting."

"Did you travel with Mr. Audubon for very long?"

"For several years. I assisted him with his paintings

of large numbers of birds, Emerald—pelicans, cormorants, canvasback ducks, grackles. Beautiful paintings these were, too. Masterful, unforgettable. He was a strange, wandering man, Emerald, so interested in everything around him, so eager for experience. He taught me much."

"But what brought you West?"

Mace frowned, his eyes becoming distant. "Eventually Audubon returned to New York, and I moved on. I'd learned all that he could teach me, and I wanted to do my own work—only I wanted to paint live animals, not stuffed ones. It's a difficult task, Emerald, to capture the grace and delicacy and strength of a wild animal when you can only observe him for hours, then sketch him as best you can. But I refuse to kill an animal unless I have to for food.

"Eventually I ended up in the Rockies—scouting, trapping when I had to survive, living off the land so that I could do my work. I love the West, Emerald. Love it deep in my bones and brain and gut. And I have an ugly feeling about this land. Sooner or later man is going to discover it and move in and change it all. And the animals who live here and own it will be no more."

"But it's so bare here—so open and empty. I can't imagine—"

Mace's eyes held sadness. "It will happen, Emerald. Perhaps only in a generation or two. Wagon trains like this one are only the first. More wagons will come, and more after that. Eventually the animals will have to struggle for survival. But I'll have them in my paintings. And someday my work will be published for everyone to see."

Mace said this with such fierce conviction that Emerald believed him.

"And your father?" she asked at last. "What happened to him? Is he still teaching on the plantation?"

A look of pain crossed Mace's face. "He died, Emerald, shortly after I left Charleston. He was all the family I ever had, and he's gone. For all of our disagreements, he really loved me in his way. And that is the one real regret I have in this life—that I left home so young, that I never knew my father better."

The campfire had flickered down, the dishes were scoured, and Mace took his leave, walking thoughtfully away, leaving Emerald to wonder just which elements of his life story he had left out. He had not mentioned women, or love at all. Had there ever been a girl, someone who had loved him? Or had his life consisted only of lonely wandering and work?

Today they would cross the Platte. They had risen earlier than usual, and Emerald, out searching for buffalo chips, was still rubbing sleep from her eyes. Wood was scarce, and they often had to burn dried buffalo dung, euphemistically called "chips," in pits dug in the ground. The idea made Emerald feel squeamish but she didn't want to be a complainer like Katje, so she kept silent.

Emerald was bent over, collecting these chips, when she heard voices and the gay, carefree sound of a man and a woman laughing together. Looking up, she saw Trude and Mace Bridgeman huddled close by the corner of the VandeBusch wagon. Their faces were easy with shared merriment. Emerald bit her lip and looked away, flinging a hard, dry chip into her gunnysack with unnecessary force.

She moved out of sight of the wagons. A few moments later, when her sack was almost full, she heard footsteps behind her and turned to see Mace.

"Hello, Emerald. I see you're engaged in one of the less savory chores of camp life. Do you need any help?"

"No," she told him, lifting her chin. An odd, hurtful pang stabbed in her chest. "The bag is almost full, thank you!"

Mace shrugged. "Too bad, then. I would have been glad to assist."

"I don't need your help!" After she had said this, Emerald could have bitten her lip, for the relaxed look disappeared from Mace's face, leaving it blank and noncommittal. She could have flung up her hands with vexation and with anger at herself for behaving like such a fool in front of him. Just because he had talked with Trude VandeBusch, had laughed with her . . . Surely Mace had a right to speak with any woman he wished.

Now she realized that he was speaking to her again. "Remember when we talked about the stars, Emerald? Would you like to watch them with me some night after supper?"

He was asking her to walk out with him, to—

"I—I don't know." Her heart was slamming erratically. "My—my employer, Margaret, is getting near her time now and doesn't feel well. I should stay near her in case she needs me."

The gray eyes, focused so intently on her, made her shiver. "Surely her husband can stay with her. Aren't you entitled to a bit of fun?"

"I—I don't know. One of the men in camp—" Emerald thought uneasily of Zelig York. "One of the men has been rather too bold with me. I've felt safer staying near the wagon, near people."

"Which man?" Mace advanced toward her, a scowl

transfixing his features. "Has any of them dared to touch you? If they have, I—"

Emerald swallowed hard. She thought of the burly strength in Zelig York's long arms, the firearms that all the settlers carried in their wagons and on their persons. This wasn't a city, with a constable to handle lawbreakers. If she told Mace that Zelig had nearly raped her, Mace might take matters into his own hands. With the fury now dawning in his eyes, she could imagine anything happening. The two shooting at each other, fighting.

"No," she managed to say. "It was nothing, really. And I'm sure it won't happen again."

"If it does, I want you to promise to tell me." Again that curious light in Mace's eyes, the warmth radiating out from him until she felt weak.

"I—I will."

"Good. Then perhaps tonight, Emerald, after we cross the river? They'll all want to celebrate then, anyway. We'll have a fandango by the fire, and our friend Wyatt can give us the medicine show he's been promising. Afterward . . ."

"I don't know." She looked up to feel the hot searching of his eyes.

"Did you think, Emerald, that I would forget the way you looked coming out of the river that night? You looked like a—I don't know how to express it. Like a wild woods creature. And a beautiful one."

Trude had been in that river, too, a cold little voice reminded her. Trude, with her full, soft breasts. But she put that thought aside.

"I'm afraid I'm just an ordinary girl. And I shouldn't have been bathing there at all without a guard, as you were kind enough to point out to me."

"Emerald."

He came nearer to her. Numbly, she stood holding the gunnysack full of chips, her heart pounding in her ears.

"Put that damned thing down, will you, Emerald? You can pick it up later."

She dropped her arms and let the sack slide to the ground from suddenly nerveless fingers.

"Hey, there." His hands were at the back of her neck, fumbling with the pins that she used to discipline her heavy dark curls into their knot. "You have lovely hair, did you know that? Sometime I would like to see it flowing all about your shoulders. That would be a pretty sight."

"I—" She swallowed hard. She felt as if she were paralyzed, mesmerized by his closeness. Everything in her seemed to respond to this man without reason or caution. Did she love him? She wasn't sure. She only knew that her eyes needed to see him and her hands ached to touch the strands of light-brown hair that were constantly falling into his eyes.

"Well, come here. Stars be damned. We don't need them, do we?"

He kissed her, and the sensations were even more intense than on their last encounter. Emerald responded fully, pressing her body into his with a knowledge she had not known she possessed. She felt his hands press into her back, sliding down to the fullness of her buttocks. But, unlike Zelig's, his touch wasn't repulsive. She wanted more. . . .

"Emerald! Emerald!" A high-pitched, childish voice rang out. It was Susannah, skipping through the long grass. "Em, Ma wants you to come with the chips! Pa's waitin' for his breakfast!"

Reluctantly Mace let go of her. "Tonight?" he whispered.

"I—I can't."

"I'll see you after supper. You want to come, you want to see me, and you know it."

"No," she whispered.

He turned and strode away. Slowly Emerald picked up the gunnysack, added a few more chips, and walked with Susannah back to the wagon.

Tonight, she thought. But no, she couldn't. She felt a heavy wash of blood staining her cheeks. If she met Mace, she knew she wouldn't be able to control herself. She'd do things she would regret.

Susannah tugged at her hand, chattering about the herd of buffalo they had seen the previous afternoon. At least four hundred beasts there had been, huge, shaggy, untidy animals who made a flowing blot of brown across the grass.

"Timmie says he's going to go out and shoot one," Susannah prattled. "He says he and Pa are going to shoot at least ten or twenty—even more than they got yesterday. We'll have more than we can ever eat, Emerald!"

"It will be a change from antelope and beef, won't it?"

Emerald let the child's talk flow over her. *Perhaps he'll marry me,* she was thinking. Immediately, doubt overwhelmed her. She couldn't quite picture Mace in formal coat and cravat, presiding at a long table filled with his own wife and family. He seemed made for the outdoors, for slouching along on his gelding, the hair under his hat blowing in the prairie wind. He was never in one spot for long, and spent his nights on the open grass, rolled up in a blanket. Sometimes he would be gone from camp all day, to return with an easy look about him, as if he had somehow communed with the world he found out there.

No, Mace would not be easy to tame.

But surely love would change all of that, Emerald told herself. Most men eventually settled down, and Mace would, too. It was the way things happened, the way they always had happened.

They reached the Wylie wagon.

"It's about time you got back," Orrin said irritably. His face was already dusty and perspiring.

"I—I had to look for the chips." Emerald busied herself laying the fire, hoping he would not notice the color in her face, or her hastily pinned-up hair. Susannah had already squatted by the wagon wheel, crooning to her cornhusk dolls.

"Well, I want to get a good start this morning. The water's high, and this may take all day."

"The river won't be bad, will it, Orrin?" Margaret came out of the wagon with slices of buffalo steak, killed yesterday, to fry in flour and fat.

"The Lord only knows. All the streams we've crossed have been high. Bridgeman says the river's a bit high, too, on account of spring flooding, but we ought to be able to get across if we're careful. I don't want to sit around here waiting too long. We have to get to California before the winter snows, or we won't make it at all."

Margaret began dredging the meat in the flour, her fingers white-coated. "That river does look fearsome," she said. "Like a sea, almost, it's so broad."

"It ain't a sea, though. Maybe a mile across at its widest part, and we're findin' a place that ain't so wide. We should be all right."

Orrin's voice did not hold full conviction, for rumors had been passing along the wagon train that the river was full of quicksand which would swallow up any wagon that became stalled in the crossing.

110

Margaret shivered visibly. "Some say there's quicksand—"

"Maybe there is," snapped Orrin. "But if the good Lord got us this far, He'll see fit to get us over that, too." He got up to touch his wife's shoulder. "I got faith, Margaret. Otherwise, I wouldn'ta got us this far. We got to go on and trust to God. It's all we can do."

Yes, he was right, Emerald thought, getting out the plates. All the same, she was glad that Mace Bridgeman was along.

Later, Emerald was to remember this river crossing in a swift blur of impressions—the stiff breeze that whipped the water into choppy waves, the pewter sky overhead, thick with the promise of rain. The emigrants gathered on the muddy bank, talking uneasily among themselves. Even Trude seemed subdued, her light hair skinned into braids and her bonnet on her head for once. Zelig York and Billie Colfax whispered together in low, tense voices.

After some hesitation, Orrin decided that the water was shallow enough to drive the oxen across, letting them pull the wagons behind them. Mace and Matt Arbuthnot would ride ahead, their horses testing the depth of the water. Mace's portfolio would ride in the Wylie wagon, well-swathed in waterproof oilcloth.

As they were waiting to start, Mace caught Emerald's eye. Slowly, deliberately, he winked. Confusion flooded through her. Yet she felt warmed, too. With Mace along, everything had to be all right, she told herself.

The Wylie wagon was the first one in line. Orrin, shouting and cracking his lash over the heads of the oxen, managed to get his team started. Forelegs splashing up brown water, the animals began to pull.

For about thirty yards, all went well. Then the lead pair began to balk at the feel of the water lapping against their bellies. They tossed their heads and jerked at the yoke, trying to turn back to shore.

Orrin, screaming and cursing, managed to get them righted just before the wagon, teetering on the soft river bottom, could overturn. Emerald, Margaret, and Susannah, huddled together in the wagon, clung to the wagon bed as it gave a sickening lurch, then righted itself just in time.

"Ma! Ma!" Susannah gripped Margaret, fingers clutching her cornhusk doll.

"It's all right, honey, really it is. Do you think Pa would take us across if it weren't all right?"

"Ma, we're going to tip over, I know we are! We'll drown in the quicksand!"

"No, we won't, Susie. It'll be just fine. You wait and see."

"I want to go home!" screamed Susannah, her face red. "I want to go home!"

"Well, we can't go home." Margaret's eyes met Emerald's. Would they ever get anywhere? Or would they all founder and sink into the mud?

They were nearing the center of the broad expanse of water now. Charles Morris, on foot, waist-deep in the water, was second in line behind them. They could hear him urging on his oxen.

The train was not taking a straight line across the water, but was twisting in a semicircle to the left because of a deeper area in the center where the water flowed slightly faster.

With dismay, Emerald saw that, although Orrin was shouting so loudly that his voice was nearly gone, the oxen were slowing up. They slipped and skidded, almost on the verge of swimming, their heads tossing in panic.

"Gee! Gee!" Orrin shouted. "Gee, you bastards!"

The wagon lurched again. Its left wheels were sinking, and a stream of water began to trickle through a crack in the caulking. Susannah buried her face in Margaret's lap.

Then they heard a shout from Matt Arbuthnot, and saw him wheel his mount about, waving and gesturing toward a point behind the Wylie wagon.

"What is it?" asked Margaret nervously.

"I don't know." Emerald crawled over Susannah's legs and climbed among the piles of goods, attempting to see out of the back.

"It's Charles Morris," she reported. "His oxen are out of control. They're heading off to the right."

"But isn't that the deeper part?" Margaret asked in dismay. "Why doesn't he stop them?"

"I don't know. I don't see him."

Mace Bridgeman came riding past them, his horse moving awkwardly through the waves, his pants wet to the waist. His lips were set, his face grim.

"Where's Morris, dammit?" Emerald heard Mace shout to Matt Arbuthnot. "In the water?"

"We'd better look."

Shocked, Emerald clung to the wagon bed, feeling suddenly cold. Her eyes searched the water, seeing only the brown expanse of waves, touched with silver in the grayed morning light. She thought of Charles Morris as she had last seen him, laughing by the campfire, twirling a buffalo tail and boasting of the three animals he had shot.

Her mind could not accept what had happened. The water was shallow, she kept telling herself. How could a grown man simply disappear in it without a trace? Oh, surely Charles had to be somewhere.

It was a frustrated search party that tried to comb the brown, opaque water. The horses and restive oxen stirred up the muddy bottom, so that little could be seen. All of the men and boys who did not have oxen to control were there. Trude, too, had joined the search. Even Timmie, wide-eyed, paddled about on Windy.

"He's got to be here somewhere!" she heard Mace explode angrily. "This damned water is only shoulder height in that hole, and everywhere else it's just three feet. He can't have drowned!"

"It only takes a pail of water to drown a man," Ben Coult said.

"Morris was a man, not a pewling baby!"

"Well, it's been more than twenty minutes. If we haven't found him by now, then he's dead."

Long minutes passed. Finally Mace let out a cry. Then, with Matt Arbuthnot's help, he pulled the body out of the water and laid it across his horse. The corpse was pale, its mouth and eyes open, water dripping from its hair and clothing.

"Poor devil. Poor damned devil." Mace's voice held a sorrowful anger. "To come all of this way, only to be bested by a river. And a shallow one at that."

"Emerald," Susannah began, from inside the wagon. "Em, what is it—"

"Close the wagon flap, Emerald," Mace ordered. "This is no sight for a child."

Emerald did as he asked, shivering violently.

It was their first death. Nausea rose, metallic, in Emerald's throat.

As if to compensate for this tragedy, the rest of the crossing went smoothly. Emerald stood on the muddy riverbank and watched as the rest of the wagons lurched across.

As they arrived, the emigrants began to cluster in small, shaken groups. Mace deposited Charles's body on the ground, where it lay, limp and obscene, like an adult-sized rag doll.

Ben Coult knelt by the corpse, his ear to the dead man's chest. "He's dead, all right." He pulled a blanket up over the sodden face.

"But how? How could it have happened?" Emerald burst out.

"I don't know. Maybe he was knocked over by an ox and panicked. Or maybe something else happened to him—a seizure or a heart attack. Perhaps if we had found him sooner we could have saved him. I just don't know."

They held the funeral services that night after supper. Billie Colfax stood over the opened grave in which Charles lay, still wrapped in the same blanket. His rolled form looked stiff and anonymous.

Billie read the service from a large black Bible. *For thou art the resurrection and the life . . .* The sonorous phrases seemed to disappear like smoke into the gray air.

They had divided up Charles's effects among the emigrants. Orrin would keep his small stock of money and personal things, in case relatives were ever found.

Margaret, standing close to Orrin, burst suddenly into tears. She clung to him as if her legs would not hold her up.

"We'll leave him here," she wept. "In the middle of nothing, in the middle of a wilderness. We'll leave him and go on. And he's only the first. There'll be more, Orrin. I feel it, I feel it in my bones. . . ."

"Hush, Margaret. Don't talk like that.'"

"But it's true."

They all stirred uneasily.

Matt Arbuthnot shoveled dirt over the grave, then rolled rocks over it so wild animals or Indians could not molest the body. Emerald closed her eyes and turned away. With a few shovels full of earth, life ended.

She began to walk quickly, toward the top of the ridge. Although the sky still threatened, it had not rained, and the air was full of an oppressive moisture, matching the blackness of her own mood.

She had set forth on this journey with a feeling of excitement and adventure, certain that all would be well, that any barriers could be overcome. Now she wasn't so sure.

She stood there a long time, gazing through a blur at the rolling land. But at last she heard a noise behind her, and turned to see Ben Coult climbing the slope toward her. He wore the fresh cotton shirt he had worn for the burial, but his expression was dark and withdrawn.

"It's going to rain," he said shortly. "You should go back to camp."

"I— Perhaps you're right." She glanced quickly at him, at the knifelike, intelligent face that hid its frustration so poorly. It was as if, she thought, there were some violence in him. Something deep and violent and hidden . . .

Then she turned and hurried away from him, her feet skidding on the grass.

Chapter Nine

❦ ❧

THE sun had set. They were all sitting around the Arbuthnots' campfire singing hymns, their voices rising in a sweet harmony that tore at Emerald's throat.

Around them the night was dark and full of the sound of insects. It hadn't rained after all. Just at sundown a patch of clear sky had appeared, to reveal the red ball of sun just before it sank. It was a moment of curious melancholy, of longing for home and loved ones left behind. All of them felt it, even Timmie, leaning against Emerald's knee.

Trude sat nearest the fire, her cheeks glowing red in its flickering light. Once she leaned over to whisper something to Mace Bridgeman, who sat near her.

In spite of herself, Emerald had to suppress another surge of jealousy. She still liked Trude well enough, but anyone who could lie with Zelig York—for she was sure this was what had happened that day—well, Emerald just didn't understand it.

The songs continued, bringing back memories of church services in Baton Rouge, herself wedged securely between little Cora and Charmaine. Thinking of this, Emerald bit her lip and tried to swallow back her homesickness and put her mind on other things.

Like Mace. She looked at him—his eyes were thoughtful, almost somber. To a mountain man, Emerald knew, death was common enough, a constant feature in the stories Mace had told them of Indian skirmishes, accidents, and illnesses that befell the trappers. Yet she knew that Mace held a special reverence for life. She was sure that this first trail death had affected him deeply.

Timmie fell asleep, slumped next to her leg, and Emerald gently eased him to a more comfortable position. When she looked up again, both Mace and Trude were gone.

For a minute she didn't believe it. Only this morning Mace had kissed her, had spoken of seeing her tonight. She hadn't agreed to walk out with him, but now she sat in the midst of the singing, feeling abandoned. Surely it wasn't as it seemed, she told herself. No doubt Mace had business elsewhere, and Trude was tired.

But where could they be? Outside the circle of the campfire, the night was as dark as a blanket. And Trude loved to sing. She would never have left the fire unless something far more important had attracted her.

Emerald felt abruptly cold. She thought of Trude as she had seen her that night in the river, her body full-breasted, lovely. She remembered that Trude had stood up in the water, naked, to pull on her dress. And she had known Mace was watching.

They sang two more hymns. Wyatt Thatcher threw off the somber mood of the gathering, singing "Jimmie Crack Corn" in his deep baritone and dancing a crude jig on the cleared space in front of the coals.

Beyond the circle of the coals were endless miles of fragrant grass. Was that where Trude and Mace were?

Lying somewhere on the grass, locked in each other's arms?

Emerald sat huddled, her belly a hard, painful knot of humiliation.

That night, she slept uneasily. She tossed and turned, fighting off more of the vague, formless nightmares. She awoke the next morning feeling exhausted, and ate her breakfast bacon and biscuits without tasting them. Only Timmie, excited this morning because his father was going to take him buffalo hunting, could cheer her.

"Pa's going to let me use a rifle, he says!" Timmie was nearly dancing up and down. "I bet I bring home a great big bull, Emerald! We'll have enough meat for a year! And you can draw a picture of me shooting it, Em," he added. "We can put it in our book."

Emerald tried to smile. Charles's funeral had been only yesterday, but it was already in the past for Timmie.

The day passed slowly as the wagons rolled along. The hunting party would catch up with them later. The sun was hot, and the endless miles of prairie seemed monotonously the same. Pieert, who had been hired to drive the wagon in Orrin's absence, said almost nothing to Emerald. She did not see Mace, who was scouting ahead. And when Trude trotted past on Golden, her blond hair flying, Emerald turned away.

It was at the end of their noon rest that Orrin returned to camp. From a distance they could see the two horses, coming slowly. Too slowly, Emerald thought. Orrin was leading Timmie's pony. And where was Timmie?

As Orrin drew closer, they saw that he was carrying

Timmie slung face-down across the saddle in front of him. The boy's right foot dangled oddly.

Orrin was red-faced and near tears. Windy, he told them, had been spooked by a big bull buffalo, had reared up and fallen heavily. The pony was fine, but the boy had landed beneath him. His right foot was crushed into a bloody mess.

"Oh, *no*," Margaret moaned. She rushed to Timmie, awkward with her pregnancy. "Why did you have to take him, Orrin? Why? He's only a little boy; he's not ready for a man's work yet!"

Orrin's mouth tightened. "A boy has to be a man. Anyway, it's done now. We'd better take him down and put him in the wagon."

Timmie was half-conscious, his face pale and covered with perspiration. As Orrin lifted the boy down, he gave a sharp, animallike cry of pain. Emerald was frightened. Timmie looked so fragile, his freckles standing in dark relief against his skin. And above his leather boot was the bright red of blood.

"No . . . Oh, no . . . ," Margaret kept saying. She followed as Orrin carried the boy to the wagon, stopping to touch Emerald's arm. "Emerald. It's more than just a broken bone. It's— Oh, you'll have to get Ben Coult."

"Of course." Already people were beginning to crowd about the wagon, to ask questions and discuss the accident. But Ben Coult was nowhere in sight.

Emerald frantically ran the length of the strung-out wagons. She had heard enough of Mace's stories to know that any accident in this wilderness could be a serious thing. He had told one hideous story about a trapper he knew who had accidentally cut his palm open with a knife blade. The wound had festered, and the man, alone in his cabin, had finally amputated his own hand.

But this wasn't going to happen to Timmie, she told herself. Unlike the trapper, they had a doctor along.

Ben's wagon was near the last in line, close to Zelig's. Coals from a noon fire had been carefully extinguished with water, and a red flannel shirt, washed, lay spread on the grass to dry. A campstool was leaning against the wagon wheel. But she did not see Ben.

She climbed up on the wagon tongue and looked into the wagon, seeing the neat interior with food stacked in orderly rows, folded blankets and clothing.

"Ben!" she shouted. "Ben! You've got to come!"

"Ain't here, little lady." Emerald turned, startled, to see Zelig York advancing toward her. His yellow teeth were bared in a smile. "Would I do?"

Blackie, Billie's dog, was beside Zelig, his ears laid back. Emerald backed away. "No," she said. "It's Ben Coult I need. Timmie's had an accident."

"Now, isn't that too bad?"

"Please—"

Then she heard a sound behind her, and turned to see Ben Coult coming over a low rise, a book in his hand.

"Emerald. Is he giving you any trouble?"

"I— No—" To her relief, Emerald saw that Zelig had left. "It's Timmie Wylie," she stammered. "He fell beneath his horse, and his foot is crushed. They've got him in the wagon now, and they need your help. It— It's bad. I'm afraid for him."

Ben jerked as if she had hit him. "But I've told you. I don't practice medicine. I haven't in some time. There's nothing I can do to help you."

"Nothing you can do! You're a doctor! You've sworn to help people, to save them if you can!"

"Save them?" Ben laughed bitterly. "Half the time I think that a doctor only makes his patients *worse*. Bleedings, purgings, lancing, amputations—so much effort, yet so many patients die. So many of them . . . My own wife and baby daughter died of yellow fever, and I could do nothing to save them. Nothing!"

"No!" Emerald shouted. "Timmie won't die, he can't! He's just a child; he doesn't care about adult feelings right now—or about your *fear!*"

"Fear?" The dark eyes under his heavy forehead seemed to flash at her.

"Yes, fear. You're *afraid*, aren't you, Dr. Ben Coult? Afraid of death, afraid to take a chance, afraid something might go wrong!"

Emerald was nearly choking in her fury. "No, you're nothing but a coward, a man whose wife died and who is now afraid to stay and take care of the people who need him and depend on him. You're running, aren't you, Ben? Running away from them all! Oh, I think you're despicable. A child lies injured, and you—"

"All right!" Ben's mouth twisted. "Enough, Emerald. Still your tongue. I'll go and get my kit. It's in the wagon."

Within seconds, Ben had the worn double saddlebags in hand, and Emerald was following him back to the Wylie wagon, half-running to keep up with him. They found almost everyone clustered outside the wagon, talking excitedly. From inside came the sounds of Margaret Wylie's weeping. Orrin's voice, loud and angry, rose above it all.

"Is he in the wagon, then?" Ben asked.

"Yes."

"Stay here," Ben ordered. But when he turned to climb into the wagon, Emerald followed him.

Inside the wagon was chaos. The boy lay, twisted

122

and half-conscious, on crumpled quilts and blankets. Margaret had tried to cut away his pant leg, and pieces of bloodstained fabric lay about him. Now Margaret knelt beside him, sobbing, while Orrin berated her.

"You, Margaret, keepin' him tied to your apron strings with book learnin' night and day—don't blame me because I tried to teach him a man's work. A man has his place in the world, and it's time—"

"All right. Enough." Ben's voice cut through their quarreling. "Get out of the wagon, both of you. I want to examine him."

Margaret looked up. "I won't leave," she said quietly, although her face was very white. "He's my boy, and I want to be here."

"Get me more blankets, then. And boil some water."

"Is there anything I can do?" Emerald asked.

"What are you doing here? Just get out of here, will you? We don't need two hysterical women in here. One's more than I can handle." Ben's words were like a savage slap. Emerald stood stunned, the blood rushing to her face.

"I said out, Emerald. I've got to clean the wounds and set the bones, and treat him for shock. I don't need a silly girl around to interfere."

"I'm not hysterical. Nor am I silly." Eyes stinging, Emerald backed out of the wagon. He had no right to treat her so, she thought furiously. Just because she had called him a coward— What a hateful man he was. Hateful and hardened and bitter.

"Emerald! Em!" Susannah was tugging at her skirt. "Em, is Timmie going to die?"

"Oh, honey, no. He'll be just fine. I've brought Dr. Coult, haven't I? Now why don't you help me put some water on to boil? At least we can do that, can't we?"

Emerald picked up the child and buried her face in the little girl's hair.

To Emerald's surprise, Margaret appeared at the mouth of the wagon a few minutes later.

"Emerald, you—you've got to help." Fine beads of perspiration dotted Margaret's face. "I tried, but I can't. I'm shaking so. He wants someone to hold the basin and help him, and I—I just can't make myself. I thought I could, but—"

"He said he didn't want me in the wagon."

Margaret climbed down from the wagon. Trude and Geertrud moved to help her, supporting her to a camp-stool.

"Please, Emerald, I don't care what Ben Coult says. I want you, I trust you," she said. Orrin nodded, all of his bravado gone.

Silently Emerald walked toward the wagon.

"What are you doing in here?" Ben demanded as soon as she had climbed inside. "Tell them I want someone to help me, not a silly miss to indulge in hysterics."

"I'm not planning to indulge in hysterics." Emerald looked down at Timmie. Ben had stripped the cloth from around his foot and leg to reveal the wound. It was a mass of clotted red. Brown dirt, horse hairs, and white shards of bone protruded.

Emerald stepped back. It was horrible, she thought, sickened. It was ghastly. With an effort, she remembered why she was here.

"His mother wants me to help. She asked me to do so. Please tell me what I can do."

"Great! Just fine! Are you the fainting type? I suppose you are, like most girls of your type."

"Of course I don't faint," she snapped back. "I've never swooned in my life."

He bent over the wound, picking at it with small, sharp tweezers, his expression one of intense concentration. "Are you quite sure?"

"No, I'm not quite sure at all!" she cried, goaded beyond endurance. "But the boy's mother insists that I be here and trusts me, so you're just going to have to accept that fact whether you wish to or not."

Ben's lips pressed together. He didn't look up. "Very well, then. But you'd better not pass out on me, understand? This job isn't for weak-stomached little girls."

Choking back a sharp retort, Emerald reached for the tin basin of water. She tried not to let it tremble. "What do I do?"

"Just hold that near me, where I can reach it. I must clean out this wound, or it will suppurate. I've been giving him laudanum to deaden the pain. But dammit, he's still going to feel something. Let's hope he stays unconscious for a while."

For long minutes Ben worked steadily, while Emerald stood very still, trying to quell the uneasy feeling in her stomach. No, she thought, she couldn't be sick. He expected her to fail at this, would be scornful and angry if she did. Well, she wouldn't give him that satisfaction.

"Refill the basin. I need clean, boiled water."

Obediently Emerald went ouside for the water, and took a deep breath of the prairie air. Orrin was waiting.

"How is he?"

Emerald stared at him. Orrin looked shaken. Old.

"He's—being taken care of," was all she could reply.

Then she went back into the wagon, and Ben asked

her to hand him objects out of his saddlebags. Knives, salve, bandages, a pair of stout wooden slats with which to set the limb.

Ben's face was somber. "Had cases like this before," he muttered. "Damn shame. Won't be able to save it, of course. If I could only *see* inside, see what shape the bones have taken . . . Impossible to set this kind of thing. This foot isn't just broken, it's smashed. If the boy were a horse, we'd shoot him."

"Shoot him! Timmie isn't a— How could you even think such a thing?"

Ben looked up. "I think it because it's true. You live in a soft, pretty world, don't you, Emerald? A world where nothing ever goes wrong, where doctors can fix things and make them right. Well, let me tell you something. This boy has a crushed foot, and none of my efforts will be good enough. If he recovers, he'll be crippled for life. But chances are he won't recover at all. This wound is a dirty one, and it will infect. Gangrene, Emerald. Have you any idea what that is like? The flesh actually rots, putrefies on the bones."

She was staring at him. Her fingers almost lost their grip on the basin.

"We should amputate, of course," Ben was saying. His voice seemed to come from a long distance away.

"What?"

"I said amputation, Emerald. And even then I don't guarantee anything. But it's really his only chance. I'm going to have to go out and talk to them about it."

"But you can't! You couldn't! You couldn't do that to him!"

"I have to. Otherwise—" Ben's eyes held mute, savage pain. "Stay here and watch him while I talk to the parents. And let's hope I can get them to agree."

After he left, Emerald's knees sagged under her and

she sank to the floor of the wagon. Nausea rose in waves inside her, and she was perspiring in streams of clammy sweat. But she couldn't collapse now, not with Timmie needing her.

The boy stirred restlessly, moaning. She reached out to clasp his cold hand in her own.

"Windy—" he muttered. Then he was silent again.

In a few minutes they were back: Ben, a white-faced Orrin, and Margaret. Tears ran down Margaret's face. But her lips were set, her body tense as she crouched down beside her son.

"You won't do that to him, Ben Coult. You won't cut off my son's foot. I won't allow it! I just won't. Timmie isn't—none of those things are going to happen to him. God wouldn't permit it. Do you hear?"

Orrin was behind her, whispering to her, shaking her. Angrily she jerked away from him. "No! I tell you I won't let him do it."

"But I'm telling you that it's necessary," Ben said. "If I don't amputate, there will be a massive infection. Then I'll have to operate, anyway, or the boy will die."

"You will not amputate. He is my son, and you'll not cut off that foot." Margaret glared at them all.

For a long minute there was silence, save for Timmie's moaning.

"Very well, then," Ben said. "I'll go now. Keep him quiet and the leg elevated. Give him fluids if he can take them. Another dose of laudanum in an hour or so. And don't touch the bandages. I'll be back tomorrow to change them."

Chapter Ten

EMERALD sat on the far side of a low bluff a little distance from the wagons, her hands clasped about her knees and her unseeing eyes fixed on the horizon.

At best, Timmie would be a cripple, she kept thinking. At worst— But she didn't want to think about that. She didn't understand how such a thing could happen to a little boy only nine and a half years old. It didn't seem fair or right.

She heard a clatter and a horse's snuffle behind her, and jumped to her feet. It was Mace Bridgeman, on his big chestnut gelding, returned from that day's scouting trip, his leather portfolio carefully packed in his saddlebags.

"Emerald! Whatever are you doing here? And why haven't the wagons moved on? It's long past the noon hour."

"It's—Timmie."

Mace dismounted and came toward her. He wore his usual buckskins, a bowie knife protruding from his belt. His hat was slouched low over his eyes, and his face was dusty.

"Timmie? What's happened?"

Quickly she told him, her hands twisting the folds of her travel-worn blue dress. Her hair had escaped from its knot and lay about her shoulders, wild and uncombed.

"And so," she finished, "Ben said he'd like to amputate the leg. Only Margaret won't hear of it. She flatly refused. And she got Orrin to agree."

There was a silence while Mace's gray eyes seemed to darken and cloud. "That's too bad," he said at last, heavily. "God help the poor little mite. And this is going to hold us up for a day or two, I'm afraid."

"Is that all you can think of?" Emerald cried. "That this is going to hold us up?"

"Didn't anyone ever tell you about the Donner party?" Mace said savagely. "They were held up, too, and winter snows trapped them in the mountains. Some of them starved to death, and the survivors had to eat each other to live. Do you think that's pretty? Well, it's not."

Mace's mouth hardened. "Of course I care. I care very much what happens to the people on this wagon train. But as I told you once before, Emerald, accidents happen along the trail. People injure themselves. You didn't expect to get through to California without a few casualties, did you? A delay could be disastrous for us—much more so than any one accident, no matter who it happens to."

"But—a boy has a crushed foot and here you are talking about delays!" Emerald's voice shook. "Why, I think you're callous. You really are! So—so why don't you just go back to camp and have yourself a bath? Your face is dirty!"

For a minute Mace looked at her. Then, as if shaking off dark feelings, he threw back his head and laughed. "Good idea, Emerald. A bath is just what I need. And while we're exchanging compliments, your face is dirty, too."

Angrily, Emerald wiped her cheek.

"No. You haven't got it yet. It's a big smudge, right near your nose. There." His finger touched her face.

She jerked away. "Oh, why don't you leave me alone? Go find Trude VandeBusch. That would just suit you, wouldn't it?"

"Oh, so that's what's wrong. Trude VandeBusch. I see."

"Well? You did go with her that night, didn't you?" Emerald had spent half that night thinking of him and crying in her tent. She turned and walked angrily toward camp.

Mace caught up with her. She felt his hand on her arm. Then he pulled her about and pressed her to him.

"Emerald—"

"No!" She fought him off. beating her fists against his buckskinned chest.

"Listen, green eyes, stop that! I'm a man, not a preacher or a eunuch."

"Well, I wish you *were* a eunuch!" she flared.

Mace gave a hoot of laughter. "You don't know what you're saying, my sweet." He was pulling her along, not even giving her a chance to breathe. He pulled her behind a rock ledge, and clasped her in his arms so she couldn't get away.

"Mace, will you please stop this? You're being ridiculous! Let me alone. I—I don't want to kiss you—"

"Oh, yes, you do."

"I don't! How can you ever think such things when Timmie is hurt?"

"Emerald. Don't you see? Nothing you and I do right now can help Timmie. He has seen the doctor, he is in his mother's good hands, and he doesn't need us. Emerald . . . little green eyes . . . there are times when the attraction between a man and a woman is too strong to be denied . . . mustn't be denied. . . ."

"No, Mace—please," she heard herself protest.

"Emerald, you feel it, don't you? It's like the force of the tides, or the swell of a prairie fire. You can't deny it; you mustn't."

He lifted her off her feet, one arm under her knees, the other under her shoulders. She struggled furiously, hitting his face with her fists.

"Stop that!" he commanded. "You little wildcat—"

"I'll scratch you! I will! Let go of me! Put me down!"

Ignoring her struggles, Mace laid her on the ground and pinned her legs with his body, her arms with his strong, callused hands. Frantically she twisted from side to side, but she could not elude him.

She twisted again, but he was too strong. He held her securely, his mouth half-smiling.

"This is all such fun for you, isn't it?" she panted. "A little game you play! Are you trying to see how many women you can put at your beck and call, Mace Bridgeman? First Trude, and now me. Well, I have no intention of being one of—of your harem!"

"My harem?" Mace's gray eyes glinted with mischief. His face moved closer to hers until she could see every detail of his features, the square face with the slightly clefted chin, the small scar along one cheekbone that, he had told Timmie once, had been gouged by a half-grown grizzly cub he had been trying to sketch.

In spite of herself, Emerald's heart began to pound at the nearness of him. A thousand times she had thought of the kisses he had given her. She loved him, had wanted once to marry him. But now all such thoughts fled her mind. Now she only wanted to squirm away from him in hurt and humiliation. For it was Trude VandeBusch he really wanted, Trude he had taken that night of Charles Morris's funeral.

"All right, little Emerald. Tell me what's bothering those wide green eyes of yours. Whoever named you certainly knew what they were doing, didn't they? Your eyes really *are* as green as emeralds."

Mace's face was coming closer yet. She felt a feather-light touch on her right eyelid as he kissed her there. A soft, melting feeling spread through her belly.

"M-my father named me," she stammered. "I remember him saying that he liked the sound of it."

"Emerald. I like the sound of it, too." Mace bent and kissed her other eye. She could feel his soft breath on her forehead.

"Please—" she began again, desperately.

"Please what?" Once more he was grinning. "Is it Trude who bothers you, my sweet green eyes?"

"Then—it's true, isn't it? You really did go with her and—" Emerald stopped.

"*You* didn't wish to come with me, if you'll recall."

Suddenly Mace let go of her. Trembling, Emerald sat up, folding her skirts about her legs. He sprawled easily a few feet away from her, plucking long stems of the sweet-smelling grass and bending them into segments. They could hear the munching sounds made by Mace's gelding as he grazed. They could have been, Emerald thought, a hundred miles away from the wagon train and from Timmie.

"Let's get something straight, Emerald," Mace said. "I'm a free man, a wanderer. My work is very important to me, and I don't have room in my life for a permanent woman."

She felt her mouth grow dry. She, too, pulled a blade of grass and sat staring at it. "But I thought—"

"You thought marriage, is that it?" He reached over and tickled her face with the grass. She pulled away.

"I see," Mace said quietly. "Well, I'm afraid marriage isn't for me. I want to warn you of that. Not," he added, "that I haven't had my share of women. There was a Nez Percé girl that I liked very well. A girl in Saint Louis. But not marriage with any of them, not ever. What would I do with a pack of children? I'd be gone most of the time, and leave my wife somewhere in a soddie or a log cabin with a couple of babies to tend. Maybe I'd only see her once in a year. How could she cope? What if I never came back? No, marriage would be a mistake."

A little ball of ice seemed to form around Emerald's heart. She had been brought up to think that marriage was the joy that men and women found together, with each other. Permanent, enduring . . .

"But I—but your wife could go with you!" she pleaded. "She could go wherever you went! Then she wouldn't have to be alone!"

"Emerald . . ."

For long minutes Emerald was silent, staring down at the blade of grass, so perfectly made. At last she said, "What about Trude? Surely it isn't right for you to trifle with *her*, either."

"Trude is different."

"Different? I certainly don't see how! Surely her pa wants her to marry, too!"

"Pa VandeBusch, for all of his talk, knows exactly what Trude is. Trude told me about him, how he used her as an excuse to go to California. Oh, Trude's circumspect enough, or tries to be. She doesn't want to

cause talk. Even Martha Rigney doesn't suspect yet,
I don't think."

"Suspect? Suspect what?" Emerald's voice rose.

"Trude—well, some people might consider her a
natural-born whore. I don't happen to. Trude is different, that's all. She should have been born in some
other century, when women could be free to satisfy
their sexual urges as men do. Trude likes what she
does, it fills a strong need in her, and nothing is going
to make her stop. So why shouldn't I—oblige her? I
have my needs, too."

She should have been born in some other century.
Mace was speaking of Trude with an odd respect. Emerald felt puzzled and shaken. She remembered the
way Trude had bathed shamelessly nude in the river,
knowing that Mace or any other man might see her.
The thing she had done with Zelig York, the provoca-
tive way she moved her body.

"But—"

Mace reached for her and pulled her down on the
grass beside him. "Come, Emerald. Don't carry on so.
Don't you realize that Trude has nothing to do with
you, nothing at all? She's pretty, true enough, but she
doesn't have your sort of beauty. No one could. Only
you . . ."

She was weak. She could not have struggled away
from him if she had wanted to. She felt his fingers at
the front buttons of her dress. Then he slipped
the dress off, and pulled away her drawers and petticoats, until at last she lay naked beside him, her long
legs bared to the sun.

"Beautiful," he breathed. "Oh, my Emerald, so
lovely . . ."

Suddenly nothing mattered, except that Mace was
beside her, pulling off his own buckskins. His hands

were on her body, worshiping it, caressing it. Then he pulled her to him and entered her, lifting her beyond all her senses.

Emerald sat up. Grass prickled her bare skin. She looked beside her, at Mace lying naked on his back, his eyes closed.

Why, she thought, she had made love to a man only hours after Timmie's terrible injury. To a man, furthermore, who had no intention whatsoever of marrying her. She must have been possessed!

She reached for her undergarments and scrambled into them. She pulled her blue gown over her head, exclaiming in exasperation when it stuck halfway down.

"Here, let me help you with that." Mace sat up, muscles rippling under his bare skin, marked in places with gouged scars. Only the efforts of another mountain man had saved him from the half-grown grizzly, he had said once. Now she could see those scars, purplish in places, ridged white in others. She shivered.

"No," she said. "I don't need any help. I'll manage." Frantically she yanked at the dress.

"But I want to help. I'm good at fastening women's dresses, you know."

"I'm sure you are!" She felt his hands easing the dress down over her. His fingers seemed to burn right through her. Why, why, had she done what she did?

She combed her hair with her fingers, wishing fervently for a brush. Did she have grass stains on her skirt? She looked a mess, she knew she did. Would anyone in camp notice? Oh, she had been such a fool!

"You have grass in your hair," Mace said, almost as if he could read her thoughts. He was pulling on his clothes in swift, economical motions, as if dressing outdoors were natural for him.

"Here, let me." She felt his hand against her head, smoothing down the unruly hair.

"I—I must get back to camp," she said quickly. "I'm sure Margaret must be wondering where I am. I was so upset I just ran off. And you—"

"I'll return to camp from a different direction. No one will suspect, since I've been out scouting all day."

As they parted he touched her hand once, gently. "Don't worry about Timmie," he said. "The boy has strength. He'll come through this."

When Emerald got back to camp, she found Orrin oiling the wagon wheels from the tar bucket each emigrant kept suspended from the back of his wagon. His face was flushed an angry red.

"Go in the wagon," he told her shortly. "Where'd you run off to, anyway, Emerald? You been gone more'n two hours. You ain't got much sense to do that on a day like today. Margaret needs you in there. If you was a slave," he added, "you'd a been whipped for less than that."

Emerald felt her cheeks burning. She climbed into the wagon, willing herself not to cry.

Twelve days later they arrived at Fort Laramie.

Geertrud VandeBusch was so weakened by diarrhea that she lay now in the wagon and couldn't even do camp chores. Trude knelt beside her mother.

"I'm going to go out and look around, Ma," Trude said.

"Don't go far, hear?" Geertrud said.

"I won't, Ma."

"We're near a fort now, and it's full of men. Indians

137

all about, too, and God only knows what goes on in *their* heads."

"Don't worry, Ma, I'll be fine." Trude adjusted a cotton blanket over her mother's thin form, put a tin cup of water near her hand, and then left the campsite, her heart beginning to pound. She was wearing her best green-sprigged calico dress, a gown that clung to the full lines of her bosom and accented the unusual white-blondness of her hair.

It had been a memorable twelve days since Timmie's injury. They had passed through scenery so incredible as to be from another world. Certainly no one in relatively flat Michigan had ever dreamed of such sights. Fragmented hills, buttes, and mesas. Nightmarish rock formations, one of them pointed skyward like an incredibly long needle or chimney. "Chimney Rock," Mace had said that one was called.

As the hills drew together into ridges, ranges, and canyons, the trip grew much more difficult. Now there were snapped axles, damaged running gear, and many pauses for repairs. One such stop had been near Scott's Bluff, an area rising eight hundred feet over the Platte. But Trude had not the heart to marvel at the scenery that day, for Timmie Wylie had been—again—in pain.

Timmie, bounced about in the Wylie wagon, was not mending right. He cried with pain whenever his leg was jostled. He kept Margaret and Emerald busy bathing his foot, tempting his appetite, or swatting away the flies that clustered about him constantly. The whole camp, including Trude, was worried about the boy. And, like her mother, several of the emigrants had diarrhea—debilitating, weakening, humiliating. And one of the Rigneys' horses, worn down from constant buffalo hunting, had died.

But now they were at Fort Laramie. Here, Pa said, the traders exchanged furs and other goods with the Indians. Indians! Katje was frightened, but Trude was only curious, and now she walked toward the fort filled with pleasant anticipation. Surely something interesting would happen.

As she walked, she looked eagerly about her. The fort was a long wooden structure with a central guard tower supported by two posts and two side towers. It looked small and rather futile against the immensity of the country that surrounded it. Behind it rose low hills, and to her right a higher peak, Laramie Peak.

But to Trude the most intriguing sight of all was the Indian encampment of many tall tepees. There seemed to be hundreds of Indians, some of the men naked except for leather breechclouts, others splendid in fringed leggings, leather shirts, shell and claw decorations. The women wore short dresses trimmed with beads, fringe, or coins, their legs covered with knee-length leggings.

She thought that the Indians seemed peaceful enough, talking and laughing among themselves, or staring at her with as much curiosity as she regarded them.

"Well! Look at this, will you, Bill? A beautiful girl!" Trude turned to see two young men approaching her on foot. They wore dark woolen pants tucked untidily into tall boots, flannel shirts open at the throat, and dusty brown hats.

"Hello." She smiled at them. It had been a long time since she'd seen any other men than those with the wagon train. One was short, with a flowing mustache. The taller one, Bill, had wide shoulders and sharp brown eyes that looked up and down her figure as if enjoying every inch of it.

"Don't tell me you're with that wagon train that stopped here last night!" Bill said. "If they got such pretty girls going to California, well, maybe I'd better go there myself!"

Trude stopped to talk and banter with them, enjoying herself. She told them about the emigrants, and asked questions about the Indians and the fort. They were not soldiers, they explained, but traders. Maybe someday the United States would declare Laramie an Army fort, but it hadn't happened yet.

"Would you like to see the inside?" Bill finally offered. "We only let the Indians in in small groups. Don't want 'em to outnumber us, you know. Can't let 'em get ideas, or we might find our heads a bit bare." He laughed, but with a kind of unease that made Trude wonder if this fear might not be very real.

"I'd enjoy seeing it," she said.

She followed them on a tour of the fort's interior—a crude quadrangle with a large, dusty open space in the center. Sheds, living quarters, and warehouses formed the walls, and the many small windows could be shuttered closed. There were other white men and a few Indians walking about, some of them on a walkway that ran along the top of the wall. All of them stared at her, and Trude began to feel a bit uncomfortable.

At first as they walked, Bill was voluble, telling her of life at the fort, the monotony of it, the sparse food, the problems of dealing with the Indians. But gradually he began to talk less, and by the time they were ready to leave he was almost silent, although he looked at her hungrily.

On the way out of the quadrangle, inside the tunnellike passage that ran beneath the guard tower, Bill pulled her aside and kissed her. The other man stood near, and when Bill released her, he, too, took his turn. His mustache tickled Trude's face.

She heard them whispering about where they should take her, and had a curiously exciting sense of danger. There were several more men now. She hadn't seen them gathering. A huge sexual excitement seemed to hang in the air.

"The storeroom," someone muttered.

She felt hands cupping her breasts.

"No—I said don't do it here," Bill said, as he caressed her buttocks. She felt a spurt of alarm, for a second group of trappers was coming across the enclosure toward them. She heard a whistle, a catcall, and then they crowded about her, ten of them at least.

"Please . . ." She touched Bill's arm. He was looking down at her, his tongue coming out to touch his lips. He looked like a good American farm boy, she told herself. Like Rolf Klaus. And he knew; somehow he *knew*.

"In here," Bill said thickly. "We got a storeroom for the food and furs and guns. . . ." He pulled her arm urgently. She could hear excited laughter coming from the other men.

"Pretty little thing, ain't she, out here all alone like she is."

"Ain't goin' to keep her fer yerself, air ye?" asked another voice.

"She's got plenty for all of us, I'll wager. . . ."

They were going to take her, she knew. All of them, one after the other. How many—how much could she stand? She was afraid, yet the thought filled her with a pounding excitement. It would be better, a thousand times better, than Rolf and Klaus. . . .

Her knees felt so weak that she had to cling to Bill,

letting him pull her forward to a door that opened in the interior wall.

"Sweet Lord! What do you men think you're doing?"

Incredibly, it was Martha Rigney, hands on her hips, her mouth a grim line. She was, Trude thought wildly, the personification of every strict mother and goodbody churchwoman in the entire country. Severe, accusing, righteous.

"Where are your officers?" Martha demanded. "Don't you men have work to occupy your hands? I thought you was soldiers, not street riffraff!"

"This isn't an Army post, ma'am," someone said. "We're traders and trappers."

"Well, I don't care who you are. You have work to do here, don't you? Then go and do it!"

Almost instantly the group began to disintegrate. The men lowered their eyes, shuffled their feet, and drifted away in twos, threes, and fours.

"What is goin' on, Trude VandeBusch?" Martha asked. "Your ma said you was out, and then I saw you walkin' up toward the fort here. You ain't got no business bein' in here. You'd think your ma would have told you. This is no place for a respectable young woman to come alone!"

"I—I wanted to see what it looked like." Trude kept her eyes on the ground, on the dusty hem of her own skirt. She wanted to smack Martha Rigney in that red, wind-raw face of hers. Instead she allowed the older woman to take her arm, to pull her forcibly out of the quadrangle and back to the emigrant camp.

"I don't know *what* you were thinking of," Martha hissed as they trotted along. Her stride was almost as long as a man's, so that Trude had to half-run to keep up. "Did you think that a fort would be something like a friendly church meetin'? Well, it ain't. Don't you realize what them men were fixin' to do? I'd hate to think what would've happened if I hadn't come along. They would've—I can't even repeat it."

"Don't—don't tell my pa," Trude managed to whisper. "It would worry him."

"Worry him! He'd ought to tie you up to protect you from your own foolishness!"

"Ma's sick; I don't want my folks to fret."

"They'll fret, all right. They should fret. Maybe they'll learn you a lesson or two. I've had my eye on you, you young hussy, for some time now. You and your calf eyes—oh, yes, I've seen you makin' em at the men in camp. At my husband, Saul, too. Well, your ma says both you girls are good girls. I have my doubts on it. No, I tell you, don't let me catch you doin' anything you shouldn't, or I'll see to it that you leave this wagon train. As God is my witness, I will. I have no intention of travelin' in—in soiled company!"

Trude wanted to protest that she was a grown woman now, that she had a right to lead her life as she pleased. But they were at the wagons now, and Martha sent her toward the VandeBusch wagon with a solid shove in the middle of her back.

Pa looked up, startled. Katje, stirring a pot over the fire, glanced away.

Trude fled into the wagon. She sat down on a trunk and began to brush her hair furiously, trying not to look at Geertrud.

Chapter Eleven

✿ ❦

TIMMIE? Don't you want to try some of these cakes? I made them with raisins and dried apples just the way you like them." Emerald held up the cakes, arranged temptingly on a plate.

"No, Em." The boy turned his face to the canvas.

"But Timmie, you have to eat something. You'll waste away to nothing!"

"Don't want any cakes. Give them to Susie."

"But—"

"I can't, Emerald."

"All right, then." Swallowing back tears, Emerald adjusted the light covering over the boy's foot and left the wagon.

Timmie wasn't getting better. Emerald was growing more certain of this every day. His tan had faded to a waxy white, and the wound, although at first it had seemed to be healing without infection, was now reddened and puffy. On Ben's instructions, they had been bathing and soaking it every day. But it did not improve, and privately Emerald thought it was worse. It even smelled.

She did not mention her fears to Margaret, however.

Margaret, sustained by a burning, determined hope, persisted in thinking that with rest, the limb would heal itself.

"Maybe not so he can walk," she told Emerald. "But so that he won't have pain, at least. That isn't too much to ask of God, is it?"

The pain was the worst of it, Emerald thought. Despite the wooden splints and the blanket wrapping that Ben had devised, each jolt of the wagon jarred the loose and splintered bones unbearably. The land was getting rougher now, and with every bump and jolt Timmie clenched Emerald's hand so tightly that she was sure he would break her bones.

But he did not cry. This Emerald found both moving and pitiful. If he would only cry, she thought, perhaps somehow the agony would be easier to bear. But it was as if Timmie had pulled a numbing cloak about himself and retreated behind it.

Ben was still giving him laudanum, in sparing doses. "I've got to be careful with it," he had told Emerald. "And my opium, too, what precious little there is."

"But Timmie is suffering!" she protested.

Ben had given her a look of irritation, and she had the sudden, eerie sense of another Ben, a dark, disturbing Ben, hidden beneath the surface. "You little fool, can't you understand that I have to save my supplies for when they are needed most? We're not in Saint Louis, you know, or in New Orleans, where I could go to an apothecary's shop and buy these things. We're totally on our own."

"Oh . . ." Emerald had begun to comprehend how isolated they were. If they ran out of something, they would have, as the old saying went, to "make it, make do, or do without." *Or die,* Emerald added mentally.

They were some days past Fort Laramie now. The

wagons were no longer able to follow close to the river, and they were traversing a series of somber-looking, convoluted mountains. These were called the "Black Hills," Mace said, because of the dark cedars growing on them.

They had seen streams blocked with beaver dams and lodges, elk paths, and deer-trampled grass. They had seen wolf tracks, and heard the animals howling at night. According to Mace, the Indians believed these hills were sacred, but Emerald thought them bleak and forbidding.

But now she walked rapidly past the stopped wagons, not even seeing the bare waste of hills and pines. If only Timmie would get better!

She skirted the VandeBusch wagon, where, during the long nooning, both Trude and Katje were napping in the shade. She felt little but anger for the blond girl these days. She had heard Martha Rigney tell what had nearly happened to Trude at Fort Laramie, and Emerald was convinced this had been no accident. Trude had sought out those men, she was sure, as she had sought out Mace.

As she walked by, Emerald cast a scornful look at the sleeping Trude. The girl lay with her skirts pulled up past her ankles. Her breasts, in the tight gown, looked fuller and lusher than ever. Even in sleep, Emerald thought bitterly, Trude looked wanton.

"Emerald." Ben Coult approached her, carrying a bucket of water from the nearby stream. "How is Timmie today?"

"I don't think he's any better." Emerald looked at Ben, thinking that his interest in the other emigrants always had something to do with medicine. If they were sick, he seemed to care about them. If not, he ignored them.

She waited while he took the pail of water back to his own wagon, then began to walk with him toward the Wylie camp.

"Isn't there *anything* you can do for him?" she demanded. "It's pitiable, to see him in so much pain."

"Short of amputation? No, there isn't." Ben's voice was harsh.

"Oh." Emerald turned away from him. "It's coming to that, though, isn't it?" she whispered.

"Yes."

"Margaret won't permit it, you know. She's very much against it. Orrin is, too."

"Margaret will permit it when the time comes." Ben's mouth twisted. "She'll hold a gun to my head and beg me to do it then."

"But—surely there must be some other way! Something else you can do!"

"What, pray?" Emerald shrank back from Ben's twisted face. "Most other doctors do the same things I do. Dr. MacPherson, at Fort Laramie, often performs amputations, he told me. For head wounds he sometimes trephines the skull, letting out the pus and fluids. There should be a better way, you are right about that. But what? What?" he shouted.

"If medicine makes you so—so furious, then why did you go into it?" she asked at last.

He was silent for a long moment. "Dreams." He shrugged. "When I was fourteen, my father was gored by a bull and later died. My mother always believed that if we had had a doctor, he might have been able to save him. I—I wanted to believe that, too. When I grew old enough, I apprenticed myself to the physician in town. I even studied for a while at the Geneva Medical College, about fifty miles away from where we lived. Then I came home to Batavia to practice."

148

"How long did you practice?" she asked.

"Eight years. By then I was married, and my wife did not—" He stopped.

"I'm sorry," Emerald whispered.

But his voice went on as if he had not heard her, low and toneless. "Agnes did not want me to practice medicine anymore. She said the frustrations were eating away at me like cancer, making me do things I—I regretted later. She begged me to quit, to move away, to start over. She had some relatives in New Orleans, in the Garden District. She wanted to try city life, and there would be opportunities for me there. She begged, until finally I—" He swallowed. "But instead we found the yellow fever. It was prevalent in the city that year. Hundreds died of it, as well as Agnes and the child."

They walked a few paces in silence.

"I'm sorry," Emerald began.

"Don't waste your pity on me, Emerald Regan. I don't need your softhearted sentimentality, or anyone's." Ben stalked on ahead. "Enough of this talk—it's useless. I must see how the boy fares today."

Emerald followed him, angry at his rudeness, yet feeling uneasy. How strange Ben was! Layers of bitterness, of caring, and of savagery. She wondered what things Ben had done and then regretted later.

The Indians came into camp after Ben had finished examining Timmie and had gone silently back to his own wagon. Emerald was kneeling beside the small noon fire, mixing dough for biscuits, while the dog, Edgar, played beside her.

Suddenly Margaret came rushing around the side of the wagon, hands clutching the hugeness of her belly.

"Emerald! Em, there's Indians in camp!"

"What?" Emerald looked up. They had, of course, seen many Indians at Fort Laramie, but those had seemed placid enough, interested only in trading.

But they had only fourteen men with the wagon train—or thirteen, now that Charles Morris was dead —and they were far from the shelter of the fort.

"Well, I'm sure it's all right," Emerald said. She tried to quell the sudden, absurd pumping of her heart. "Mace said yesterday that Indians might come into camp. We're to be calm and friendly."

We'll make a good show of firearms, Mace had also added, but Emerald decided not to mention this. Margaret looked nervous enough already.

"But savages as they are—I heard of a little girl in Texas carried off by Comanches in 1836 or 1837 —they do take captives, everybody knows that—" Margaret licked her lips. "Who knows what they'll do?"

"They'll probably beg for some of our wonderful biscuits," Emerald tried to joke.

She stood up and poured a dipperful of water over her hands to clean them of flour. Then she smoothed back her hair, and walked around the wagon.

There were six Indians, two still sitting on their horses and the other four already dismounted and talking with Mace Bridgeman and Zelig York. Other emigrants were gathered about.

As Emerald walked closer, she saw that their horses were bridled in the Indian way, with a length of rawhide knotted about the horse's lower jaw. For saddles there were hide pads or decorated blankets. And there were four packhorses, laden with saddlebags and bulky bundles. The visitors wore leather clothing, hide shirts trimmed with beadwork, hair, and fringe, and carried elaborately painted buffalo robes. They all wore feathers, and carried bows, arrows, and painted shields. Two cradled muskets protected by leather covers with intricate beadwork designs.

These were men with broad faces and high, heavy cheekbones. Their eyes seemed to glitter in the sun. Even the youngest of them, a boy of about Timmie's age who remained with the packhorses, had the same stern, impassive look as the adults.

"Emerald, you mustn't get too close!" Margaret came hurrying up. "We don't know what might happen if they see a young white girl—"

So Margaret had overcome her fright to see to Emerald's welfare. Emerald felt warmed, but she couldn't help smiling. With Mace present, and the other emigrants, how could there be danger?

"They say the Indians have been known to kidnap white girls," Margaret persisted. "The little girl I told you about was only eight, with beautiful flaxen hair—"

"But my hair isn't flaxen, it's dark. And Mace says—"

"Mace, Mace! He doesn't know everything! No man does. You'll learn that fast enough."

They moved closer to the group of Indians and emigrants, and Orrin came over to Margaret.

"Go back to the wagon," he ordered. "And start makin' biscuits and some stew. We're runnin' low, but we got to feed these damned savages. And they want guns and ammunition, too, can you believe that? They say we're killin' off the game they need."

"But—" Margaret began.

Orrin gave her a push, none too gentle. "Do as I say. Martha and Geertrud are doin' it, too. We got to feed 'em and be friendly. They got firepower, too, in case you hadn't noticed."

Margaret touched Orrin. "All right," she said. "I'll

make a big pot of stew. Emerald, you'd better come, too. I'll need all the help I can get."

"Very well," Emerald said. But as she paused for one last look at the Indians, one of them looked directly at her.

He was taller than the others, and carried his body proudly. His hair was black and long, braided and tied with a decorative strip of hide. A necklace of bear claws glinted dully around his neck. His face was less chunky than those of his companions, his jaw narrower beneath the jutting cheekbones. His brows were level, his dark eyes slightly hooded, his nose straight. His mouth was wide and strongly curved, both savage and sensual.

He was beautiful, she thought. As perfectly made as any wild animal. Except that this was no animal, this was a keenly intelligent man whose eyes regarded her steadily and almost unblinkingly.

She felt Margaret tugging at her left hand. "Emerald, do come along, will you? You look as if you'd seen a ghost!"

"I—I'm sorry."

The spell was broken. Emerald looked down and drew a deep breath. "Of course I'm coming." As she turned to leave, she felt the Indian still watching her.

Later, after the party of Indians had eaten their fill and ridden out of camp, Mace Bridgeman came to the wagon to talk to them. His gray eyes looked warmly at Emerald. But his words, when he spoke, were all business.

"We've all got to be careful from now on," he said briefly. "And at night we're going to have to draw the wagons closer and set guards for the herd. The Indians are notorious horse thieves—it's a game of skill and a matter of prestige among them to see how many animals they can steal."

Emerald shook her head, unable to imagine this. "Were they a—" she hesitated—"a war party?"

Mace laughed. "They were Sioux, and they weren't a war party; they'd been trading at Laramie for ponies and hides. They're on their way back to their camp now, I would imagine, to join their women and children. But don't delude yourselves, these are a warrior people. And whites are moving in on their lands, killing the buffalo and destroying the grass. It's possible that in the future. . . ." Mace paused, his eyes looking speculative.

"But why would they stop and ask us for food? Don't they have supplies of their own?"

"I'm sure they do. They're very good hunters. But ammunition is short; they always need that and will trade for it."

"But—their guns," Emerald persisted. "Where did they get them?"

"From trade. Outfits like the Missouri Fur Company or Astor's American Fur Company."

"But they seem so. . . ." Emerald stopped, unable to express herself more clearly.

"Savage? Of course they are. And yet they have their own ways, their own codes. An Indian is a stoic, Emerald. He believes in courage above all else, and despises the coward. Those feathers they wear—each stands for a *coup,* an enemy touched in battle with a harmless stick. When they put on war paint, they paint a spread hand on their chests to show they've killed an enemy in hand-to-hand combat."

The talk passed on to other subjects, but Emerald still thought of the man whose eyes had held hers. Who was he?

Chapter Twelve

❦ ❧

IT was nearly dawn. In the first restlessness that precedes waking, Emerald stirred and snuggled deeper under her blanket. Nights were colder now; the blanket was a necessity. Unconsciously she pulled it over her, and slipped back into her dream. She was with Mace, feeling him pressed against her as they lay full-length in the grass.

Marry me, he whispered. *I didn't mean what I said about never taking a wife. I love you, Emerald. . . .*

She heard shouting, angry voices that didn't belong in her dream, that pushed Mace away from her.

"Damned horse thief! Caught him red-handed, I did, the little Indian bastard!"

"Indians . . ."

Emerald stirred, moaned, but the shouts grew louder.

"I say we oughta teach 'em a lesson!"

Emerald gave up, let the dream recede, and opened her eyes. The loudest of the voices was Orrin's. But she could also hear Pieert VandeBusch and the higher, more excited clamor of twelve-year-old Jan Vande-Busch. Something had happened, that was clear.

She sat up, groped for the brown linen gown she'd worn the day before, pulled it hastily over her head,

155

and buttoned it with flying fingers. Then she stumbled out of the tent and looked about her. The air was a pearly, indefinable shade of gray, the sun just beginning to tinge the sky with pearled pink. The shouts, she realized, were coming from the center of the grouped wagons.

She moved closer. Pieert VandeBusch, his straight, whitish-blond hair falling in his face, held an Indian boy captive. Because the struggling boy was nearly naked, wearing only a breechclout, Pieert gripped a twisted handful of his lank black hair.

He was no older than nine or ten, Emerald saw, and, if she was not mistaken, he was the boy they had seen yesterday with the Indian party.

Nearby, in angry clusters, some of the emigrants had gathered. Orrin, Red Arbuthnot, Matt Arbuthnot, Saul Rigney, Mace Bridgeman. All of them were looking at the boy.

For all his squirming, there was something defiant about the boy, Emerald thought, some proud quality that made him look almost adult. Yet his arms and legs were wiry and childish.

"Was it a game to you, eh, boy? Did you think you could get away with my pa's best stallion?" Pieert, usually so taciturn, shook the Indian boy violently, until his slender legs nearly left the ground.

Why, Emerald thought, the child was no larger than Timmie!

"Pieert!" She elbowed her way past the men, conscious that the women, too, were now assembling, in hastily pulled-on gowns, or blankets draped about their shoulders. "Pieert, don't!"

Pieert was but a year older than Emerald, a quiet, big-shouldered youth who had been polite enough to her. But now he only glared at her.

"Pieert, you must release that boy! You're hurting him. You can't treat him like that."

Pieert's lower jaw thrust out. "I can treat him any way I like. He's an Injun, ain't he?"

"He's a human being! Oh, Pieert, do let go of him, you're nearly pulling the hair off his head."

She went up, but Pieert shoved her away. She stared at him, beginning to be frightened.

She heard Orrin's voice. "Injuns ain't human like you and I are. You ask me, they ain't no better nor no worse than the niggers. And I should know, I seen enough niggers to last me."

An excited hubbub of talk arose, the gist of which was that the Indian boy had been caught by Pieert and Jan in the act of stealing one of the VandeBusch horses away from the herd. Since Orrin was captain of the wagon train, they had dragged the boy to him. The question now was whether to let the boy go or to treat him as a horse thief.

"Listen, folks. Listen to me, will you!" Mace shouted for their attention. "You all know we're passing through Indian country here. This boy was trying to do what for him was an act of courage. We can't punish him; there must be other Indians nearby, maybe within a day's ride, maybe closer. We'd better let him go and count ourselves lucky he didn't get away with the horse he came for."

"Let a damned horse thief go?" Orrin was incredulous. Unlike Mace, who was fully dressed and looked alert, he looked disheveled, his shirttails hanging out, his hair sticking up in tufts. Beside him, Margaret stood wrapped in a blanket, eyes dark with fatigue.

"Unfortunately, yes. You certainly aren't suggesting that we hang the boy, are you?"

A murmur rose from the gathered settlers, and after a moment Orrin said, "Well, no . . ."

"Then let's set him free. We'll put a bigger guard over the herd. That should stop any more thieving. Indians aren't much interested in oxen, you know, except as meat. It's horses they want."

"But it just don't seem *right,*" Orrin protested. "I mean, the Injun is a horse thief, ain't he? He would have taken VandeBusch's stallion, and that woulda been the last we'd have seen of him. And who's to say the kid won't be back tomorrow with his uncles and his cousins, ready to steal the whole damn herd?"

"It's a chance we'll have to take," Mace said. "Unless you want to hang a child." He looked contemptuously at Orrin.

"Let a horse thief go so he can come back tomorrow and rob us again? And what of the oxen? I won't stand for them damned savages butcherin' my stock, takin' out the best steaks and then leavin' the corpse to rot. That's what they'll do, all right. Then where'll we be, stuck in the middle of nowhere without no oxen?"

"I told you Indians may be about," Mace said. "I don't advise doing anything to the boy." He stood quietly, but Emerald saw that his hand rested casually near his sheathed knife.

"You told me! You're just the damned guide we hired to take us over the mountains!" Orrin shouted. "Get this straight, Bridgeman. *We* pay *you.* You don't tell us what to do; we tell you. As for them Indians, you saw how peaceful they was in Fort Laramie. They ain't been bothering anyone."

Mace's lips twisted. "I'm glad to see you're so knowledgeable. As for me, I may decide to quit this interesting and exciting job. What if I just saddle up and ride out of here? Where would you be, then?"

"You wouldn't do that. We hired you, damnit. We ain't payin' until we reach California, do you hear that? And you're going to stick with us."

Mace smiled slowly, contemptuously. "I'll do as I please."

"I'm the captain of this here wagon train." Orrin reached beneath his hanging shirttail and pulled out a dueling pistol. "This here pistol says we'll do what *I* say. And I say that I'm takin' charge of this little Injun horse thief. And I'm teachin' him a lesson."

There was an instant of dismayed silence. The Indian boy's eyes widened when he saw the pistol, but he did not cry out, even when Pieert's hands tightened in his hair. Mace's hand moved imperceptibly closer to the sheathed knife.

"Don't be a fool, Wylie," he said. "We don't dare have bloodshed. We need every man we've got—*every* man—or we're all going to leave our bones beside the trail. Put your pistol away, Orrin, and let that boy go."

"No. We won't let him loose."

"He may be an Indian, Wylie, but he's also a child, and he must have a family. Do you want them taking reprisals against us?"

"Let 'em try." Orrin gestured to Pieert. "Tie the boy to my wagon," he said.

Suddenly Margaret, who had been watching with increasing agitation, rushed forward, her blanket flapping. "Orrin, Orrin, what are you thinking of? You can't do this! Ever since Timmie's accident you've been different, full of temper. Oh, Orrin, don't do anything you'll regret later. I beg of you."

"I won't regret nothing. Get back, Margaret. And shut your mouth," Orrin said savagely and Margaret did take a step backward.

159

"Pieert," Orrin went on, "I said tie the boy to my wagon. He'll come to California with us, as my slave."

"What? As your *slave?*" Margaret was almost weeping. "Orrin, oh, Orrin, don't do this." She turned to the others in appeal. "He was an overseer, you know. He—he's always wanted a slave of his own. . . ."

"I have a right to him! This here is a territory, ain't it? You can own slaves here if you want. And I want one. Why shouldn't I have me a nice little horse thief? Serve him right, it would. And I'll have someone to help me with the work. His folks'll probably never miss him. Think he got lost or something."

Instantly voices rose, arguing, shouting, cursing. Even Pieert, fingers still locked in the boy's hair, was yelling.

Many of the emigrants, Emerald saw, actually agreed with Orrin. Zelig York stepped up to thump him between the shoulder blades. Only Mace Bridgeman stood silently, face expressionless.

Margaret's fingers gripped Emerald's. "This is insane," she said in a low voice. "Orrin has gone mad. Oh, Emerald, I can't believe this is happening. I should have known it. I should have felt it coming. . . ."

"But of course the others won't permit it," Emerald said.

"I don't know. When Orrin wants something . . ."

The men were gathered about Orrin in a tight little knot, their voices filling the air. At last Orrin backed away from them, pistol leveled.

"Listen here! Listen, I said. I'm takin' this here Injun as my slave, and no one is going to stop me. I'll defend this with all the firepower I have, and I've a lot more right here in my wagon where I can get it. Ask my wife. She knows what weapons I carry. Anyone want to try me? I've got Zelig York, Pieert Vande-Busch, and Pete Arbuthnot on my side, and that's enough. There's nothing to stop me, and I ain't going to *be* stopped."

"Oh, Orrin," Margaret moaned, but no one paid any attention to her.

"Well? Anyone got the guts to try and stop me?"

No one had, it seemed. Even Mace Bridgeman shrugged his shoulders and turned away, as Pieert herded the boy toward the Wylie wagon.

Emerald ran after Mace. She caught up with him and grabbed his arm. "Why don't you do something?" she cried. "Are you simply going to walk away and let him do this terrible thing?"

Mace turned on her. His eyes were dark, his mouth angry. "And what exactly do you expect me to do about it, Emerald? Kill Orrin Wylie? That's what it would come to. And at least four other men of this wagon train agree with him. Shall I kill them, too? Would that satisfy you?"

"Are you a coward, then? Are you afraid?" she taunted.

"No. I'm not afraid."

"Then—then, Mace, I don't understand! This is wrong! That little boy is only Timmie's age! We can't take him as a slave; it would be barbaric."

"Yes. It would be, although slavery *is* legal in these United States. You of all people should be aware of that. Didn't you live on a plantation where a nice black mammy helped you to dress every day and combed those pretty curls of yours?"

"Yes," she exploded. "I did. And you come from Charleston, where there is slavery, too. But that doesn't make it right. Why, Mace, this is kidnapping. Taking a little boy away from his family, from his people—" She was ready to weep in fury and frustration.

Mace leaned toward her. "Don't worry about it, Emerald. I don't like this any more than you do, and I won't stand for it. In an hour or two, I'll quietly cut him free. And that should be the end of the whole fracas."

"But Orrin—"

"I'll handle Orrin Wylie privately, not in front of an angry mob. He'll see reason then, I hope. And now, Emerald, I think you should get back to the wagon. From the looks of it, Margaret Wylie needs your help."

The day stretched before them, long and ugly, and Orrin stubbornly refused to change his mind about the Indian boy. The youth would be tied to the wagon, and walk behind it. Once he grew accustomed to his bondage, and they were out of Sioux territory, Orrin would train him to do some of the camp work. He could help with the oxen, carry water—Orrin would find enough work for him. The boy was still young enough to be tractable.

They ate a hurried breakfast, Orrin's rifle propped close at hand against the wagon wheel.

"It's a sickness in him," Margaret told Emerald in a low voice while Orrin was busy with the oxen. "He used to whip the slaves sometimes, when he really didn't have to. There was one man, Ruffo, almost white, whom Orrin didn't like. . . . Oh, this isn't right. I thought it would be different in California. I thought we would get away from all of that. Orrin wouldn't have to feel bad because we were poor and we didn't own any property, any slaves. . . ."

Emerald carried a plate of food and a cup of fresh milk in to Timmie, wondering how to tell him what had happened, but Timmie had heard his parents' raised voices and knew. He lay on his back on the pallet of blankets, feverish, hectic circles of red on his cheeks.

"What's his name?" Timmie demanded.

"His name?" For an instant she floundered. "Why, I don't know, Timmie. He's an Indian, and I don't think he understands our language."

"I bet he can talk in signs, though. Mace was telling me about that. He says Indians don't have to know how to read or write, or even talk the other person's language. They can just talk with their hands and arms See? This means buffalo." Timmie crooked his forefingers over his head like buffalo horns. "And this" —he extended one forefinger—"this means moon."

"Well, perhaps you can talk with him, then, if Mace shows you the symbols." Emerald looked at Timmie. She hadn't heard him say so much in days. "Now please try to drink your milk, Timmie," she said. "It's Bossie's best. You haven't been eating enough."

"I don't want milk. I want to come out and see the Indian boy."

"Well, Timmie, I don't know. . . ."

"I bet you're going to see him, aren't you, Em? Are you going to draw him for our book?"

"I—I don't know. Do you want me to?" Emerald had barely glanced at her sketchbook since Timmie's accident.

"Oh, Em, please! I wish you'd draw me a picture of him so I can show it to my friends when we get to California. And—and I wish I could go out and see him. Is he my age? Is he bigger than me? Does he wear a big Indian war bonnet? With lots and lots of feathers?"

Emerald tried to smile. "No, actually he's rather naked. And he has no feathers, just a hide cloth around his waist. And I would say he's slightly smaller than you."

"Smaller?" Timmie's face lit up.

"Why, yes. I think he's around nine or ten years old. He—" But there was little else that Emerald could say about the Indian boy, who squatted in the grass at the end of his rope tether, his eyes almost black and filled with a burning, adult anger.

"I want to see him, Emerald. Please, I do! Could you and Ma carry me outside the wagon today? Just for a minute or two? I want to be out. My leg won't hurt much, I don't think. I could close my eyes and hold my breath, and you could move very carefully, and maybe it wouldn't."

"Oh, Timmie, do you really think we should?"

"Yes," he said. "I promise you it won't hurt me."

But of course it did, and Emerald, seeing Timmie's white face and hearing his stifled cry, could have wept. But at last she and Margaret lifted him out of the wagon and laid him on a blanket at the rear of the wagon.

As soon as they made him comfortable, Timmie turned and stared at the other boy.

"Hey," he said tentatively. "Boy . . ."

The small Indian looked up. His eyes met Timmie's. Then he looked down at the ground.

"What's your name? Mine's Timmie Wylie. It was my pa who took you, but never mind him; maybe after a while he'll let you go. You'll know how to find your way back home, won't you? Mace Bridgeman says Indians are good that way. They can read the skies and the rivers and the animal tracks like I can read a book. Do you know animal tracks? Could you teach me? After my foot gets better, that is?"

For the first time, Timmie seemed to falter. Then he went on, "I wish you could see Emerald's pictures. She did one of my horse, Windy, that made him look almost real. . . ."

Leaving Timmie to chatter to the silent Indian, Emerald went to help Margaret draw a last bucket of water from the stream. When she returned, the brown boy was squatting near Timmie's blanket, drawing pictures in the dirt with his big toe, for his hands were bound.

Timmie looked up excitedly. "Em! Ma! He says his name's Feather. Something like that, anyway. I think there's more to the name, but I couldn't get it all."

"Feather," Emerald repeated. "That's a very nice name. But you'd better come back in the wagon now, Timmie. Your pa has the oxen yoked and wants to get started."

"Aw, Em. Ma, do I have to? I want to talk to Feather. Can he ride in the wagon with me? Can he? He wouldn't be too heavy."

"No, Timmie," Margaret said. "Your pa wouldn't like that. You see, Feather is a slave. And slaves don't ride."

Timmie's face fell.

"Son, I'm sorry."

Emerald quickly patted Timmie. "Don't forget the nooning rest," she comforted. "We'll bring you out of the wagon then. If you can bear it, that is."

"Oh, I can bear it, I can!" But Timmie's eyes clouded, as if in anticipation of pain to come.

At last they had him back in the wagon, where he settled himself on the familiar blankets with resignation.

"Em? How's Windy?" he asked suddenly in a voice so low that she almost didn't hear it.

"Oh, Windy's fine. Jan and Bob are taking special care of him for you."

"I wonder if he misses me."

"Of course he does."

"I'll never be able to ride him again, will I, Emerald? My foot will never get any better, will it?"

"Oh, of course it will!" she told him. "What are you talking of, Timmie? If you'll just get plenty of rest, and drink all of your fresh milk—"

"Milk won't help. I know that, Em. You don't have to lie to me. They're going to cut my foot off, aren't they?"

"Cut your foot off!" Emerald was horrified that Timmie should be aware of this possibility. "Who told you a thing like that? Why, no one is going to do such a thing to you. Your parents would never allow it."

But she couldn't help thinking of what Ben had said, and had to look away.

"Yes, they will. They'll allow it."

"They will not! Oh, Timmie, don't say such a thing. Don't think it. You're going to be just fine, I know you are. Ben said so."

"Ben was lying. I don't like him. And you're lying, too." Timmie turned his head and stared dully at the stained canvas.

Emerald felt like quailing before Timmie's grim certainty. "But Timmie—" she began.

"Go away, Em. Go away. Pa wants to start up the wagon train now. You said so. And I just want to lie here."

There was nothing for her to do but back out of the wagon.

Chapter Thirteen

❦

THE Indian boy would not walk.

Orrin, shouting hoarsely at the lead pair of oxen, had started his wagon rolling, and the dark-skinned boy had allowed himself to be pulled over onto his side and dragged along in the dirt.

Emerald was standing at the rear of the wagon with Susannah, who usually walked the first few miles until she grew tired. She had bent over to retie the little girl's bonnet when she saw Feather fall.

"Orrin!" Emerald screamed, and ran forward. Orrin, in dusty nankeen shirt and felt hat, was beginning his daily trudge, whip in hand. "Stop the wagon! Stop! The Indian boy's fallen, he's being dragged along!"

The wagon drew to a creaking halt. Margaret peered out of the back to see what was happening.

Emerald followed Orrin back to where the Indian lay in a tangle of bare arms and legs. "He tripped, I think," she said. "I'm sure he didn't mean any harm."

Orrin ignored her. He jerked the boy roughly to his feet. The child's entire right side was streaked with dirt and abrasions. His eyes were hard, defiant brown stones.

"Dammit, you little savage, you watch your footing, will you?" He shook the brown shoulders.

Emerald stepped forward. "Please, he's only a boy. He'll be all right now, I'm sure he will."

"He'd better be," Orrin grunted. But he let go of Feather and went forward once more to crack his whip over the heads of the patiently waiting oxen. "Giddap, you mangy beasts! Giddap!"

The wagon lurched forward, the rope snapping taut. And once more the Indian boy fell to the ground, and was pulled along like a sack of potatoes, his long black hair dragging in the dust. This time Emerald was sure he had fallen deliberately.

"Feather!" She lifted the boy and set him upright. "Oh, Feather, you mustn't do this to yourself. You'll hurt yourself terribly. You must walk, you must."

The boy turned and looked at her, his eyes unreadable. He let his knees sag so that Emerald had to support him.

"Feather! Please!" She was gasping from the exertion. "You can't do this. You must walk, or——"

"What the *hell's* going on here?" Orrin, carrying the long-handled ox whip, had walked back toward them again. He looked irritable. "Won't that Injun walk?"

"I think he will if I can—can only convince him," Emerald panted.

"Leave go of him. I'll convince him." Orrin raised the whip.

"No! Please——"

But Orrin gave her a push. "Get back, Emerald. I guess I got to tame down this here slave of mine."

There was a loud crack as the whip came down on the boy's back.

The Indian boy stood and bore it stiffly, his eyes

168

fixed on the horizon. His features hardened as if he was determined to bear any amount of pain. Only a slight quiver of his lower lip betrayed him. A welt marred his bony, dusty back.

"Please!" Emerald gasped. "Don't treat the boy so." She looked at Susannah, clutching her cornhusk doll, thumb in mouth. "Not—not in front of your daughter."

"What the hell does that have to do with it? I don't plan to hurt him none, just teach him a lesson."

Again he raised the whip, and lashed the bare brown back. Emerald turned away and hugged Susannah until both of their bodies were shaking. She could not stand it.

Once more, the whip left a welt but no blood. Orrin was breathing fast. "Well, that should do it. Now we'll just see. If he doesn't want to walk this time, then he can damned well be dragged. He'll learn quick enough."

Emerald's mouth was dry as she watched Orrin stalk forward once more. Margaret had seen all this, too, from the wagon, and her eyes were bright with anger.

For the third time, Orrin started the wagon moving. And for the third time, the Indian boy fell to the ground.

Emerald screamed.

Almost instantly, her ponderous body moving faster than Emerald could have dreamed possible, Margaret was out of the wagon. In her hand she carried a knife, the very knife Emerald had used to slice the bacon for breakfast.

Margaret ran to the taut rope and cut it. As the Indian boy collapsed, Margaret slowly bent over and picked up the severed end of the rope.

"A dog's leash," she muttered. "This is like a dog's leash."

Orrin ran toward them, his face choleric. "What the hell are you—"

Margaret looked at him. "I cut the rope, Orrin. Your slave is going to ride in the wagon with Timmie." Deliberately she thrust the butcher knife into the waistband of her apron. "Why? Because God told me to do it this way. God, remember Him? Now go along with you."

Without another look at her husband, Margaret bent over the Indian boy. "Emerald, help me with him. We must get him in the wagon and put salve on his wounds. He mustn't infect."

Wolf Dreamer stood at the top of a rocky outcropping, looking with narrowed eyes at the clouds that lay in a long band across the horizon.

He believed in clouds, had seen much in them, and considered them to be a part of his power. But the major part of his power was in his dreams, which he had been having since he was ten, the age of Small Feather.

He had gone into the hills alone, and there, far from his people, he had fallen from a cliff and broken his leg. Lying on the gritty earth with the flies buzzing over him, he had his first vision. Hordes of silver wolves had come running toward him, and their paws were made of fire. They kept coming, more than he could count, and everywhere their feet touched, the ground was left black and smoking.

He would have died there, but a man on horseback found him on the second day. He was a white man, the pale shade of his skin making Wolf Dreamer think of his vision, of the silver-white wolves. The man had sheltered the boy from the searing sun, had given him water, and had splinted his leg. He was a fur trader, the man had explained in sign language.

For two days the man had stayed with him, until Wolf Dreamer's father, Running Horse, found him. The leg healed, and his father gave him his new, adult name when he heard about his dream.

Wolf Dreamer. It was a good name. He had had many dreams since that day, and had become his tribe's most powerful medicine man. He could heal, and he could predict the future. He was greatly respected, but he often rode alone, for he was Wolf Dreamer, and his dreams were terrible and strange.

Today, he did not like what he saw in the clouds. Small Feather, his brother's son, had been missing for two days. This was not a matter for great concern, but his brother's widow, Sun Comes Up, was fretting.

As Wolf Dreamer stared at the shifting clouds, his eyes began to water, but he did not blink. And slowly he saw the outline of Small Feather's face take shape, then gradually shift into the form of a wagon wheel.

Yes. It was so. The boy was with the wagon train they had seen two days before.

Wolf Dreamer frowned, remembering the green-eyed girl he had seen with them. Her skin had been pale, her eyes the color of spring grass. He had seen her in his visions . . .

Two days had passed, but Mace had not been able to release the Indian boy, for the youngster's injuries were too severe to leave him alone on the prairie.

Emerald, rubbing salve on the child's lacerated back one nooning, whispered fiercely to him, "In a few days, Feather. When you're well, Mace and I will

171

let you go, I promise. Oh, how I wish you could understand me!"

The wagons rolled again, and the hours seemed to inch by. It was as if Emerald had always trudged by the Wylie wagon, its sounds always in her ears: the oxen bellowing, the wheels squeaking, Orrin shouting, the whip cracking.

Dust, stirred up by the herd and by the wagon wheels, was everywhere. They ate it, breathed it, slept in it, felt it gritty in their clothes. They rotated places every day, for those in the first wagon ate the least dust, those in the last wagon the most.

Beyond Laramie Fork, the country became very rough. The trail hugged the Platte through what seemed an endless desert of gullies, sharp ridges, greasewood, and cottonwood. Wagons tipped over and were righted. Axles and running gear broke—for the dozenth time—and were yet again repaired. Heavy, nonessential items like rocking chairs and tables were discarded.

"We behave as if the entire world were our garbage heap," Mace remarked one day. "Fifty years from now, our old pots and pans and featherbeds will still be here, drying in the sun and wondered at by wolves."

But Orrin and the other emigrants ignored such talk. To them the world was huge, the expanse of land limitless, and Mace's objections incomprehensible.

There were small, fresh streams threaded among cottonwoods, and Mace was kept busy scouting ahead to find them. They had hit what he said was their first alkali water, a bitter-tasting liquid that could poison cattle, horses, and dogs. Some, in fact, had already died.

More of the emigrants were sick with diarrhea now,

even Emerald, who usually considered herself to be as healthy as a horse. Geertrud VandeBusch was now constantly ill, and Trude did all the cooking and camp chores.

In spite of Emerald's growing dislike of Trude, she had to admire the way the other girl could work. Trude's mare, Golden, was sickly from the bad water and from being run too hard, so now Trude, like Emerald, had to walk. At the noon rest, Emerald would see her collecting fuel or setting up her cooking tripod. Pa VandeBusch even boasted to the other men of what a good cook Trude was.

Mace, too, seemed to notice, and Emerald was convinced that he was still seeing her secretly. *But I'll make him forget her,* she vowed. *I'll make him love me. And marry me, too.*

Timmie continued to be ill. Ben Coult came to the wagon several times a day to change Timmie's dressing and to rub fresh salve into Feather's rapidly healing abrasions. Each time, Ben seemed more irritable, more somber. Several times he again mentioned amputation.

"Amputation! Why must you keep harping on that topic?" she asked him one night, as he was about to return to his own wagon. Evening sounds—of cooking, a fiddle, quiet talk—filled the air.

Ben looked at her. "You persist in your foolish daydreams, don't you, Emerald? You see the world as a fairy-tale place where everything always ends happily."

"I'm not a child!" she retorted furiously. "Of course I know that bad things happen. I'm just thinking of the boy's future. In a place like California, where every able-bodied man will be needed—"

"Future?" Ben's voice was a rasp. "Isn't that just

173

fine? He won't have any future if we don't take off that foot. Can't you see that it's infected? That it's getting worse every day instead of better? He's running a fever, you little fool. That's why his cheeks are so red and his eyes so bright. Gangrene is setting in, Emerald, and you dare to hope for a good future for that boy!"

"No," she whispered. "You must be mistaken; I'm sure you are. Why, Timmie's fine. You saw how much pleasure he is taking in Feather. He's learning to talk to him. It keeps him alert and gives him something to put his mind on. He can't be getting worse."

"He is. One of these days you people will admit it."

That night they reached the north fork of the Platte. It would be a hard crossing, Mace warned them all. The water was too deep for fording, so the wagon beds would have to be ferried across, the animals swum. It would be tricky at best, and they were sure to lose some oxen.

Emerald shivered, thinking of their last bad crossing, when they had lost Charles Morris. And now, with Timmie so sickly . . .

But there was no choice, she reminded herself. They had to go on. Independence Rock lay ahead, Mace had told her, a great gray mass of rock rising above a broad valley like a stranded whale. For years the mountain men and emigrants had been inscribing their names on the rock. Mace, too, had carved his name, and he had promised to show it to Emerald when they passed by. She tried to keep this in her mind and not show her fear of the river.

They camped overnight on the riverbank, planning to rise early the next morning to prepare the wagons for the crossing. Wyatt Thatcher brought out a deck of cards and a faro box from his wagon, and some of the men played, their voices loud in the night. In the far distance they could hear the wolves' hoarse howling.

It was at dawn, with the sun a huge red ball barely over the horizon, that they discovered Feather was missing.

The Indian boy had been sleeping beneath the wagon, his wrists tied to one of the axles. Orrin himself saw to the knotting of the rope each night. And it was Orrin who discovered the boy missing. His bellow brought Emerald dashing out of her tent with her dress half-buttoned.

"Where is he?" Orrin roared. "My slave—someone's gone and cut him loose!" He held up the frayed rope end.

"Orrin, whatever is wrong?" Margaret emerged from her and Orrin's tent, and Susannah crept out of the wagon. All of them stared at Orrin sleepily.

"I said the damn Injun's gone!"

"He was here when I went to bed last night," Emerald ventured. "I know because I went to take him a blanket. He was cold."

She felt exultant. By now the boy would be far away and would join his people again.

"That damn savage was just waitin' all along to cut hisself loose," Orrin raged. "He knew damn well we were going to cross this river and he'd be left stranded with no way to get back to his people but swim. So he jest—except I don't see how. . . ."

Orrin walked around the wagon, jabbing with his boot toe at various scrapings in the dust.

"None of you approved of me havin' a slave, did you?" he said almost to himself. "None of you.

175

Oh, I saw the way you looked at me. Like I was some kind of a inhuman beast."

"Of course I—I disapproved," Margaret choked. "But I didn't—"

"They *say* Injuns make good, tractable slaves," Orrin went on as if he had not heard her. "But you folks wouldn't believe that, would you? Even Timmie—"

Orrin stopped and picked something up. "If this ain't Timmie's shirt button, I'm a monkey's rump."

Timmie! Emerald and Margaret looked at each other, remembering the long hours Timmie had spent with the Indian boy.

"No, Orrin," Margaret began.

"Leave me be, woman. I lost my slave, and I got a right to know why. I got a right to know who's the traitor in my own wagon."

"But the boy wouldn't—he couldn't have done such a thing! He's too sick, Orrin, you know that. It pains him too much to move."

"He don't have to move much to slip the Injun a knife, does he?"

For punishment, Orrin gave his son ten smacks across the palms of his hands with the whip handle.

Chapter Fourteen

※ ⅗

IT was the hottest day Emerald had yet seen, and they were riding on a crude raft that the men had lashed together of cottonwood logs. They had removed the wheels from the wagons and would lash each wagon bed in turn securely to the raft. Now Margaret, Emerald, Susannah, and Timmie clung together on the raft while Orrin and Wyatt Thatcher alternately paddled and poled.

Edgar barked fiercely at the brown, swirling water.

"Aw, Edgar, it's only water," Timmie told him. "Em, do you think we're going to make it?" They had made a soft pallet of blankets for him, and covered him with canvas so he would not get wet.

"Of course we will!" Emerald said. "After all the rivers we've crossed? Why, we're veterans at it now, aren't we?"

But this crossing, she saw, didn't look quite so easy. Leaves, twigs, and branches swirled by the raft in the current. Horses and oxen struggled and floundered, while men astride other mounts screamed at them and cracked whips.

Downstream, limp and wet and brown, floated the body of Orrin's lead ox. And Emerald could see other beasts weakening. Some jerked their heads about, trying to keep their noses above water, their eyes rolling in fright. She felt sorry for Wyatt Thatcher, now grimly poling. He had already lost two of his six oxen and now had no spare team.

"Orrin, oh, do be careful," Margaret pleaded.

But Orrin was concentrating on the difficult task, and barely nodded.

Suddenly, reaching out to dip his paddle, Orrin lost his footing. For a moment the raft lurched precariously as he struggled to regain his balance.

"Ma!" Susannah screamed. "Ma, my dolly! My dolly!" Her cornhusk doll had fallen into the water.

"We'll make you another one, Susie," Emerald said quickly.

"But I don't want another one. I want this one. I want my dolly!" Susannah crawled toward the edge of the raft and reached out for the doll.

"Susie— Be careful—" Emerald started toward the child, but the raft lurched again and Susannah lost her balance. Screaming, she pitched into the water.

Emerald, still on awkward hands and knees, could not believe it had happened so quickly. Orrin and Wyatt were intent on poling, and Margaret was encumbered by her pregnancy. They could not help her.

So Emerald had to do something, though she could not swim.

She threw herself into the water. It smacked her like a wet, cold slap. She had intended to hold onto the edge of the raft, but the current jerked her away.

Water flooded into her mouth and nose as she struggled and kicked. Her chest burned.

She was going to drown, she knew dimly. Hers,

Emerald's, would be the next funeral to be held along the trail. *No,* she thought angrily. *I don't want to die—*

Then something hard jabbed her in the side. The pain seemed to wake her, and she instinctively clutched with all her strength at whatever had touched her.

"Emerald, you damn little fool, just what were you trying to prove?" It was Mace Bridgeman. He pulled her across the slippery, moving back of his horse as if she were a sack of wheat.

"Susannah!" she choked. She coughed up water and clung to the saddle horn. Beneath her she could feel the movements of the swimming horse.

"She's all right. See—Orrin's got her. With the paddle."

Emerald looked. Orrin, by some miracle, had managed to jump into the water and was holding the horns of a swimming ox, while extending the makeshift wooden paddle to Susannah. The little girl, wet and sobbing, clung to the paddle end. Other hands already reached for her.

"Oh . . . Thank God . . ."

"You can thank God when we get you ashore, you little idiot," Mace said in her ear. "And pull your legs astride, will you? Never mind your modesty, I don't want you falling off this horse."

Numbly she did as he asked, feeling his strong arms about her, holding her securely.

"What did you think you could accomplish?" he demanded. "Jumping in the water when you can't even swim? Did you want us to have two drownings instead of one?"

Emerald twisted about. She could feel his chest pressing into her back. "Oh, be still, Mace Bridgeman!" she snapped. "I was just thinking of Susie. I couldn't sit there and watch her go down, could I?"

There was a short silence. Then Mace said, "No, I guess you couldn't."

The horse continued to swim for the far shore, seemingly not disturbed by its extra burden, and Mace's arm continued to encircle her, even after they had reached the shallows. Then she felt a soft whisper of lips touching her cheek.

"Never scare me like that again, little Emerald."

Did he really say that? Or had she only thought she heard it in the noisy confusion of their arrival, the hands reaching to pull her off the horse, the excited voices rising? Mace immediately left to help with the other wagons. But Emerald, huddled in someone's miraculously dry nankeen shirt, felt warmed, and very confused.

It took them nearly all day to ferry everything across the river, making trip after trip with the raft. Four oxen and one mare were lost. Windy, Timmie's pony, had a raw scrape on one haunch, but Orrin made a salve out of wagon oil, and the animal seemed contented. Emerald was relieved to learn that Bossie, the little milch cow, had survived the crossing, for they depended on her milk.

During the crossing, Billie Colfax and Zelig York had taken almost fanatic care of their wagon. What was it about those two? Emerald wondered for the dozenth time. No minister she had ever seen had eyes like Billie's. And no preacher she knew would travel with a man like Zelig.

They made camp early, for everyone was tired and the animals needed rest. Emerald woke Timmie for supper, and noticed that his cheeks were two hot circles, his eyes unnaturally bright.

Emerald backed out of the wagon and rushed to find Margaret, who was cutting up buffalo meat for stew.

"I think Timmie is a—a bit feverish tonight," she said.

"Is he?" Margaret looked up. Her hand holding the knife wavered. "Well, we must be sure he drinks his milk for supper. That should help him. They say milk is good for sick people."

"I'll go and milk Bossie, then."

"And I think I'll start sponging his forehead," Margaret said. "I don't think we need bother Ben Coult with this, do you?"

Emerald hesitated. "No . . . of course not."

She found the milk bucket and walked over to where the herd milled about in its ever-present dust cloud. *I don't think we need bother Ben. . . .* The words seemed to float in her head, ugly and ominous.

She found Bossie and hurried toward her. Zelig York was squatted down a short distance away, fussing with one of his oxen, who had gone lame in one foot. She shivered and tried to hurry on past him. She hadn't told anyone in the wagon train of his advances toward her—she felt too ashamed.

She kept her head averted as she set the bucket under the cow, who lowed, plaintively.

"Well, I see you made it across the river safe enough."

"Yes, I—I did make it across."

"Well, how's about a little celebration, then?" He came closer to her, and she could smell whiskey on his breath. The neck of a bottle protruded from his back pocket. "I got enough for two here."

"Please. Don't bother me. I—I must milk the cow so that Timmie can have milk for his supper."

"Milk?" Zelig laughed unpleasantly. "That kid don't want no milk. Pretty soon he ain't going to be around to drink nothing at all."

"What do you mean?"

"You know what I mean, honey." Zelig made a chopping motion across his throat. "And, say, when are you and me goin' to get together again? How about tonight? I'll meet you over there, by that rocky rise."

"No! I have no intention of 'getting together' with you, as you say. Can't you understand that? I—I don't like you, and I wish you would just leave me alone."

Just as Zelig started to advance toward her, growling with anger, they heard another voice, cold and dry.

"Zelig. Enough."

It was Billie Colfax, accompanied by the dog, Blackie. His eyes were the pale blue of a December sky.

Zelig began to protest, but Billie's eyes narrowed. "I said enough. You and your women have got us in trouble before this, and I don't want it to happen again. Now, back to the wagon as we agreed."

Each of Billie's words was as hard as a whip crack. He waited, idly petting the dog, until Zelig turned and left.

"Th-thank you," Emerald stammered.

The colorless eyes looked at her without expression. "That's quite all right. However, I would advise you to stay with your wagon. That's the safest place for you."

Emerald shivered. She opened her mouth without thinking. "What church did you preach at before you came on the trail?"

The gray eyes flickered. "It was in Chicago," he

said. "On State Street, near the College of Saint Mary's of the Lake. Why do you ask?"

"Why, I—I just wondered."

"Curiosity is not always wise, nor is it godly. But don't worry. I am well qualified to preach, and I am planning to carry my calling to the great country of California."

"Oh. That's good. . . ."

Embarrassed, Emerald began to milk the cow as Margaret had shown her. And when she looked up next, Billie Colfax was gone.

Timmie's fever grew higher that night. Margaret and Emerald took turns sponging him, working by the light of the oil lamp that Margaret used only in emergencies.

"Mama . . . Ma," Timmie mumbled, his head tossing from side to side. In the flickering light, his face seemed bone-thin, the freckles faded, the flesh melted away. "Windy . . . Ma, get Windy and saddle him, Ma . . ."

"I'm here, Timmie. And Windy is fine." Margaret dipped the rag into the pan of water, wrung it out, and laid it on his forehead. "Windy is with the herd, son. Safe and sound. You can ride him when your foot gets better."

"Won't . . . won't get better." The voice was a whisper.

"I should get Ben Coult," Emerald said.

"No! No, I don't want that man here. I won't have him."

"But—"

"No, I won't have him. We're sponging the boy, and that should help. Sooner or later the fever will break. Then Timmie will be fine."

"No, I don't think so." Emerald had the strange

183

feeling that at this moment she was the grown woman, Margaret the young girl. "No, Timmie won't be all right. We need Ben. He's the only one who—"

"I said I won't have him here!"

Emerald turned away and stumbled out of the wagon, nearly falling in the darkness. Orrin squatted by the small night fire, listlessly feeding a buffalo chip into the yellow flames. He looked grim and alone.

Emerald knelt beside him. "Timmie is worse," she whispered impulsively. "We can't get the fever down. We've been sponging him for hours."

Orrin looked at her. His eyes, in the firelight, seemed red and swollen. "I didn't mean for it to happen like this," he mumbled. "It was God who showed me the way to come to California. And now He's makin' me pay the price for what I done."

Emerald didn't understand what he meant. But now they must save Timmie.

"I think we should get Ben Coult and have him— do the amputation," she went on recklessly.

"Amputation." Orrin licked his lips. His square hands trembled.

"Yes. You could talk to Margaret. You could make her understand. She doesn't seem to realize that Timmie might—might die."

She had said too much, Emerald knew. There was a long silence. Emerald could hear a dog bark, the distant howl of a wolf.

"All right, then. Go get Ben Coult. I'll see to Margaret. Go on, will you? What are you waiting for?"

Emerald hesitated. She looked upward at the sky, at the massed stars above her, so many of them that they were like dusted sugar.

Then she ran to get Ben.

Chapter Fifteen

❦

EMERALD stood leaning against the side of the Wylie wagon. Her head whirled.

Ben Coult was in the wagon with Timmie, with his bag full of surgical knives, herbs, salves, and bandages, examining Timmie's foot, deciding where and how to do the amputation.

Emerald drew deep, shaking breaths. She had a wild urge to lift up her skirts and run away into the night. To be anywhere except here. Oh, she had to stop this! She had to get control of herself.

"Emerald? Are you all right?"

She turned. Trude was behind her.

"I'm all right." Emerald pulled away. Trude was wearing a dress hastily pulled on and buttoned crookedly over her full breasts. Her hair, looking now as white as paper, streamed down over her shoulders, giving her a wild, eerie look.

"Are you sure? You were swaying; you looked sick." Trude hesitated. "I woke up and saw the lantern lit. It's Timmie Wylie, isn't it? We've all been so worried. He must be worse, or Ben Coult wouldn't be here."

"Yes. He is worse." Why didn't Trude go away and leave her to her misery? Emerald wondered angrily. Wasn't it enough that she had taken Mace away from her? What more did she want?

"I came to help," Trude said.

"We don't need *your* help!"

Trude smiled sadly. "I think you do. If there's surgery to be done, you'll need plenty of people around. My cousin, back in Michigan, had to have his hand cut off once. They fed him whiskey until he nearly passed out, and it still took eight men to hold him down. My pa and my brother helped. I'll never forget that day."

Eight men? Emerald stared at Trude, feeling her knees turn to butter beneath her.

"It won't take very long, though," Trude went on. "That's the mercy of it. And maybe Ben has something better to give Timmie than whiskey. We can hope that he does. . . ." She touched Emerald's arm tentatively. "Take deep breaths, Emerald. It'll help. . . ."

Emerald jerked back as if Trude had stung her. "I'm not feeling faint! I'll be fine."

"Good." Trude went on in a lower voice, "My ma isn't going to be able to help much, I'm afraid. She still has the dysentery, and she's worse than ever. And Katje, she always did have a weak stomach at the sight of blood. But I did stop and wake Martha Rigney. She's getting dressed now; she'll be as strong as any man. And Ben'll want help, I'll wager."

In spite of all her protestations, Emerald swayed again. As if from a long distance, she heard Trude's voice. "You'll be all right in a minute or two. Better get the faintness over now. Then you'll be ready to help. Take deep breaths."

Emerald did. After a moment, the faintness seemed to abate. She saw that Martha Rigney was coming now. Behind her came Wyatt Thatcher, his shirttails hanging out.

"Martha said you might need me," he mumbled.

Emerald looked about her. They were quietly gathering, all of the adults of the wagon party who were not sick or occupied with herd duty. Mace Bridgeman lounged near the wagon wheel, having emerged from the shadows so silently that she had not even heard him. Pa VandeBusch rubbed eyes still glazed with sleep. Pieert VandeBusch stood with his father, white-blond hair hanging in a forelock, looking frightened.

Only Billie Colfax and Zelig York were not accounted for. How strange that a preacher would not be here to offer comfort and prayers.

But she didn't have time to wonder about that now. Mace Bridgeman stepped forward. In the dark his face looked strong, yet weary. "Well, folks, I'm afraid our doctor here is going to need some help from all of us if we're going to get this job done. We'll need men to hold the boy down. All the oil lamps we can find, and people to hold them. And someone to act as the doctor's assistant."

He looked at Martha Rigney, obviously intending that she should be the one.

But before Martha could reply, Emerald heard her own voice ring out. "I'll be the assistant. I have a strong stomach, I swear I do. And—and Timmie loves me. He needs me."

Mace tightened his lips. "Emerald. You can't want to put yourself through that. Martha Rigney has lived on a farm; she's seen plenty of accidents—"

He stopped, for Margaret Wylie was climbing out of

the wagon. Her belly seemed grotesquely large compared to the small, wan oval of her face.

"I want Emerald to help," Margaret said, in a high, thready voice that Emerald could barely recognize. "Emerald knows Timmie, and I—I want her to help. In my place. I trust her."

"But Martha Rigney is experienced in such things," Mace began.

"I don't care. Emerald helped with his leg before, didn't she? She's nursed him. I want her now. And I mean to have her."

"Very well, then," Mace said quietly, his voice full of pity. "But I would advise you, Mrs. Wylie, to go elsewhere while this takes place. For the sake of your unborn child. There's no need for you to stay and watch."

"No! I—"

Then Margaret choked. She put both hands to her mouth. They heard her footsteps as she ran off into the darkness that surrounded the wagons.

Emerald drew a big breath of the fresh night air. Suddenly she felt strong, ready for anything. Hadn't she helped Ben before, when Timmie's leg was first injured? If she could do that, she could help again. Somehow she could control her horror and nausea.

Timmie needed her. It was enough.

In an emotionless voice, Mace organized it. He dispatched people for oil lamps, for spare oil and clean rags. He told Trude to boil water. He assigned men to hold the boy down—one for the shoulders, one for each arm, one for each leg.

Then they carried Timmie outdoors and laid him carefully on a pallet of blankets. Bob Rigney was assigned to tend Susannah, who had awakened crying.

He carried her, wailing, to the Rigney wagon. The helpers stood by, feet shifting uneasily, while Orrin paced.

Timmie, who had been immersed in a heavy, moaning sleep, opened his eyes. "Em? Are they going to do it? My foot, I mean?"

Emerald swallowed. "Yes. But we're all going to be here to help you. And—and Dr. Coult will give you opium to deaden the pain. He's saved it for this."

Timmie nodded. His face, in the wavering light of the oil lamps, looked like a miniature adult's. "Where's Ma?" he asked.

"She—she went for a walk," Emerald managed. "I'm sure she'll be right back."

"She don't want to look," Timmie said knowingly. "Are you going to be here, Em?"

"Yes. I am," Emerald whispered.

They were ready. Ben came to give Timmie the medication, a sheen of perspiration gleaming on his forehead and upper lip. Numbly Emerald watched as the doctor knelt by the boy and held the opium to his mouth.

Then her glance caught Mace's. The gray eyes were somber. "Don't worry, little Emerald," Mace leaned over and whispered to her. "Timmie Wylie is a strong boy. He'll get through this. You have courage, too. Whether you know it or not."

"I—I hope so."

His hand reached out for hers, squeezed it. And again Emerald felt a strengthening in her, the little heart-jumping thrill that happened every time she was near him or touched him.

Then Mace stepped back, toward Timmie's head, readying himself for what lay ahead.

"All right," Ben Coult said harshly. "Take your

places, please, everyone. We'll allow the morphia a few minutes to take effect."

In later years, Emerald's memory mercifully dimmed the picture of shadowed figures braced about the small, prone body, the corded arms of the men strained against Timmie's struggles. The three oil lamps, held overhead by Trude and Martha, cast wavering light, their smell thick and unpleasant.

Surely all of this was just a bad dream, Emerald told herself. But it was real enough. Mace's features, grim, twisted, his jaw clenched tightly, were real.

"I want you here, Emerald, by his leg. Just so." Carefully Ben Coult placed her, told her what to do, which of the sharp instruments he wished handed to him. There was, she saw with terror, a blunt saw in his saddlebags.

They were all crowded together with barely room to move, the air thick with the smell of fear. *We are all afraid,* Emerald thought. Mace, Ben, all of us.

Then there was no longer any time to think. There was only Ben's voice in her ear, giving quick orders, curiously impersonal. Her own hand, reaching for the saw, the knives, the basin, the ligatures made of waxed thread, the slender pincers, the clean rags and sponges.

It was, as Trude had said, over quickly. Timmie's entire body arched and strained at the hands that held him. His scream rose hideously.

"Hold on, Emerald. Hold on." Mace's voice came from very far away. "Grab your courage, girl, and don't let it go."

Vomit surged at the back of Emerald's throat, but grimly she pushed it back, her teeth biting furiously into her lower lip. She couldn't fail now! For this, she knew, was the most important part of her job. She had to help while he stemmed the bleeding and made a flap of skin to tie off the veins and arteries. And still Emerald's hands moved mechanically, knowing exactly what to do, following Ben's orders precisely.

They bandaged the stump. Then they carried Timmie, wrapped in blankets, back into the shelter of the Wylie wagon. Trude VandeBusch and Ben would sit with him, and Emerald, gone suddenly weak now that her job was over, sank to the ground.

"Emerald? Are you all right?" She felt hands lifting her, setting her on her feet again. It was Mace, his familiar buckskins smelling of horses and dust and wilderness, and of something else, too, the musky scent of healthy male.

"I—I guess I'm all right."

"You should go to your tent and try to sleep. We still have a few hours until morning."

"Sleep? I can't."

"Of course you can. Do you think that going without sleep is going to help Timmie Wylie or anyone else? You'll be needed tomorrow to nurse him."

She clung to him, savoring the warmth of him, the nearness. She could almost forget Trude. She could forget everything except that his arms were about her, pulling her close.

"You must get your sleep, little Emerald," he repeated gently.

"But I couldn't. I can't possibly."

"Look. Either the boy lives or he dies. But whatever happens, you won't help by staying awake all night when you don't have to." Mace's teeth showed in a fleeting smile. "Take care of yourself first, Emerald. Then attend to others. That's the way to survive in the mountains."

She stared up at him, at the face now losing some

of its somberness and relaxing into jaunty good humor. "Why, how can you say that? You don't really care about that boy at all, do you?"

He frowned. "Of course I do. I care very much. But remember this. If there are two men in the mountains, and one deteriorates into illness, then if the other needs his help, he won't be able to give it. Then both die."

"I don't think you really believe that," she said. "Or follow it, either."

"Believe whatever you wish." For an instant Mace's face looked sad. Then he bent down and kissed her, his body pressing into hers urgently.

But as quickly as it had begun, the kiss was over. Mace released her, gave her a pat on the bottom and a push toward her tent.

"Sleep, Emerald. You've a right to. You performed well, better than any man here would have. Go on. Get some rest. Morning will be here fast enough."

Emerald did as she was told. She stumbled into her tent and fell on her blankets. The memory of the kiss still sang through her veins. She had time for one prayer. *Timmie—God, please take care of him and make him well.*

Then she fell deeply asleep.

A dog barked, high, yapping, insistent. Emerald stirred and turned over, pulling the rough woolen blanket over her ears. But the barking persisted, to be joined by someone laughing and the distant crack of a rifle as someone shot at game.

Unwillingly, Emerald opened her eyes. A pale light pervaded her tent, touching the water-stained canvas.

Morning, she thought. Another day of trudging beside the wagon in the hot sun. Then she remembered. *Timmie.*

She sat up and threw off the blanket, discovering that she was still dressed. Only a month earlier the gown, blue, long-sleeved, and trimmed with ribbon, had been one of her prettiest. Now its hem was frayed, its cloth covered with grease stains, dust, and blood. But she didn't care what it looked like; she was thankful only that she didn't have to waste time dressing.

Timmie! She should never have slept. She should have been at his side throughout the night. Guiltily, Emerald jumped up and went outside.

It promised to be another brilliant Western day. The sky was already an eye-hurting blue, the rising sun a white ball. It would be hot later; another day of choking dust and brassy, burning sun.

Emerald looked about her at the wagons pulled into a rough circle, the emigrants tinkering with running gear, starting breakfast fires, or putting away tents and bedding. Perhaps, she thought hopefully, Orrin would call a rest day. If they tried to move Timmie—

She hurried to the Wylie wagon and rapped on its side. Margaret peered out. Her face was seamed with weariness, and old-looking in the harsh morning light.

"Oh, it's you, Em. He's still asleep. But I think his fever's down. If God is good to us, he's going to be all right."

"Oh! That's wonderful!"

Margaret nodded. "Ben Coult left just a few minutes ago. He says the incision was clean, and if we're lucky, it'll heal fine. He said a lot depends on whether Timmie wants to get well." Margaret pushed distractedly at her auburn hair.

"But of course he'll want to get well!"

"Will he? Sometimes I wonder. A boy with no foot . . ." Margaret blinked her eyes rapidly. "Well, enough of that. Orrin says we're to stay here and rest another day. Timmie isn't the only one sick. Geertrud hasn't been right in days. And Katje, too, still has the dysentery. They've had it worse than anybody else." She motioned to Emerald. "You might as well come in and see him. Trude went back to her wagon to sleep, so you and I will sit with him today."

Emerald knew better than to suggest that Margaret should rest. For the first time she was glad that she herself had slept. Mace had been right. She would be fresh today, and her nursing skills would be needed.

She crept into the wagon, her heart pounding absurdly. Timmie was a small mound under his blankets. His breathing was shallow but regular. His face looked fragile. Emerald thought of him as he had been at Council Bluffs, vibrant, full of energy, galloping about on Windy. Now he was a cripple, or would be, if he lived through the shock of the amputation.

But he must live, she thought fiercely.

"I think his fever is down," Margaret repeated, as if to reassure herself. "My ma used to say that children often have marvelous recuperative powers. That they are capable of recovering very quickly, if they don't die. Oh, Em—" Her voice broke.

"We must cook some special dishes to tempt him," Emerald said quickly. "A good meat broth. And perhaps some dried apple pie. He always did relish that."

"I'll put some apples to soak. I think I have enough. Or I'll borrow some. Surely Trude will have extra. Her father is such a big eater that they came extra well supplied."

Trude. Even Margaret expected nothing but generosity from the blond girl. Again Emerald felt that mixture of hate and hurt. She might have liked Trude in spite of her sexual habits. But now whenever she looked at the girl, she could only see her in Mace's arms.

She offered to stay with Timmie while Margaret had breakfast and rested.

"Rest? No . . ." Margaret twisted her hands together, unconsciously rubbing them over her huge belly. "Of course, I might go and see to Susannah. She was so frightened last night. . . ." Margaret's lips shook.

When Margaret left to find Susannah, Emerald sat down near the stacked barrels of flour and bacon to watch Timmie. She reached out a hand to touch his forehead.

Still hot, she thought in dismay. Although it was not as hot as it had been. She lifted the blanket that covered him, thinking to cool him a bit.

The boy sighed and moaned in his sleep.

"Ma . . ." he muttered. "Emerald . . ."

Emerald leaned forward. "I'm here, Timmie."

Timmie opened paper-white eyelids. "Em? They took it off, didn't they? My foot—I remember it hurting. Like a hundred knives."

"Yes. They took it off. But only to make you better, Timmie."

He was silent, the pupils of his eyes almost black. He looked like a very old man, a man whose body has given out and who is ready for death.

"Timmie," she whispered. "It isn't as bad as it seems. Really." She stopped, her throat convulsing. What could she say to comfort him? Nothing, really. In this unimaginably large wilderness, where a man's physical strength and stamina were so essential, Timmie would be a cripple.

She must not think that way. She mustn't even let Timmie sense such thoughts. If he did, he would never want to get well.

"Timmie," she said rapidly, "I have some pictures to show you. Do you want to see what I've been sketching? I've some pictures of Windy, and of Susie with her doll. And—and of Feather, sleeping in the shade." She tried to laugh. "I've even got fat old Pa VandeBusch, huffing and puffing to push his wagon uphill. . . ."

Timmie did not smile back at her. He said nothing.

"Shall I go and get my book? And maybe after breakfast we can carry you outside the wagon. Maybe Jan and Bob will come and visit you. . . ."

Her voice trailed away. Timmie wasn't paying any attention. His eyes were focused blankly, as if he had withdrawn to some secret place in himself.

Emerald sighed. "Does it hurt? Do you want to sleep some more? Then go ahead. Rest will be good for you. It will help you heal."

Obediently he closed his eyes.

The day of rest had ended, and another day had gone by as well. They were back on the trail, trying to make up for lost time.

The trail had begun to head slightly south, and they could see ranges of mountains, rounded and low to the northwest, and in an almost solid line to the south. The creeks that entered the Platte had odd names, like Poison Spider Creek or Poison Creek. This was because of the alkali, Mace said.

Emerald stared curiously at the shining white beds. These were alkali flats, Mace told her, and some of the emigrants scraped up bits of the white stuff and used it, like saleratus, in their biscuits.

They passed a contorted rock formation that Mace called Red Buttes, its rocks a dozen different shades of vermilion, carmine, crimson, orange. The sight was breathtaking, but it also made Emerald realize that they had entered a strange, arid, vacant world. It was as if Baton Rouge and the people she loved there no longer existed.

The trail soon left the Platte and crossed over to the Sweetwater River, named, so Mace told her, when a mule carrying a party's sugar fell into the river.

"Why, naturally! Sugar would make sweet water, wouldn't it?" But Emerald's attempt to be light-hearted fell flat. She was too full of worry these days. Timmie's stump was healing extremely well, Ben said. But his mind was not.

He would speak to no one, not even Margaret. His eyes looked blankly ahead, and he didn't even complain of pain. Once, when Emerald had dared to mention Windy, he had uttered a hoarse, frightening cry and had burrowed even further under his blanket.

They reached Independence Rock in time for their nooning rest one day. This was a huge, turtlelike mound of reddish-gray stone rising up almost out of the river. Proudly Mace took her to the spot where he had scraped out his name: "M. Bridgeman, 1844."

He showed her the scrawlings of other mountain men he knew, some of whom had signed with an "X." Many emigrants, too, had left their names. Some initials, written with axle grease, were only dark smears now.

"It won't be long, I'll wager, until this rock has hundreds more names on it," Mace said. They climbed to the top of the rock, from which they could see an alkali flat and many huge, strangely shaped rocks. Mace narrowed his eyes at this vista, as if it pleased him. "People are starting to settle in California and Oregon Territory now. Each year, more of them come."

"I wonder what their lives will be like," Emerald said thoughtfully, thinking of their own wagon train and the vast distance it had traveled so far, the hot, dusty, weary miles.

Mace's eyes were distant. "Backbreaking work and hardship, of course. What else, Emerald? They'll live in soddies or log houses, and when their shoe leather wears out, they'll make themselves moccasins or go barefoot. They'll work harder than they ever did in their lives, and if they're lucky, they'll survive. . . ."

"And you?" something made her ask. "What will you do once we reach California?"

"Why, I'll get back to my animals and my paintings, Emerald. There's plenty to do—half a continent out there, waiting for me. There's a lake in the Sierras, Emerald, so beautiful that it almost stops your heart. Nearly twenty miles long, bluer than a piece of fallen sky, and swarming with trout. They say it's bottomless. . . . I may go there."

Emerald watched him with a pang. Was she being a fool to dream of capturing such a man? He was as wild and free as the wilderness itself. And as untamable.

Yes, she told herself. She was a fool. But she couldn't help it, she wanted him. In spite of Trude, in spite of the dozens of other women he must have had, in spite of all good sense or prudence, she wanted him. There would never be any other man for her.

She felt Mace take her hand. "I have a knife," he said. "Let's climb down a bit, and you can scratch your name, too. There's room below mine."

They climbed down to where he had left his signature, and he pressed the bowie knife into her hand. The pressure of his fingers was so strong that it sent a little thrill through her.

"E. Regan," she carved. "1847."

Then, with an odd, impish grin, Mace took the knife away from her and carved a large, crooked heart around the two names.

"There," he said with satisfaction. "That carving should last a long time. A hundred years from now, Emerald, people will come to this rock, and our names will still be here. Stone is very strong, Emerald. It can take and hold many things."

Their names, enduring a hundred years . . . forever. She followed him down to level ground, refusing his offers of help, a huge, aching sadness spreading through her.

Chapter Sixteen

❦

IT was easy to follow the trail made by the wagon train. Even a child of two summers could have done it.

Wolf Dreamer dismounted and stood staring at the ruts and skid marks defacing the earth. Across the surface of a rock, a wheel had left a raw, reddish scar. He touched it contemptuously with his moccasined toe, picturing the trail the wagon train had left behind, the miles of scars and ruts, the abandoned campsites littered with garbage.

Wolf Dreamer's lips tightened. He thought of the camp two days previously, where one of their fires had been left smoldering. Did not the white man know of the terrible dangers of grass fires in this land? A fire could burn on for days, destroying the grass and many animals, and the men who hunted them would starve.

In their passing, the men of the wagon train had discarded many objects. Some were familiar to Wolf Dreamer—food supplies, odd bits of shoes and clothing. He had learned about the white men's things during his seventeenth summer, when he had wintered in the mountains with a white trapper.

That year, out of necessity, he had learned the white man's talk. English, it was called, a tongue that Wolf Dreamer found very strange. The language had many words all meaning the same thing, and some words meaning more than one thing. There were many words denoting color, but few describing the hunt.

Some of the articles discarded by the wagon train he had picked up and taken back to camp. One was a heavy, carved wooden box with a white area marked by black lines, which opened to reveal intricate metal parts that made clicking sounds. "Clock" was the English word for this thing.

He had taken the clock to Sun Comes Up, his brother's widow, to comfort her with its small, secret voices. She had been quiet and silent since Small Feather's return, except to whisper of killing. Her words had been echoed by others of the people.

But Wolf Dreamer would wait, he told them, and see if a dream would come to tell them what to do. Besides, he reminded them, most of the warriors were on a scouting party to the north. They must make any move carefully.

But still, by himself, he followed the wagon train, seeing the strange discards—the soiled cornhusk doll, the half-eaten barrel of maggoty bacon, the dead oxen, the buffalo wantonly shot and left where they had fallen, with only the choicest steaks cut out.

He followed, and he waited for a dream to show him what to do.

Grimly the wagon train pressed on, thankful for the respite that the valley of the Sweetwater gave them. Here, though peaks and ridges were all around and the blue-and-purple snowcapped Wind River Mountains were in sight, the valley offered easy passage. There was plenty of water and grass. There were antelope and buffalo, as well as easy grades for the wagons.

"It's as if God meant us to come this way," Orrin said.

Orrin seemed to have recovered his spirits after Timmie's surgery. The fact that Timmie did not speak did not seem to bother Orrin, who was preoccupied with the fact that he had lost another ox, and now had only four. He would have to put the milch cow in the yoke if one more ox died.

They had passed a place called Devil's Gate, where the river had cut a deep gorge, with perpendicular walls and high cliffs on each side. They found an odd spot named Ice Slough, where you could dig down through a foot of muck and come to layers of ice, even in summer. Jan and Bob, joined by Trude and some others, amused themselves by chipping out ice and throwing it at each other. But Emerald, worried about Timmie, could not summon such gaiety.

One morning, as she was adding fuel to the breakfast fire, Mace Bridgeman came by the wagon to see Timmie. Afterward, he spoke to Emerald, a suppressed anger in his eyes.

"I don't like it. According to Coult, that stump is healing perfectly, better than I'd dared hope. Yet the boy doesn't seem improved at all. In fact, I'd say he's worse—mentally, anyway. I don't like this."

Emerald stared at him, her heart sinking, for he voiced her own fears.

"When I lived in Charleston," Mace went on slowly, "the slaves at Kingdom Come whispered strange things among themselves. It seems that if a person —especially someone very old or ignorant or young—

begins to believe that his life is over, something happens to him. He begins to slow down, like a clock stopping. And then—he dies."

"But surely Timmie— You said yourself that his stump is healing perfectly, that he—"

"He is not getting better." Mace's voice was sharp. "A melancholy humor has come over him. And if something doesn't happen soon to bring him out of it—" He picked up a small rock and scowled at it.

Sudden anger filled her. "But what? What can bring him out of it? He won't be read to, he won't look at my sketches, and he doesn't want to visit with the other boys. He won't even pet his dog!"

"Then we must think of something."

"If only we could get another leg for him," Emerald mused. "If only we could. Not his own, of course, but a wooden one, some device that we could strap on so he could get about—"

"A peg leg? It might work."

"Of course it'll work!" she said excitedly. "And we can get Saul Rigney to help us. He is a cabinet-maker, and I'm sure he has the proper tools somewhere in his wagon. And— And— Oh, Mace, it's worth a try, isn't it?"

Emerald berated herself for not thinking of this solution sooner. Timmie had been lying helpless in the wagon for so long that they thought of him as an invalid. No wonder he was so depressed and silent!

She hurried to the Rigney wagon with her idea. Saul Rigney, his brown hair looking unkempt, his nose and lips peeling from the sun, looked up from an antelope carcass he was butchering. "I ain't never done nothing like that before," he said flatly.

"But that doesn't mean it can't be done. Oh, please,

do help us. Timmie must have some way to get around. We can't just let him go on as he is."

"A human leg ain't like a table leg, you know."

"But—it's almost the same thing, isn't it? I mean—"

"Besides, I got to find just the right piece of wood for the job, and where do you think I'm going to get it around here? We ain't exactly got a big pile of seasoned lumber ready to build with." But Saul was beginning to look thoughtful. "Of course, if someone had a good piece of oak or maple in one of them wagons . . ."

"Oh, I'll find something!" Emerald promised. "If only you'll do the work. Please?" She gave him her prettiest smile.

"You get the wood, and I'll make the leg."

Emerald made a tour of the wagon train, with Susannah trailing along behind her. In the end it was Trude VandeBusch who produced a sturdy oak table with thick, rounded legs.

"My grandfather made it," she told Emerald. "But take it. With Ma and Katje riding in the wagon now, there's too much weight for the team to pull, anyway. We'd have had to lighten up somehow."

"I—thank you," Emerald said with difficulty. "If we can get Timmie walking again, perhaps he'll be all right."

"Why not? Anyone would be happier out of that wagon, I would think." She helped Emerald carry the table back to the Rigney wagon.

Saul worked on the foot at nooning, and at the evening camp. Various members of the wagon train drifted by to offer opinions, but, oddly, Zelig York provided the best suggestion. He had known a man in Chicago with a peg leg, and had helped him take it off one night when the man got drunk. He remembered how it had been made. They would need plenty of padding, just here . . . and leather straps. . . .

When Saul finally put the strange-looking device into Emerald's hands, she thanked him profusely.

Saul nodded and ducked his head. "Still looks like a table leg to me," he said. "But maybe it'll work. Martha says not. She says that there wood is going to rub the boy raw acrost the stump. That's why she made this."

He held out something, and Emerald saw that it was padding, carefully made of flannel. Martha must have worked several hours on it.

"Thank you," Emerald blurted. "Oh, tell her thank you."

With mounting excitement, she went back to the Wylie wagon and climbed inside. Timmie lay on one hip, staring fixedly at a butterfly-shaped water stain on the canvas. It was all he had looked at for days.

"Timmie?"

He did not reply.

"Timmie, I have something that I want you to try." Abruptly all Emerald's optimism vanished. Margaret and Orrin had given her permission to do this, and Margaret had even been enthusiastic. They were ready to grasp at any hope. But her heart sank as she realized that, in the end, everything depended on Timmie.

"Timmie. Saul Rigney has made an—an artificial foot for you. I'd like to show it to you."

More silence. His face, looking more fragile than ever, was averted from her.

"Timmie, please, you must listen to me. We—we can strap on this artificial foot, and you'll be able to walk again. You can go outside the wagon and"—she drew a deep breath and plunged on—"and you might be able to ride Windy again. Would you like that?"

Still, Timmie did not reply. If only he would turn and speak to her! If only she dared strap the leg on and *make* him wear it!

"Timmie," she pleaded, "you certainly don't want to spend the rest of the journey lying in the wagon, do you? Why, Mace Bridgeman says we're coming to the Great Divide soon. You can look out and see snow on the mountaintops. Snow, Timmie! You'd enjoy seeing that. You could, if you'd—"

"No," Timmie said hoarsely.

"Timmie." She put her arms around him. But he was stiff, and she could feel him straining away from her.

"But Timmie, why? Why don't you want to wear it? It—it was made to help you get about. You won't be helpless anymore. You'll be able to do almost anything you want to do."

"Don't want a peg leg."

"A—peg leg?"

Emerald felt stunned. She had been so proud of her idea, so pleased with herself, that she hadn't noticed the other emigrants referring to the limb as a "peg leg." The boy had overheard, of course. She could imagine the thoughts that must be running through his head. A grotesque, lurching figure, laughed at . . .

"Timmie, Timmie, it isn't a peg leg. We don't have to call it that at all. It's an—an artificial foot. It will help you, don't you see? You mustn't be frightened by it—"

It was no use. The boy's body was absolutely rigid, and he glared at the stain on the canvas. *"Won't have no peggety leg."*

Emerald felt crushed. "Maybe you'll change your mind, Timmie, when you've had time to think about it."

He didn't move or speak. Aching inside, she left the wagon.

It was nearly dusk. The day, colored by Timmie's refusal to try on his limb, had been a discouraging one. Now Emerald hurried toward the river, a bucket swinging against her skirts. Margaret wanted to brew extra coffee for Timmie, and they had decided to make more nourishing broth. And if they could warm enough water, they would bathe him. When he felt better, perhaps he might change his mind.

This was strange country, she thought as she walked. Night fell very swiftly. One minute the sun would be shining brightly, the next it would fall behind some peak and the temperature would drop suddenly. Yesterday morning she had awakened to find a white rime of frost on her tent, and a skim of ice in the water bucket.

She reached the river's edge and stood gazing at the swift current pouring over tumbled rocks. For all its danger, this country was lovely, too, she reminded herself. Magnificent and lonely.

But these days she hardly noticed the scenery. There was always something more immediate to think about—her own tired feet, the chores that must be done, Timmie. Sometimes she would look right at blue-misted mountaintops and not even see them.

She picked her way among scattered rocks, dipped the bucket, and stood for a moment holding the full pail, wishing she could bathe. She had been washing herself from a bucket at night for too long.

Well, why not? she thought boldly. No one was about—the others had filled their buckets long ago. She wouldn't need a guard if she bathed quickly. The current was too fast here, but farther up the river there might be a pool where she could have some privacy.

She rounded a bend, still lugging the full water bucket, and saw Mace Bridgeman splashing in the river.

He was nude, standing thigh-deep in the water, revealing solidly muscular arms and chest, a wide chest curving down, a triangle of belly.

Her heart squeezed. He was beautiful and as full of lean, proud grace as the antelope he painted.

"Emerald?" Mace suddenly turned toward her. "Is that you? I thought I heard a grizzly. I was about to run for cover!"

"Oh—I was just getting Margaret some water—" she stammered in confusion.

"Oh?" Mace threw back his head and laughed. "Well, the tables are turned, I see. First I come upon you bathing in the river, and now it's your turn to come upon me."

"And you didn't post a guard, either!" she said pertly.

"No, darling. I didn't." He strode out of the water and easily, gracefully, shrugged into his buckskins. Then, droplets of water shaking off his damp hair, he came toward her.

"Emerald," he whispered. "Emerald, did you like what you saw?"

"I—"

"I think you did, little green eyes." With one swift gesture he pulled her to him, and weakly she allowed herself to be pressed against his body. He whispered into her collarbone, nuzzled her neck until soft quivers melted her.

"Emerald. I want you. I want to lie with you again, the way I did once before. I want to hold you. My

God, how I've wanted you, Emerald. You've been in my thoughts ever since then, no matter how hard I tried to push you out."

"Is Trude in your thoughts, too?" The sharp retort popped out of Emerald unbidden. "Do you try to push *her* out of your mind, too? Or do you let her in?"

Abruptly Mace pulled away from her, scowling. "I told you about Trude! We're friends, good friends, no more."

"Sexual friends!"

Mace sighed. "Yes. I see it's hard for you to understand. Trude is a good woman, a fine person. She likes me, and I like her very much. But . . ." He paused. "You, Emerald, you've been in my mind ever since Council Bluffs. But you—you're young, you expect certain things from a man, things I can't give you."

There was a fierce, agonized look in his gray eyes, a look that pulled her to him, that drew her and held her. She was electrically aware of his hand as he touched her again.

"Mace," she whispered huskily. "I—I don't care about that. I don't care about—about anything. . . ."

"Emerald. Oh, my Emerald."

He kissed her mouth, crushing her to him until their bodies and heartbeats seemed to merge.

He tugged at the fastenings of her gown. Feverishly, wildly, she helped him, and then crept with him underneath the trees, where shadows covered them like blankets as they lay locked together in passion. . . .

"You'd better put your dress on." Mace sat up and began to gather their scattered clothing.

"Oh . . ." Emerald sat up, too, one hand trying to straighten her hair, which had come loose from its pins and ribbons. "My hair—and my gown! I must look terrible!"

Mace laughed softly. "You don't. You're beautiful, Emerald, inside and out, and it doesn't matter whether your hair is combed or your dress spotless."

"But—" she began. "Margaret—the others at the wagon train—they'll be wondering—"

"Don't worry, it's dark now. No one will see you when you go back to camp. You can tell them that you slipped and fell. You can limp back and tell Dr. Ben Coult that you sprained your ankle. I'm sure he'll rig up a bandage for you."

Emerald stopped in the act of pulling on her dress, struck by a careful note in Mace's voice.

"Ben?" she repeated.

"Don't you know, Emerald? The man is in love with you. He has been for a long time."

"Ben Coult? In love with me?" She was bewildered. "Oh, but surely you're mistaken. He—he's too bitter inside to love anyone."

"Perhaps. And perhaps not." Mace's voice was grim, thoughtful. "At any rate, I think we'd better get a move on. I'll escort you partway back to camp. You'll need your sleep, Emerald. Tomorrow is going to be another long day."

Chapter Seventeen

TIMMIE finally walked after they crossed the Great Divide.

They had begun the day climbing the easy grade toward the South Pass. The pass itself was a broad, flat, windswept meadow, not at all spectacular, and it was difficult to tell when they finally reached the summit, although the view of snowcapped mountains to the north was as vivid as anyone could wish.

As she walked, Emerald felt Susannah tugging at her skirts, trying to get her attention.

"The mountains— Oh, look, Emerald! They're white on top."

Emerald tried to smile and make conversation with the little girl. Timmie should be with them, she thought, seeing the mountains, too.

Impulsively she called inside the wagon to Margaret. "Couldn't we bring Timmie outside? It's the Great Divide, and he's been riding in the wagon for so very long. . . ."

Margaret's face appeared at the flap of the wagon, then withdrew. A moment later she was back. "He says no," she told Emerald. "But I've left the—the artificial foot beside his pallet." Margaret's jaw squared stubbornly. "Perhaps I'm being cruel, but I told him that sooner or later he'll have to wear it. I've a mind to force him, Em."

Emerald nodded, and caught up with Susannah again, her heart aching. It seemed there was nothing they could do for Timmie. None of Ben's potions or medicines worked against such depression.

On the downward grade, they stopped to make the evening camp. As Emerald was building the fire, she saw Mace Bridgeman riding toward her, leading another horse by the bridle.

Emerald smoothed her hair and checked the row of pearl buttons that fastened her green gingham gown, trimmed with narrow lace at collar and cuffs.

As Mace rode closer, swaying easily in the saddle, she saw that he led Timmie's pony, Windy. She hurried forward to meet him.

"Mace! Why are you leading Windy? Is he hurt?"

Mace smiled crookedly. "Hello, my little Emerald."

She blushed, and wondered angrily what was wrong with her. Fluttering just because he had said hello to her!

"What's wrong?" Mace said. "Your cheeks look red."

"They're not red at all!"

"Aren't they?" Mace grinned down at her from his high seat. "Well, Windy is fine," he said. "Now it's the boy I'm thinking of."

"The boy?"

"It's high time he was back on his horse, Emerald."

She stared at him. "But you know Timmie isn't in any shape to ride. He barely speaks to anyone. Even if you could get him into the saddle, he's too weak to ride."

"He'll ride," Mace said. He dismounted and pushed back the brim of his dusty felt hat. "Leave it to me."

"To you? But—"

They found Margaret sitting on the campstool beside the wagon, trying to brush Susannah's hair. The little girl, crouched by her mother's knee, yelped with pain as the brush found a snarl.

Margaret looked up. "Hello, Mace," she said. Her eyes widened as she saw Windy behind him. "There'll be coffee in a minute," she added. "And will you stay for supper? It won't be much, but Emerald made some soda bread yesterday."

"Thank you, Mrs. Wylie. I always enjoy sampling Emerald's cooking. But first I have something to do. May I talk to Timmie, please?"

"Why—yes. He's in the wagon."

Mace climbed into the wagon, and Margaret lowered the hairbrush as if all the strength had gone out of her. Susannah ducked under her mother's arm and dashed off, sun-streaked yellow curls—snarls and all —flying.

Margaret looked at Emerald. "Oh, I don't know what's to become of Timmie. I've been praying for him until no more words will come. If only—" She fell abruptly silent.

If only we hadn't come. This, Emerald knew, was Margaret's thought.

The minutes passed. The noises of the evening camp surrounded them. Then a sound came from within the wagon, a wooden, knocking noise. Both women looked up. They heard Mace's voice, encouraging. Then the stumping sound again.

"Timmie," Margaret whispered.

The boy appeared at the front flap of the wagon like a small wraith. Mace's hands were at his elbows, supporting him, and Timmie's eyes were two intense blue coals, filled with triumph.

"Look, Ma . . . Emerald. . . ."

He swayed back and forth, held up only by Mace's grip, yet he was standing. In her gladness, Emerald even forgot to look at the artificial foot protruding from Timmie's pant leg.

"I'm going to walk," Timmie said wonderingly. "And I'm going to ride Windy. Mace said I could."

They both stared as Mace lifted the boy out of the wagon. The sun was going down, sending out yellow rays to touch Timmie's hair with fire. Mace lifted the boy onto Windy and adjusted the stirrups as if it were the most natural thing in the world to put a sick boy onto a horse.

"No—" Margaret, recovering from her shock, rushed forward. "Whatever are you thinking of? Timmie isn't strong enough! And Windy hasn't been ridden in days. He'll throw the boy off—"

Mace pushed Margaret back firmly. "The horse needs exercise, Mrs. Wylie. And who better than his owner to do it? Timmie won't fall. Nothing will go wrong. You'll see."

Emerald watched as Timmie unconsciously took his old, easy position in the saddle. But with the wooden foot, how could he sit a horse properly?

"Go on! Git!" Mace slapped the pony's rump, and Windy obediently began to canter across the wide expanse of meadow.

Emerald held her breath, watching as horse and rider circled the length of wagons, then veered back. If Windy should be spooked by the artificial foot, or if Timmie, weakened by illness, should sway and fall—

Mace was smiling.

"Aren't you worried?" she burst out to him. "Aren't you concerned that he'll fall? You know that Windy hasn't been ridden in days!"

Mace looked at her. "Windy has been ridden regularly. I did it myself."

"But—"

"We couldn't let the animal run wild, could we? I figured one day Timmie would want to ride again. I kept him disciplined enough. And today I gave him a good run before I put Timmie on him. Don't worry, he isn't frisky. And the boy will do fine. He has his responsibility, you see."

"Responsibility?" Emerald looked at Margaret.

"Why, of course. He has his horse to care for. Every mountain man knows that his life depends on his horse, and that he can't let the animal get soft or out of condition."

"So that's what you told him in there," she said softly.

"He's been coddled overmuch, I think." Mace glanced at Orrin, who, talking with Red Arbuthnot on the far side of camp, had paused to stare at his son in astonishment. "And blustered at, too. Blustering won't get a man—or a boy, either—to help himself. Responsibility will."

"Oh?" Emerald suddenly felt, in the midst of the wagon train with people about, as if she were alone with Mace. She wanted to trace the curve of his jawline and touch the slight cleft in his chin.

"Brings to mind the day after I was clawed by that grizzly cub," he said. "I lay there on my blanket, knowing that I would never get up again. Every move

217

was agony; muscles had been torn, ligaments damaged. My partner, Jim Briskin, had dragged me back to the cabin and cleaned my wounds as best he could, with boiling-hot water.

"We were low on food, and Jim went out fishing. Eight hours went by, and he didn't come back. And I kept thinking of that bear—a half-grown cub, it had been. Where was the mother? And where was Jim? Finally I had to drag myself up and off those blankets. Every move was pure agony. I was dizzy and sick; I was sure I was going to pass out. But I didn't. I stood there taking deep breaths until I was able to get my gun and go looking for Jim."

"And did you find him?" *Take care of yourself first,* Mace had said. Emerald tried to reconcile it with what she was hearing now.

"I found him, all right." Mace chuckled. "He'd been treed by the mama bear—about a ton of angry grizzly! I had to shoot her, of course; I hated to do it, but I had no choice. Later we took the pelt. But the more I dragged myself about, the easier it was to move and the better I felt."

Mace squinted into the setting sun. "It was responsibility for my partner that got me moving; I figured a taste of it might work for the boy, too." He touched her lightly. "Don't worry, he won't fall. That boy is a natural rider."

Emerald relaxed, as if she had taken a drink of heady wine. "So you told him that story in the wagon."

"Yes!" Mace was smiling. "And now how about that soda bread I've been promised? Are you a good cook or aren't you?"

In a few minutes Timmie was back, cheeks flushed with pride and exertion. He dismounted awkwardly.

Margaret was about to rush over to help him, but Emerald held her back.

"I think he must do it on his own," she whispered.

Timmie hobbled to the campfire. His walk was awkward and none too steady, but Emerald could have cried with gladness to watch him.

From now on, she told herself, only good things would happen to Timmie, and to the entire wagon train. God could not possibly allow anything further to go wrong.

Emerald was asleep, and dreaming. In her dream she lay naked in the tall prairie grass with Mace. He touched her breast, sending hot flames into her groin. She wanted him—wanted him as she had never desired a man before—

Then, suddenly, as so often happens in dreams, she noticed a wolf sitting and looking at them. It was a large and beautiful beast, its coat thick, its skull broad and intelligent. Its eyes were brown and gold, with infinite depths, so that she felt drawn within them.

She awoke then, to discover herself lying crookedly in rucked-up blankets, her petticoat tangled about her legs. Her muscles ached, as if she had held them tensed for long minutes.

She sat up and shook her head, trying to clear it. Involuntarily, she remembered the Indian with brown-gold eyes, the one they had seen after leaving Fort Laramie. Strange that she should think of him now. She shivered, reached for a dress, and pulled it on quickly. Then she made her toilette and brushed her black, unruly curls.

By the time she emerged from the tent, she had already forgotten the dream. She looked about her, drawing deep breaths of the thin, heady mountain air.

219

She began to take down her tent and fold her bedding. Margaret and Orrin's tent, she saw, was still standing, although Orrin was already up, rubbing a salve on the shoulder of one of the oxen.

"Well, good morning."

She turned and saw Mace coming toward her. His cheeks were freshly shaved, and he looked relaxed and cheerful.

"Good morning," she mumbled. She dropped the blanket she was holding and bent to pick it up, feeling the hot blood in her cheeks. The dream she had had, of the two of them. . . .

"Are you ready for some hard going today?" he asked.

"Hard going?"

"Why, yes, didn't Orrin tell you? We're at Big Sandy now, and beyond here there won't be any water until we reach the Siskadee."

"Siskadee?"

"It's a Crow word meaning sage hen. It's what trappers call the river. It won't be pleasant going, and we may lose some of our oxen. Everyone must cut grass to carry along, and fill all the jugs and kegs with water."

"Oh." She remembered her confidence, two days ago, that all their troubles were over. How foolish she had been! Now she thought of all the water the animals needed, the water for coffee, for drinking and washing.

She tried to smile. "It's odd, but just thinking about a shortage of water makes me thirsty!"

He gave her a grim, twisted smile. "Well, drink deeply while you can, little green eyes. We'll have two days of hard going."

He left and walked toward the VandeBusch wagon.

Emerald watched him, and made a mental list of all the containers they possessed that would hold water. Normally, of course, they did not carry large amounts of water because of its weight.

She thought carefully. There was the bucket. And a large keg that had once held bacon, plus another spare barrel that Orrin had prudently saved. Cooking utensils. And the tin chamber pots . . .

But she quickly discarded *that* idea. They certainly would not be desperate enough to drink out of chamber pots!

She must go and wake Margaret, she decided, so that they could get started on the work. Susannah could help, too, she decided. And Timmie. Although he had only been up and about a few short days, Timmie seemed to be filling out right before their eyes. His appetite had returned, and she had even seen him giggling with Susannah over the antics of a small, quick lizard.

Margaret came out of her tent. "Emerald? Was Mace Bridgeman just here? What did he want?"

Margaret looked pale, as if she had not slept well. And, Emerald noticed, she had forgotten to fasten one of the button loops at the front of her dress.

"He came to tell us that we'll be without water for a time, perhaps two days. We are to take plenty of water, and as much grass for the animals as we can."

"Oh? Will you see to it, Emerald?"

"Of course."

"You must fill everything you can find. Everything."

"Yes, but"—Emerald hesitated—"you don't mean the chamber pots as well?"

"The animals can drink from them. They aren't as fastidious as we." Margaret's mouth curved in a half-smile, and her right hand came to rest on the mound of her belly. For an instant she stood tensed, as if waiting for the kick of the infant inside her.

"Very well," Emerald said. "But are you sure you're feeling all right? You seem tired."

"It's just the—dysentery. It struck me again last night. But don't be concerned about me. Just see to the water." Margaret turned to go back into the tent, moving more slowly and heavily than ever.

An hour and a half later, they had loaded the wagon with water and with as much grass as they could cut. Timmie insisted on helping and, seated on the ground, managed to pull surprising amounts of grass.

Then, like so many days before, they began the long walk. Orrin walked beside the oxen, cracking his whip and shouting until his voice was hoarse. Farther back was Emerald, with Susannah skipping at her heels. The little girl was now able to walk a full day. A week previously she had celebrated her fifth birthday and was now, in her own mind, a "big" girl. Margaret rode in the wagon, and Timmie had insisted on riding Windy, although Emerald made him promise that he would go inside the wagon as soon as he grew tired.

They were the second wagon in line today, behind Ben Coult. Mace Bridgeman, of course, rode far ahead. Behind them, wheels churning up dust, were the others—the VandeBusches, the Rigneys, Arbuthnot's two wagons, Wyatt Thatcher. Last in line, lagging because of its heavy weight, came the wagon owned by Zelig York and Billie Colfax. And milling beside the wagons was the herd, urged along by Jan VandeBusch and Bob Rigney.

How small the herd was getting to be, Emerald

thought. Many oxen had collapsed of exhaustion, or had drowned. Beef cattle had been butchered and eaten. The VandeBuschs' milch cow had died, along with Trude's mount, Golden, and Katje's horse, Henry.

And the train itself was extremely small, she realized for the first time. By now she had heard enough of Mace's stories to realize that many wagon trains were composed of dozens of wagons and perhaps a hundred or more people.

Eight wagons, headed into a sagebrush plain, hideous with alkali, a dry, hot wind, and endless sun. Twenty-three people, including some who were weakened or sick.

She stared ahead to the horizon and tried not to think about being thirsty.

Chapter Eighteen

MARGARET Wylie sat in tho wagon, staring out at the arid, dusty land, swept by the never-ending wind. First the mountains, she thought slowly. Then, almost before you could draw breath, this desert. The gray-green, stunted sage bushes were dry and brittle-looking. Alkali salts glared like snowfields in the hot sun, shimmering with heat waves. And there were mirages, cruel visions of pinewoods or ponds or bayous.

How sick of it all she was—the enormous, cruel sun, the wind, the odd illusions of distance and heat, the gritty, corrosive dust that reddened her eyes and irritated her skin.

Margaret licked her lips and tried not to think of the water they carried in the wagon bed only a few feet away from her, in kegs and pans and jugs.

Two days of this desert, she thought. Two days. Her only comfort was that Timmie seemed on the mend. And, of course, there was Emerald. The girl had proved her worth a hundred times over. She worked hard and rarely complained, and, God knew, there was enough to complain about. She had acquitted herself well during Timmie's amputation. Even Orrin had admitted that.

It was odd, she thought, how much she had come to love the green-eyed girl. How dependent she had become on her. Well, she thought, California would offer plenty of chances for a girl like Emerald. She would have her pick of any man she wished. In fact, there were men right here in the wagon train who might be willing to have her. Any fool could see Ben Coult was drawn to her.

And Mace Bridgeman. A tough, complex man who was in some ways almost as wild as the animals he painted so skillfully. But he was a good man, too, she decided, a man with vast reserves of love for the right woman if she were willing to accept him for what he was. Was Emerald such a woman?

Margaret arched her back as another cramp twisted through her. She sat rigid until it was over, then relaxed. Common dysentery, she told herself. She had been bothered by it for days.

She looked at Orrin, who was plodding ahead beside the oxen, perspiration shining on his face. He had constantly to flick the whip over the backs of the team, who were starting to lag. If the beasts foundered or failed them— They could all die out here.

She saw Orrin glance back at her, then lift his free hand in a half-salute. She felt a small, answering smile spread across her features. For all of Orrin's stubbornness and madness, she still felt love for him. Nothing had been able to eradicate it. Not his stealing the money, not his enslaving the Indian boy, not even his punishing Timmie while he lay ill.

God help her, she had tried to hate the man, but couldn't. They were too firmly bonded together, by all the years of sleeping spoonlike, belly-to-back, by all the times they had joined their bodies in lovemaking.

As late as four days ago, they had been together, Orrin's body lowering itself onto hers with slow care. And she had reveled in it. Such things might hurt the baby, some women said. But privately Margaret didn't think so. How could a thing so good, so healing, be hurtful?

"Margaret? How are you doing? Is your dysentery any better?" It was Emerald, at the mouth of the wagon, one hand adjusting the green goggles she wore. They had all bought goggles in Saint Louis on the advice of a woman they had met in one of the stores. Now the goggles, protection against the corrosive dust, were priceless.

"I'm fine," she said. "How much farther, does Orrin say, until the noon rest?"

"I don't know. He wants to press on a little farther. But it will be something to look forward to, won't it? A long drink of water . . ." Emerald made a small, valiant face. "There I go again! No matter what I start out to say, it always ends up that I'm talking about water."

Margaret nodded, trying to smile. Her tongue went out to touch her cracked lips. "Where is Timmie?" she asked. Again she felt the crampiness, and she sat carefully erect.

"He's ahead, riding with Mace Bridgeman."

"He must come into the wagon at nooning. I don't want him to get sunstroke. All that riding can't be good for him."

Emerald smiled and moved away to resume her walking. Margaret closed her eyes against the pain. *This isn't dysentery,* she thought. It was the baby. All along, she had sensed that the pains were far too regular to be diarrhea. But she hadn't wanted to admit it.

She had always had long labors, eighteen hours with Timmie, twelve with Susannah, ten with the little boy, Orrin, Jr., who had died at birth. The child would probably be born—she calculated rapidly—after they had made their evening stop.

It couldn't come any earlier, she knew. For if it did, they would have to stop the wagons and wait for her. And they shouldn't do that. If they delayed here, more oxen would die. Perhaps even humans as well. She thought of the pathetic, almost illegible little marker they had seen days earlier, on the prairie: *"Mary Ellis. Died May 7th 1845. Aged two months."*

No, she didn't want to be responsible for any deaths, of beasts or people.

Margaret braced her feet against the hard, unyielding plank sides of the wagon bed. She, Margaret Wylie, would not be the cause of stopping the wagon train just yet. They must keep going for as long as they possibly could.

They had stopped for the noon rest, but there was little water to give the oxen, and the beasts knew it. Some bellowed restively, while others stood in their yokes with heads lowered and eyes dulled. They must save the water for tonight, Mace had told everyone, overriding some protests. The animals would pull harder if they thought water lay ahead.

Emerald stood and watched the men argue. Their faces and clothes were coated with dust.

How they had all changed, she thought. The dust, the heat, the wind, and the endless incredible distance had changed them. They had elected Orrin in good fellowship, but now, no matter what decision he made, someone objected to it. If Orrin wanted to stick close to a river, Zelig York growled that a detour would be shorter. If Orrin decided to camp at one stream, Wyatt Thatcher would say that there was better water three miles ahead.

Only Mace Bridgeman could hold them in any sort of order. By bickering over routes, he pointed out, they were wasting time and energy. Too many other wagon parties had collapsed in dissension, or had lagged about like tourists, taking time off to hunt or sightsee. An hour lost here, another hour wasted there—these could add up to whole days frittered away.

They were all feeling the chill nights now, weren't they? Winters in the mountains were dangerous, and the Sierras were ahead, beautiful but dangerous.

Susannah had changed, too. In Council Bluffs she had been a babyish sprite of four, clinging to her dolls. But now she was five, and somewhere along the way she had grown hardy. Her legs were slim but strong, her face tanned leather-brown, so that her eyes looked like blue chips of stone. She ran everywhere, romping with Edgar, gawking at prairie dogs, climbing rocks, and chattering incessantly, as if this were the most wonderful experience of her life.

Geertrud VandeBusch had diminished from a worn but still vital woman to a gaunt specter with tallow-yellow skin who rarely left her wagon.

Katje, thank heavens, was beginning to recuperate from her dysentery. But the ordeal had left the fifteen-year-old dried up and wizened, her beauty faded. Katje had even stopped complaining.

Red Arbuthnot, once a hearty sixty-five, now had hands that shook uncontrollably. He suffered from what Mace called "mountain fever," as his old heart and lungs struggled to adjust to the higher altitudes.

Matt, his son, had become gaunt and hard, and had grown a ginger-red beard.

Ben Coult was tanned almost black, his nose red, his lips cracked and sore. His eyes seemed to follow Emerald when he thought she was not looking. But he talked to her seldom, and when he did, it was usually to make a bitter or caustic remark.

Since Timmie's amputation, Pieert, the oldest VandeBusch boy, had turned even more quiet, and once Emerald had come upon him talking to himself. She knew he was frightened by the bigness of everything, the huge, implacable wilderness around them. He felt like a grain of sand among mountains, a speck so small that God could not notice.

But some of the party, she reflected, had not changed. Zelig, Billie Colfax, Trude. Rob Rigney and Jan VandeBusch, the two half-grown boys, were as boisterous as ever, untroubled by thoughts of death or large skies or human disaster.

She herself . . .

But abruptly she tired of thinking. It was no use. They had come this far; they must go on.

"Go ahead, then, but I'll do what *I* want. My beasts need waterin' and they're goin' to get it!" Zelig's voice was defiant. He strode back toward his wagon, face twisted.

· Emerald watched him, and shivered. Bitterly she regretted not telling Margaret about Zelig, but she had been so ashamed. And anyway, what could they have done? The only law here was that of the rifle and the pistol. To discipline Zelig, they would have to kill him.

Mace Bridgeman left the group of men and stood alone, eyes shaded against the noon sun. And Trude left the VandeBusch wagon and was walking toward him. The blond girl's brown dress clung to every line of her body, nipping in at the waist so that the full curves of her hips seemed even more voluptuous. And Trude's hips swayed invitingly when she walked, as if she knew that every man in camp had his eyes fastened on her.

Trude reached Mace and stood talking to him, her hand on his arm, looking up at him.

Friends, Emerald thought, physical friends. She could not bear to look. To her surprise she felt tears well up in her eyes, sudden wet tears in this dry and arid land.

She turned and hurried toward the Wylie wagon. She wouldn't cry, she told herself fiercely. She just wouldn't.

But when she got back to the wagon, busying herself with rationing out small drinks for Timmie and Susannah, she cried, anyway, lowering her eyes so that the children wouldn't notice.

Mace, she thought miserably. *I wish I didn't love you at all.*

Margaret was not sure how far apart her pains were. But they kept coming, grinding and twisting in her until she gripped the edge of the wagon bed to keep from crying out.

Timmie was back in the wagon with her. She had insisted that he was too weak to ride all day in the sun, and he seemed happy enough, curled on the quilt with one of Emerald's books, the artificial foot worn nonchalantly.

"Ma? Don't you feel good?" Timmie asked. She must have made a noise, she realized, for he had not looked up from his book. Children, she thought. Only days ago she had been convinced that Timmie would die. Now here he was, his cheeks already turning brown again, reading his book as if he were a bored steamboat passenger.

"I'm fine, son." She forced a smile. The wagon creaked, jogging her from side to side.

"This is a good book, Ma. This Mr. Poe, he makes a person feel all shivery and scared inside, like a ghost story."

"Yes. I—I shall have to reread him. It has been a long time since I've done any reading, I'm afraid."

"I wish we had more books."

"Yes, well, perhaps there will be some in California."

"I don't think so. Mace says they don't have very much of anything there. Shoe leather or tools or anything. The boats come in with goods, but I don't think they'd be bringing books, do you? Mace says they wouldn't."

Margaret managed a more genuine smile. The boy had begun to follow Mace Bridgeman about, asking a thousand questions and listening avidly to the tales of wild animals and mountain life. She wished Orrin would spend that kind of time with Timmie. But Orrin was obsessed with the wagon train, the oxen, the weather, and the route.

She bit her lip as another contraction came. It seemed to last for a long time—vivid, sharp, red pain. When it finished, she was wet with perspiration and could hear her own breath panting.

"Ma? You sure you feel good?"

"Yes, Timmie. I—I'm fine. Just read your book, will you? I want to think."

"Yes, ma'am." He gave her one hurt look, then buried himself in Mr. Poe, whom he was reading for the fifth or sixth time now.

Awkwardly Margaret shifted around, trying to ease

the aching of her back. If only she dared ask Emerald to come in the wagon and rub it for her. But if she did, they would stop, and all the wagons would wait in the hot sun for her to give birth.

She looked about her, at the wagon surroundings she had seen so often before. The soiled, dusty, stained canvas, hung here and there with objects, and with pockets she had sewn to store valuables and other small things. The goods piled up, the crumpled brown wool blankets, the patchwork quilt her mother had pieced.

Another pain dug at her with metal fingers.

She closed her eyes and clutched the rim of the wagon bed until splinters of wood pierced her fingertips. She tried not to groan. She mustn't make any more noise. . . . Seconds ticked on. Or was it minutes, hours?

What would it feel like to die? she wondered. Would death be more agonizing than this? Or would she just slide out in a slow lapsing of consciousness, quietly?

The pain was gone, leaving only an ache in her back. She would die, the thought came. She would die with this baby she had not really wanted very much.

She had barely given a thought to this child, she realized miserably. She had worried about Timmie, prayed for him. But never for this baby. She had not even thought what to name it. She had not even asked herself what sex it would be. When it had kicked, she had only thought, "Oh, it's kicking," and nothing more.

Would God punish her now by letting her die in childbirth?

Margaret lifted up her right hand and looked at it carefully. It was shaking. This labor was going faster than the others, she realized. She was well along now. But all she had to do was hold on and keep her mouth closed so that she would not groan. Hold on. . . .

"Ma! Ma!" Timmie was shaking her. "Ma! What's wrong? You're sick, aren't you? You're making funny noises."

"No . . . I'm not making noises. . . ."

The pain gripped her again. It picked her up and would not let her go. She tried to breathe in quick, short pants. She must not make any sound. . . .

When she opened her eyes again, the regular jouncing of the wagon had stopped and Timmie was not there anymore. Orrin's face was in the opened flap of the wagon, Emerald's behind him, silhouetted against the sun, so that she couldn't see their features clearly.

"Margaret! Margaret, is it your time? Oh, Jesus . . ." That was Orrin. She heard the words without understanding them. She was in a dark red pit, a well of pain. She had to concentrate on not screaming—

"I'll get Ben Coult," Emerald said.

"Can't you women handle this? Birthing a baby is women's work."

"I don't know anything about babies, and Ben Coult does. I think Margaret should have a doctor. She wanted him to help her."

They were arguing over something, Emerald's voice stubborn. Then the faces disappeared.

"Mrs. Wylie, how long have you been having your contractions?"

She opened her eyes and looked up. Ben Coult seemed different now than when she had seen him in Council Bluffs. His face was tanned dark, his features knifelike and gaunt.

"I . . . don't know." She touched her belly. It was a hard, solid ball.

"Did they start after breakfast?"

"Yes . . ."

"How long after breakfast?"

"I—I don't know."

"And how far apart are they?"

". . . don't know . . ." Another pang came. It was larger than the others, more awesome. In spite of herself, Margaret moaned.

"Don't hold the screams back, Mrs. Wylie. Go ahead and yell if you have to."

"But— No, I can't— They mustn't stop the wagons—"

"They have stopped the wagons."

"But we must go on—"

Ben shook his head impatiently. "We'll go on soon enough. But for now I've got to have the wagon still so you won't be tossed all about." He turned to Emerald, who had again entered the wagon, and said, "Take some clean rags and wash her."

"Yes."

They were in and out of the wagon, first one person, then another. Orrin looked in, then hastily retreated. Now Emerald bent over her with a rag moistened with the precious water. Impulsively Margaret found Emerald's hand and squeezed it.

"It's all right," Emerald said. "I don't mind. Squeeze hard. It'll be over soon, and you'll have a beautiful baby to take care of."

Baby. Again the guilt. But she didn't have time to feel guilty for long, for now the great-grandmother of all the pains was upon her. It was no longer sharp and twisting, but a full, powerful, frightening pressure, as if she were trying to evacuate a melon.

Dear God—

She arched, writhed, no longer seeing anything or

anyone, completely concentrated inward. Dimly she was aware that she clutched a hand—hard enough to break bones. That she was lying on her back, knees brought up and apart.

Then it came again. Bigger and stronger than ever, relentless. She screamed.

"Push!" Ben Coult shouted. "Take a deep breath. Margaret, and push! Push the baby out!" He was pushing down on the bulge of her belly, helping her.

Pressure, exploding in her.

Then the miracle happened, the birth miracle she remembered. The pressure begin to ease and change as she pushed.

"Push!" Ben yelled.

It came sliding out of her in that great satisfying surge, the baby flowing out of her, wondrously created by her even as it came.

She heard small, angry squalls reverberating against the canvas sides of the wagon.

"My . . . baby . . ."

"It's a boy," Ben Coult said. He was holding the baby by the feet. It was small and red, covered with a white substance, wriggling and crying. "He's a big one, and healthy. A healthy boy."

Margaret wept.

Chapter Nineteen

✥ ❧

TWO days later, Margaret named the baby. They had reached the bluffs above the Green River and had made the difficult descent to the joyousness of water and grass.

Never had Emerald been so glad to be anywhere in her life.

"If Heaven has any earthly look to it at all," she told Margaret, who sat in the wagon nursing the infant. "It must be like this. Green grass! Trees! Pine forests!"

"Yes," Margaret sighed. "Isn't it wonderful? We are very lucky."

Emerald nodded. The last day in the desert had been very hard. There had been agonizing hours of waiting while Margaret had the baby. Then plodding beside the weary oxen, all of them, people and beasts alike, thirsty and longing for water. But somehow they had withstood it, even Margaret and the red-faced infant who now nuzzled aggressively at her breast.

"What are you going to name him?" Emerald asked. She felt nearly as proud of this baby as if she had given birth to him herself. For hadn't she been there as the small, dark head emerged?

"I don't know." Margaret looked down at the baby, frowning. "I'm ashamed, but I haven't really thought."

"Well," said Emerald. "He was born on the way to California, wasn't he? That should count for something."

"Yes. He's a California baby, that's true." Margaret lifted the infant to her shoulder to burp him, and kissed him softly. "I think . . . yes, I'll call him California, then. The name might bring him some luck. He'll be Cal for short. How does that sound to you?" She looked anxiously at Emerald.

"Why, that's fine. It's a good name."

California. Cal. Emerald felt like jumping up and down with sheer childish excitement. They had passed through a bad stretch of desert, losing only one ox. Even the milch cow had lived. And they were on their way to a new land, a land where wonderful things could happen.

Yes, Cal was a good name. She would make a crayon sketch of the baby this afternoon, she decided, as soon as she had had her bath. For Orrin had declared today a rest day. A whole day, she thought luxuriously. A day to wash her body and her hair and her clothes, a day to do as she pleased . . .

She lingered a few more minutes talking with Margaret, then bundled up her soiled clothing and went down to the river. Others were already there, arguing over who should bathe first, the men or the women.

"All right, folks!" Wyatt Thatcher, waving his arms about theatrically, was trying to settle it. "Step right up to the greatest and most luxurious bathing facility in the entire Western Hemisphere. Cool, medicinal waters, soothing to the body and the mind alike. Ladies, step right up and take advantage of this wonderful offer. Gentlemen, you will follow the members of the fairer sex at the time they are finished."

There was laughter and a few jibes at Wyatt, whom most of them liked.

"Oh, why not all of us together?" came a laughing cry from someone, to be quickly shushed by Martha Rigney. But eventually the men turned back toward camp, leaving the water to the women. Only Mace, Emerald saw, had not been there at all.

Emerald hurried toward the river, eager to wash the days of accumulated dust from her hair and skin.

She nodded politely to Katje and Martha Rigney, who were kneeling at the water's edge, starting to scrub a huge accumulation of soiled clothing. Beside them Susannah played, paddling her toes in the current. Of the women, only Margaret and Geertrud were not present.

"Water! Water!" Trude gloated. She was stripping off her dress. For an instant she stood in her petticoats, pulling the pins out of her white-blond hair, so that it fell forward onto her shoulders. Her skin, where her dress had covered it, was as pale as a bowl of light cream, and her breasts jutted forward, full and womanly.

Had Mace touched those breasts? Kissed them? Emerald was astonished at the bitterness of her own feelings.

Martha Rigney had looked up from her scrubbing, too. "Surely you're not goin' to bathe buck-naked!"

"Why not? It's the usual way to take a bath, isn't it?" Trude began pulling off the rest of her undergarments.

"It's a whorish way to take a bath, in my opinion.

239

Out in the broad light of day—it's shocking, I say. And I don't intend to put up with it."

"Oh?" Trude was entirely naked now, arms akimbo on her hips, eyes dancing with mischief.

"Look at you! Showin' off your— Why, I never saw the like! Never thought I'd see the day when I'd be travelin' with the likes of you! A buck-naked whore, that's what you are!"

But Trude ignored her, and waded into the water gaily. "Ohh! It's cold! Do come in, Emerald. It feels good!"

Emerald hesitated.

"Oh, do come," Trude urged. She splashed water over herself and scrubbed her arms and thighs.

"*You* ain't going in there like that, are you, Emerald?" Martha demanded.

Emerald stared at the tall, rawboned farm woman. "Yes," she said. "I am."

"Well! I never! I always did think you were no better than you should be, Emerald Regan. But now this proves it. Well, go and join that—that floozy. Yes, go and display your body. We all know that God is watching. He'll see you get your just deserts, mark my words."

Martha gathered up her wet and dripping laundry in one fierce motion. "Come on, Susannah, Katje. We'll bathe later, and we'll do it decently!"

They left, and Emerald watched them, feeling furious and shamed. Oh, she hated Martha Rigney and her thin, pinched, poisonous mind.

Trude giggled, sounding once more like the girl Emerald had met in Council Bluffs. She ducked beneath the water and shook herself like a puppy.

Impulsively, Emerald pulled off her own dress and peeled away her petticoats and underwear, which suddenly seemed far too tight. In a moment she stood naked. She felt the sun warm on her breasts and belly.

Defiantly, she waded into the river. Let Martha Rigney call her anything she chose. She was doing nothing wrong.

She found an area a distance from Trude and, mindful of the current, sank beneath the surface so that the water came up to her chin. It felt luxurious, the water touching every part of her body with cool fingers.

"So you finally decided to take a real bath," Trude said.

"Yes . . ."

"It's fun, isn't it? And women let themselves miss all of this pleasure."

"I suppose they do."

"You know it's so, Emerald. What's wrong with having a bit of fun now and then? Men do; why can't we?" Trude splashed herself, humming.

Emerald stared at her, suddenly hostile. "I suppose you're hoping that Mace Bridgeman will come to the river and see you bathing, as he did before," she said sharply.

"So? And what if he does see me? It won't be the first time."

Emerald flushed angrily.

"You don't own the man, you know," Trude went on calmly. "Mace isn't married; he's free for the taking."

"Perhaps *you* should get married," Emerald said coldly.

"Married. Not me. And not Mace, either, I'm afraid. He's not the marrying kind, and both of us know it."

"He is!" Emerald burst out. "He is, he will be, if only—"

"You're a little fool, Emerald Regan. Mace is a roamer, a wanderer, and his work is far too important to him to give it up for a woman. For you or for me." Trude cupped water in her hands and laved it over her creamy shoulders.

Emerald thought of Mace's arms about her, the powerful strength in them, the warm, tender lovemaking that could stir her so deeply, so completely.

"No," she whispered. "It's not true. He will, someday. . . ."

"Someday? Never is more like it." Trude laughed.

Her cheeks stinging with anger and confusion, Emerald began to wade toward shore. *He's not the marrying kind, and both of us know it.* She hurried out of the water, yanked her clothes from the young cottonwood where she had hung them, and pulled them on as quickly as she could over her wet body. She tugged angrily at her petticoats, wishing she knew who to be angry at—Trude, Mace, or herself.

"What's this I hear? Two lovely girls arguing?"

It was Mace, of course, grinning at her with a teasing glint in his eye. Emerald jumped backward, feeling a rock jab into her bare feet. What had he heard?

"This spot was set aside for the *women* to bathe in," she snapped. "You're not supposed to be here!"

Mace laughed. "Come, Emerald, I didn't mean any harm. Your voices were so loud that I just stepped down to see what the trouble was. I didn't know this area was set aside for the women to bathe. I was washing myself downstream."

His hair was damp and freshly combed, his face newly shaved. He looked relaxed, his eyes gleaming with a disconcerting, teasing light. And Emerald was miserably aware that Trude was still disporting herself in the water.

"I'm sure you have a good excuse," she managed. "And now I must get back to camp. There's work to do."

"Emerald—"

"I said I have to go now!" She could barely control her fury. "But that shouldn't bother *you*. After all, Trude is still in the water, and that should please you mightily, shouldn't it?"

Mace turned swiftly, and for an instant Emerald was frightened by the fierce power of his anger. She stepped backward, her heart pounding.

Then Mace looked toward the river. "Trude isn't in the water," he said.

"Of course she is! I was with her. Maybe she's farther downstream. Or perhaps she's gone ashore."

"Gone ashore? Then she must have done it naked, for her clothes are still here. Dammit, Emerald, she can't swim. Why couldn't you have paid attention to her?"

Emerald flushed. But before she could speak, Mace had pushed past her and half-run, half-waded into the water. Then, in a sudden piking motion, he dove under the surface of the water. Emerald stood on the bank and watched, suddenly terrified.

Mace's head appeared above the surface again, his wet hair streaming into his eyes. "I can't see her. And these damned clothes are weighting me down."

Like an eel he wriggled out of them and tossed them toward Emerald. The fringed shirt landed in the shallows, followed by the buckskin pants, the heavy leather belt, the bowie knife.

"Well, don't just stand there and gawk!" Mace

shouted at her. "Look about, will you? She may have floated downstream."

"I—I can't swim," she whispered.

"Then walk along the bank, you little fool! Unless you want to see the girl dead, is that it?" He plunged under the water again, and this time she could see his pale shape moving with the current.

Frightened, angry, she began to stumble along the rocky bank. "Trude!" she called. "Please, Trude! Where are you? *Trude!*" Her scream echoed among the trees and tumbled boulders. A bird called, its voice a liquid treble. Insects hummed. A dog barked back in camp. "Trude! Oh, please come out!"

Then she spotted a gleam of white on the other side of the river, near two tilted-up rocks. Something was caught there, something that shone yellow-white, like blond hair.

Emerald swallowed, feeling sick. Then she screamed, "Mace! There! Over there!"

He swam through the water with strong, scooping strokes. He reached the shallows on the other side, stood up, and began running through the water, the curve of his buttocks muscular and beautiful. At last he reached the rocks, and Emerald saw him bend over and lift Trude in his arms.

Chapter Twenty

WOLF Dreamer knew that his brother's widow, Sun Comes Up, was waiting for him to decide about the wagon train. The whole camp, following after him at a slower pace, waited, too.

Sun Comes Up was a desirable woman, tall and lithe like an antelope with large and liquid eyes. Wolf Dreamer had been planning to take her to wife, as was the custom for a brother's widow.

But he had not. He had become obsessed with the green-eyed woman who traveled with the wagon train, and could think of no other. Her strange eyes seemed to draw him to her.

He purified himself in the sweat lodge so a dream might come. It was a sixteen-stone bath, breathlessly hot and moist. When the dream came, it was of a coyote. Its fur was yellow-gray, and it had gone rabid, snapping and slavering, biting its own tail. In the dream, Wolf Dreamer, with Small Feather at his side, crept over the top of a ridge and saw the coyote below, worrying insanely at its bloody stump of a tail.

"There." The boy pointed, his body stiffened, nostrils flaring. The sun caught the reddened scars on his back, turning them to gold.

Then, before Wolf Dreamer could move or speak, an enormous ball of fire came rolling along the rock-strewn slope, and passed like a prairie fire over the coyote. When it had gone, there was nothing left but the animal's charred body, and the corpse bristled with arrows, as if a hundred warriors had shot it.

Wolf Dreamer told the dream to the others in the camp. Sun Comes Up smiled, her eyes bright for the first time in many days. The men nodded, talking excitedly. They began to prepare.

Trude lay limply in Mace's arms, the creamy color of her skin gone bluish. Raw, bloody gashes marked her hip and side, and she looked forlorn and cold.

But she was alive.

"Get her some dry clothes!" Mace snapped. "Right away! I don't want her to take pneumonia."

"Very well," Emerald said dully. She found Trude's clothes and, when Mace laid the gasping girl on the ground, managed to pull them on her while Mace shrugged into his own buckskins.

Then she watched as Mace lifted the girl with rough tenderness. Desperately Emerald tried to quell a painful stab of jealousy. She was glad that Trude was alive; of course she was.

But why, she wondered, did Mace have to look at Trude so tenderly?

"I'm so cold . . . so cold," Trude whispered, turning her pale face toward Mace's buckskinned chest, her eyelids fluttering.

"Hold tight, Trude. We'll get you back to camp and a warm fire, and you should be fine." Mace's voice was husky. "To think that you might have drowned—"

"I don't swim very well," she whispered. "Mace . . . darling . . ."

Mace bent his head to the girl's face and whispered something to her, something that Emerald could not hear.

Numbly, stumbling over rocks and hummocks of grass, Emerald followed the two back to camp, where a shocked crowd gathered to stare. Trude looked battered and wet, yet her breasts thrust out the wet fabric of her dress even more noticeably.

"This here accident is nothing but the Good Lord expressing His displeasure," Martha Rigney said sharply. "And *she* knows *why!*"

Emerald waited with the others, a numb feeling of hurt in her chest. Mace had held Trude so tenderly, so caringly, as if she meant a very great deal to him. As if he—loved her!

Ben Coult arrived, and Mace lifted Trude into the VandeBusch wagon for treatment.

Emerald stumbled back to the Wylie wagon, as Mace still lingered near Trude. Slowly, dully, she began to collect the Wylie laundry to wash in the river.

"Well, young Emerald." Martha Rigney's voice rose behind her. "You needn't think *you're* so smart. You saw what happens to girls who bathe buck-naked—they get their comeuppance, that's what!"

"But—" Emerald looked up blankly. "But no one saw us—"

"*God* saw you. And God will punish you. And if I see such wantonness again, I promise you I'll take action. We know what to do with loose girls back where I come from!"

"Oh?"

"Seen it done myself. Little hussy back home thought she could get away with stealing another woman's husband. Well, we proved her wrong. Aye, stripped her and got out the tar bucket and a comforter full of feathers. Heated up the tar good and hot—"

"Oh—" Emerald put a hand to her mouth, turned, and ran toward the wagon, hearing Martha Rigney's derisive laughter behind her.

Another day had passed. Fortunately, Trude had recovered quickly from her near-drowning. They were traveling among high ridges now, with pine forests, good streams and springs. It was easier than the desert crossing, yet this was hard country, too. Often the wagons had to be lowered with ropes down a steep slope, or hauled up one. Saul Rigney broke another front axle and had to make emergency repairs. Orrin, too, fretted about the condition of his wagon. The wheels were going, he said, and the front axle, repaired twice already, was very weak.

The baby, Cal, was doing well. But Margaret was recovering slowly from her childbirth, and exhaustion added new, deep lines to her face. Sometimes Emerald thought this Margaret was an entirely different woman from the pretty, auburn-haired person she had first met in Saint Louis.

"Now, Emerald, don't fret so about me," Margaret said. They had stopped for the noon rest, and were eating cold biscuits and rice, washed down with milk. "I'm just fine. It's natural to feel worn down after having a baby. And I—I'm kind of old, I guess, to be birthing children."

Old, at thirty-four.

"Perhaps we should stay here and rest for a day or two more," Emerald began.

"No! I don't want any extra rest, and I won't hear of it. I'm tired, yes, but I can go on."

However, to Emerald's surprise, Orrin himself announced, the following morning, that the entire wagon train would rest another day.

"Rest? We done rested up already, and now you want us to lay about some more!" Red Arbuthnot's blue eyes flashed.

"I got to repair an axle," Orrin insisted.

"So? We all got repairs. We're all hanging on by the skin of our teeth, but we all keep goin', don't we?"

Orrin reddened. "And I say we stop. Remember, I'm the captain of this here train. You elected me back in Council Bluffs."

"And we can un-elect you, too. Maybe that's what we ought to do. It don't strike me you're too good as a leader. If you ask me, you're more bluster and bellow than you are good sense."

Orrin took offense, and the argument boiled higher. After half an hour of debate, it became clear that the majority of emigrants sided with Red and wanted to push on.

Orrin cursed under his breath. "Well, then, dammit, you folks can do what you want. Me, I'll drop back a day or two, and then catch up. I got my wagon to see to." Then he added, "And my wife."

Through this discussion, Mace had been stubbornly silent. Now he pushed one hand through his unruly brown hair and scowled. "What do you think this is, Wylie, the Boston Post Road? We're in the wilderness. This is Snake Indian country."

"So? I got work to do."

"Then do it at the night camp."

"Aw, why should I? We ain't seen any Indians in the last two weeks, and we've had no trouble to speak of. You yourself said the Snakes was friendly enough."

"Friendly, at the moment." Mace pressed his lips together.

"Well, listen here, Bridgeman, it was us hired you to do our guiding. You don't tell us what to do—we tell *you*. If you want to get your money at the end of the trail, that is."

There was a long silence.

"Very well. Have it your way, then, Wylie. Wallow in your own stupidity if you must. We'll go slowly, and we'll leave an easy trail for you. See that you catch up in one day's time, is that clear?"

Mace stalked off.

The other wagons left, and Timmie and Susannah went down to the stream to play, while Orrin began tinkering with the iron wheel rim. Margaret spread a blanket on the ground and napped there with the baby. Edgar, the dog, snoozed beside them, while Windy and the other animals grazed nearby.

It was peaceful, but Emerald felt restless. She realized that she missed the comfortable sensation of having many people about her.

"I'm going to pick up some firewood," she said to no one in particular, found a soiled gunnysack, wandered away from the wagon. She skidded down a steep incline strewn with loose rocks, then climbed laboriously up another one. Soon the wagon was out of sight, but still she kept climbing, putting an occasional stick or branch in her sack.

She looked up to see Mace walking toward her, leading his gelding by the bridle.

"What are you doing here?" she asked in surprise. "I thought all of you had left."

"I came to try to talk some sense into you, Emerald Regan, even if Orrin Wylie is beyond hope."

"Sense?"

"Yes, you little fool. This country may not seem dangerous to you, but it could be. I want you to join the main wagon train, now. Then you'll be safe and I won't have to concern myself about you."

"Oh?" Emerald tossed her head. "Well, you needn't *concern* yourself over me."

"Well, I do! I'm getting paid to worry about you. You and all of the others are my responsibility."

"As Trude was your responsibility the day she nearly drowned in the river?" Emerald snapped.

She was instantly sorry, for Mace's face went cold.

"And what did you expect me to do, Emerald? Let the girl drown? She is my friend. You seem to think that I belong to you, that I'm somehow your personal property. Well, delectable as you are, I don't belong to you, or to anyone."

Emerald burned with humiliation. "How very wrong you are!" she cried, clenching the rough gunnysack until her fingers hurt. "I don't consider you my property! What makes you think I would want you at all? Because I don't! I—"

To her horror, she was crying. "Oh!" She turned and ran away from him. Her feet skidded and slipped, catching the hem of her gown.

"Emerald! Wait!"

But she didn't look back.

Chapter Twenty-one

❦ ❧

MARGARET Wylie slept away the morning, the baby snuggled close to her side, and dreamed that she was meeting Orrin once again on the wooden walk outside the school in New Orleans where she had once taught.

They had stood silently for a moment, each wondering what to say to the other. Each was conscious of the current running between them, so strong that it seemed as if they *must* touch.

"I want you to marry me," he said abruptly.

"What?"

"I said, I want you to marry me. I can't go on like this, meeting you here in town. I've saved enough to take a wife, and I want to take you."

Forthright—that was Orrin. Stubborn, too, she knew by now. If he wanted her for a wife, she would be his. Her knees felt weak as she realized that he was going to kiss her. Right out on the street, with carriages and drays rumbling past, and a mulatto woman stopping to gawk at them. . . .

The baby stirred beside her, and started to cry.

Margaret moved drowsily, trying to burrow back to her dream.

I want you to marry me.

But Cal was crying louder, bending his little legs and kicking her rib cage insistently. She sighed, turned over, and scooped the infant to her chest.

But the cries did not stop, so Margaret fumbled at the buttons of her gown and gave the baby her breast.

His mouth closed down on it instantly. She felt the drawing pull as he began to nurse.

I've saved enough to take a wife, and I want to take you.

Odd, she hadn't thought of Orrin's words in years. But it was just like him, she told herself, to take so much for granted. If she could have looked into the future that day and seen herself thirty-four years old and already middle-aged, would she still have married him?

Probably she would have, she admitted to herself. She looked down at the baby's intent little face, eyes closed, mouth sucking. If she hadn't married Orrin, her life might have been different. She was sure it would have. But she couldn't wish her children unborn. She had them, and she was glad. She would do it again, all of it.

She began to blink her eyes rapidly, and felt a surge of disgust at herself. How weepy she had been lately. Crying over a sharp word from Orrin, or nothing at all. It was the feeling that came to a woman after she had given birth, Margaret knew, but it seemed to make no difference. She cried, anyway.

She switched Cal to the other breast. She could hear Timmie and Susannah giggling to each other as they splashed in the river, and Orrin scraping something as he worked on the wagon wheel.

Then, amid these peaceful sounds, Margaret looked up and saw the Indians coming silently toward the wagon. There were eight or ten of them, and they were nearly naked, painted with red hand prints and ocher markings on face and chest and arms. She had an impression of exotic feathered headdresses. They were like birds of prey, wingless, ferocious birds.

Fear came upon her in a sickening, gut-wrenching rush. Margaret clutched Cal to her bare breast and began to scream.

Mace had left her more than an hour ago, yet Emerald still sat in the curve of the rock formation, staring dully at the vista of near hills and farther ones, shaded in tones of green and hazy gray, with the blue, intense sky above. Nothing mattered to her except Mace, and she had sent him away.

At last she stood up, shaking away her thoughts, picked up her gunnysack, and headed back toward the wagon, following her own trail with difficulty. She had not realized that she had come so far. But at last she found the river.

She hesitated, then heard Susannah's shout of laughter. With relief, she turned upstream.

She found the two children standing knee-deep at a spot where the river widened. They had been building a castle of sand and rock, and both were soaking wet. Susannah's dress was damp to her chest, and her hem was dragging in the water. Timmie, too, was wet, and had waded into the water while still wearing his wooden foot. Heaven only knew, Emerald thought exasperatedly, what the dampness would do to the wood.

She ran to meet them. "Timmie! Susannah! Have

you been playing here all this time? And what are you making?"

They both looked up together.

"It's a fort," Susannah said. Her forehead was streaked with mud.

"A trading fort," Timmie added. "Like at Fort Laramie. These stones here are the Indians, and these are the traders. They're having a war, see, and the Indians are coming in their bullboats and shooting arrows at them. . . ."

Emerald slipped off her shoes and lifted the hem of her dress. "Can I help you? We could dam up some of the water, and I could help you get some more rocks."

"Sure, Em," Susannah said. "You can move that rock over there. It was too heavy for us."

Emerald started toward the rock, and, as she stood in the chilly water, her skirt lifted to her knees, she heard a scream cutting through the clear mountain air.

Margaret's scream flew on the air, bright and high, then died. She heard it with surprise, as if it came from far away and did not belong to her. Somewhere, Edgar barked frantically.

She looked toward the wagon, where Orrin lay on the ground tinkering with the right forward wheel. He hadn't lifted his head. Had he even heard her?

"Orrin!" she screamed. "Orrin!"

The fantastic painted figures swept toward them. One of them glanced at her, seeing the infant, the bared breast, and instantly discounted her.

Margaret jumped to her feet, thrusting the baby into the folds of her bodice. Disordered thoughts overwhelmed her. The baby, his head so wobbly and helpless. Her breast showing. The children. Orrin. What was she going to do?

Guns, she thought rapidly. Guns. In the wagon. She must get to the wagon.

She began to run, her left arm supporting the baby and instinctively hiding him.

She reached the front of the wagon and saw Orrin. He was already dead. He lay like a bundle of rags, with an arrow protruding horribly from his back. One of the Indians knelt beside him, knife in hand. Before Margaret's horrified eyes, the Indian took a grip on Orrin's hair and sliced into the scalp. Red appeared. Bright red.

I've saved enough to take a wife, and I want to take you.

Abruptly Margaret was full of anger. She thrust the baby through the flap of the wagon, then, screaming hoarsely, she threw herself at the Indian who was scalping Orrin. Dreamlike, her fingers clawed. She bit down, tasting salt and dust and male human.

The Indian twisted beneath her, greasy with paint. Orrin's dead eyes looked up at them.

Margaret felt strong. She would kill this man who was scalping her Orrin. She would make him pay. Euphoria filled her, sang in her. She was laughing; she was crying.

When the arrow hit her in the back, she felt it only as a blow, as if a rock had slammed against her.

Orrin, she thought, startled.

Then, like watercolors blurring, the ground in front of her seemed to tint red, then gray. Margaret felt very tired. Suddenly she was weary of fighting.

She sank into featherbed darkness.

Chapter Twenty-two

❧ ☙

THE scream cut through the placid noises of wind and water. Emerald, Timmie, and Susannah stood frozen as the chilly water swirled around their ankles.

"Em?" Susannah asked.

Emerald felt as if the pit of her belly had fallen out. *Margaret,* she thought. It was Margaret screaming.

"Stay here," she whispered. "Stay here and *hide,* in the bushes or *somewhere.*"

She splashed out of the river, feeling the small, sharp stones cut the bottoms of her feet. Her dress was wet and clung to her legs.

She saw the Indians as soon as she came over the rise. They were on foot, their brown bodies elaborately painted. She stopped, hand to her mouth. Every instinct screamed out to run. They were concentrated on the wagon and hadn't yet seen her. Yet something held her there as an Indian drew his bow and loosed an arrow, in one swift, deadly motion.

She could see a dark outline lying on the ground on the far side of the wagon. Dark pants, dark flannel shirt: Orrin. And then she saw Margaret, pierced by an arrow, blood welling red.

The children, was her first, feverish thought. Were they hiding? Dear God, Timmie couldn't run!

She turned and ran toward the river, but drew back with a shriek. An Indian faced her, the same man she had seen outside Fort Laramie. She was sure of it, for he had the same full, sensual mouth, the same yellow-brown eyes. But this time he was nearly naked, wearing only a breechclout. His chest and arms were painted with long red stripes, and his chest with two red hands.

For an instant they looked at each other, his eyes narrow.

Then she realized that three other Indians had started toward the river, where Timmie and Susannah were.

"No!" she screamed. "No, please! No!"

The Indian said something she did not understand and took a step toward her. Suddenly, four Indians stood in a circle about her, blocking her escape, looking at the first one as if awaiting his orders.

She choked back another scream. She couldn't let them see her fear, yet she saw lust in their eyes. They wanted her, she was sure of it.

Oh dear God, she prayed, please . . .

Then she heard shouts coming from the river. Shouts and a high-pitched, childish shriek.

She turned and wildly tried to run through the restraining wall of Indians, beating her fists against them. Hands gripped her; fingers cut into her arm. She heard laughter. They would play with her, she thought furiously, like a cat with a downed bird, until they tired of their sport.

Well, she would show them. She wouldn't give up too easily.

She kicked out with her bare foot, feeling pain as

the kick connected. She clawed, bit down on some-one's hand, tasting the salt of blood. A voice cried out angrily, and someone else laughed.

Emerald twisted and kicked frantically. The man she had bitten lunged toward her, and she aimed an-other kick at the bulge of his breechclout. Her kick landed. He gave a high, agonized scream, and lifted his painted, decorated war club.

Was there a shout from the Indian who seemed to be their leader? She didn't know. For the club came down, and there was only the blinding red-blackness that consumed her.

Distantly she heard voices, felt the sun's warmth on her skin. And pain. Always there was the pain, a heavy iron band squeezing her skull. She moaned.

She must be dreaming, she decided dazedly, dream-ing that she was riding face-down across the back of a horse. It was a very vivid dream, for the horse's movements jolted her, took away her breath, became part of the agony and pounding in her head. Beside her face she saw a beaded, quilled moccasin, a bare leg. Was there a hand holding her securely on the horse?

But she didn't know or care. She slid into uncon-sciousness, where pain was mercifully absent.

When she awoke again, she was lying on a litter slung between two poles. A horse was dragging it roughly along the ground. She tried to move, but she was tied in, arms and legs, like a baby. Above her hung the noon sun, huge and white and hot. Her head pained savagely.

Emerald remembered the Indians, creeping across the clearing. Timmie's shout. Orrin and Margaret dead. The arrow in the center of Margaret's back, bubbling up red.

The children: were they alive or dead? Emerald wanted to cry with fright and pain and grief, but the muscles of her face would not move. A black, fuzzy haze gathered at the back of her mind. She willed it to come closer, and fainted.

Consciousness came back very slowly. Her first awareness was of sounds, so many sounds that she could not sort them out. She lay very still, eyes closed, letting them wash over her.

Gradually, some became distinct. There were the familiar noises of horses, of dogs barking. Children shouted rhythmically, as if playing a game. A woman screamed shrilly. Other voices, both male and female, talked more softly. Someone laughed.

Camp sounds, she thought dazedly. She was in a camp.

With an effort, she opened her eyes. At first she saw only a blur. But gradually she was able to see the smooth walls of tanned hide, with daylight filtering through them. The walls slanted upward, narrowing to a hole at the top. Damp, hot clouds of steam filled the tent like marsh fog.

Emerald tried to move her legs. To her surprise she realized that they were bare, and that she seemed to be restrained at the ankles. Her hands, too, were tied behind her back.

She was frightened, but when she lifted her head, she felt excruciating pain and dizziness before she could see again.

She was lying in an Indian tepee, stripped naked except for a deer skin laid across her pubic area. Her hands and feet were tied with rawhide thongs, and she lay on the fur side of a buffalo robe. Steam filled the tepee in white billows.

She put her head down and closed her eyes, trying to think. How long had she been here? By the dry, cracked feel of her lips, she guessed she had been here many hours, perhaps a day or more.

Vaguely she could remember the journey here to the Indian camp, the gaining and losing of consciousness as she was moved from horse to pole-carrier. Then at last there had been the softness of buffalo robes and a female voice questioning. The voice had been young, throaty, lovely, yet there had been anger in it. Then hands had moved her again, had fastened the thongs about her ankles and wrists.

She shifted, and tried to bend her cramped knees. She ached all over, but her head hurt the most. There was, she noticed, something heavy on her left temple. A bandage?

How long had she been lying here helpless? Where were her clothes? How many people had seen her in her nakedness? And where were Timmie and Susannah and the baby?

She blinked hard to force back tears. No matter how terrified she was, she knew she mustn't show fear. The Indians despised cowards, Mace had said once.

Then, slowly, she became aware that there was someone else in the tepee. He had begun a low, singsong chant, begun it so softly that at first she thought it was a part of the camp sounds.

She turned her head, risking the dizziness, and saw him. He was dressed in an eerie costume, with paint and shells and claws. A big wolf pelt covered his head and shoulders. He beat slowly on a painted hide drum.

"Who—who are you?"

He said nothing.

263

"Please——"

His eyes glowed amber-yellow, and with a start Emerald realized that this was the Indian she had seen near Fort Laramie, the same man who had raided the Wylie wagon.

"Oh, please," she whispered again.

But he ignored her, turning aside and doing something she could not see clearly. She tried to struggle up, and again the dizziness overtook her. She felt as if she were falling, falling.

The Indian began to chant again, and the sound of his voice and the drum filled the tepee. She could smell burning sage, aromatic, bitter.

Pain throbbed in her head. Minutes passed, or perhaps hours. Tied and helpless as she was, she could only lie there and listen to the eerie, hypnotic voice. It rose and fell, filled with an odd, quivering intensity.

Four times the strong, yellow-painted hands took a forked stick and placed hot stones into a pit in the center of the tepee. Four times the man dipped a horn spoon into a full skin beside him and poured water onto the hot stones. Great clouds of steam rose. The heat grew more intense. Perspiration poured down Emerald's face, breasts, and thighs. And still the voice chanted, more intense now, ringing and clear.

Emerald lay as still as she could, frightened by a supernatural feeling that grew stronger with each minute. It was, she thought wildly, as if there were spirits in the tepee, evil spirits brushing about her like cobwebs.

But the voice, the rhythmic, chanting voice, stood between her and the cobwebs. Slowly, slowly, its inflection rose. The formless evil seemed to hesitate. And still the Indian chanted.

His voice rose about her like incense, filling her

ears and her senses, quickening her heartbeat with insistent power. Higher, higher, urging, commanding.

And then, suddenly, the chanting stopped. Emerald lay stunned and shaken. The evil, whatever it was, seemed to be gone and with it had gone the pain in her head.

Emerald heard a child laughing outside, and then a dog's high, yapping bark.

She felt herself lifted and carried in strong arms. Then, without any warning at all, she was plunged into the cold water of a stream, and icy liquid burned her.

Chapter Twenty-three

❦❦

A day had gone by. Miraculously, the squeezing pain in Emerald's skull had vanished, as if it had never been. Even the wound had begun to heal and no longer throbbed.

She sat outdoors, on a buffalo robe near the entrance to the tepee. Nearby, one of the young Indian women, her face expressionless, was painting a design on a tanned buffalo hide that was stretched on a frame. Idly Emerald watched her, admiring her deft artistry.

The sun, hot and high in the cloudless blue sky, dazzled her eyes after being kept in the tepee for so long.

They had given her clothes, Indian garments, but she thought the soft elkskin dress rather pretty. Its yoke was embroidered with seed beads and quills; its seams and hem were heavily fringed. A leather belt cinched the dress at her waist, to reveal her breasts and the full, female curve of her hips. She had also been given soft leggings and moccasins embroidered with beads in an exquisite design.

Two older women, their brown faces wrinkled with

years, had come into her tepee an hour ago and dressed her. They had washed her and rubbed herb-scented grease into her skin. Then they had plaited her hair into two braids to fall over her breast, and had fastened them with beaded thongs. They had been amazed by her green eyes, staring into them and exclaiming.

They had rubbed vermilion into her cheeks, and then helped her to dress in the soft, strange clothes. It was as if they dressed a bride.

Now, sitting outside the tepee in the sun, Emerald tried to push back her grief and fear, and looked about her. The Indians had chosen a natural meadow for their camp, enfolded by rough hills covered with pines, and big, tumbled rocks. A swift little stream, hidden by grass, ran through the meadow.

The camp was busy. Women cooked, scraped hides, and tended babies in elaborately decorated cradleboards. Men repaired their weapons. A group of little girls played a cheerful game, throwing small objects into a woven basket.

Emerald watched them, still fearful. She didn't understand. The Indians had injured her and taken her captive—yet they had worked to cure her injury. Then they had dressed her in this beautiful costume, taking great pains that her beauty should be visible. They had not, however, untied her hands, although her feet were free.

What did it all mean? Orrin and Margaret were dead. But where were Timmie and Susannah? A cold lump filled her chest, and she fervently hoped the children were still alive. Indians sometimes took young children as captives, she knew. But they were also capable of killing them.

And there was the baby, Cal. Had the Indians

found him? Or had he been left in the wagon to lie there alone, cold, hungry, with no one to hear his cries but the wolves and the coyotes. . . .

Emerald shuddered. Surely someone from the wagon train had come back and found Cal in time. Mace would have come looking for them. She felt tears again in her eyes, and blinked them away.

The young Indian woman dipped her bone brush into a little paint cup, giving Emerald a sidelong glance of hatred.

"You—you're doing beautiful work," Emerald said, although she knew the girl couldn't understand.

The Indian girl shrugged. She was lovely, Emerald saw, tall and willowy, with small breasts and narrow hips. Her braided hair was black and glossy. She had a firm, straight nose and full lips, her cheeks artfully vermilioned. She was ageless in her beauty—she could have been eighteen or twenty-eight—yet she looked at Emerald with hatred and jealousy.

Emerald sighed, trying to position her wrists so that the thongs didn't rub. Well, she thought, she didn't care what this Indian girl thought of her. She didn't care about anything. Margaret was dead, and the Wylie children probably were, too. Her chest felt tight, aching with a thousand held-back tears. If only she could throw herself down on the buffalo robe and cry, and sob and pound her fists.

No, she must not think like that!

"Please, tell me. What is your name?" she asked the girl.

The girl looked at her and muttered something in a throaty, rich voice. It was the same voice Emerald had heard once before, when she had arrived at the camp. Now the girl looked up and down Emerald's body in frank female assessment.

Emerald flushed. "You don't want to tell me your name. And I see you don't want to be friendly, either. But why? What have I done to you? I wish I could speak your language."

The Indian girl gave Emerald one more long look, then deliberately turned her back.

A high-pitched shouting came from the far end of the camp. Emerald turned to her left, and saw a group of about twelve young boys pouring out of one of the tepees. They ranged in age from about eight to twelve and were naked except for breechclouts.

Suddenly, she recognized Feather among them. Feather! Feather, the Indian boy Orrin had captured and dragged behind the wagon. Of course, she thought, these were Feather's people. After his escape, he had found his way back to them. Glad as she was of that, she realized that the Indians must have followed the wagon train, waiting for a chance to take revenge. And that chance had come when the Wylie wagon dropped behind. . . .

She stared at Feather. Even from this distance she could see the reddened scars from Orrin's lash, the abrasions from where the boy had been pulled along the ground. No wonder they had wanted to kill.

Then another boy came out of the tepee. He was paler than the other boys, and walked with an odd, lurching gait.

Timmie! Emerald sat bolt upright, stifling a glad cry. He was safe, he was still alive! Had Susannah been captured, too?

Please, Emerald prayed. Let it be so. Let Susannah be alive, too. And Cal.

"Timmie!" she called out. "Timmie, it's me, Emerald! Are you all right? Oh, Timmie—"

Timmie's lean little body tensed. She saw him look about the camp, searching for the familiar voice.

"Em!" He started to hobble toward her.

Then one of the Indian boys reached out a swift foot and tripped him.

Timmie went sprawling into the dust, his arms flying. For a moment he lay there, his attitude curiously resigned. Then, slowly, he got up. Keeping his face averted from Emerald, he walked with the others to a cleared space near the farthest tepee. He did not look back.

Emerald drew her knees up and sat awkwardly huddled on the buffalo robe. Suddenly she felt very cold.

More Indians joined the group at the clearing, some of them staring openly at Timmie's wooden foot. Even from this distance Emerald could sense the excitement in the air, the tension.

The men, woman, and children surrounded the young boys, so that Emerald could no longer see them. The Indian woman touched her roughly on her upper arm, and gestured toward the gathering, her meaning plain.

Emerald was to go there, too, and watch whatever was happening.

Slowly she got up and followed the Indian girl. Apprehension soured her stomach. She was afraid something was going to happen to Timmie.

The Indian girl gripped her arm as if with hawk talons. Although the sun was hot, Emerald felt chilled. Her hands were perspiring.

The grim-faced boys had formed two rows, which faced each other. Each held a buffalo robe draped over his left arm.

Timmie, too, stood among them. He equaled most

271

of the Indian boys in size, and he was strong and wiry from a summer of riding Windy. It was only his wooden foot that handicapped him. He looked toward Emerald once, without recognition.

In the row opposite Timmie was Feather, his dark eyes flashing. His scars seemed faded now in the intense sunlight.

The crowd hushed expectantly.

It was a game, Emerald thought. These boys intended to play some sort of rough game, and they were forcing Timmie to take part.

In the pause, interrupted only by the yapping of a scrawny camp dog and the whickering of a horse tethered nearby, Emerald had time to be proud of Timmie. Only she, who knew him so well, could tell that his lower lip was trembling slightly.

Then Feather chanted a string of rhythmic words, and the two lines of boys began to move warily forward. Each boy held up his buffalo robe like a shield. They had obviously played this game many times. Only Timmie seemed puzzled, and he hung back behind the others.

One boy lashed out with his right foot at the knee of a boy in the opposite row, and suddenly the scene turned into a melee. Everywhere boys were dodging and kicking out at opponents. Only Timmie stood alone. There seemed to be no rules, for the boys attacked whoever was closest, and often two boys jumped one.

Many of the kicks, Emerald saw, were aimed at the back of the knees. A boy hit squarely would fall and squirm away as best he could. Was the object of the game to knock a boy down?

The Indians—more women than men—crowded about Emerald, watching with high excitement and placing bets. This was a nightmare, she thought wildly, pitting children against each other like gamecocks.

Then another boy fell, and his attacker threw himself astride the fallen boy, grabbed a big handful of hair at each temple, and began to knee him in the face. Streams of blood gushed from the fallen one's nose.

The two began to roll in the dirt, punching each other. And now a second pair was down, and another boy's nose bloodied.

Two boys approached Timmie warily, robes on their left arms raised for defense. They looked just like miniature warriors, Emerald thought. Then she saw that Feather was one of them, his lips straight and unboyishly grim. For an instant she thought she saw an apologetic look pass from the Indian to the white boy.

Then Feather kicked out at Timmie, catching him on the side of the knee. Timmie staggered backward.

Feather kicked again, and Timmie flushed an angry red. Now, Emerald saw, there were three boys challenging him. Was the real purpose of the game to test Timmie?

Suddenly Timmie took the initiative. Balancing adroitly on his good foot, he kicked out with the wooden one, hitting Feather's kneecap, and knocking him backward.

A second boy, taller than the others, missed a kick, but a third circled to Timmie's back and aimed savagely at his knees.

Timmie fell heavily. And before he could scramble to his feet, the three others were on him, brown arms and legs moving quickly. Robes and dust flew.

Then Emerald heard Timmie shriek angrily. The four boys were still tumbling in the dusty grass, and a long streak of red flowed from Timmie's nose, but his features were screwed up with rage. He had begun to fight back. Kicking, yelling, kneeing, he lashed out at his attackers. Amazed, Emerald saw that he had managed to roll on top of Feather. Now it was Timmie who gripped Feather's long black hair and bloodied Feather's nose.

Oh, Timmie, she thought, how much longer could this go on? For all his courage, Timmie was still weak from the amputation. And there were others left to fight—youngsters hardened by years of rough-and-ready games.

Then, as abruptly as it had started, the game was over. One of the Indian boys, fighting silently and viciously with another, called out, and all the boys stopped fighting. Some got up, holding scrapes or bloody noses. Two lay on the ground, obviously in pain but stoic.

Timmie sat up, looking about him dazedly.

Feather smiled at Timmie, and after a moment Timmie smiled back.

Thank heavens, Emerald thought, it's over. Then, sensing someone watching her, she turned. A man was walking toward her. He was tall and lithe, and wore a painted hide shirt, the upper half blue, the lower half yellow. The man's eyes, a rich shade of amber-brown, regarded her with an expression she could not understand.

Emerald shivered. It was the wolf-costumed medicine man who had cured her wound.

Frightened, she tried to look away, but found that she could not.

He spoke. "That was a warrior game." His voice was full and pleasing. "The boys play the swing-kick game until they bleed. It makes them good warriors and courageous in battle. The captive boy, too, was brave. It is good."

"But you speak English!"

"I lived with a white trapper one summer. I learned the white man's talk from him. Now I can talk to you, Green-eyed Woman. You will go with the woman Sun Comes Up. You will go to her tepee. I will let you talk with the young captive. Then I will come."

He turned and left.

"Timmie! Oh, Timmie!" Emerald embraced the boy, and cried unashamedly. The Indians had untied her wrists and had left them alone together in the tepee. There was no one present to see her break down.

For an instant, Timmie clutched her. Then he pulled back. "Em, you'd better not let them see you crying and carrying on. They won't like it."

She tried to wipe her eyes. "I—I suppose not."

"I *know* you can't cry. Because I did it, and they whipped me. To them, crying's for babies, or cowards. They won't even let their babies cry. And they hate cowards."

"Oh, Timmie, that awful fight. Are you all right? Were you hurt?"

She held him away and looked at him. Blood clung to his swollen upper lip. His chin was scraped, and one eye was purple-black. But other than that, Timmie looked amazingly his old self.

" 'Course I'm all right. Did you see the way I got Feather with my knee?" he asked triumphantly. "I rolled right over him and beat him!"

"Yes. You did. Oh, Timmie—" She hugged him again, thinking of all that had happened.

"Timmie, where is Susannah?" she asked at last. "And Cal?"

"Cal? I—I don't know."

"But Susannah? Surely you must have seen what happened to her?"

"I hid her."

"You what? Oh, Timmie! But where? Is she all right? Did the Indians find her?"

"There were some big bushes leaning over the water, around the bend, and I shoved her in 'em. I figured if she squatted down real tight, she'd be all right. Then I started running away from her, so they wouldn't find her. I figured they might not guess there were two of us. And I was right. They didn't see her."

"Timmie, Timmie." She stared at this brave boy, who was not quite ten.

"It was my foot the Indians liked," Timmie went on, his voice trembling a little now. "They'd never seen anything like it, I could tell. They picked me up, and they took it off and looked at my—my stump, and then they put the straps back on, and they watched me walk around on it a lot. I fought 'em and hit 'em a bit, but they only laughed at me. That made me mad. I walk pretty good on this foot now. I've been practicing."

Emerald hesitated, then said, "You know, don't you, Timmie, that your mother and father—"

"Yes, Em. I know."

For a moment they looked at each other. Emerald had the odd feeling that she was facing an adult Timmie, the man he would one day become. Then, abruptly, Timmie flung himself into her arms and cried.

For a long time she held him. Gradually his sobs grew fainter, and at last he pulled away from her.

"The thing I hate, Em, is that they got Windy. They've got him somewhere in camp. I think they're going to let one of those Indian boys ride him."

"Oh, no, Timmie."

The small mouth tightened to a hard, adult line. "I'm not going to let 'em. We're going to get out of here, Em. We'll escape somehow, like Feather did. We'll ride Windy back to the wagon train. And we— we'll shoot 'em all for killing my ma and pa."

Emerald bit her lip. The Indians were a strong warrior people, hardened to survive in a harsh land. She and Timmie were heavily guarded, weaponless, and helpless.

But we're not helpless, she told herself, summoning her last shreds of courage. *We have each other, and we have hope. We'll get away somehow.*

"Tell me more about what happened," she said. "Tell me everything you can remember."

The story Timmie told was brief. He had been held by the three Indians at the riverbank for about twenty minutes, while they exclaimed over his wooden foot and forced him to demonstrate its use. Then they had made him walk back to the wagon, where they had strapped him tightly to the back of one of their horses.

Mercifully, or perhaps intentionally, he had been tied facing away from the wagon and couldn't see the bodies of his parents. Emerald was not sure he realized that they had been scalped. He had not seen Emerald at all until they had arrived at the Indian camp.

"But what about Cal?" she persisted. "Surely the Indians must have found him."

"They did. They picked him up, took him over by the horses, and looked at him for a while. One of them sort of tossed him around a little, like he was a ball. And then—then this big Indian, the one with the funny yellowish eyes, he took Cal away from the other Indians. He was mad or something. And then he put Cal down in the wagon again, real gentle-like. Cal cried just a little bit, and then I think he went to sleep. Anyway, I don't know what happened to him after that."

"Oh. And what about the milch cow?" she asked after a long pause. "And the other animals?"

"I don't know about Edgar. I didn't see him. But Bossie, I guess she's all right. When the Indians came, the oxen scattered. They slaughtered one of 'em, I think, but it must have been Ben or Sam, not Bossie. I think they loaded up some meat and took it back with us, but Bossie, she must of run away."

"Thank God for that." Emerald closed her eyes and tried to think. Susannah, she decided, would have waited in the river until the Indians had left. Then she would have crept up the bank and seen—

But the wagon would be the only place that Susannah could go. And there she would find the baby, where the Indians had left him.

"Do you think they'll be all right, Em? There's wolves in the mountains, and grizzlies. . . ."

"Of course they will be! Don't you worry about them one bit, Timmie. Why, Mace Bridgeman will get worried when the wagon doesn't show up, and he'll ride back and find them. Then he'll know what happened to us, and they'll all come and—and rescue us!"

It was a fantastic thought. The wagon train was small, the emigrants weak and tired farmers. Emerald didn't expect them to even try.

But Timmie did.

"Sure, he'll come," he said happily. "Mace will.

They've got lots of rifles and pistols, and thev'll come and get us, Em. All we have to do is wait, and do what the Indians tell us, and not cry."

Silently Emerald pulled him to her.

Chapter Twenty-four

✦✦

TRUDE VandeBusch sat near the warmth of the campfire, a shawl pulled about her shoulders, and watched Mace Bridgeman eat. It was dusk, the air chilly. Somewhere a coyote howled.

"Well," she said. "How is the stew? I used bay leaves to flavor it. And some of the sweet basil leaves Ma brought. It lends a good flavor, they say."

"The stew is fine," Mace said. He ate quickly, and she was sure that he did not taste any of it.

"You don't look as if you're enjoying it very much."

"Oh, leave the man alone, Trude, and let him eat," Pa said, reaching for a third helping. "He's got things on his mind."

"Yes, I can see that."

But she felt restless. She got up, fetched the coffeepot, and offered Mace some more coffee.

"No, thanks. I've had enough." He wiped his mouth and stood up. Trude knew he must be worried about the Wylie wagon. The Wylies should have caught up tonight, but they had not.

Trude followed him as he left the circle of the campfire.

"Where are you going?" she asked.

Mace hesitated. In the moonlight his face looked washed with silver. "That damn fool Wylie."

Trude frowned. "I thought you said he insisted on staying back. It was his decision."

"Yes." Mace walked rapidly toward the quietly grazing herd.

"Where are you going, Mace?" Trude persisted.

"Back there. To the Wylie wagon. I want to see what's wrong. I'll be back by morning."

"But—" She wanted to ask if she could come with him.

"I'd better saddle up," he said. "Tell them I'll be awhile."

He disappeared among the grazing oxen and horses. Trude felt hot color spread up from her bosom to her face. *So,* she thought. So.

She arrived back at the wagon and found her family still sitting there. No one had lifted a finger to start clearing away the meal.

Sighing, she began to clear away.

Emerald sat in the tepee toying with the fringe of her elkskin leggings. She had been here nearly three hours since they had taken Timmie away.

Her guard, a strong-looking middle-aged woman, crouched on her heels just outside the entrance to the tepee. The woman, her face broad and wrinkled, had peered in several times, and each time Emerald shrank back. For the woman, hideously, had no nose.

Emerald wanted to cry. But Timmie was right; she had to show all the courage she could, no matter how afraid she felt inside.

For the hundredth time, she looked around at the sparse furnishings of the tepee. There was a fire pit, placed a third of the way back from the door flap. There were beds of folded buffalo robes, each with its own willow backrest. Soft leather storage bags were folded in a stack, and a brightly painted shield hung from a pole at the back. A cloth, painted with figures of warriors and horses, hung on the walls from shoulder level to the floor. And rich brown buffalo robes, fur side up, covered the floor.

This was all comfortable enough—if you were an Indian, she thought. But she wanted to be back with Mace, where she belonged.

She tried to keep her mind busy so that she would not be afraid. She tried to think of Mace. She could remember the feel of his arms around her. *You expect certain things from a man . . . things I can't give you . . .*

Over and over she turned the words in her mind, hearing them as vividly as if Mace were here.

There was a rattling noise at the front of the tepee, and the entrance flap was raised. It was the old woman again, peering in fiercely. Emerald gazed back, trying not to flinch. At last the woman nodded and withdrew.

Shivering, Emerald remembered the pains the women had taken in dressing her. The vermilion for her cheeks, the oiling of her body with scented grease, the beautifully decorated clothing. As if she were to be a bride . . .

Emerald closed her eyes. Indian men, Martha Rigney had claimed, lusted after white women, most especially those with blond hair. Oh, nonsense! Emerald thought. Anyway, she didn't have to worry, for her own hair was black.

But she did have green eyes. She remembered how the women who had dressed her had looked into her eyes, marveling, as if they had never seen such a phe-nomenon before. And the medicine man had called her "Green-eyed Woman."

Emerald heard another rattling sound, and when she opened her eyes, the yellow-eyed medicine man was there. He had made no sound, entering the tepee as noiselessly as campfire smoke. He sat cross-legged, clad in the painted, fringed, two-color shirt.

His face looked as if it had been carved out of some rich, dark wood. His nose was arrogant, the cheekbones carved high, the mouth sensuous. His eyes were brown-yellow, the colors seeming to move and change.

"Oh!" She struggled to conceal her shock at seeing him, and—yes—her attraction.

"What is your name, white woman?"

"Emerald Regan."

"Emerald," he repeated. "Is not the emerald the precious stone that your women wear?"

"Yes, that's right," she said nervously. "It is a green precious stone that women often wear. I—I have one myself, an emerald pendant, given me in his will by my uncle."

She had given the pendant to Margaret to keep for her, and supposed it was still hidden in the wagon, in one of the canvas pockets. Unless the Indians had taken it.

"The—stone is green," she said. "That's why my father gave me the name. Because of my eyes, you understand. Green eyes are rare, even for my people."

"Yes." The man's eyes held sorrow and knowledge, and looked too deeply into hers.

She felt acutely conscious of her appearance, with her hair braided in the Indian way, and the soft leather dress revealing the shape of her body.

"Who—who are you?" she asked at last.

"My name is Wolf Dreamer. I am a Wicasa Wacan, a holy man, and I dream of our brother the wolf. Few others of my people have dreamed so."

"Why have you taken us captive?" she asked. "Surely it would harm no one if you returned Timmie and me to our people. We don't belong here."

"We shall see where you belong."

"But—you can't expect us to stay here! We don't know your ways. I—I'm a white woman, and Timmie is a white boy." As she talked she began to regain her courage. "You attacked us for revenge, didn't you? But it was Orrin Wylie who made Feather a slave. Timmie and I had nothing to do with that! It was Timmie, in fact, who set Feather free!"

"Yes. We know that. We know, too, that you were kind to the boy."

"Then let us go, please! Timmie's only a child! He has his whole life before him!"

"You need have no fear. The boy will live out his life as the spirits ordain." Wolf Dreamer spoke slowly and with dignity.

"What spirits?" Emerald challenged. "Yours? Or his own God? Timmie and I don't belong with you. How can you repay an act of friendship by keeping us here as your prisoners?"

Wolf Dreamer put his hand up. "Enough. It shall be decided."

Frightened by the flash of anger in the man's eyes, Emerald subsided.

For a further moment they sat in silence. Then Wolf Dreamer lifted an object he had been holding in his lap. It looked like a flute, carved out of rich, dark wood and polished. It had five finger holes, and an air vent that could be closed with a movable piece of wood carved like a horse's head.

"What is that?" she asked.

"It is the Big Twisted Flute, made by a shaman who dreams of the buffalo. Buffalo Dreamer heard its music in his dream. This flute has great powers in matters of love, and it will help a captive decide if she wishes to stay here and be my wife."

Emerald felt stunned.

So this was why she had been so carefully and seductively dressed in Indian costume! She *was* intended to be a bride!

"But—but that's impossible, of course!" she cried. "I couldn't ever be your wife. It's not that I— But I belong with my own people. I want to go back to them at once!"

"That will be decided by the spirits."

"But I don't love you! And I don't want to marry you!"

He ignored her. Slowly, as if he were lifting a sacred object, Wolf Dreamer put the flute to his lips and began to play it.

The music was rich, low, insistent, utterly different from anything Emerald had ever heard. It was as if each note touched her like a soft fingertip. She tingled with the song's vibration.

Her eyes fastened on the flute, on the effigy of the horse. She couldn't look away. Unbidden, erotic thoughts began to seep into her mind. A stallion, mounting a mare, pounding into her with enormous power . . .

She shook her head and tried to push away the image. Why on earth had such a thought come into her head?

Yet again the thought came, and this time she could

almost see the stallion, roan-red, haunches rippling with muscles, shining with foamy perspiration. . . .

And still the compelling flute music continued, probing and sensual. Emerald could feel the soft, caressing fingers touching her. Warmth spread through her. She sensed that she should stand up, and did so, moving in a graceful, Indianlike way. The flute music filled her mind.

She was outdoors, walking through the camp, walking past painted tepees. The ground, scuffed with footprints, moved beneath her, but she could not feel her body. She floated over the grass and dust. Wolf Dreamer walked before her.

They entered another tepee. Something dark loomed up, and she saw that it was a man in a buffalo mask, horns rising up like the spirit of the bison. Yet she felt no fear, for the music was with her, touching her with sensuous fingers.

The buffalo man lifted a pipe filled with herbs and puffed smoke toward her. She breathed the smoke.

She felt as if she were expanding to the size of a giantess. She would burst through the hide walls of the tepee. Yet she was small, too, as small as a prairie dog, and the tepee was enormous, stretched above her to infinity, stars caught in its upper vent like jewels. . . .

She fainted. When she came to, someone was pouring a strange, bitter drink into her mouth. She choked, gulped, and tried to spit it out. But again the bone spoon was thrust between her lips, and she had to swallow.

She looked up and saw Wolf Dreamer's face above her, strangely distorted.

"The flute has power," he said. His rich voice was deep and echoing.

"Once a woman has felt such power, the strength of the horse, the most ardent of all animal lovers, she cannot resist. And when a woman of the Sioux hears such a flute, follows the music, and finds herself in the shaman's tepee, she considers herself a married woman."

"A—married woman?" Emerald heard her own voice, thick and slurred. She remembered following the flute, but now she felt so relaxed. And the warmth was still in her, blooming in her groin like a flower.

"Yes. Do you consider yourself married now, Green-eyed Woman?"

Emerald moved her head from side to side. All she could think of was the eerie flute music caressing her, stroking her. Nothing else mattered. Not Timmie or the wagon train or even Mace. All of them were far away and unreal.

"Are you my wife now, Green-eyed Woman?" Wolf Dreamer repeated more insistently.

She heard her own voice replying.

"Yes," she whispered. "Yes . . ."

Chapter Twenty-five

❧ ❧

FOR Emerald, the next hours passed in a fuzzy dream, as if she had been given some strange drug. She was taken back to the first tepee and made to wait there. After a time, three women came and dismantled the tepee, ordering her to stand outside it while they worked.

They folded its huge bulk efficiently and tied the bundle onto a pole travois. They piled more bags on the travois and lashed others to the horse's back. They worked very quickly, and finished breaking camp in fifteen minutes.

The noseless old woman kept looking at Emerald, who finally conquered her revulsion and plucked at the woman's arm. "Please, could you tell me where we are going?"

The woman looked away, her leathery face expressionless. So Emerald stood quietly, shaking her head and trying to clear her mind. There must have been some powerful herb in the smoke she had breathed, she decided. Or in the bitter medicine.

Sometimes she thought she could still hear her own voice, consenting to be Wolf Dreamer's wife. "*Yes* . . .

Yes . . ." What on earth had made her say such a thing?

But she had. For all practical purposes, she was Wolf Dreamer's wife. Or at least he thought she was. And, oddly, this thought did not disturb her greatly. For she thought she could almost hear the tantalizing notes of the flute, still. Stroking her skin, enflaming her senses, until she forgot everything . . .

She heard a pebble rattle behind her and turned to see Sun Comes Up, the girl who had been painting the buffalo robe, walking proudly toward her. She wore a fine elkskin dress, like Emerald's, with tiny seed beads in an elaborate pattern, and long fringes that swayed seductively.

Around her neck, mingled with the shell bangles of her necklace, Sun Comes Up wore something that sparkled green in the late afternoon sun.

"My pendant!" Emerald cried. "That's *my* jewel you're wearing!"

The Indian girl understood at once. Her mouth twisted slightly. She said something in her own language, her right hand touching the emerald possessively. Her eyes flared triumph.

"But you have no right to wear it!" Emerald stormed. "It's mine! My uncle left it to me—it's my name-stone. And your people stole it—they must have taken it right out of the Wylie wagon, like—like common thieves!"

But Sun Comes Up only smiled and lifted the pendant away from her neck to examine its brilliance, its faceted gleam. Then, abruptly, she let the pendant drop.

She had seen Wolf Dreamer walking across the camp toward them. As he came, Emerald experienced another wave of dizziness. The Indian camp, with its rows of tepees, its tethered horses, seemed to tilt sideways. She flung out her arm for balance. Then, slowly, the world tipped upright and was normal again.

Sun Comes Up turned abruptly and walked toward a tepee farther down the row. Just before she entered the tepee, she looked at Emerald triumphantly, fiercely. *He is mine,* the look seemed to say. *Don't think that you can ever have him, for he belongs to me.*

"Come," Wolf Dreamer said. "We are ready to depart."

"But where? Where are we going?" She looked at the loaded travois horse, at two extra horses that had been brought for herself and Wolf Dreamer. The smaller of the horses, a dark roan mare, had a painted saddle with a high, built-up horn, and was obviously intended for her.

"Not far. We will be alone together for some days. We are well provisioned. I will not have to hunt."

In the presence of these other people, Wolf Dreamer spoke quietly and hardly looked at her. Yet she sensed his pleasure in her, his attraction to her. An attraction that was somehow more than sexual . . .

"What will Sun Comes Up have to say about this?" she blurted.

Wolf Dreamer scowled. "She is a woman. She does not tell a warrior what to do." He motioned toward the small mare. "Come. We will go."

Knowing that she had no other choice, Emerald mounted. Swaying against a new spell of dizziness, she gripped the saddle horn like a novice, flicked the halter rope, and felt the mare begin to move beneath her. She felt an instant's clear panic. She didn't belong here, dressed as an Indian, with this Indian man. She belonged with Mace Bridgeman.

But with a grim effort of will, she forced her face into a calm expression. If she wanted to live, she must not show fear.

They made an odd wedding procession, riding across the meadow where the Indians were camped, Wolf Dreamer leading, Emerald behind him, and the cut-nose woman leading the travois horse at the rear. Emerald bit her lower lip until it hurt, trying not to think of what must come next.

They rode slowly to keep pace with the cut-nose woman on foot. The sun was low now, shining into Emerald's eyes and making them water.

"Where are we going?" she asked Wolf Dreamer again.

"Not far."

"Oh. I was wondering. . . ." He was not taking her back to the wagon train, and she had been a fool to think it even for an instant. Carefully she glanced at Wolf Dreamer, but he ignored her, his face expressionless.

Uneasily, Emerald looked back at the Indian woman, who plodded along as tirelessly as a pack animal, perspiration gleaming on her brown face.

"The woman who is with us"—Emerald could not keep silent any longer—"what is her name?"

"It is Cut Nose Woman."

"Oh!" she exclaimed. "What a cruel name! And— whatever happened to her nose?"

"She was an unfaithful wife."

"Oh!" Emerald felt a hot surge of blood in her face. Had Cut Nose Woman once been as lovely and young as Sun Comes Up? Had her husband done the thing to her? Had it hurt? Had she cried?

They rode in silence for a while, Emerald trying to quell her pity, fear, and anger.

"Do you think it evil to cut off the nose of a woman who is not faithful to her husband?" Wolf Dreamer asked. She turned, startled, to look at him, but his dark, exotic face showed no emotion.

"Why, I— Yes, I do! The poor thing has to go through the rest of her life looking like that, just for one mistake! No other man would ever look at her again. Yes, I think it's cruel."

"We have always done it thus. Some among us, at least. With us, a woman who has been married only once and has been faithful is considered better than any other. Is that not true with your people?"

"Well, I—" Emerald could not look at him. How could she explain white society to this Indian? And, she wondered ashamedly, by his standards, what would Wolf Dreamer think of Emerald herself? A woman who had given her body to a lover, a man not her husband?

But Wolf Dreamer said nothing more, and within a few minutes they reached a grove of tall pines, the ground beneath them thick and soft with pine needles. The place looked curiously like a fort. The grove was backed by a rounded, perpendicular cliff and protected on two sides by more high rocks.

Wolf Dreamer dismounted and motioned for her to do the same. This was to be their camp, she realized. They were only a mile or two away from the main Indian encampment, yet they could have been a hundred miles away, so quiet was it here. Only an occasional bird and a small stream trickling down the cliff broke the silence.

Wolf Dreamer adjusted his painted robe about his shoulders and stood aside as Cut Nose Woman unloaded the travois horse.

"You must help, too, Green-eyed Woman. It is woman's work," he said.

Emerald tried to obey, but she was not sure what to do, and Cut Nose Woman obviously scorned her help. So she ended by doing nothing.

Within minutes, it seemed, Cut Nose Woman had set up the tepee and carried the bundles inside. She laid a fire outside the tepee and lit it with flint and steel she must have received from a white trader. She produced a buffalo paunch and propped it up with a forked stick at each corner. Then she filled it with water and dropped in six stones that had been heated in the fire.

When the water began to boil, Cut Nose Woman dropped in a chunk of meat, wild onions, prairie turnips, and peppermint leaves. She then produced a mushy substance that smelled of gooseberries.

Wolf Dreamer ate his meal first, while the two women watched; then it was their turn to eat. Emerald tried to drink the hot, unsalted soup, but each sip reminded her that she was a helpless captive among strange people. Her stomach felt dry and cramped.

"You must keep up your strength with food, Green-eyed Woman," said Wolf Dreamer.

"I—I'm not hungry. And my name is *Emerald*."

"I call you Green-eyed Woman." His amber-yellow eyes looked at her, then away. In the presence of Cut Nose Woman his eyes seemed to avoid hers. And yet Emerald could feel the bond between them, growing stronger with each minute. The tension was almost unbearable. She shivered, and spilled soup on her hand.

Cut Nose Woman cleared up the remnants of their meal, and left, walking downhill the way they had come, one foot plodding in front of the other. Emerald and Wolf Dreamer watched her until she disappeared from sight behind a rocky ridge.

"Come," Wolf Dreamer said. "We will go inside the tepee now."

Emerald lay naked on the luxurious fur rug of the tepee, looking across at Wolf Dreamer's sleeping body.

They had been in the tepee for several hours, or perhaps it had been longer, she didn't know. Time had passed in a blur, punctuated by sharp, sensual images.

Wolf Dreamer had pushed her into the tepee, for she had been unable to move. She had stumbled inside and fallen to her knees on the buffalo robe.

Then he produced a bone cup filled with more of the bitter drink she had taken earlier. She pushed it away angrily, but he forced open her mouth and poured it in as if she were a recalcitrant child. Finally she had to swallow or choke.

"I—I hate that stuff!" she cried. "And I hate you! I don't want to be your wife—I want to go home!"

"But you are my wife," he said calmly. "Often captive women become wives. It is good that it should be so."

"Good! For you, perhaps, or for your people. But not for me! I'm different. I don't belong here!"

"Perhaps." At first she could not read the expression on Wolf Dreamer's face; then she thought she saw a puzzled look. "I saw you in my dream, but all was not clear. The dream said I should make you my woman, but beyond that I do not know. It seemed as if there was something else. . . ." He stopped.

"Do you do everything by dreams?"

"Yes. It is our way. How else would we know what the spirits intend for us?" Wolf Dreamer looked squarely at her, and she sensed a warmth radiating from him, as intense as sunlight. Now that they were alone, he seemed subtly different. Less stoic, and more like a man filled with desire for a woman.

Thickly, as if in a dream, she heard him asking her to undress. He wished to see her body, he said. She began to comply, her fingers moving awkwardly. The bitter potion had begun to work on her, and she felt more and more removed from what was happening. It was as if her body, naked now and luminous in the firelight that shone through the door flap, belonged to another woman.

"You are beautiful," he said. She felt his hands on her breasts, touching her nipples. They tightened and tingled. Then his mouth was on hers, devouring her.

He undressed, and she saw his smooth, bronzed skin, the chest marked with white, raised scars. He was a big man, his wide chest and shoulders tapering to a narrow, tight waist. Helplessly her eyes were drawn to his nakedness. She could not look away, and didn't want to. She breathed his musky odor, sharp and pleasurably masculine.

Then he was upon her, rolling with her on the fur rug, his hardness pressing against her. For a second she fought him, teeth bared, fingers clawed. But then all of her struggle was gone, and she lay in a half-trance. She felt as if she were somehow above everything, looking down at the nude humans, their forms curiously beautiful in the filtered light of the tepee.

Then she was clinging to him and riding with him upward, upward, exploding. Then floating downward to soft darkness.

Mace, her spirit seemed to cry out, at the height of her passion. *Mace . . . darling . . . where are you?*

Trude VandeBusch was awakened that morning by an uproar in camp. Dogs barked and oxen bellowed. There were shouts, exclamations, a high, squalling sound, and rising above it all was her own father's voice, loud and excited.

Trude sat up, flung off her blanket, and hastily pulled on her old gingham gown. The dress stretched tightly over her bustline, and usually attracted long, hot-eyed looks from men, but this morning Trude did not even think of that. Her fingers flew over the buttons. Then she ducked out of the tent and ran toward an excited group of settlers.

Mace Bridgeman was at the center of the excitement. He stood by his gelding, his hat flung back and his face dusty. The front of his shirt bulged.

Trude pushed past the other emigrants until she could see what Mace was cradling inside his buckskin shirt. It was the Wylie baby. And at his side was Susannah Wylie, clinging to his leg, her face white, her hair snarled, and her dress stiff with dried mud.

"It was Indians, all right," Mace said. Trude had never seen his face so grim, his eyes so bleak.

"Orrin and Margaret Wylie are dead, both of them," Mace said, his mouth twisting. "Shot with arrows and scalped, right where they fell."

Voices rose, shocked, angry, questioning.

"The only bodies I found were those of Orrin and Margaret," said Mace. "Susannah was hiding in the wagon. And this little fellow was alive and crying." He handed the baby to Trude, who cradled it to her breast.

"I think Emerald and Timmie were captured by the Indians," Mace continued. "There was a lot of blood on the ground, but I'm pretty sure it was ox blood—they butchered one of Orrin's oxen for meat. Timmie's pony was gone, too, but I did find the milch cow and brought her back. We'll need her for the baby."

Mace told the rest of the story in a flat voice. Susannah had hidden in the river beneath some overhanging bushes until the Indians left. Then she had gone back to the wagon and found the crying baby, and the bodies of her parents. The little girl had climbed into the wagon with the baby and stayed there until dark. The infant had finally fallen asleep, exhausted, in Susannah's arms.

Mace had found them asleep together on Margaret's patchwork quilt.

"But what are we goin' to do?" old Red Arbuthnot demanded. "They killed Orrin and Margaret—and you know what them savages do to their captives. We've all heard the tales."

Mace clenched his jaw until the powerful muscles knotted. *"Some* Indians, Red, treat their captives savagely. Others do not. I don't hold with killing, not unnecessarily. But I'm going after Emerald and Timmie. I think we have no other choice."

Voices rose in argument. Some of the emigrants were frightened, others angry. At last Trude saw that Susannah was leaning against Mace's thigh, half-asleep.

"Come, Susie, come with me. I'll put you to bed in our wagon. And Cal, too. Perhaps Ben Coult has something we can use for a nursing bottle."

For an hour or more, the camp was in turmoil as

the men talked, cleaned firearms, and packed up the horses. They had decided to go after the Indians—as Trude had known they would. For Mace Bridgeman there could be no other possibility.

Chapter Twenty-six

❦ ❧

EMERALD'S dreams that night were chaotic and frightening. She and Wolf Dreamer had finally fallen asleep on separate fur-covered beds, naked and exhausted. But even in her sleep she could not escape him. The flute music, vibrating and sensual, seemed to follow her into her dream.

During the night she half-awakened to find Wolf Dreamer again inside her, stroking slowly and rhythmically, bringing her to a climax so swift and intense that she cried out.

Then she sank again into darkness.

She dreamed again. She stood outside the tepee, under a sky with tumbled silver clouds. She shivered, for the scene was eerie and lonely.

She was not alone. A wolf crouched at the far edge of the clearing beneath the sheer cliff. Its eyes were amber, their pupils contracting, dilating, holding her in a hypnotic gaze.

A shot rang out. The wolf's chest exploded and gushed blood.

Emerald awoke to the first light of dawn, whimpering with fear. She sat up, her heart pounding. She had been crying in her sleep, for her face felt wet and sticky. She was still in the tepee, with its well-tanned hides, its dewcloth painted with the figures of warriors charging into battle.

Slowly, her eyes turned to where Wolf Dreamer slept. He was naked, lying on one side. In sleep he looked as any man would, vulnerable and defenseless.

Emerald looked down at herself, at the whiteness of her thighs, the round, voluptuous curve of her breasts. She remembered the notes of the flute, the taste of the bitter drink, the feel of Wolf Dreamer's hands and mouth upon her body. . . .

She curled up, burying her face against her knees, shame and dismay taking possession of her.

The bitter drink! *Of course,* Emerald thought. It must have contained some native drug, an herbal potion that had acted as a sexual aphrodisiac. And the flute, the hypnotic, twisted flute, endowed with magical Indian properties, had completed the seduction.

No wonder she had responded to him.

And, she thought, Wolf Dreamer regarded her as his wife and could keep her for the rest of her life if he wished. If he kept giving her that drug, it would make her willing enough.

Eventually, she knew, she would be assimilated into the life of the tribe. She would learn the language. She would wear Indian clothing, learn to tan and decorate buffalo robes, and to prepare food the Indian way. She would become pregnant by Wolf Dreamer and bear him a half-Indian child. Perhaps she would come to accept her fate. She might even grow fond of Wolf Dreamer. . . .

She sat bolt upright, feeling panic. If she stayed with the Indians, Mace might go on to California without her, thinking her dead. He might marry some-

one else, perhaps even Trude VandeBusch. She would
never see him again.

Their captors would make an Indian of Timmie,
too. They would force him to participate in their war-
like games. They would teach him to hunt and to
make weapons, to count *coup* and wear feathers on
his head. Timmie was young and impressionable, and
he had the kind of courage that the Indians admired.
Eventually he would become like Feather, and forget
his white heritage. . . .

That must not happen, she thought. Somehow they
must both escape.

But how? What could she possibly do?

For long minutes she crouched there, beside the
sleeping man, trying to think, to plan. But nothing
came to her. How could a girl and a young boy escape from the Indians? In the first place, she didn't
know where Timmie was, for they had kept him apart
from her. But even if she could find him and get
away, they had no horses, food, or water, and they
would still have to find their wagon train. Or be
doomed to wander this vast wilderness until they died
of starvation or thirst, or wild beasts killed them.

Escape was only a wild hope, Emerald knew, but
she and Timmie would have to try.

Slowly she slid off the fur-covered bed, but before
she could get her clothes, Wolf Dreamer awoke. One
moment he was lying curled up in seeming slumber,
and the next he was sitting up as silently as a lynx.
His eyes seemed to glow at her.

"Oh!" Emerald recoiled and covered herself with
her hands.

"Where were you going, Green-eyed Woman?" He
spoke calmly, and Emerald shivered. No human man,

she told herself, could awaken so quickly and completely, like a cat.

"I—I was just going to get dressed!" she said. "It's cold without anything on. And—and my name is *not* Green-eyed Woman, it's Emerald. Can't you understand that? I'm Emerald!"

"You are Green-eyed Woman. It is your Indian name."

"But I don't want an Indian name! I want my own name! And I want to go back to the wagon train, to my own people, where I belong. Just as you belong here."

"You will stay here and be my wife. I have seen it in my dream."

"Your dream! Oh—poof on your dream!" She knew she was being reckless, but she couldn't help herself. "Dreams are superstitious nonsense, that's what I think!"

Wolf Dreamer's face darkened ominously. For an instant she thought he would hit her. Instead, he reached for a breechclout and fastened it around his waist.

"Cover yourself, Green-eyed Woman." His face was stern and implacable.

She grabbed the elkskin dress and impulsively threw it into a corner of the tepee.

"I want my *own* dress!" she stormed. "Where have you put it? I don't like Indian clothes. I want my own back. Do you hear me?"

Wolf Dreamer looked at her contemptuously as if she were an unruly child throwing a tantrum. "You will wear Indian dress or none at all. My wife will follow Indian ways."

Emerald stared at him. For an instant she wavered.

Then, reluctantly, she retrieved the dress and pulled it over her head. She tied the belt with a jerk.

"Why take *me* to wife?" she retorted. "Why don't you marry that other girl, Sun Comes Up? I'm sure *she* is willing."

Wolf Dreamer's mouth twisted "She is my brother's widow, and will become my wife, too. It is custom. With more wives I will have more hands to work for me. Sun Comes Up is a skilled woman. She will make many beautiful robes."

Polygamy! Emerald thought, horrified. Yet pride made her say, "Well, I, too, am skilled with my hands. I can draw and paint very well. *I* will make beautiful robes, too."

"I am sure you will."

He smiled, and she realized that he had wanted her to say that. She was already slipping into the Indian ways of thinking.

Blindly, searching for some way to set him off balance, she remembered her dream of the night before, of the wolf with the amber eyes.

"You said they call you Wolf Dreamer?" she asked him.

"Yes."

"And you dream of wolves?"

"Yes."

"Well, I, too, have dreams of a wolf. I dreamed of one last night—a wolf with yellow eyes like yours."

She pointed at him dramatically, and was pleased to see him recoil for a second, as if she had touched him. But quickly he recovered his composure. "Tell me of your dream, Green-eyed Woman."

"I dreamed that I was standing outside this tepee. Or perhaps it was not here at all, I'm not sure. Anyway, there was a wolf crouched about fifty feet away from me. He was watching me. He—he watched me for a very long time, silently, not moving at all. His eyes were yellow-brown, like yours. And then—then suddenly there was a shot. The wolf was wounded. And he—" She hesitated.

"Go on. I wish to hear all of your dream."

"And then he died," she said slowly. "The blood gushed out of his chest, and he lay down and died."

Wolf Dreamer drew himself up proudly. "That is all?"

"Yes."

He rose, opened the flap of the tepee, and went outside. "Make the morning food, Green-eyed Woman. I am hungry."

Emerald sat very still, alone in the tepee, staring at the hanging flap, which still swung back and forth from Wolf Dreamer's exit. What was she going to do now? She did not know how to cook the Indian way, and there was no one to show her. She did not know how to do the Indian women's work, and she didn't want to learn.

Despair overwhelmed her. She would remain with the Indians forever, she was sure of it. She would *become* an Indian. She would never see Mace Bridgeman again, or shelter herself in his arms. Never again blend her body with his. She would never see California, with its rich, fertile farming valleys, its warm, balmy climate.

She almost cried out with pain. But she did not. With all of her strength of will, she pushed away the agonized thoughts, the despair.

Then she followed Wolf Dreamer outside.

Somehow she managed to contrive a crude boiled meal, using the leftovers from the previous night. To her surprise, after they had both eaten, Wolf Dreamer told her that they were returning to the main Indian camp.

She looked at him. He had put on his impressive painted shirt, the claw and shell jewelry, the bone breastplate and feathered headdress. He seemed an exotic, bronzed creature again.

"But we just got here——" she began, then stopped. It was obvious that Wolf Dreamer had originally planned to enjoy a "honeymoon" of several days. But now he wanted to go back. Was it because of her dream? If so, she would be happy to go back to the main encampment, and be closer to Timmie. She didn't plan to escape without him, and maybe the boy would have some ideas. . . .

"Take down the tepee, Green-eyed Woman," Wolf Dreamer said. He sat down in the shade of a tall pine and stared at her expectantly.

"Take it down?" Her voice rose. "But I——I don't know how. Your women——Cut Nose Woman and the others——did it before."

She looked in dismay at the tepee. It stood about thirteen feet high and looked as solid as granite.

"You can learn."

"But——"

"My wife must learn to do woman's work," he repeated implacably.

Emerald glared at him. "Woman's work! I'd like to thank you for all the detailed instructions you've given me!" She stamped toward the tepee. She knew he was watching her with amusement, which made her even madder.

So he wanted her to do "woman's work" without even showing her how. Very well, she would do it.

She would show him that a white girl could do anything.

She drew a deep breath to calm down, and looked around the camp. The travois horse was grazing peacefully at one end of the clearing, his front legs hobbled with rawhide. When she got the tepee down, she would load it on the travois as the Indian women had done.

She stood for a minute looking at the tepee. It was constructed of a big piece of buffalo skin, made by piecing individual hides together, wrapped around a cone of poles. Above the door, the two sides of the buffalo skin were fastened together with wooden pins.

She decided to unfasten the pins, and did so with difficulty, and the aid of a long stick. Then she pulled at the hide, and it slid down the poles in an untidy heap. A skeleton framework of ten poles was left, rising above the messy-looking mounds of furs and leather bags of belongings.

Emerald took a good grip on one pole and heaved upward with all her strength. First one pole tilted, then the others, and they all clattered to the ground in a puff of dust.

"Good enough," Emerald muttered to herself with satisfaction. *"That's* done." She glanced at Wolf Dreamer to see if he had noticed her progress. But he was walking toward the downward slope that was the only approach to the fortlike clearing.

Emerald perspired as she dragged the heavy, sewn-together hides flat upon the grass and folded them. It was really a job for two women. But at last she made a huge, awkward bundle and dragged it over toward the travois horse.

He whickered at her, rolling his eyes and showing his teeth, but Emerald was too furious to be afraid of him. Nearby she found the saddle, managed to get it on the animal, and tightened the girth. Then, struggling, she lifted the two travois poles and fastened them to the saddle. She dragged the folded tepee onto the travois and tied it securely.

Then she carried all the flat, decorated leather bags and furs to the horse, loaded some on the travois, and packed some on the horse's saddle.

So this was "woman's work," she thought, wiping away sweat. Putting up and taking down tepees, and doing every other sort of heavy camp work, from carrying water to butchering animals, while the men relaxed as Wolf Dreamer was doing. The Indian women, true, seemed to accept their lot, and even to enjoy their work. But Emerald didn't, and she never would!

Grimly, she doused the fire and picked up scraps lying about the camp, to make sure the site looked just as it had when they arrived. She would show him how well she could do!

She found Wolf Dreamer a short distance from the camp, squatting down to examine a scuffmark in the dust. He was frowning.

"I've finished loading the tepee," she said.

He nodded, barely noticing her, and Emerald's cheeks reddened with anger. In her own society, such heavy work would have been *man's* labor.

They saddled up and rode back to the main camp, Emerald eagerly looking forward to seeing Timmie.

But when they arrived, she couldn't spot Timmie anywhere. And she immediately had to put up the tepee again, this time with the aid of Cut Nose Woman, who laughed uproariously when she saw how ineptly Emerald had loaded the travois horse.

Sun Comes Up came out of a tepee and laughed, too. She was still wearing the emerald pendant.

"Laugh all you wish, you—you jewel thief!" Emerald panted angrily. "I'd like to see how well you'd do if you were back in Baton Rouge, trying to run a big house!"

Just as the tepee was nearly finished, Emerald heard shouting, and turned to see a group of boys running into camp. Timmie was with them, naked save for a breechclout.

Emerald paused in her work to watch him surreptitiously. He was handling the wooden foot even better than he had before, she saw. Although his way of running was awkward and lurching, he managed to keep up with the slowest of the boys. He was laughing at something Feather had said.

We must escape quickly, she thought. Timmie genuinely liked Feather. He would adapt to the Indian way of life very soon, and then he would not want to leave them.

She knelt outside the tepee and began pegging down the bottom edge, following the example of Cut Nose Woman, who had started from the other side. She had driven two stakes when there was a commotion on the opposite side of the camp. A man rode up, his horse lathered, and spoke to Wolf Dreamer in low, excited tones.

Wolf Dreamer's body grew tense, more alert. He asked the man a short, staccato question. The man replied with a long string of words, gesturing with his hands.

Cut Nose Woman and Sun Comes Up were listening, too.

Wolf Dreamer turned and said something to them, a short phrase that was unmistakably an order. Emerald cried out with surprise and pain, for Cut Nose Woman grasped her braids in two strong hands and pulled her backward toward the stream at the edge of the encampment.

Emerald screamed and fought, but Cut Nose Woman merely released one of her braids and clapped a hand over her mouth. Her hand smelled of sweat and Indian food.

Emerald twisted and tried to kick Cut Nose Woman, but she was stolid and strong from a lifetime of heavy work, and simply dragged Emerald along. Sun Comes Up was helping, too, pulling Emerald's arms.

The hand covering her mouth and nose wouldn't let her breathe. Emerald fought frantically, kicking, lashing out with her elbows. Her lungs hurt, and her scalp felt on fire.

Choking, strangling, Emerald went limp. Red, concentric rings seemed to swoop in front of her eyes, but just before everything went black, a thought flickered. Mace was coming to rescue her and Timmie!

Then she was unconscious.

Emerald awoke sprawled flat on the ground, her face shoved into dirt and grass. She could hear water nearby. The two Indian women crouched on either side of her, winding a gag roughly about her mouth.

Distantly, she heard a shot.

Her heart leaped. *Mace!* she thought, *Mace, I'm here! Oh, please—*

She pulled the gag away and fought Cut Nose Woman frantically, surprising herself with her own ferocity. She didn't care about anything except getting free.

She twisted, wriggled, scratched, clawed. Her breath came in ragged, gasping sobs.

But there were two Indian women, both of them

strong from years of vigorous activity. One of them smashed her face, and a stabbing pain shot up her nose. They grappled with her. Their combined weights forced her flat onto the ground, slowly, agonizingly. They sat on her.

"No! No!" Emerald screamed.

The women tied a band of leather around her mouth, cutting cruelly into her lips. They shoved her face into the dirt. She smelled the rich, rotting odor of leaves and humus. A small stone bruised her chin.

All at once her strength left her, all of it spent in the wild struggle. She let her body go limp. She bit her lower lip until it bled, determined not to cry in front of these two women. Sun Comes Up laughed softly, obviously pleased by Emerald's submission and discomfort.

A few seconds passed. Emerald drew a long, shaky gulp of air and tried to relax. She lay helplessly, weighed down by the two Indian women lying across her.

They started to dig up the earth with their bare hands. Dirt, handfuls of half-rotted pine needles, and old leaves fell in Emerald's hair and slid over her neck.

Ugh, she thought, and twisted to avoid the rain of debris. But Cut Nose Woman grunted at her and shoved her face into the ground again. Emerald tasted and breathed dirt.

Then she began to understand. The women were trying to hide her and themselves with a rough camouflage. The emigrants would have to come close to spot them.

The undergrowth was so thick here, Emerald thought with a sinking heart, the plan might work. The rescue party would be frightened off without finding her. And she and Timmie would have to stay with the Indians forever.

The digging was completed, and the three women seemed to melt into the soil, animallike. Pinches and rough pokes in the ribs told Emerald to lie still.

Despair filled her like icy rainwater. She and Timmie would never get away, ever. They would stay here for the rest of their lives. Emerald shook with sobs, and tears burned her eyes.

Sun Comes Up pinched her sharply and hissed in her ear. Emerald knew Sun Comes Up hated her and wanted to kill her. If it were not for Wolf Dreamer, she would probably do just that.

Then something changed inside Emerald. Her tears were gone and she could almost feel the fury growing in her. She managed to twist about and glare at Sun Comes Up.

The Indian girl certainly did not look lovely now, Emerald thought with fierce triumph. Her hands were crusted with dirt, her nails broken and bleeding. Soil and humus stained her face, clung in clumps to her hair, and ruined her elkskin dress. She looked more like a grubby and primitive animal than a human woman.

But, Emerald realized, she herself must look every bit as bad. Whatever would Mace think when he finally found her?

If he found her, she added despairingly.

Chapter Twenty-seven

❧ ❧

THEY lay there for some minutes before they heard another shot. It seemed to come from across the encampment, at a point where the meadow narrowed between two bluffs.

Emerald could feel the two Indian women tense, but she could see nothing but the dirt under her nose and the dense underbrush surrounding them.

She could hear the two women breathing heavily. Wind rattled the leaves of an enormous cottonwood overhead. A puppy yapped in camp; the little stream splashed; a bee hummed. But all else was silent.

Emerald shivered with dread and excitement.

Then she heard a horse galloping through the camp.

"Emerald! Emerald! Oh, Em!" Timmie was screaming at her. She was sure it was his voice. She heard the horse crashing through the undergrowth nearby.

She began to struggle violently, heaving the Indian women off her. She got one hand loose, ripped desperately at her gag, and managed a muffled scream.

Cut Nose Woman dug fingernails painfully into her

arm, forcing her to the ground. But now hope surged through Emerald, wild and uncontrollable.

With a sudden movement, she twisted to her side and jammed her knee into the Indian woman's stomach. Cut Nose Woman gave a startled grunt and doubled up.

Emerald elbowed Sun Comes Up in the nose, feeling the squashy give of flesh and warm blood.

She jumped to her feet and looked frantically around. A dark roan pony stood a short distance away, and, although the animal wore an Indian blanket and halter rope, she was sure it was Timmie's Windy.

A hand was twisted in his mane. And now, as the pony wheeled and headed toward her, she saw Timmie himself clinging precariously to the pony's right side, Indian-style.

She drew a quick, panicked breath, and began to run to meet Timmie. Then the first arrow winged swiftly through the air. It curved toward Windy and barely missed him.

As if the first arrow had been a signal, more arrows filled the air.

A gun fired from the bluff, sending out a white, floating puff of smoke. Many guns fired. A man screamed and fell forward.

Time seemed to stand still as Emerald ran. Another arrow arched toward Windy.

"Em! Em!" Timmie cried.

But behind her came running footsteps. She ran on, her breath coming in agonized gasps, hearing an arrow whiz past her.

She had almost reached Windy when Sun Comes Up tackled her. She felt the impact of the other woman's body, and fell heavily. Rocks and sticks cut into her skin.

She fought desperately. Elbows, fists, teeth, nails. She was a cornered animal, fighting for her life.

As if from an enormous distance, she heard Timmie screaming, "Em! Em! You've got to come! Hurry, it's our only chance!"

But she couldn't come. She was locked in combat with this man-strong Indian girl, this girl who hated her and wanted her dead. Her head slammed on a rock, over and over. Agonizing pain shot through her skull and she felt a surge of nausea.

Sun Comes Up's face hovered over her, dirt-stained, certain of victory, eyes glinting with ferocity. And with pleasure, Emerald realized with horror.

Timmie was still shouting at her, but now his cries had no meaning. Emerald wanted to tell him to go on without her, to leave her behind. But she couldn't. No words would come.

But just as she started to slide into unconsciousness, someone tore the other girl away from her.

Someone lifted and held her. Someone who wore fringed buckskin and a brown felt hat, and who held a red bowie knife.

"Mace," she whispered, "you're really here." His face, with its slightly cleft chin and its broad, humorous lines, was so dear to her that she wanted to weep. She wanted him to hold her for a long time.

But he pushed her away. "Get on Windy and go back along the stream bed. Both of you. Get out of here! I'll cover you."

"But—" Dazedly Emerald looked at Sun Comes Up, who crouched on the ground staring at her slashed bloody hands.

"Can't you hear? I said get going, dammit. Now!" Stumbling, Emerald did as she was told.

They arrived back at the wagon train by nightfall.

Never had Emerald been so happy to see the dusty and tattered canvas tops, the wagons in a circle in a small meadow, the herd grazing peacefully nearby. There was a small campfire, its smoke carefully sheltered. And, incredibly, someone had strung a rope line from one wagon to another. Hanging on it, stiff from laundering and white from the sun, was a row of diapers.

Emerald wanted to cry with joy.

On the trip back, riding double with Mace, she had learned how the ten emigrant men had trailed the Indians back to their camp, then waited two days for the right opportunity. Mace himself had crawled up the stream bed to within only a few hundred yards of the Indian camp. He had crouched in the heaviest clump of underbrush, and had nearly been surprised by one old crone in the midst of her morning ablutions.

"Oh!" Emerald gasped, thinking of the danger he had been in. "Oh, the risk, Mace! What if one of their dogs had scented you? You shouldn't have chanced it! You—"

"I was in the stream water," he told her. "That killed my scent. Anyway, I had to do it. I wanted to be sure I had the right group of Indians and that you were with them. No sense attacking until we knew that."

Emerald fell silent. Many men, she knew, would have attacked the Indians—any Indians—without knowing or caring whether they were the right ones or not.

"Why so quiet?" Mace said after they had been riding for a while longer. She could feel the warmth of him against her back.

"I was just thinking of Sun Comes Up, the girl who was trying to kill me."

"What about her?"

"She—she painted buffalo hides beautifully. Do you think she'll be able to use her hands again?" Emerald could not get the picture of the Indian girl out of her mind as she had last seen her, staring in horrified surprise at her bleeding hands.

Mace frowned. "I imagine she will. I hope so. The Indians are a tough people, Emerald. They can set broken limbs, and they have their own curative herbs, some of them surprisingly effective."

"I—I suppose so."

"All right, Emerald. What's wrong? Does it bother you that I slashed the woman's hands? What did you expect me to do, let her kill you? She was trying her best to do that. You were already passing out when I got there. If I hadn't cut her, you would have died."

"I know, but—"

"I could have killed her, you little fool." Mace's voice was harsh.

After that, they rode in silence. Emerald was miserably conscious of Mace's nearness. Yet his thoughts could have been a thousand miles away. The last time she had seen him they had quarreled—she had said some ugly things about Trude. Was he thinking of that now? And how much had Mace observed of the Indian camp life? Did he realize that she had been Wolf Dreamer's "wife"?

"Mace," she began once. "Mace, I should tell you—"

"You don't have to tell me anything, Emerald. I'll never ask that of you. It happened, it's over now, and you'll never have to think of it again."

She choked back a sob, thinking of the wild night

with Wolf Dreamer, the frenzied pleasure he had been able to draw from her body. "Yes . . . I—I suppose you're right. . . ."

The miles passed, and they were back at the wagon train. Timmie and the others had lagged behind.

"You go on to camp, Emerald. They'll be glad to see you. I'll ride back and make sure the others are all right. Thatcher's horse is lamed and may need some attention."

Unwillingly, she dismounted near the edge of the wagon circle. Mace waved at her and galloped away, and Emerald hurried toward the wagons. It was dusk, the long shadows purple.

She saw Trude VandeBusch first, sitting on a camp-stool near the VandeBusch wagon, feeding Cal from a crude, homemade bottle. Trude looked up, saw her, and sprang to her feet.

"Em! Oh, Em!" Susannah came rushing out of the wagon, curls flying. She threw herself into Emerald's arms. "Em, you came back! Oh, Em!"

She was home.

The other emigrant women began to crowd about, their voices rising in anxious questions. Where was Timmie? Were the men all right? Haltingly, Emerald assured them that all was fine, that Wyatt's horse was lame but Mace and the others were coming shortly.

Trude seemed to sag with relief. "So Mace is all right, then," she said.

"Yes. He is."

Trude lowered her eyes. "We—we buried Orrin and Margaret yesterday. Reverend Colfax said the service over them. We made a rock cairn for them."

"Oh . . ."

For the first time, Emerald noticed the curious stares of the others, their eyes going up and down her figure, taking in her clothing and appearance. Slowly she became aware of how she must look. She was covered with bruises, welts, and scratches. Her lips were sore from the gag. There was dirt in her hair, and on her dress and arms.

"Why, you're wearing Indian dress!" she heard a female voice—was it Katje's?—say in surprise.

"Yes. They took away my own clothes. I don't know what they did with them," Emerald said wearily. Suddenly she had had enough questions. All she wanted to do was crawl into a tent, wrap herself in blankets, and cry until she could weep no more.

But still their eyes lingered on her, even Trude's.

"I won't ask you any more questions," Trude whispered. "I imagine you'll want to forget."

The two girls looked at each other. *She knows*, Emerald thought. She knows at least something of what I've been through.

She felt dirtied, the joy in her homecoming somehow gone. She had been thinking of baby Cal on the way home. She had longed to cradle him, to see for herself that he still lived. But now her heart felt leaden.

"Cal has been so good," Trude said. "At least, since we made him the bottle. We made it from an old syringe that Ben Coult found in one of his saddlebags. It works well enough."

Emerald sat down on the ground and took the infant in the crook of her left arm as Margaret had taught her. He was clean and dry. His head wobbled. Two little fists jerked and waved in the air.

"Hello, Cal," she said.

The baby looked at her. His slate-blue eyes were as bright and alert as a bird's. And there was something in them that made her suddenly think of Margaret.

Emerald bent her head and, still holding him, began to cry.

The others arrived within minutes. Emerald put the baby down in his basket and went to meet them. Almost instantly she and Timmie were at the center of a jostling, excited group of emigrants. All of them—those who had stayed behind as well as those who had helped to rescue her—stared speculatively at her.

Wyatt Thatcher had nearly taken an Indian arrow, he informed them all gleefully. But he had killed two Indians and wounded one more.

" 'Fore it was over, we killed six or eight of them damned savages, maybe more," he exulted. "You should of seen 'em run! Like prairie chickens they was, scatterin' in twenty different directions. We near cleaned 'em out, their menfolks, anyways. Mace wouldn't let us get the women and children. Said they wouldn't harm nobody none. Me, I think an Injun's an Injun."

Emerald stared at him, horrified. She and Timmie had waited far downstream in a clump of thick bushes. They had heard gunfire, but they had not seen any of this. And Mace had not mentioned it on the way back.

"You don't mean that you wiped out the—the entire camp?" she said faintly, thinking of Wolf Dreamer.

"Near about." Wyatt was grinning. "We tried to, anyways. Hey, what's wrong with you? Don't tell me you're feeling *sorry* for them savages?"

"I— no . . ."

"After what they done? They must of treated you like a queen if you can look so mad at the thought of a couple of 'em getting killed."

She flushed. "No, they didn't treat me like a queen. They—"

"They scalped Orrin and Margaret Wylie, in case you'd forgotten, you young baggage." Martha Rigney's voice rang out accusingly. "Or were you too busy making up to them Indian bucks to notice?"

Her eyes raked Emerald.

"I didn't ask to be taken by the Indians," Emerald said defiantly. "Surely you don't think that I did?"

"Well . . ." Martha sniffed. Her stare at Emerald, at the Indian costume that she still wore, was curious, knowing. Emerald felt the heat rise to her cheeks.

She was relieved to feel a soft, hesitant touch on her shoulder.

"Come, honey, come to our fire," said Geertrud VandeBusch. "You can rest there, and clean up, until they go and fetch the Wylies' wagon back. Trude has a gown that'll fit you. And don't you pay no attention to Martha—she has a filthy mind that can only think one thing. An unmarried girl sticks in her throat—especially one as pretty as you."

Night had fallen like a gray woolen cloak. The sky was scattered with stars and lit by an enormous moon. Emerald sat before the VandeBusch fire. She was shivering, even though Geertrud had given her a brown knitted shawl to put about her shoulders.

She had bathed in a bucket as best she could. She had even washed the dirt out of her hair with a precious bit of soap Geertrud had given her. Now her curls streamed damply down her back, making a wet circle on the gown Trude had lent her. The dress, a faded plaid with carved wooden buttons, was frayed at the hem and under the arms. But it was clean.

"Honey? Are you feeling all right?" Geertrud asked

in her soft, worn voice. "You look real pale tonight. Pa and Pieert ought to be back soon with what's left of the Wylie wagon. Then you can take a look and see what the Indians left you."

Geertrud threw on another stick of firewood. Trude was in the wagon, bedding down the three Wylie children, who were to sleep there tonight. They could hear her talking to them, her voice filled with laughter.

If it were not for Mace, Emerald thought, I could like Trude. Perhaps I do like her, I don't know.

But there *was* Mace. And only an hour ago Emerald had gone to get another bucket of water from the stream and had seen Mace and Trude together, embracing.

She had hurried by them, angrily letting the bucket bump against her legs. And now she sat by the Vande-Busch fire, feeling more alone than she ever had in her life.

Trude started singing to the baby inside the wagon. Geertrud was dozing where she sat. The homely, ordinary sounds of the camp filled Emerald's ears. Oxen bawling, a horse whickering, someone laughing, the clink of metal plates and spoons, the melancholy strum of Red's violin. She had thought she would never hear those sounds again.

But one question had been bothering her ever since Wyatt Thatcher had described the attack on the Indian encampment.

Was Wolf Dreamer dead?

She tried to picture his lithe, vital body lying still, a bullet hole exploded in his chest. She remembered her dream of a wolf shot like that, but believing in dreams was foolish. And anyway, she could not imagine Wolf Dreamer dead.

He might try to take her back again.

The thought made her jerk upright, cold beads of moisture springing out on her forehead. Of course he wouldn't find her again, she reassured herself. Mace wouldn't permit it. As long as she was with the wagon train, Mace would keep her safe, no matter what Trude meant to him.

She leaned forward and rested her head on her knees. She could see the stars, dusted across the sky like granulated sugar. Once Mace had told her they would watch the stars together. How long ago that seemed, though it was really only a few short months ago.

Her eyes drooped shut. Then she fell asleep, her head cradled on her knees.

Chapter Twenty-eight

❧ ❧

THEY were headed, Mace said, for Fort Hall, which was a minor fur-trading post of the Hudson's Bay Company.

But much had changed. Sometimes Emerald would turn quickly, expecting to see Margaret, enormously pregnant, sitting in the wagon. Or Orrin, yelling, cursing, and cracking his whip at the lead oxen.

But Margaret and Orrin were dead, and this was no dream, it was real, as real as the sun that baked them, burning their faces and blistering their lips.

Emerald had insisted that the Wylie children not be parceled out among the other families. She would care for them herself. It was, after all, what she had been hired to do. She hired Pieert VandeBusch to drive the Wylie wagon for her, and paid him from a small stock of money that Margaret had sewn inside a secret canvas pocket, which the Indians had miraculously missed.

Each day Emerald walked behind the silent Pieert. He did not even curse at the oxen. He just cracked the whip and walked along, occasionally tossing his long, white-blond hair, so like Trude's, out of his eyes.

At Geertrud's suggestion, Emerald had rigged up a cloth sling for the baby, and carried him snug against her right breast. He seemed to enjoy this mode of travel, looking about alertly, or else sleeping. He rarely cried, making her think of the quiet Indian babies she had seen strapped into their cradleboards.

But Indians were something she wanted to forget. So she pretended that she had never lain with Wolf Dreamer, that she had never been captured.

Timmie and Susannah seemed to resume their normal life—during the daytime, at least. Timmie rode Windy much as he had always done, and Susannah walked with Emerald, chattering to her. Sometimes Timmie would take his sister onto Windy's back with him, and the two children would gallop about, Susannah's shrieks full of excitement.

But their memories bothered them at night. Susannah slept restlessly and cried out often in her sleep. Sometimes Emerald would awaken in the morning to find that the two older Wylie children had crawled into the tent with her and the baby—Timmie on one side, Susannah on the other.

If only Margaret were here, she would think fiercely, pulling the children to her. Margaret was irreplaceable. It was hard, being in sole charge of three small children, one of whom was only an infant. Emerald felt both frightened and inadequate. Sometimes she daydreamed of settling down in California with Mace. But somehow in those dreams the Wylie children were always there.

Orrin's loss affected the wagon train greatly. There was much arguing and bickering over who was going to be the next captain. One faction supported Mace Bridgeman. He, they said, was the logical choice, with his vast wilderness experience. But Mace declined the job. He had been hired as a guide, he told them, not as captain.

Ben Coult was also mentioned, but he refused abruptly. So the contest was between Red Arbuthnot and Billie Colfax, who had, surprisingly, joined the argument and nominated himself.

Emerald, watching Billie for the hundredth time, felt a shiver. What was it about this man that made her want to shrink away, though he called himself a man of God?

But Red Arbuthnot was the one finally chosen, to the delight of Bob Rigney and Jan VandeBusch, who both idolized him. Emerald cheered, too. Red's health was improved now, and for all his rough ways, the freckled old man with the pinkish-white hair did have plenty of experience. And everyone liked him. With a crude, boisterous joke he could settle an argument between two angry men so that both were left laughing. It was a skill much needed these days, for the emigrants were trail-weary and nervous.

The days passed. At Bear River the trail swung northward again. The going was good, except for a few places where canyons forced the wagons away from the streams into hilly country.

It was beautiful country, Emerald thought. There was deep grass, clear water, cottonwoods, timbered hillsides. They were able to rest and fatten the oxen. And the children whooped and played around the bubbling soda springs. One was called Steamboat Spring, Mace said, named for the chugging sound its waters made.

Once again Emerald got out her sketchbook—for, to her relief, the Indians had left this intact—and began to draw. She depicted Timmie sitting on an enormous boulder covered with ocher Indian drawings hundreds of years old. She drew Susannah helping to start the noon fire, and Cal snoozing on a blanket in the sun.

Leafing through earlier pages of the book, she found drawings of Orrin and Margaret, and decided to give her sketchbook to Timmie and Susannah at the end of the trail. It would be all they would have to remember their parents.

As they neared Fort Hall, they traveled through more sagebrush land, broken by plains of black lava. Sharp lava rocks cut the animals' feet and made the wagons torture to ride in. And along this dull, monotonous stretch, Emerald and Mace quarreled.

It began simply enough, after a long, dreary day of walking. They had pulled up to make camp, and Emerald had made an antelope stew.

Watching the stew, she rubbed her temples and sighed, for she had the beginnings of a headache. She had not been sleeping well recently. Strange, disjointed dreams of Wolf Dreamer kept interfering with her slumber. Was he alive or dead? Would he come back to steal her again? The dreams—and the questions—would not let her alone.

Then, to fray her nerves still further, just as the stew started to boil, Susannah tripped and cut her knee on a sharp rock. Up to this point, the little girl had been brave enough about losing her parents. But now, looking down at her bleeding leg, Susannah began to scream for her mother.

"Susie, Susie, I—I'm here," Emerald said.

"I want my ma, not you, Em! I want my ma to come back!"

"But— Oh, Susie, she can't come back. You know that. You know she's dead now."

330

"I want her back! I want her back!"

At last, with Geertrud's help, Emerald managed to get Susannah bandaged, hugged, and put down for a nap in the wagon.

"I'll sit with the children for a while," Geertrud offered. "And I can watch the stew pot, too. Maybe you'd like to get away for a little while, Emerald. I know this has been hard on you."

Emerald nodded gratefully, took her sketchbook, and walked away from the camp. She picked her way among the scattered, dull-green sage bushes. Perhaps she might find some small animal to draw—one of the small, lively lizards, or a rabbit. Or maybe she would just sit. At least she could be alone for a few minutes, after day upon day of being with the children constantly.

She walked quickly, wanting to get away from the wagons altogether. The sun was almost down, a huge red ball on the edge of the horizon.

She would have to hurry, she told herself. As soon as the stew was done, the children would need to be fed, and Cal given his bottle. . . .

It was then that she saw them. Mace and Trude, walking together, intimately close. Mace wore his usual buckskins, and Trude's blue gown was tight-fitting, its cut accenting the lush curves of her body. Her hair was pulled into a knot at the back of her neck, from which loose hairs caught the light of the setting sun like a halo.

Emerald stopped short. They had not yet noticed her. Trude was looking up at Mace with a teasing expression. And Mace was smiling down at her, his eyes crinkled in the way Emerald loved so well.

Suddenly, abruptly, Emerald could stand it no

longer. She picked up her skirts and hurried toward them.

"Well, look who I've found!" she heard herself challenge. "Are you perhaps making plans for your wedding?"

It was a rude and preposterous thing to say, and Emerald knew it. She felt ashamed of herself, yet she couldn't seem to stop. She felt so old tonight, so weary and lonely and discouraged.

Both of them looked at her.

Emerald's cheeks were hot. "I said," she repeated, "are you planning your wedding? Or don't you plan to marry her, Mace? Perhaps you plan to go on to California and find still more girls who will be perfectly contented to become your mistresses!"

To Emerald's perverse satisfaction, Trude's mouth fell open. She started to say something, but Mace put a hand on her arm. "Go back to camp, Trude."

"But I want to stay! It's me, too, that she's insulting—"

"I asked you to please go back to camp. I'll deal with this."

Trude glared angrily at Emerald, then left, walking at first, and then picking up her skirts and running toward the wagons, her hair tumbling down in a white mass over her shoulders.

"Now, what's this all about? All this nonsense about weddings?" Mace seized Emerald's upper arm painfully, but she did not try to struggle away.

"I—I suppose I shouldn't have said such things. . . ." Shame washed over her. And now she had to face Mace's anger, his hard mouth and his cold eyes.

"No, you certainly shouldn't have. We were just having a quiet conversation. Did it ever occur to you,

Emerald, that Trude and I might possibly be friends? That I might enjoy her company—with or without sex?"

"I—" Emerald felt confused and humiliated. 'It—it isn't fair," she whispered.

"What isn't fair?"

"Why, you've trifled with my affections. You—you made love to me, and now Trude—"

"Trifled!" Mace's eyes were as cold as granite. "Wherever did you learn that word, Emerald? From the nice, proper ladies of Baton Rouge? For God's sake, must you be forever wanting to tie a man down and sew him into a neat little bundle? I have my work, Emerald. My painting, my animals. My life doesn't have room for a permanent woman. Can't you get that through your head?"

"I—I—" Her voice trembled. She bit down on her lower lip, hard, to stop the sobs that threatened to well out.

"Emerald, you may not like Trude, and you may not like me to be with her, but you had no right to say such things in front of her. What devil possessed you? Haven't I told you that I plan to marry no one?"

"But I thought—" Emerald whispered. She stopped, unable to go on. *I thought you loved me,* she wanted to scream. *I was so sure you did.*

"Emerald, Emerald . . ." Mace's voice was husky. "Can't you see? Marriage just can't become part of my life. What would I do with a wife? Start a rancho and leave you there while I travel about the wilderness? I have my work. It's important to me—"

"And marriage is important to me!" Emerald shouted. "Maybe I'm wrong to feel that way, but I do. I—I'd be a good wife to you, Mace, if only you'd let me! You know we'd be good together—you said

333

yourself that I mean more to you than Trude— I could be a friend, too, I could—"

He looked at her, his mouth curved in a sudden, sad smile. "Emerald, did you know that when you're angry those eyes of yours narrow like a cat's? Sparks almost jump from you." He stepped toward her, reaching for her. "Darling . . ."

For an instant she felt his lips brush against her face, the strength and security of his arms. And the magical, leaping force that bound them together.

Then she pushed him away so violently that she nearly lost her balance. "No! No, Mace, don't touch me! I—I'm not a girl like Trude, I'm not controlled by my—my sexual desires alone. I—I need love. Real love, married love, Mace. I can't couple with a man out on the prairie like—like a wild beast. I—I love you," she sobbed. "I always will. But I can't live this way, Mace, I can't be your mistress. I want marriage. And—and so we're finished, you and I. Do you hear that? We're through."

"Emerald—"

"I mean it, Mace." She could not believe her own voice could be so cold and so final. "I really mean it. I never want to have anything to do with you again."

There was a strange expression on Mace's face. "Very well. You've made yourself quite plain, Emerald. And I'll abide by what you've said." Then he turned and walked back toward camp.

Emerald stood and watched him go. Slowly she brought her hands up to her face and pressed her fingers against her cheeks. There was a hot, stinging sensation at the backs of her eyes.

Mace! she thought. *Mace, my darling, I didn't mean it.* She wanted to cry out, to race after him, to throw herself into his arms.

But she hesitated, and the moment passed. He was gone.

Another day went by, a day much like all the others. The sun beat savagely down upon them. Emerald trudged beside the wagon with Susannah, forcing herself to respond to the little girl's chatter.

Mace had ridden ahead, scouting the territory for water and for the best route. Riding free, Emerald thought dully, as she knew he loved the best. And perhaps, if he found the chance, he would even sketch one of the wild desert jackrabbits or rodents.

She could not rid her mind of his light hair blowing, his eyes crinkled against the sun, the gray eyes that could be serious or light up with a smile. In spite of Trude, in spite of all good sense, she knew that she still loved him. And, she added bleakly to herself, she probably always would.

Some women, she thought with a pang, were like that. There was only one man with whom they could be fully intimate, in mind and in body. And it seemed that she herself was one of them. For her, there could be only Mace Bridgeman.

But I won't be his mistress! she vowed. I won't be like Trude, content to have only the physical, not caring what other people think. I won't be a slut, a mistress. I want more.

That night, after the evening meal, Timmie sought her out as she was scouring the tin dishes with sand. Edgar, Timmie's dog, his fur matted from days of running in the sagebrush, thumped his tail happily. Edgar had somehow managed to evade the Indians—who, Mace said, might have eaten him—and two days later had turned up at camp, starved and limping. Timmie had been overjoyed to see him.

"Em, you haven't drawn any more pictures," Timmie said now.

"I haven't?" Emerald tried to smile. "I guess it's because I'm tired. It seemed a long walk today. And I do miss your mother and father."

"I know."

"Would you like me to draw you something now? I could get my pencils if you'd like."

"No . . ." Timmie seemed to sigh. "Could I look through your book, though? I want to see the picture you made of Feather."

Emerald found the sketchbook, and Timmie leafed through its pages until he found the sketch. She had caught Feather's angry, yet yearning expression.

"I guess Feather wanted to go home as much as I did," Timmie said.

"Yes."

"That's probably why he let me have Windy. Because he remembered."

"What?" Emerald stared at Timmie. "Timmie, did Feather somehow help us to escape?"

"Sure. They were taking Windy away, and Feather crept up and turned him loose. And then he showed me how to ride him like the Indians do. I know he meant for me to escape, Em."

Emerald went to bed that night in a mood of deep depression. Mace had come back to camp and had taken his meal that night with the VandeBusches. As she lay in her tent, she could still hear bursts of laughter coming from their wagon.

They camped the following night by a small, swift little stream that emerged from black lava rocks.

After she had started her fire, Emerald put Cal in his carrying sling and went to the stream to fill her bucket. She felt restless, hot and dusty. Perhaps she could find a place deep enough to bathe, she told herself. Or at least to wade.

She wandered upstream, picking her way among the sharp rocks.

Cal gurgled, reminding her of his presence. She bent to kiss his fuzzy scalp. "Don't worry, Cal, we're going back to the wagon in just a minute," she told him. "I just want to fill my bucket first."

She found a good spot and was dipping her pail when she saw Zelig York. He, too, carried a bucket.

"Well, if it isn't little Miss Emerald."

"Hello, Zelig." She had managed to avoid him for a long time.

"Fillin' your bucket?" The small eyes glinted at her.

"Yes, but I must get back to camp. Timmie is waiting. And—and Geertrud. They're expecting me."

"Oh, are they now."

"Yes." She began to edge backward, nearly stumbling over a boulder.

"Please," she begged. "Please leave me alone. I have to get back to camp. The baby is hungry."

"Aw, even I know that you don't have to feed a baby unless it's screamin'. Whyn't you jest set him down somewheres? And you and I c'n get together. Been watchin' and thinkin'. What'd they do to you, them Indians? They better than a white man?"

"What—what are you talking about?" But Emerald knew. She was afraid she would be sick.

"No— Please—"

She dropped her bucket and tried to run among the rocks that littered the stream bank. She slipped, caught herself desperately, and hurried on. Cal's sling cut into

337

her neck, and she put one arm around him to steady his fragile head. She shouldn't have brought him! And if she fell . . .

Zelig was following her. She could hear him among the rocks.

"Please—" she panted. "Please just leave me alone, will you?"

He grabbed her arm. She cried out and tried to struggle free.

That was how Martha Rigney found them. Emerald, burdened with the baby, trying to fight back against the hot, hard strength of Zelig's hands. The bodice of her gown was ripped, revealing part of her right breast.

Chapter Twenty-nine

❦

WHAT on earth is going on here?" Martha Rigney asked, outraged.

"It isn't what you think," Emerald began. "He——"

But Zelig interrupted her. "I was comin' up the stream with my bucket there, when *she* stopped me. She was a-flirtin' so, and carryin' on, that I hardly knew what to think. I——I couldn't help myself. . . ." There was a fawning, slobbering note in his voice.

"Oh? She flaunted herself, did she?"

"It's a lie!" Emerald burst out. "Zelig followed me here! I was just——"

"A likely story, if you ask me." Martha set down the two filled water buckets she carried and now stood with her hands on her hips. "Oh, he might of followed you, all right. But who egged him on, eh? Who begged for it?" she asked triumphantly.

"Begged! I didn't beg! I didn't do anything of the sort!"

Martha pressed her lips together. "Seems to me you've been mighty calm-hearted, young woman, for a girl who was carried off by the Indians. God only knows what those savages did to you. I had my suspicions of you before. But now——"

"Are you saying that because I was kidnapped by the Indians, I would *welcome rape?* Is that what you're telling me?"

The woman scowled, her eyes avoiding Emerald's. "I don't know about that. I only know that I've come upon you and a man in a mighty compromising situation. That's all I've got to say."

"But it wasn't my fault! I've told you! Look at my ripped dress! Do you think *I* did that?"

"Seems to me it's a mighty poor thing for a young unmarried girl to be on the loose as you are, without a mother or a chaperone, and no husband to keep her occupied."

While Martha was talking, Zelig quickly adjusted his shirt and left. He did not even give Emerald a backward glance.

"It don't seem as it matters much what one man does, or another, or what excuses you can cook up," Martha went on. "Fact is, you're here, sluttishly free to do as you please. You're a burden to all of us, a poor example to the innocent children in your charge, and a constant temptation to the God-fearing men of this wagon train. Now, if you was married to one of them—"

"Married!"

"And why not? It's sinful, your carrying-on in the sight of God. Bathin' naked, carrying on with men. I for one don't intend to put up with it. No, as far as I can see, the best thing is for you to marry. When we get you under the control of a husband, maybe you'll settle down. Not that you'll make much of a proper wife, of course. I have my doubts about *that*."

Emerald moistened dry lips. "I was hired to care for the Wylie children and to help with the camp jobs, and that's just what I plan to do. Until we get to California, at least. I promised Margaret I'd help her, and I will. Why should I need a husband to do that?"

"You need one because—why, all women need husbands! Besides, you're a constant temptation to men, that's what! They all look at you, and they think about what you did with the Indians, and they—"

"And just what *did* I do with the Indians?"

"Why, I—everyone knows what those Indian bucks do to white women. That's all they think of, getting a white woman. . . ." Martha licked her lips. "Never mind about that. We all know what happened to you, and you needn't bother to deny it."

"So that's it. I didn't ask to be kidnapped by the Indians. But because I was, you all assume I'm a wanton. Well, I'm not!"

"Well, miss, you'd better fix that dress of yours and get back to camp. The baby needs feedin'; I heard him crying when I come. And you'd better start thinking about who you're going to marry. And it better not be any son of mine," she added hastily. "My Martin ain't old enough for the likes of you."

"Oh?" Emerald glared at the older woman in contempt. "Perhaps Zelig York, then. Would that satisfy you? To see me married to a man like that?"

"It would satisfy me to see you acting properly in the eyes of God, that's all."

Emerald took Cal and stumbled back to camp, concealing the damage to her dress as best she could. She climbed into the wagon and changed, brushing off Timmie's questions.

But as she began to feed Cal, he persisted, "Em? You look funny. Why was your dress torn? And your face is all scratched—did you know that?"

"It's—nothing, Timmie."

"Did you get in a fight, Em? If you did, you should

have told me about it. I would have come and hit 'em right in the nose. Pow! That's what I would have done."

She forced a smile, patting him on the shoulder. "I'm sure you would, Timmie."

After a minute or two, he went out to play. She leaned against the wooden side of the wagon. Cal had fallen asleep on her lap, surfeited with milk. Through the thin canvas she could hear Martha arguing loudly.

She tried to ignore her, and carefully settled Cal in his basket for the night. Then she went outside and began setting up her own sleeping tent. Night had fallen, the sky clear and cloudless, scattered with stars.

Within a few minutes, however, Timmie was back. "They're talking about you at the VandeBusch wagon," he announced with a worried look. "They're saying you got to get married."

"What? They are?"

"Yes, Martha Rigney says it. She says that Zelig York tried to—'get' you, or something like that. And it was your fault. And now you have to get married because it isn't proper for you to be without no husband."

"Without *any* husband," she corrected automatically. But a cold feeling spread through her.

"Yes, without no husband," Timmie went on. "It's sinful, they said. They said it's too hard for you to take care of us all by yourself. You need a man to help you. A man to drive the wagon. If you do get married, Em, where will Susie and me and Cal go? Will we come, too?"

"Of course you will!" She hugged him. "Anywhere that I go, you'll go, too. But I'm not going to get married. That's nonsense. They're wrong if they say that, because it just isn't true. No one has even asked me."

"But you *could* get married." Timmie's face was troubled. "Maybe Mace Bridgeman would marry you, Em. I don't think I would mind that. I like him."

Her heart twisted. "Hush, Timmie. I'm not going to be marrying Mace Bridgeman or anyone else. So you mustn't fret about it. Now, you go and find Susannah and tell her it's time to get washed up before bed. Then I—I'll tell you a story or something if we've time. Hurry, now!"

He ran off, seemingly satisfied. But Emerald finished putting up her tent with trembling hands.

The next morning Geertrud sought Emerald out as she returned from milking Bossie.

"Emerald?" Geertrud's dress, like those of all the women, was frayed and much mended, its hem permanently stained with dirt. It hung loosely on her, for Geertrud was more frail than ever. Yet her eyes were determined. "Emerald, might I talk with you?"

So, Emerald thought. Geertrud, too. She turned so violently that some milk sloshed from her pail.

"I know what you're going to say! Timmie told me! You people think I should get married, don't you? Married to one of the men in the wagon train so I'll be respectable and you won't have to fret yourselves about me anymore!"

Geertrud sighed. "Yes, I—I'm afraid we do think that best. Under the circumstances. You see—"

"No. I don't see! Under what circumstances? Do you mean that because Zelig York tried to—to attack me—" She floundered.

"Oh, is that what happened? I rather thought so. Martha seemed very excited. . . ." Geertrud smiled at Emerald faintly. "Emerald, honey, I'm afraid Martha might have some good reasons for what she says. Both Pa and I think so."

"But *why?* Oh, it isn't fair. I don't need a man to get to California. I can get there by myself!"

"Can you?"

"Of course I can! I won't be alone; I'll have Pieert to drive the wagon—you promised him to me. And he said he would do it if I paid him."

Geertrud looked at her with pity, and Emerald felt frightened. "I'm sorry, Emerald, but Pieert— Well, I don't think he wants to do that job anymore."

"He doesn't! But why not?"

Geertrud hesitated. "I'm not sure. Perhaps it's because of what Martha said. Or—other things. But Pa doesn't think it's such a good idea anymore. He feels if we refuse to let Pieert work for you, then you'll find yourself a proper husband. A man who can take care of you, so that you and the Wylie children won't be a burden to the rest of the wagon train."

"But we won't be a burden! Why should we be? If necessary, I'll drive the wagon myself. Or Timmie can. Timmie is a good helper. He—"

"Had you forgotten Timmie's bad foot, Emerald? He walks well enough, but I'm not sure he could keep it up for more than an hour or two. And he's not capable of repairing the wagon. As for you, you've a newborn infant to care for. No, I don't see how you can do it, Emerald. You need a man. He can protect you from men like Zelig York. Once you're married, the other men will let you alone."

Emerald had a thousand protests to make, a thousand objections. Instead, she whispered, "But I—I want to marry for love." It was all she could say.

Geertrud was silent for a long minute. "Emerald," she said at last, "what did you expect to do when you reach California? Had you given any thought to that? It's wild country, filled with Indians and Spaniards and rough men, no place for an unprotected woman. You would have to marry someone, sooner or later."

Emerald's eyes filled with tears. Geertrud was right, she realized numbly. She had not thought about what she would do after arriving in California.

"You'll come to see that we're right," Geertrud said gently. "I'm sure you will. And you'll thank us."

"I don't think so."

"After you've had time to think, you will. Someone in the wagon train will make you a good husband, I have no doubt. You're a desirable girl. And wives are scarce in this country."

Indeed, Pieert did not appear that morning to drive the wagon. When Emerald sought him out, Trude told her that he had gone back to herd duty.

"But he said he'd drive my wagon!"

"My pa told him not to." Trude lowered her eyes, and Emerald stared at her in fury. Trude, too, was an unmarried girl who was a "temptation" to men. But Trude had the protection of her family.

"Well, I'll manage somehow," she said. "I'll find someone else to do it."

"Who? Martin Rigney? His mother has already said she won't let him near you. And the Arbuthnots have all they can do with their two wagons."

Blindly Emerald turned away, knowing that Trude was right. They wouldn't give her any help. They would force her into marriage.

She found Timmie and Susannah trying to load the wagon, Timmie issuing orders to his sister in a high-pitched voice. Timmie turned to look at her. "Red says we're next to last in line today," he said importantly.

"That's fine," she told him. "Where is the whip? I'm going to drive the oxen myself today."

"But where's Pieert?" Susannah's eyes were wide.

"He's not going to help us anymore. Come on, Timmie. It won't be so bad. You'll ride Windy, just as usual. And Susannah, you can help me with the baby. You're a big girl now."

"Yes, big," Susannah agreed.

It was a disaster from the start. Emerald could not handle the whip, although she had seen it used often enough. Once, by mistake, she lashed the oxen hard, and cried out in horror. She had always hated to see animals whipped.

She marched back and put the whip in the wagon, determined to do without it. But the big, slow-moving beasts were accustomed to its steady crack. Without it, they lagged, tossing their heads restlessly. So she had to go and get it again, avoiding the oxen's big brown eyes.

Cal, too, was a problem. They had begun the day with Susannah carrying him in the sling, for Emerald did not feel she could manage the whip with him about her neck. But after an hour, Susannah was stumbling.

"Em, Cal is too heavy!" she insisted. "He makes my neck ache!"

They put the baby in the wagon. But he was not happy there, and screamed furiously. Besides, the springless wagon jolted him unmercifully, and Emerald was afraid he would be injured.

Grimly she walked over to the VandeBusch wagon to ask for help. She found Geertrud sitting in the wagon bed with some knitting.

"If someone would just help me with the baby," she said. "Could Katje perhaps come and carry him? Or could you hold him in your lap?"

Geertrud flushed. "Emerald, I know you think we're being cruel. But don't you see that this isn't going to work? You have a baby to care for, a baby to take up most of your time. What are you going to do if the wagon breaks another axle? Suppose it happened to-day—now? Do you know how to fix it?"

"Well, no . . ."

"Then how will you repair it?"

"Why, I—I imagine one of the men will come and help me."

Geertrud sighed. "The men have their own responsibilities, their own worries—and plenty of them. And what will you do, Emerald, when we reach another river? Or a steep hill? Or what if one of the men approaches you again as Zelig did?"

"I don't know," Emerald said miserably.

"I'll take the baby for today," Geertrud said, reaching for Cal. "You don't have to worry about him. I'll care for him, as long as I'm here. But I want you to go back and think about what I've said. Will you?"

So Emerald did. She pondered as she trudged over the rough ground, covered with scattered sage, creosote bushes, and buffalo grass. She thought as the wagon jolted from side to side, once hitting a rock and nearly knocking the shaky left front wheel off.

Twice she had to oil the wheels from the bucket hanging at the rear of the wagon, getting grease all over her dress and hands. No one offered to help her; they all had their own jobs to do. They were all busy, she realized; all of the wagons needed constant attention.

At noon they pulled up, and thankfully Emerald

got out the flint and steel and started to make the fire. Her entire body ached. She knew she looked frightful. Her hair had escaped from her sunbonnet in damp, dusty ringlets. Her face was covered with perspiration. Her dress, too, was soaked, and there were grease spots on her skirt.

Looking down at herself, she laughed bitterly. Perhaps no one would desire her, looking as she did.

But the notion was little comfort.

Timmie, too, seemed dispirited. He sat down in the shade of the wagon without his usual questions and talk. Susannah squatted beside him, playing with some small stones she had picked up along the way. Both children avoided her glance.

Emerald washed her face and began to boil water for coffee. As she got out some cold leftover rabbit pie, the men began to saunter past. One by one all the single men of the camp came to look at her.

First came Ben Coult, tall, embittered, withdrawn, humorless. Even though she knew he loved her, there was something about him that made her uneasy. An odd kind of violence in him. No, she could never marry Ben.

Next was Martin Rigney, eighteen years old, tall, with the gangling awkwardness of adolescence. He looked at her furtively as he went by the wagon. If she married him, she would have to live with the Rigneys and endure Martha Rigney day after day.

No, she thought. She couldn't bear that.

Red Arbuthnot walked by with his two sons. They were talking and pretended that they didn't notice her. But she could sense them appraising her as if she were goods for sale in a shop.

Well, there's a choice, she told herself wryly. Red, sixty-five but still vital—if you liked men that old.

Matt, ginger-haired, freckled, and steady. Peter, much like Matt, but duller. They were all good enough men, she supposed. But there would be no love, no sharing, no passion such as she had had with Mace. Such a marriage would be like a business deal, an exchange of services.

Wyatt Thatcher was next. He was an inch shorter than she was, jaunty and wiry, like a little fighting cock. He was a drifter, a gambler, a charlatan, eager to reach California with his gambling equipment, his patent medicines. She tried to picture herself presiding with him at a blackjack table, or a medicine show, and stifled another bitter laugh.

Even Billie Colfax found an excuse to walk past her and stare. Emerald did not even try to imagine marriage with him. Zelig York was the last to stroll by "accidentally." Only Mace Bridgeman did not come.

She knew Mace was back in camp, for she had seen him repairing a spare bridle. But he had ignored her, and soon went to take his noon meal with Wyatt Thatcher. He had taken her at her word, she realized bitterly. He would do nothing to save her.

The noon rest seemed interminable. Emerald barely tasted her food, and moved about the ever-present camp chores barely aware of what she was doing. *Mace,* a little voice in her mind kept crying out. *Oh, Mace!*

But soon they started up again, and then all her thoughts were on the trail itself. Never had the walking seemed so long or so difficult. The sun beat down on her until every step was a major effort. She found that she was watching the wagon fearfully, remembering how Orrin had fretted about the wheels and axles. If only they would hold!

At least Cal was with Geertrud, she thought thankfully. But what would she do with him tomorrow? And the day after that?

As the sun grew low, one of the weaker oxen began to lag. Emerald lifted the whip and cracked it near him as best she could.

But the animal, swaybacked and gaunt, only stared at her dully.

Emerald wiped dust off her face, tasting it gritty on her tongue. If he died, there would only be five oxen left. She would have to lighten the load, to throw out some of the tools and food. And what if more oxen died?

No wonder Orrin had fretted so, she thought suddenly. No wonder he had seemed ill-tempered.

When they made camp that night, she sought out Geertrud.

"I—I am afraid you're right," she admitted in a voice so low that Geertrud had to lean forward to hear it. "Perhaps I—I do need a man to help me. . . ."

"I thought you'd come around to it," Geertrud said. "I'm so sorry, honey."

Chapter Thirty

❧⟨❧

W OLF Dreamer was tired. He sat loosely on his war horse, feeling the throb of his bullet wound, which still festered despite the herb poultices he had put upon it.

It was only a wound in the upper arm, and should not have troubled him much. After all, he had received many wounds in the past, both from accidents and from tribal rites. But this injury came from the white man. Perhaps that made it more poisonous.

He had left the Indian camp, alone, leaving the women to regroup and care for the dead and wounded, and had been following behind the wagon train for some days now, through the hot springs area and the sagebrush land, always keeping a day behind so that he could not be seen.

The white men were as innocent as two-summer babes, he thought scornfully. They tried to conceal the smoke of their fires, but he always saw it. And, of course, their trail was plain. Other wagon trains had passed, leaving deep wheel ruts, and others would pass again. But Wolf Dreamer could see the fresh marks and the discarded garbage and goods, scattered wantonly wherever the train had passed. Their horses and oxen had grazed wide swatches into the brown summer grass, what little there was of it.

But he knew the white men did not care what they did to the land. Why, he wondered, did they not stay in their lands to the east? Why must they always have more land?

He was not really sure why he was following this wagon train beyond the lands of his own people and into the territory of the Blackfeet and the Bannock. Was it anger for his murdered warriors, for the slashed hands of Sun Comes Up?

Or was it Green-eyed Woman? He had asked her, as was often the custom with captives, if she wanted to become his wife. She had said yes. But she had not meant her words. And at the first opportunity, she had escaped.

A pang of loss went through Wolf Dreamer as he thought of her. Her skin, pale as snow-tipped mountains. Her eyes, like spring grass.

He missed Green-eyed Woman. He wanted her back. He had dreamed of her four times since—odd, distorted dreams in which he crawled through underbrush, reaching out for her with a kind of numb desperation. But in his dream she had stood frozen and still.

He did not know what the dreams meant. And he knew full well the dangers involved in following the wagon train alone as he was doing. For all of their stupidity, the white men possessed guns that were accurate at long distances.

There was one white man, too, who was as clever and wily as an Indian. He had crept close to Wolf Dreamer's own camp, had lain in the stream for a full day without detection, a feat worthy of any Sioux.

He was the one who had freed Green-eyed Woman and had hurt Sun Comes Up.

Wolf Dreamer thought he would enjoy facing this unknown white man in battle. To best a man of such courage and daring would be a great triumph.

No, Wolf Dreamer didn't know what drove him. Perhaps it was the dreams. Or maybe it was something else, something that ran deeper still.

But it didn't really matter. Something, beyond dreams, beyond explanation, told him to follow the wagon train.

He obeyed.

Word of Emerald's decision to marry spread like prairie lightning through the camp. That night after the evening meal, the men again made excuses to come by the wagon as she sat with the children.

Zelig was first.

"How about it, Emerald, eh?" He gave her a look that was such a combination of belligerency, lust, and longing that Emerald shivered. "I'm gonna need me a wife in California."

She stared at him incredulously. "I can't believe it. For you to do what you did—and then you ask me to marry you!"

Zelig reddened. "That's what you say—now. I'm gonna be rich in California. You'll have plenty of money to spend—and you'd like that, wouldn't you?" Zelig grinned at her, his sour, gamy odor drifting toward her. "When I want a woman, I get her. You remember that, girl. Hear?"

He stomped off beyond the circle of the firelight, and Emerald pulled her shawl closer about her shoulders.

When I want a woman, I get her. Uneasily, Emerald remembered what he had said. What had he meant when he said he would be rich? Where would a man like Zelig get money?

Fifteen minutes later, Matt Arbuthnot appeared, ostensibly to ask whether she had any dried fruit he could borrow. He hemmed and hawed, making awkward conversation, until Emerald felt acutely uncomfortable. If only he would just ask! she thought in exasperation.

At last, after half an hour of talk, Matt did ask. "Emerald, I know this may sound odd to you, but I —I do admire you, and I—was thinking that maybe after I get to California I might be settling down and taking a wife. My first wife died, you know. In childbirth, the baby with her. And I've been wondering, since you're in need of protection. . . ." He paused expectantly.

Emerald lowered her eyes. Of all the single men in the camp—with the exception of Mace, of course— Matt Arbuthnot would make the best husband. The freckled Matt was a kind, gentle man. He would be considerate, dependable, and a good provider. Although he was shy, he had a wry sense of humor that she liked.

But she felt no physical attraction toward him at all. How could she ever sleep night after night with a man who did not arouse her senses?

"Matt, I—appreciate your asking," she said at last. "But I'm not sure."

He brightened, evidently taking this for a half-hearted consent. "Well, take your time, Emerald. I don't want to hurry you."

"Yes. I—I'll do that."

Most of the rest found excuses to walk past and talk with her. She received proposals from Ben Coult and Wyatt Thatcher. Even young Martin Rigney, gulping and swallowing until his Adam's apple bobbed, told her he "allowed as how she'd make a pretty good wife," and that he was sure his mother would "come around after a while." As he said this, he looked furtively toward the Rigney wagon, as if to reassure himself that Martha wasn't listening.

Emerald heard them all in a numbed daze. How many other girls received *five* proposals in one day?

She caught Katje VandeBusch staring at her jealously, and she longed to go over and tell the younger girl the truth; she didn't want to marry *any* of the men who had proposed. Mace Bridgeman was the only one she wanted. And he had not asked her.

Night had fallen, and Timmie and Susannah had already gone into the wagon to sleep when Emerald finally took the baby and got up to prepare for bed. Her eyes felt sore from the blowing dust of the trail, and from the tears she had held back all day.

With a catch in her throat, she thought of Margaret Wylie. If Margaret were alive, she would have thought of something, would have done something.

But Margaret was dead. And Emerald had no other friends in the wagon train—not really. None but Mace. And he was no longer her friend, either.

Desolately she crawled into her tent, settled the baby in his basket at the foot of her pallet, and crept under her blanket.

In the morning, Martha Rigney came over to the wagon and demanded to know what Emerald's decision was. Which of the men did she plan to marry?

Emerald stared at her. The emigrant woman looked as she always did, gaunt, brown-skinned, and formidable.

"I can't marry any of them," Emerald said. "I—I thought I could, but I can't."

Martha's lip curled. "What, none of them? You think yourself too good for them, is that it?"

"No! I—"

"Well, we don't need a footloose girl around here to tempt the men and set a bad example for those poor little Wylie children. Not to mention the fact that your wagon is going to be a constant burden to the rest of us. When your axle breaks down, you'll be begging for help with it fast enough."

Martha's eyes glittered with ill-concealed triumph. "No, I expect to see you married by the time we reach Fort Hall. Or we'll find a husband for you there, that's what we'll do. And we'll leave you there with him. How would you like that?"

"But—you couldn't!" Emerald gasped. "The Wylie children—they have an uncle in California. We must go there and find him. I owe it to them. And they—they'll miss me. . . ."

"They'll get along rightly enough. We'll take the two older ones with us, and leave you with the baby and the milch cow. If any relative is found, he can send back for the baby. That will suit well enough. The trail is too difficult for a young infant, anyway."

Emerald could not conceal her fright and dismay. She had heard enough about Fort Hall to know that it was even smaller than Fort Laramie, a barren building set in the midst of sagebrush and mountains. Half-wild traders, trappers, and Indians congregated there. Any woman left at such a place would lead a hard life. She would end up either as one man's bedmate-slave-wife or as prostitute to them all.

The thought made Emerald sick.

"Oh, you'll manage well enough," Martha said,

seeing Emerald's dismay. "Your kind always does. Unless, of course, you want to be a bit less choosy and take one of the men here. We've had enough of you and your like! Next thing we know you'll be making eyes at my own Saul. If you haven't already. Flirtin' with him, flaunting your body at him—"

"I've never done such a thing!" Emerald gasped.

"No? Well, you're not goin' to. I'll see to that. You'll be married by the time we reach Fort Hall. Or you'll marry there."

Martha went back to her own wagon, and Emerald stood swaying, her fingers clutching the rim of the wagon wheel. How could Martha ever believe that she, Emerald, had designs on prosaic Saul Rigney? A man of forty-five with two big sons.

Slowly she began to understand. Even as a girl, Martha must have looked much as she did now, plain and gaunt. She envied and hated all young girls with shapely, pretty bodies. Especially did she hate Trude, who smiled at Saul, who flirted with the man as she did automatically with all men. But Trude had a family to protect her. Emerald had no one.

Agonizingly, the day inched on. Geertrud again took Cal with her so that Emerald would be free to drive the wagon. Emerald had long since stopped admiring the scenery, the profile of distant mountains, the hard sky arched over sage and sparse grass.

Now the land was only something to be trudged over, one foot in front of another. There was no longer any joy in her steps, for she knew that at the end of a day or two, she would end up marrying a man she didn't want.

To add to her desolation, she did not see Mace at all. He was scouting ahead of the wagon train, searching out water. He knew what she was facing, she told herself. How could he help but know? Yet he did nothing.

She hated Mace Bridgeman, she told herself. Hated him as she had never hated anyone.

Hard lava rocks cut into the soles of her leather shoes. But she kept walking, swinging the whip over the backs of the oxen—growing more skilled each time she did it—until perspiration dampened her dress and streamed down her sides.

They reached Fort Hall, where they would camp for a few days of rest, badly needed by oxen and humans alike. Here the emigrants could buy a few extra pounds of flour—at exorbitant prices—or a slab of dried salmon. Or they could trade six worn-out oxen for four healthy ones.

This Zelig and Billie did. They were the only members of the party to trade for fresh oxen. As Billie explained to everyone within hearing, "We got that equipment to haul, and I mean to get it to California no matter what I have to do."

Fort Hall covered roughly half an acre of ground and was surrounded by an adobe wall more than a foot thick, above which could be seen the tops of cooking chimneys. The fort flew a red flag lettered "HBC," for "Hudson's Bay Company." Inside the stockade were dwellings, stores, and barns, all overshadowed by a two-story, grim-looking blockhouse.

"All kinds of people come here, Em!" Timmie told her excitedly. "All kinds!"

"Oh?" It was two hours before dusk, the sun still a rich yellow ball in the brilliant sky. Emerald was cutting strips of dried beef for supper. She had not been inside the fort yet, and did not expect to.

"Yes, Mace said so! He says the Spaniards come

here, and the French-Canadians, and the missionaries, and even priests! And they all drink whiskey made from wild honey!"

"The missionaries, too?" Emerald asked dryly. She had caught glimpses of the men who lived in the fort—bearded, unkempt, sun-blackened men who laughed too loudly and stared at all the emigrant women. Once Mace had told her the interesting facts about the areas they passed through. Now he did not speak to her at all.

"And do you know that flag, Em? That red flag they're flying?" Timmie continued. "Well, Mace said that the trappers say those initials HBC stand for 'Here Before Christ.' Don't you think that's funny? I wonder if any Spaniards are at the fort now? I'd like to see one, wouldn't you, Em?"

"With all of them wearing beards, I don't think I'd know one if I did meet him," Emerald said. "We'll see plenty of Spaniards in California. Is that all you can talk of, Timmie? What Mace Bridgeman tells you? Haven't you anything better to do?"

Timmie looked hurt. "I like Mace. He tells me lots of things. What's wrong with that? I wish you'd—" He stopped.

Emerald patted the boy's shoulder, already sorry for her sharp tongue. "You wish I'd what?"

"Why, marry him. They said you were going to get married, Em. Aren't you?"

Emerald looked down at her shaking fingers. "I—I don't know, Timmie."

"But they said you had to!"

"I know; I'm aware of that."

Mace doesn't want me, and he's the only one I want, she wanted to add. But she knew she couldn't

359

say such a thing to Timmie. He would run back and tell Mace, and her pride couldn't stand that.

"But Martha Rigney said so," Timmie persisted. He picked up one of the strips of beef and began to nibble at it. "I heard 'em all talking about it this morning. Wyatt said he was going to get you. He and Zelig nearly got in a fight!"

"Oh?" In spite of herself, Emerald hoped Timmie would say more. "Did he?" she asked encouragingly.

"Yes, and Ben Coult and Pa VandeBusch had to stop 'em. Zelig, he was yelling that he'd have you, and damn to everyone else. Or something like that." Timmie regarded her cheerfully, his jaws still chewing. "Boy, that was one fight I wish I could have seen. Zelig, he could have taken Wyatt and twisted him up like a doughnut!"

Emerald choked back a laugh. "I suppose he could. But it isn't nice to talk like that, Timmie. You sound so bloodthirsty. You wouldn't want to see Wyatt hurt, would you?"

"No'm. But they woulda stopped 'em in time, before *that*. Anyway, they were saying you were bein' so choosy, you wouldn't take any of 'em. So then Martha Rigney said they were going to leave you in Fort Hall if you didn't pick out one of 'em." Timmie paused. "I didn't believe her, though. That old bitch doesn't know what she's talking about."

Emerald stifled another giggle. "Why, Timmie, where did you ever learn a word like that?"

"From my pa." Timmie shrugged. "But Em, they wouldn't leave you here in Fort Hall, would they? Why, there's nothing here but sagebrush and Indians!"

"Timmie, I—I don't know."

360

"But can they make you? Mace'd stop them, all right! He wouldn't let 'em!"

"Don't be too sure about that." Emerald turned to hide the sudden anguish on her face.

"But Em, you don't have to worry, they won't be leaving you in Fort Hall, anyway. See, Wyatt Thatcher, he had this idea on how they could decide it."

"Idea?"

"Sure. He's got cards in his wagon, cards and gambling stuff. So they'll just use the cards to decide it. That's what he said."

Emerald stared. "They plan to *gamble* for me!"

"Why, yes, I think that's what they said. They were all laughing about it. Tonight they'll do it, after supper. Em? Why does your face look so funny? Em?"

Somehow Emerald said something to satisfy Timmie and sent him elsewhere. She finished preparing the meal automatically.

So the men planned to gamble for her as if she were a piece of property without a mind or feelings!

It was an incredible idea. Trust Wyatt Thatcher to think *that* up, she thought angrily. But she could see how it would appeal to the rest of the emigrants. It had been a dull and exhausting journey, and they might all yet perish. A bit of gambling would serve as amusement for men who had gone too long without fun.

She had heard, of course, of the high-stakes gambling that went on in New Orleans and Baton Rouge among the wealthy gentlemen who could afford such pleasures. Who hadn't? Whole fortunes—coffles of slaves, plantations, entire sugar crops—had been won or lost on the turn of a card. She and Aunt Anna had laughed nervously about this, saying they certainly hoped Uncle Calvin didn't get the notion.

And now she, Emerald, was to be the prize for a group of trail-weary emigrants who had suffered too much hard work and not enough recreation.

Well, she wouldn't let them do it! she decided furiously. She would put a stop to it at once.

But what could she do? Mace wouldn't marry her or help her.

She could hardly run away into the wilderness. She would be captured by Indians or die of starvation. If she stayed here at Fort Hall, she'd probably live—if she didn't mind being whore to the whole fort, or slave-wife to one man.

Her thoughts ran on feverishly. What about the Wylie children? She could hardly desert them now. Certainly the other emigrants would care for them and get them to California safely, but Timmie and Susannah loved her and depended on her.

She would have to marry.

But she would choose her own husband, her own fate. She would choose Matt Arbuthnot. Her life would be dull with him, but she would have a husband who was steady and considerate. Many women, she assured herself, had made such marriages and had eventually become fond of their husbands. She was sure she could be fond of Matt. Eventually.

Her heart seemed to cry out. Fond! Was that lukewarm emotion all that she was to have out of life?

After supper, she went to find Martha and Geertrud and the others and announce her decision.

Chapter Thirty-one

❧ ❧

THE stars were coming out overhead. A hot evening breeze pressed Emerald's skirt against her legs as she walked. She shivered, despite the heat, and pulled her shawl tighter about her shoulders.

She had hoped to speak to Geertrud alone, but found most of the emigrants gathered at the Rigney wagon, sitting or standing about the campfire. Red Arbuthnot had his fiddle out, and was bent over it trying to repair a broken string.

Two trappers from Fort Hall had joined the group, looking like ruffians in their dirty buckskins and full beards.

Everyone looked up as she approached. She was glad the darkness concealed the flush of her face.

"So it's you, miss," said Martha Rigney. "Come to tell us what you decided, eh?"

"Yes. I . . ." Emerald's voice was barely a whisper. She could see Matt Arbuthnot sitting on a campstool behind some of the others.

"Speak up, girl, we can't hear you."

"I said. . . ." Emerald looked frantically for Geertrud, but she was talking to Katje at the fireside.

"Could I please speak with you alone?" Emerald asked Martha. "I can't—with all of these people about—"

"Very well." Smoothing down her apron, Martha led Emerald a short distance from the wagon. "Well, and I suppose you've made up your mind, have you? Or do you find yourself taking a liking to Fort Hall here?" The woman looked contemptuously at Emerald as if she were a slut or a street woman.

Emerald bridled. "Why, I think you're enjoying this, aren't you?"

"How dare you! Whatever you get, miss, is none too good for you, that's what I say."

"But—"

"Speak up. What have you decided?"

"I—I will marry Matt Arbuthnot," Emerald whispered.

"Matt, eh?" Martha gave Emerald a grudging look of respect. "Well, at least it isn't my Martin, and for that I'm thankful. Are you going to tell him yourself, or shall I?"

This couldn't be happening, Emerald thought half-hysterically. "I don't care. You can do it if you wish," she said.

"Very well." Martha turned and started back toward the fire and the gathered emigrants. Emerald hesitated, knowing she should follow, but unable to do so. Everyone—even Zelig and Billie, who rarely left their wagon unattended—were there.

She waited. There was the sound of some night creature crying out in the brush, the distant, eerie howl of a coyote. She heard an out-of-tune note on the fiddle. Then there was a rustle among the emigrants as Martha made her announcement. It was followed by a hubbub of excited, angry voices.

"But it ain't fair!" That was Wyatt Thatcher. He had just arrived from his wagon, faro box in hand.

"Yeah, what about the rest of us? We want a woman, too!" That was Zelig.

More voices rose, and boisterous, deep male laughter.

They sounded drunk, Emerald thought with growing dismay. But where had they gotten the whiskey?

Then she remembered the two men from the fort who had joined them, and what Timmie had said about whiskey made from wild honey. Of course! The traders had brought whiskey to sell. And after long weeks of abstinence, the emigrants were drinking out of control.

Emerald squeezed her cold hands together, wishing she were elsewhere. Surely her decision to marry Matt Arbuthnot should not cause such commotion.

Unless, she thought, they did not accept her decision.

She felt as if a cake of ice had blocked her throat. And soon her fears were confirmed, for she could hear the men shouting.

"Ain't fair! We ain't going to be cheated—"

"—want to get me my chance, too, dammit, no matter what *she* says—" Martin Rigney, Emerald thought, appalled. Rebelling against his mother, wanting to show himself a man among these trail-worn men.

"Keno, will it be? Or faro? We got to get the game that will—" That voice was Wyatt Thatcher, of course, trying to organize things. She even heard Ben's voice, strangely thick.

And now there was a new voice, more slurred than the others. "Been a year since I had me a white woman. Better'n a squaw, anyway, no matter what they say about them Indian women. Hell, why not marry me a white gal? Then I'd have myself some white tail anytime I wanted it—"

One of the men from Fort Hall, she thought.

Quickly, so quickly, it had gotten out of hand. One minute they had been a group of men drinking together; a little loud, perhaps, but orderly enough. Now there was an ugly excitement in the air. And where was Mace? Emerald scanned the crowd for him, but he was not there.

Geertrud stood, her light cotton apron standing out white against the flickering firelight. She rubbed her hands together nervously.

"It's wrong," she began. "Wrong what you're doing. I did want the girl to marry, true. I do think it best. But not like this. Why, this is a terrible thing. Give the girl a chance to choose the man she wants. It's not fair. Pa—" Geertrud crouched and plucked at her husband's sleeve, but he shook her off roughly.

"Aw, hell, Geertrud, let the folks have some fun, will you? God knows, they need it. This is all harmless enough, ain't it? At least she'll get a husband out of it. That's a lot more than some women ever get!" He threw his head back and roared with drunken laughter.

"But Pa, you *know* this isn't right. You know—"

"Go back to the wagon, Geertrud, if you don't like it. And take the womenfolk with you. We don't want no women around here, nohow." Pa VandeBusch laughed again, uproariously, and staggered against his wife with such force that he nearly knocked her over.

"But—"

"Aw, go on," Wyatt added his shout to Herman's. "All churchgoers back to their wagons. Maybe you can do some prayin'!"

"This is—why, it's ungodly, that's what it is!" To Emerald's surprise, Martha Rigney began an indignant protest.

But male voices drowned her out, and the women began to leave. Geertrud, with Katje lagging behind her, and Timmie and Susannah at her skirts, emerged from the circle of the firelight.

Susannah spotted Emerald and began to sob. "Em! Oh, Em, where were you, I was looking and looking for you but I couldn't see you. Oh, Em, I don't like it. Their voices are so loud. And they said—"

"—they said they're going to have a card game, Em—" Timmie put in.

"—and somebody's going to win you—"

Both children flung themselves at her, and Emerald knelt down and hugged them, trying not to cry herself. "I'll be all right," she whispered. "Please, don't worry about me. I promise I'll be fine."

"You'd better come back to our wagon." Geertrud touched her arm. "You'll be safer there. They're all drunker than lords, every one of them, including our precious Dr. Ben Coult. And even Reverend Colfax, I'm mortified to say. All of them, drinking that whiskey the traders brought! I've never seen the like, and I never hope to again. But let them do their drinking. Let them do whatever they wish. They'll be sick and sober enough in the morning."

Yes, Emerald thought. *And if they have their way, by then I'll be married.*

Shouts and raucous laughter rose from the campfire around which the men were huddled, passing a whiskey bottle from hand to hand. Their merriment drifted back to the farthest wagon, where Geertrud and the other women had taken shelter.

Emerald crept cautiously away from the wagon, making sure that she was safely hidden in the thick darkness.

Holding her breath, she edged a few yards closer until she had a clear view of the men and their gathering. She couldn't help it, she told herself defiantly. She *had* to see, *had* to know what was happening!

Minutes passed, tense minutes for Emerald. She watched while the men shared the bottle and opened another, money exchanging hands. Wyatt Thatcher went into the darkness, and returned with the faro box. Someone added fuel to the fire, so that it flared up brighter. And there was now an oil lamp, its light casting a dancing yellow glow on the faces nearest it.

More drunken laughter rose, and the burnished wood of the faro box caught the firelight. The men crowded about the cards, all of them clamoring at once.

Emerald swallowed hard, feeling sick. Then, within the safety of the sheltering darkness, she sank to the ground, her hands pressed together so tightly that her palms hurt. *Mace . . . oh, Mace,* she cried inside. *Why did you have to pick tonight of all nights to disappear?*

She could hear the men arguing now. Zelig York wanted to play poker, while someone else—one of the men from Fort Hall—was yelling that they should play blackjack. Faro— Monte— Abruptly, one of the men from Fort Hall got up and left the campfire. He staggered slightly, fumbling at the front of his pants and humming to himself off-key.

He came straight toward her. Desperately Emerald flattened herself on the ground and began to crawl under the nearest wagon bed, hoping he would not see her.

Hard lava rocks scraped her hands and knees. In the darkness she bumped her head on the bottom of the wagon and stifled a cry of pain.

The man stood and urinated against the wagon wheel, only inches away from Emerald's shoulder.

He must have had a very full bladder, she thought half-hysterically. For it seemed an eternity that the stream lasted, sending the hot stench of urine to her nostrils. She had her eyes screwed tightly shut, for she could not possibly look. If she opened her eyes, she would start screaming.

The stream stopped, and the man adjusted his clothes.

Then she felt a hand grasp her shoulder and jerk her out from under the wagon. There was a loud, startled exclamation. Then the man thrust a big, warm hand into the bodice of her gown, cupping her breasts.

At first she was paralyzed. Then she found her voice. "Oh— No! For God's sake, please—"

But the man only laughed and began dragging her toward the campfire. She kicked, struggled, and tried to dig her feet into the earth, but he only lifted her up so that her shoes could not touch the ground.

"Hey, look here! Look what I found under that there wagon! A nice little bit of female flesh! Is this here the piece we're a-gambling on?"

He pulled her into the circle of the light, laughing loudly, obviously pleased with the discovery. He reeked of whiskey and of unwashed body.

"Ain't she something? Oh, yes, ain't she? And look at the build on her. She'd make any man's bed a happy one, wouldn't she?"

Their faces were all turned up to her. Emerald was ready to sob with shame and fright. The man from

369

Fort Hall grabbed the front neckline of her dress and tore it away.

"Don't you dare, you—you—" she stammered with fury, wishing that she could remember more of Orrin's curse words. She snatched the torn bodice of her gown and covered herself as best she could. Why had she been such a fool as to want to watch this? She would have been safe with Geertrud and the other women.

"Aw," laughed the big bearded man who had found her hiding. "Don't cover 'em up, honey. They're too pretty for that."

She shrank away from him, feeling like a trapped rabbit as she stared about her, looking for a way out. But all she saw was the scattered cards, the faro box, the faces around the flickering oil lamp.

At first the men looked back at her. But then Pa VandeBusch glanced away from her and would not meet her eyes, as did Ben Coult. Matt Arbuthnot looked as if he were about to protest, but Zelig York jabbed him in the ribs angrily.

"I can't believe this is happening," she began in a low, furious voice. "Stripping away my clothes! Gambling for me! I thought you were all decent men. But I see you're not. You're lower than the—the lowest of the scum in the gambling dens of Natchez or Baton Rouge!"

As hoarse cries went up, she raised her voice to be heard above them. "You're drunk, all of you! Well, I have no intention of being a gambling prize for a group of drunken pigs who ought to know better! I have every right to choose my own husband, and that's exactly what I intend to do. If any of you are worthy, which I doubt!"

She stopped, breathless. There was an instant, indignant roar. They didn't like being called drunken pigs. It had been a mistake to talk to them so angrily. Emerald knew that they had stopped thinking or reasoning.

"Hey, now, honey." The bearded man, like a big, playful bear, grabbed her arm and pulled her up against his chest. "That's no way to talk, now, is it? Why, you can't blame us for makin' the best of a good thing, can you? We didn't mean no *harm*."

With each word he pulled her closer. She could see the drink-glazed blue eyes, the rather thick lips.

"Get away from me!" She pushed at him. "And leave me alone! I won't be pawed!"

"Is that so, honey? Is that just so?"

As the others roared and hooted, he crushed her to him and planted a huge kiss on her mouth. She struggled and wriggled, but his mouth devoured hers, his strong arms lifting her off the ground. She could feel the hard bulge of his erection against her.

She could hardly breathe. Her heart was pounding in sick fright. Right now they were all laughing, but she sensed danger. These men could be driven to rape her. They were, in fact, very close to it—drunken, boisterous, all inhibitions gone.

If she did or said the wrong thing—

She staggered backward as the bearded man released her. The ripped dress fell away from her breasts again, and she grabbed the cloth and covered herself.

The men began to crowd about Wyatt again, clamoring for him to name the card game and get it started.

"Faro!" he screamed. "Faro it'll be. And the man who bucks the tiger—gets the lady!"

More shouts, jubilant with hope.

They had forgotten her.

Emerald, her heart slamming in her chest in panic, edged toward the safety of the darkness, and the other

371

wagon where Geertrud, Martha, and the others waited.

She was almost to the edge of the firelight when her captor saw she was missing. He lunged toward her, grabbed her arm, and pulled her forward again into the light.

"Hey, girl! Where you going? You're the prize, you gotta stay here and watch us play! Me, I'm the one's gonna win you, and I plan to walk away with my winnin's as soon as I can."

He winked. "What a prize," he gloated. "What a *prize*. And to think we got ourselves a preacher right here, to make it all legal."

"He can't be much of a preacher if he would consent to gamble like this!" she heard herself snap.

The bearded man shrugged. "And what difference does it make? He's here, ain't he? Who cares if he's saint or sinner? This ain't Boston, you know!"

With this, he shoved Emerald down onto a campstool. "Stay put, woman, and don't you dast move. Because if you do, you know what's going to happen to you?"

He bent forward and whispered into Emerald's ear. The blade of a bowie knife flashed for an instant in the firelight.

She barely heard the obscenity he mouthed. She felt weak. If she could only faint, she thought desperately, but she had never fainted in her life. She would have to watch them gamble, whether she liked it 'or not.

"All right," Wyatt Thatcher said, taking charge. "We'll have Pa VandeBusch the casekeeper, since he's already married and not too drunk. Saul Rigney can be the lookout. Sorry we ain't got no fancy layout, boys, but this ain't exactly the *Mississippi Queen,* is it? Although we got ourselves a mighty pretty little queen right here, don't we? And she's gonna make it all worthwhile."

The game began.

Chapter Thirty two

❧ ❧

THE game of faro was sometimes called "bucking the tiger." It was, Emerald knew, essentially a guessing game. Mace had explained it once, for he had played the game often during his wanderings with Audubon and later.

There was a dealing box, from which one card at a time was dealt and exposed at the top of the box. The casekeeper kept a running tally on an abacuslike device that showed the number of cards and each denomination that had been played.

The game itself was simple enough. You called out a card, such as "queen," betting that the second of two cards drawn at random would match it. Cards were dealt in pairs—but only the second of any pair could be a winner.

Eventually only three cards would be left in the box. Because of the abacus, everyone would know which they were. Then bettors would "call the turn," or guess the order in which the last three would appear.

"But there are fifty-two cards in a deck!" Emerald had protested. "Where is the last card?"

"Oh, that's called the 'soda card,' " Mace had said.

"It's the first card dealt and doesn't count." He had smiled at her. "This game has lots of odds to figure. And, believe me, the inveterate gambler has figured them all. But you don't have to worry about it, Emerald. The only ladies who play faro are not very nice ones."

Mace seemed very far away now. She had given up hope of his appearing in time to help her. He was staying out overnight, she was sure. Or somehow he had known this was going to happen, and was staying away on purpose, leaving her to her fate.

After arguing at length over the details, the men started to play. They had decided to use Ben Coult's watch fob as a timer, and to play until midnight. At that time, the high winner would take the prize.

Zelig York won ten dollars on a jack, Wyatt Thatcher fifteen dollars on a queen. Ben Coult, his voice more slurred than she had ever heard it, doubled the bet. All conversation stilled as they waited for Pa VandeBusch to deal.

"Jack! Come on, that's my lucky card!" Zelig York spat on his palms and rubbed them together. "Come on, baby! Win for me—win big!"

Ben Coult was silent, his tall, lean body swaying as he lifted a tin cup and downed a swig of whiskey.

The winning card turned out to be a ten, and Wyatt Thatcher was the first man of the night to win anything. He raked in the coins gleefully, while Emerald's heart sank. To be married to this bandy-legged little man, a drifter and a gambler. . . .

The minutes passed, punctuated by groans and shouts from the intently playing men, who paused now and again to drink from tin cups or directly from a third and fourth bottle, reused and filled now with the home brew. Ben was drinking steadily, which surprised Emerald.

She found that she was alternately watching and shutting her eyes. She didn't know which was worse—to know that Zelig York had just won twenty more dollars, or not to know.

More minutes passed. Emerald ripped off a strip from her petticoat and made crude repairs to her dress. She had just finished this when she heard a scraping, scratching noise on the ground behind her.

She turned, startled and frightened, and saw Timmie Wylie wriggling along the ground.

"Timmie!" she whispered. "Timmie, stay where you are. Don't come into the light. I don't want them to see you."

"I wanted to see what they were doing," Timmie whispered back. "We can hear their voices as plain as day. They're all drunk, Geertrud says. She's worried. And Katje's crying. Geertrud is going to take Trude and Katje and Cal and me and Susie away a bit, so they won't find us if they come looking. Martha's coming, too, and Jan Rigney. We'll be back in the morning, when they've sobered up."

"Oh . . ."

"Geertrud wants you to come, too, Em. She says you'd better come before it's too late."

To be with Geertrud and the others, safely in a group! Emerald felt a fierce pang of envy. But, she saw, the bearlike man was staring at her suspiciously. He had appointed himself her watchdog, and rarely glanced away from her except to look at the cards. No, she didn't dare to make a move now.

"I—I can't," she whispered to Timmie. "They're watching me. At least that man from Fort Hall is. And —and I'm frightened of him."

"Wow! Is he a soldier?" Timmie exclaimed.

"Hush. No, I don't know just what he is. Maybe a trader. But Timmie, you'd better go," she said urgently. "You shouldn't be here."

"But Em—"

"I said go!"

She was relieved to hear Timmie leave, but she felt more lonely than ever.

The game progressed, and the men got drunker. Voices were louder now, more raucous.

Ben Coult, Zelig York, and the bearded man from Fort Hall were now in the lead. Zelig York's face was coated with drops of perspiration, which kept running into the hairs of his beard. Ben, too, was sweating, the gaunt hollows of his cheekbones more pronounced than ever.

Emerald could not stop staring at Ben Coult. It was the whiskey, she was sure. Ben must be one of those men to whom liquor is poison, and the thought made her feel cold.

"Only twenny more minutes!" roared Pa Vande-Busch. "Come on, men, let's see your money! Can't accumulate if you don't speculate! Lessee who's gonna be the winner, eh?"

The contenders bent even more intently over the faro box. Their faces in the flickering oil light shone silver with sweat. The Arbuthnots were still playing, but were losing heavily, as were most of the others. Of the men, only Saul Rigney, Pieert VandeBusch, and Pa were not playing at all. Young Bob Rigney, forgotten in the excitement, crouched behind the others, watching it all avidly.

The minutes ticked by. With each one, Emerald felt sicker. Zelig, she saw, had a big pile of coins and bills stacked in front of him. But so did Ben Coult and the bearded man, whose name, she had learned, was Julian.

"Midnight, men! Time's up!"

There were loud groans. Emerald held her breath. She was clammy with perspiration.

"Now we got to count it all," Pa said. "And we got to make it honest. So Saul and I, we'll take our time, and you'ns can wait to make sure it's all legal. And it better *be* legal, too. I got a pistol back in the wagon says it is."

There was a tense silence as Pa and Saul Rigney counted the winnings of each contender. Emerald heard coins clinking together, bills shuffling. This was money, she thought, saved up so carefully, carried over long miles of trail, intended for the purchase of needed items in California.

Far away a coyote howled.

"Well," Pa said at last. "I guess there's goin' to be a weddin' around here."

The shout went up. Emerald stood up, holding the front of her dress together precariously.

"It's our doctor friend here who's got hisself a purty little bride," Pa said, enjoying himself. "Dr. Ben Coult. So what d'ye say, men? We got the preacher; we got the girl; we got the whiskey, too. So how's about havin' us a weddin' tonight? A little celebratin'!"

Ben Coult. Emerald felt stunned. The men surged around Ben, shouting in anger, surprise, or jubilation, slamming him on the back and tossing the cards up into the air. She barely saw Zelig York's fearsome scowl, or Martin Rigney's disappointment.

She knew only that Ben's eyes had claimed her, his features expressionless, and that suddenly she felt very frightened.

Ben. He had saved Timmie, had doctored them all.

Desperately she approached him. "Ben—" Her voice was a whisper. "Ben, you don't really mean for this to take place, do you? This—this is a travesty of a wedding, a mockery—"

"I won you, didn't I, Emerald? Fair and square." Ben's eyes gleamed at her, and he stank of whiskey.

"But you're a doctor! You can't let this happen!"

She felt possessed by a wild sense of disbelief. The darkness pressed around them; the men shouted and reeled drunkenly.

"What does my being a doctor have to do with it? Didn't you hear them? They're fixing to have the wedding right away." Ben leaned toward her, his mouth twisted mockingly. "In only a few minutes, the beautiful Emerald Regan will be my wife."

"You're all drunk!" she burst out. "Drunk and ugly! And I'm going back to Geertrud and the others to wait until you sober up. We'll have the wedding tomorrow!"

She turned away from him, but he suddenly grasped her forearm with hard strength.

"No, Emerald. No, you don't. I may be drunk—but I still want to marry you. I always have. And I'll do it now, tonight. What difference does the time or place make? I want you, and you need a man."

"No—not like this. Please, Ben, this is preposterous. Please, let's just wait until tomorrow, when you can think clearly."

"I'm thinking clearly now. I want you, and I mean to have you."

"Do you, Ben Coult, take—take thish woman—"

Billie Colfax's whiskey-hoarse voice made a grotesque parody of the marriage vows. All of the men

380

were gathered about, still drinking and still spoiling for fun.

Emerald stood rigidly beside Ben Coult, hearing him reply to Billie's query in a deep, resonant voice. Billie asked the ritual question: Did she, Emerald, take this man to be her lawful, wedded husband?

"Well?" Billie said. "Come on. Ain't you going to say it? *I will*. Go on, say it."

The flaring firelight made grotesque shadows on Billie's face, giving him a demonic look.

"I said you got to say *I will*," Billie repeated.

"Oh. I—I will." Her voice was barely a whisper.

"Then I now pronounce you man and wife," Billie said perfunctorily, and turned away. Men crowded about them, whooping, pushing, shouting. Someone started to bang on a pan bottom with a wooden spoon.

"Come on! Come on! To the bridal tent! Let's have the chivaree! It's a wedding!"

Emerald stood paralyzed next to Ben, not daring to look at him. Her husband. Someone was blowing across the mouth of a whiskey bottle. Wyatt Thatcher strummed on his banjo and Red Arbuthnot played a wild jig on his fiddle.

"Come on, li'l bride! To the bridal tent for the m-marital rites—" Wyatt Thatcher's mouth was open and wet.

Ben took her arm and urged her toward his wagon, to the accompaniment of bangs, whistles, shouts, and obscene ribaldry. Martin Rigney carried the oil lamp, its light swinging in wild arcs.

The small canvas tent was set up neatly near Ben's wagon, as usual.

"A kiss from the bride! We want a kiss! A kiss!"

But to Emerald's vast relief, Ben turned to them

and growled, "Not on your life," and pushed her inside the tent before anyone could protest.

It was pitch-black inside, and Emerald felt instant claustrophobia. She could hear Ben's rapid breathing, smell the strong, sweetish stench of whiskey.

The others surrounded the tent, shouting. It was a chivaree, she thought. Trude had told her about such wedding horseplay—kidnapped brides, parties that lasted two and three days, objects put in nuptial beds, banging and knocking at doors. At the time she had pitied the bride who had to endure such rough pranks.

"Well, Emerald Regan," Ben said. "I won you. What do you think of that?" His voice was thick and slurred.

"I think this whole wedding is a travesty! I'm amazed that you went along. I—I thought you were a gentleman!"

"Did you?" She sensed him moving in the darkness, and then he shoved her backward onto the blankets that neatly lined the floor of the tent.

"Please—" She beat at him with her fists, knowing that to scream would be useless. Who would hear? Or care? Any screams would be drowned out by the chivaree outside the tent, the pot-banging, the twang of the banjo and fiddle.

Again she shoved him. Ben—this drunken Ben— was a stranger.

"Dammit, Emerald, will you stop struggling and listen to me? You're my bride now. Didn't they just make it legal? God knows, I've wanted you, ever since that day I first saw you. Wanted you no matter how whorish you were—"

"Whorish!"

"Do you think that I don't know of your love affair

with Mace Bridgeman? I've seen your face when you look at him—and I've seen his. But it doesn't matter. Even spoiled fruit tastes good if you're hungry enough. And I'm hungry. Besides, you'll be virtuous now that you're my wife. I'll see to that. You're mine, and I'll get all I want of you. Do you hear?"

There was madness in Ben's voice, obsession. He touched her, and Emerald fought back, kicking and scratching. Her toe hit something soft, and Ben screamed with pain.

"You bitch— I'll show you—"

His hands were on her shoulders, pushing her backward, jerking her petticoats up, pulling at her undergarments. In her ears was the din of the chivaree, louder now, as if the men were standing right outside the tent.

"Ben—" she gasped. "Ben, please, not like this! So —so ugly, with them out there, laughing and shouting and carrying on—"

Ben's breath was ragged and hoarse. "You're my wife, Emerald. I've waited for you, waited a long time. I won't be denied now!"

And then Ben was on her. Like a savage animal, she thought dazedly. Like an animal.

It did not last long—or perhaps it lasted forever, his body crushing her down, overpowering her. She could hear him panting in her ear and groaning. Then, just as he started to climax, the tent collapsed on top of them, smothering them in its folds, outlining their bodies in canvas. The men outside the tent let out a shout of joy.

Horribly, horribly, Ben continued.

It was over. Ben rolled off her, sat up, and fumbled until he had found the tent poles. Then he lifted them up, and the canvas tautened once more as it stretched over them.

Emerald crawled to the far corner of the tent and curled herself into a ball.

Chapter Thirty-three

HOURS had passed. Ben lay snoring where he had fallen asleep. And Emerald still huddled as far away from him as possible, her eyes wide open.

The revelers had gone back to their own wagons, or had passed out wherever they were. For it was quiet outside the tent now, save for the natural night sounds, the distant howl of a wolf or coyote, the scraping noises of insects. A horse, tethered with the herd, whickered.

She was married, Emerald kept thinking dully. Married to this man who had virtually raped her. She blinked her eyes and wiped away tears, fearful that any movement might wake Ben.

She wished that he would stay asleep forever. How could he have changed so? she wondered. Or—had he always hidden ugliness beneath the surface of his personality, waiting for alcohol to release it?

The first faint twitter of a bird interrupted her thoughts. Emerald stiffened. Dawn was approaching. How could she face the other emigrants after they had seen her humiliated, after they had seen her and Ben having sex beneath the folds of the tent?

There was another sound. Someone was walking wearily into camp.

Mace! It must be Mace!

But where was his horse? What had happened? Emerald sat up and began to crawl toward the flap of the tent.

Her husband stirred, groaned, and turned on his side. She froze, waiting with a frantic heart, until he had settled into regular breathing again. Then she pulled open the tent flap and crept out.

She looked about her. Dawn shaded the eastern sky a tint lighter than the west. The camp, with its wagons drawn crudely together, was still. No one was in sight, save for Martin Rigney, who lay sprawled in sleep about forty feet away, his flannel shirt stained with vomit.

Emerald stood and walked quickly around the bulk of the Rigney wagon. Then she saw Mace coming down a slight incline strewn with sage bushes and buffalo grass, his pack slung across his back. In the dim light she saw that he was carrying his saddle and bridle. The left thigh of his buckskin pants was stained dark, and he was limping.

"Mace!" In her joy to see him, she forgot to lower her voice. She ran toward him, her skirts flying.

"Mace, oh, Mace, where have you been? What happened to you? Where is your horse? Oh, Mace—"

She flung herself into his arms and began to weep against his chest, her body shaking.

For an instant she felt the unyielding hardness of his body. Then his arms went around her and held her.

"Emerald. What's wrong? Why are you crying? And why are you up at this hour? It isn't even real dawn yet."

He held her back, his eyes examining her face. She knew what he must be seeing. Her curls were matted and tangled, and she knew her eyes were swollen from crying.

But that didn't matter, she thought. Nothing mattered except that Mace was here.

"I—I don't know how to tell you." Her breath caught in a sob.

"Tell me what? Everyone is all right, aren't they?" His voice was sharp. "It isn't Indians, is it?"

"No—"

"Then what, Emerald? What is it? I've had a long walk back here. My horse got bitten by a rattlesnake, and he fell on me. I had to shoot him. Now I'm tired, and I'd like to catch a bit of sleep before the wagons get rolling again."

"It—it was the whiskey," she said. "The whiskey the men from Fort Hall brought—"

She told the story in quick, bald sentences, rushing over the worst parts.

He gripped her until her shoulders ached. "Do you mean to tell me that those bastards *gambled* for you? As if you were some slut in a gambling house?"

"Yes . . ."

Mace's lips tightened. The gray eyes were like cold chips of ice. "And so you're married to Ben Coult. Are you glad about it, Emerald? Happy?"

"Happy!"

"Well, are you?"

Did he blame *her?* she wondered incredulously.

"You don't understand," she cried. "I didn't want to marry any of them, Mace Bridgeman. I only wanted to marry you. You knew that, didn't you? That's why you stayed away from camp! You were willing to make love to me, all right, but you didn't want to marry me!"

"Emerald." He held her. She felt the physical warmth of him, smelled the musky odor of maleness, of sagebrush and wild grasses and horse.

"Emerald, I didn't know this would happen, I swear it. Not like this. We quarreled, you and I. I—I thought perhaps it would be better if you were married to someone else, a man who would take care of you and make you happier than I could. I figured you'd find someone, a girl as lovely as you. Figured this would force you to make a choice—"

"A choice!" She could have screamed at him. "What choice did I have? I was virtually bought like a slave! Or a—a shipment of sugarcane! That's how much choice I was given. And now I'm married. Married to a man who horrifies and disgusts me, a man I never wanted and never would have chosen in a hundred years! And it's your fault—"

She collapsed against him, weeping into his shirt.

For a long moment he held her, stroking her hair with his trail-roughened fingers that caught on her curls. "Emerald, I'm sorry. Do you hear me? I'm sorry."

"I wanted you to help me," she sobbed. "I prayed for it. I waited for you, thinking you might still come back before it was too late—"

"Emerald! Oh, God. I would have been back but for my horse. I said I was sorry. Darling—"

She jerked away from him. "Being sorry isn't quite enough! It's too late for that. I'm married to a man who raped me on my wedding night. *Raped* me, did you hear that?"

Mace looked shaken and angry. "Ben raped you? That bastard! Emerald—I swear I didn't mean for this to happen."

388

"Are you so sure of that?" She didn't know what drove her to say such a cruel, lashing thing. But she could see by the stunned look of his face that she had hurt him deeply. "Mace . . ." she murmured. "Mace, I . . ."

He pulled her to him and kissed her, a long, slow, gentle kiss that seemed to cleanse her, erasing all the ugliness of Ben. A kiss tender and healing.

"Emerald." Gently he released her. "Go back to your old wagon—the Wylie wagon—for now. I'll take care of Ben Coult. You may be married to him, but he won't mistreat you again. I'll see to that."

She clung to him frantically. "But—but I don't *want* to be married to him!"

"You are, though. You're Mrs. Ben Coult now. And whatever kind of man I am—and that's not always so good—I am not a coldblooded murderer. So, as much as I'd like to take out my rifle and shoot Ben Coult right between his filthy eyes, I'm not going to do it. But he'll be sorry enough. Mark my words."

When Mace left, Emerald stood swaying. Then, slowly, she walked toward the Wylie wagon.

Morning had come. Emerald stared out at the hot glare of day fighting a sensation of unreality. Surely, after all that she had been through, the sun could not look the same. The sage bushes could not be the same dull green.

As Mace had instructed, she had crept back to the familiar Wylie wagon. Now she moved about beneath the canvas, trying not to think of the previous night, trying not to think of anything at all. She washed her face and brushed her hair, stopping to peer into the small square of looking glass once owned by Margaret. She stared at herself critically—at the green eyes smudged with heavy shadows, the cheeks marred with a dark bruise. She was married now. Married. The knowledge was a dull heaviness in her.

She put down the mirror, her hands shaking. And it was then that she heard the angry voices coming from Ben Coult's tent.

Loud voices, filled with hatred.

Her heart thumping, Emerald climbed out of the Wylie wagon into the hot sunlight. Mace was arguing with Ben, with tightly controlled fury.

"If I were a murdering man, Coult, I'd kill you for what you did last night. You're despicable; you're no better than dirt. Taking a woman into your care and then treating her as you did Emerald—"

She heard Ben's muffled reply.

"You have a wife, now, Coult, and you'll treat her right or I'll see that you suffer. Suffer long and slow—"

Smack.

She heard Ben's stifled outcry, and then there was another hard, smacking crack.

The ox whip, she thought in horror. Mace must be lashing Ben with an ox whip.

Before she could stop herself, she was running toward Ben's wagon and the tent that was still pitched beside it.

"Mace—Mace—you mustn't! You mustn't!"

The two men were facing each other. Bright streaks of blood ran diagonally across Ben's back and soaked through his shirt. Perspiration ran in rivulets from her husband's face, and there was a look Emerald had never seen there before—naked fear, mingled with hatred. Hatred, Emerald knew, for Mace and for her.

Mace's voice was a rasp. "Don't waste your pity on him, Emerald. I'm not going to hurt him badly—just enough to let him know what will happen to him if he ever dares to harm you again."

"Please," she begged. "Please, Mace. Whether I like it or not, Ben is my husband now. This will only make things worse between us."

Mace lowered the whip, his eyes stony gray and impenetrable.

"Very well, Emerald. As you wish." He turned and strode off toward the low sagebrush hills, his back stubborn and very erect.

"Mace—" She started after him, and then abruptly stopped. She had no right to follow him now. She no longer had any right to love him, to seek the shelter of his arms. She was married to someone else.

"Emerald—" Ben Coult began, starting toward her. Bloodstains were spreading on his shirt.

"Leave me alone!" she snapped. "I have chores to do."

The sun rose higher. The air—as always—was dry and hot. Dully, Emerald started a fire, brewed coffee, fried bacon, and made cornbread from the stores that still remained in the Wylie wagon. The others—Geertrud and the rest—would be coming back to camp soon. They would all be hungry. And the baby—

She ran to milk the cow, and brought back a half-pail of thin, warm, foaming milk. It had an odd flavor, and she knew that Bossie had been nibbling on sagebrush. She would have to set Timmie to pulling grass for the cow. If her milk turned bad, the baby would starve.

Emerald went grimly about her chores, not looking anywhere except at what she was doing. She did not want to see Pa VandeBusch, yawning and groaning and rubbing his head. Or Martin Rigney, staggering up from where he had fallen, to look about bewilderedly. Or Wyatt Thatcher, picking up the scattered cards and putting away the faro box.

No, she didn't want to see any of them. She would never forgive them.

She heard pebbles crunch behind her, and whirled about. It was Ben Coult.

She shrank back. His once-clean butternut shirt was plastered to his body with blood and perspiration. His coarse hair hung in his eyes, and his face looked more bitter than ever. His lips formed an expressionless straight line. She saw, too, that he was carrying his medical saddlebags.

"Wash my back," he ordered.

"What?"

"I said, wash my back. You're my wife now, aren't you?"

She gave him a long, defiant look.

"Emerald, I asked you to wash my back and clean my wounds. Don't you think that it's the least you can do?" His words were heavy with sarcasm. "Here are some bandages and salve."

"Very well." She reached for the bandages he held out to her, the bottle of greasy ointment. "You'll have to take your shirt off."

Silently, Ben stripped off his shirt. His skin was marred by three diagonal cuts, raw and angry-looking. They would scar, she supposed, but she didn't really care. Ben was lucky to have only three whip cuts. Mace had been so furious. . . .

She treated the cuts grimly.

"Emerald."

She reached for the wad of bandages and unrolled them savagely. "Yes?" she snapped.

"I—I don't know what to say," he muttered after a moment.

"Then don't say anything! There's nothing you could say to me that I would want to hear."

"I just want to tell you that I'm—sorry about what happened last night."

Now she did look at him, her mouth open in ridiculous surprise.

"Sorry! For raping me!"

"It was the drink," he said in a low voice. He moved closer to her and tried to take her right hand. She jerked it away from him and moved to the other side of the cookfire.

"Emerald, I tell you, it was the drink. I—I shouldn't have taken any. I have a problem, as you saw. I'm fine if I take no liquor at all. But sometimes the notion to drink gets so strong in me that I can't help myself. And then—"

"And then ugly things happen, like rape. Is that what you're trying to say?"

"Yes." Ben hesitated. "It was one reason I decided to go to California. My wife's death, of course. But also—this. I thought if I came to a new place—they said the climate was salubrious—"

Emerald felt an instant's wrench of pity.

"I wager this wasn't the first time you raped a woman," she said thoughtfully. "You attacked your wife, too, isn't that true?"

It was if she had hit him. Ben's face suddenly darkened, and he glared at her. He was so close to the Ben of last night that she instinctively stepped back.

"Enough, Emerald!" he snapped. "I lowered myself by telling you I was sorry. I promise it won't happen again. Isn't that enough for you?"

"Very well." She let her voice match the coldness of

his. "But let me tell you something, Ben Coult. Don't you ever take another drink of whiskey while you're around me. Ever! Do you understand?"

There was a silence. Then Ben looked away from her. "Well?" he said sharply. "What are you waiting for, girl? The water is boiling, and you still haven't bandaged me properly. After my wounds are dressed, we'll talk about the disposition of the Wylie wagon and oxen."

So, Emerald thought, the marriage—if you could call it that—was to be a joining of two enemies. She would perform "wifely" duties, and Ben would see her and the children safely to California. As long as he did not drink, he would be tolerable.

But if he drank, he would change into the Ben she had seen last night. And she would always live with the fear of that change.

She bandaged Ben's back silently. He did not thank her, but left for his own wagon, for which she was grateful.

A few minutes later, Geertrud, the other women, and the children came walking back from where they had spent the night. Their small figures were dwarfed against the glaring blue sky, lugging blankets and canteens. Trude was carrying the baby.

Emerald rushed out to meet them. Timmie and Susannah ran to her, and the others crowded about. Cal was crying, his voice a hoarse, pitiful croak, punctuated by hiccups, as if he had been crying all night.

"Emerald? Are you all right?" Geertrud was anxious. "I worried about you all night. We all did. We barely slept."

Emerald glanced at Martha Rigney, who flushed. Trude, too, looked ashamed, and her eyes seemed to plead with Emerald for understanding.

"I—I'm all right," Emerald said at last. "I'm married, though. To Ben Coult."

"Married!"

"Yes," Emerald said flatly. "Billie Colfax performed the ceremony last night, so it's legal enough. Ben is my husband now. I hope it pleases all of you."

Let them make what they would of Ben's bandaged back, of the scattered whiskey bottles and sodden men. Or let Pa or one of the others tell them the whole story. She no longer cared.

"Well," Geertrud said. "That's a good thing, at least. You'll have a man to help you, and that's what you needed all along."

"A man. Yes." Emerald's voice was bitter.

Chapter Thirty-four

✺⟡✺

LATER that morning, Emerald had to sort through the Wylie wagon and decide which goods to keep, which to abandon.

"We can't haul two wagons," Ben told her. "First, we don't have enough fresh oxen. With the Forty-Mile Desert coming up, it'll be hard enough for our oxen to pull one wagon. And we don't need two sets of tools and household goods. That's wasted weight."

Ben had put on a clean shirt, beneath which the bulge of his bandages barely showed. Emerald, looking at him, could hardly believe that she had been virtually raped by this clean, reserved, bitter man. Had it only been a nightmare?

"But Margaret's things—her quilt, her books—" she protested.

"I have plenty of blankets. As for books, they are a luxury we may have to do without."

"But reading matter is going to be scarce in California! I've noticed *you* reading; you have books. Why shouldn't we have some? I have no intention of leaving them along the trail when Timmie and Susannah are going to need them for lessons later."

"Very well. But they will have to go, Emerald, if the oxen start to flag. I hope you understand that."

She pressed her lips together. "I understand."

So, grimly, Emerald sorted through the food, the tools, the cooking gear, the clothing, blankets, tents. She packed her own sketchbook, of course, and her drawing materials. She refused to leave them behind. She also took a few small personal items of Orrin and Margaret's—a little mirror, some letters, a Bible.

At last the Wylie wagon stood empty and forlorn, its wheels askew, its canvas stained and torn. The discarded goods lay in a pile beside it.

Timmie had lain in pain in that wagon, and Margaret had sat on the front seat, knitting a sweater. That sweater would never be finished now. Emerald's eyes burned.

They were ready to go. Today she and Ben would be third in the line of wagons, a line now shortened by one. The wagon train had always been too small, Mace had said once, and now, she thought, they were perilously small. A tiny group trusting their lives to this big land.

"Well, Emerald," Ben said behind her. He was already dressed for the trail, wearing felt hat and green goggles, and carrying his whip. "Why are you just standing there? Call the children. We have a long day ahead!"

It was as if they had been married many long years, Emerald thought. If Ben felt pain from the lashing, he was concealing it well. She stared at the eyes masked by the goggles. "Very well," she said at last.

She found Susannah playing in the dust with the dog, Edgar. Timmie was with Bob Rigney near the herd.

"Timmie, it's time to get started," she told the boy.

"We're late enough today. We'll not cover many miles, I'm afraid."

"Em, is—" Timmie hesitated. "I don't like Ben Coult so well. Are Susie and I and Cal going to live with him and you now? I mean, forever?"

"I—I don't know. Your father said once that you have an uncle somewhere in California, maybe near San Francisco. When we get there, we'll have to try to find him. He is your relative, you know."

"But—" Timmie's eyes watered. "Susie and Cal and I, we don't want—"

"Timmie," she said gently. "I would never leave you with someone who wouldn't be kind to you. And perhaps this uncle, since he's related to your mother, will be as nice as she was. You'd like him then, wouldn't you?"

"I—yes, I guess so."

But he sounded dubious. "Don't worry," Emerald said, hugging him. "We have a long time before we must start thinking about that!"

From Fort Hall the trail went westward along the south bank of the Snake River, where the water cut a channel through rough, dark lava rock, often with perpendicular sides.

Once more, Mace's services as guide were needed, for it was necessary to choose camping places with care. The riverbanks were so steep that often, although water flowed tantalizingly below, it was unreachable from above.

"Folks have been known to camp here and go thirsty all night, within sight of water, just because they couldn't get down to it," Mace said one night, as he was eating his night meal with them.

It was Ben's obligation to feed Mace in his turn,

but the meal was an uncomfortable and unhappy one, shot through with undercurrents of tension. Only Emerald and the children spoke to Mace, while Ben sat scowling at a distance.

Her second night in the tent with Ben had been another nightmare.

Emerald lingered by the fire as long as she could. Ben sat on the other side, reading a medical book by the light of the flickering flames, frowning at its pages.

"Well," he said at last. "You had better get to bed, hadn't you?"

"I—"

"Don't worry. I won't rape you tonight."

She scurried into the tent, not knowing what to say. How abrupt and frightening his moods were! She left her petticoat on, and lay down on the rough woolen blankets. She lay there for a long time and waited for him to come to her.

It was nearly half an hour before he came. She heard him opening the flap of the tent and moving about as he took off his clothes. The smell of soap and medicinal salve came from him.

At least he was clean, she thought wildly.

He spoke to her. "Tomorrow, Emerald, I'll want you to clean my wounds again. I'll need more salve on the raw places."

"Yes."

He went on, in the same cold, quiet tone of voice. "And, since we're married, I will demand what is rightfully mine. I'm sure you understand what I'm talking about?"

"I—yes," she whispered.

"Well? You needn't worry, I promised your *friend* Bridgeman that I wouldn't mistreat you again, so you need have no qualms on that score. Or should I call the man your lover?"

"It—isn't any business of yours," she managed.

"Oh? You are my wife now. Or had you conveniently forgotten that?"

"No, I hadn't forgotten."

"Then strip off your clothes, girl. And do it willingly this time. I want to sample you again, and this time without a struggle."

He was waiting. She lay there, a shriek frozen in her throat.

Ben's hand touched hers. Lightly, very lightly. "Why are you trembling, Emerald? Surely you're not frightened of me? Why should I want to hurt my *wife?* My sweet little wife, who was responsible for the whipping I received? Eh?"

She could not speak.

"Well, Emerald? I trust you're thinking over what I've just said."

"Yes . . ."

"Then take off your petticoat. I want to enjoy that ripe body of yours. Surely it's a husband's prerogative."

"Is it?" From somewhere she found a last, reckless vestige of courage. "What about love? The sharing between husband and wife? You know there's no love in our marriage! It's a sham—a travesty—"

"Plenty of marriages take place without love. Undress, Emerald, or I'm going to take your clothes off myself."

The contempt in his voice was like a whiplash, and she knew that Ben had begun to take his revenge on her, a revenge that would undoubtedly last for many years.

She lay down, holding herself rigid. Then she felt

his hands on her breasts, cupping them, moving urgently over her.

Emerald lay and fought her shame. She forced her thoughts elsewhere. She would think of Mace, she decided.

Of Mace's lean, beautiful body, of his mouth on hers, of his voice, gentle with love . . . Tender, fierce . . .

Emerald lay beneath the pumping, panting body, and felt nothing, nothing at all. And when it was over, she rolled away from him as quickly as she could. Once more, she pulled on her clothes. In spite of the heat, she wrapped herself in a blanket.

Only later, after Ben had fallen asleep, did she allow herself to cry.

The miles of trail wore on. During the long days, trudging well behind Ben so that she would not have to speak to him, Emerald had little to occupy her mind but her restless thoughts. Was the rest of her life to be like this, so joyless, so bleak?

They had crossed a little stream called the Raft River, where, Mace said, the trail split. From here, some people went on to California, and others turned toward Oregon.

They found here a ragged cotton doll lying discarded near a rock, a remnant from a previous wagon train. The doll was faded from days of lying in the intense Western sun.

"It—it looks *dead*," Susannah whispered. She would not go near the doll.

"Oh, Susie, what nonsense. I'm sure some little girl is missing her doll baby right now. Maybe she dropped it as the wagon went by this spot."

"No, I don't think so," Susannah insisted. "No, the dolly is dead. I don't want to look at her."

They went on, but Emerald had to stifle her feelings of unease. Surely the doll could not be anything so sinister as an omen. . . .

Each night, in the tent she shared with Ben Coult, she suffered dreams that disturbed her sleep, and she woke in the morning covered with clammy sweat. In some dreams, she relived the night of the faro game and her marriage to Ben. Several times she dreamed of a gray wolf. Twice she saw the wolf shot again in the chest, blood flowing obscenely red.

One morning, Ben asked her what was wrong.

"Nothing," she told him. "I had a bad dream."

"You've had too many dreams lately. You even cry out in your sleep. Do you want me to make you a sleeping draft?"

"No. I don't want anything. I'll be all right."

"Are you sure?"

"Yes," she said dully. "I'm quite sure."

Now that he had established his mastery over her, Ben treated her with a hideous sort of kindness, like that of a farmer for prized livestock, she thought. He saw to her comfort and did the heavy camp jobs. He watched her constantly, and followed her when she left the campsite to fetch water or fuel. And he enjoyed her body at night, while she lay acquiescent and trembling, her mind fixed grimly on other things.

The days went on, and Emerald lost weight, and felt gaunt and tired. They had reached a desertlike region, and had seen some Indians whom Red Arbuthnot called "Diggers." These were dirty, unkempt, primitive people who, Red insisted, ate whatever they could get their hands on, including grasshoppers and rats. You had to watch them, he advised, or they would steal anything in sight.

Seeing them made Emerald think of Wolf Dreamer, who was himself anything but primitive. For a time she had been able to push him out of her mind. But now he was back. Nearly every night she dreamed of the gray wolf she associated with him in her mind. Sometimes she glanced back over her shoulder, as if a wolf might be following them.

They traveled now along Mary's River. Or, as Mace said its new name was, the Humboldt River.

It was a long, monotonous, rather unpleasant stretch, which wore away at the nerves. Everyone was a bit sharper with his companions, more irritable. But Emerald did not really blame them. Because of impassable canyons or high water, the trail wove from one side of the river to the other, so that they were constantly having to cross it.

And, with each mile they traveled, the quality of the water deteriorated. It became more tepid, salty, and alkaline, its color going from chalky-white, to yellow-green, to putrid brown. Zelig York's dog, Blackie, died from drinking alkali water—and all of them had to be careful. As Wyatt Thatcher complained, "It ain't water I'd ask a dog to drink, but I got to drink it myself, and, worse yet, I got to be thankful for it, too."

Dust devils plagued them—fine dust stirred up by the wind. There was the problem of finding grass. The meadows still held good grass, but sometimes they could find it only in low-lying, swampy areas, where the men had to go out and cut it by hand.

And Emerald had never realized how important water could be, how anxiously her eyes would search the arid hillsides, gray with sagebrush, looking for signs of it. Sometimes there was spectacular scenery, but Emerald had seen mountains and fantastic rock formations before; if they did not have a stream bubbling out of them, she was not interested.

When they reached the Humboldt Sink, they stopped for a few days of rest. Here the river ended, and sank into a maze of sloughs, swamps, salt lakes, and marshy meadows.

There was sufficient grass and water, and they could rest for the pull that lay ahead. Rest, fatten the oxen, and bathe, if you didn't object to the stench and unpleasant color of the water.

One night, drawing some of the bad-tasting water, she met Mace Bridgeman. She was alone because Ben had been called to look at an ox's infected foreleg.

"Hello, Emerald." Mace was on foot and had evidently been washing his hair, for his head was damp. He looked more weary than Emerald had ever seen him before, and somehow older. The sun wrinkles about his eyes were grooved even deeper, and his face had lost some of its jauntiness and confidence.

"Hello," she said. How many times, as Mace rode by, had she prayed he would stop and talk to her! But she hadn't seen him except for the obligatory meals he took at Ben's wagon.

"Are you doing all right?" he asked her after a moment.

"What do you mean? I'm exhausted, my gowns are worn nearly to threads—what few dresses I have left, that is. I'd give anything for a lobster salad or a baked ham or some fresh-squeezed lemonade! I don't sleep well at night, and I'm married to a man I hate. And you ask me if I'm doing all right!"

"I'm sorry. I didn't mean to offend you. I only wondered if he—if Ben was treating you well."

"Yes. I suppose he is. By his standards."

"You haven't looked very happy lately," he persisted. "Emerald, are you? Happy, I mean? I wanted you to be."

"No, I'm not happy. Did you expect me to be? I—"
I love you, not Ben, she might have gone on. But her pride would not let her.

A spiteful little impulse, born of all the heat, of the long, weary walking, popped up in her. "I suppose *you're* getting along well enough, though, aren't you?"

"What?" Mace seemed to stiffen.

Recklessly, she went on. "After all, you always have Trude to console you, don't you?"

"I haven't spoken to Trude since the day you got married." His voice was cold.

"I don't believe you."

He shrugged angrily. "Believe me or not, Emerald, as you wish. It's true. Trude and I had a friendship, nothing more. You never would accept it—you never wanted to accept it. But that's what it was. And now it's over. I'm not quite sure why, but it is."

Emerald picked up her bucket of brackish water and went back to camp, leaving him standing there. He was lying, she told herself. A man like Mace didn't go without a woman. Not when a girl like Trude was available.

And yet, when she saw Trude later that night as she went to take Geertrud some biscuits, she was struck by the change in the blond girl. Trude looked thinner, more tired, and her eyes were red-rimmed. Had Trude been crying?

Well, Emerald thought, turning away. What Mace and Trude did was none of her business now.

She must never forget that she was married to Ben.

Zelig York stirred. He opened his eyes and groaned. Slowly, warily, he sat up. He put a hand to his head, feeling the headache squeezing his skull like a rawhide band.

It was that damned patent medicine of Wyatt Thatcher's, he thought. It was foul stuff. But he was so damned thirsty and it was all there was to drink, except for that hellish water. And, as Wyatt had assured him, winking, it might even cure his catarrh.

It was well past dawn. He was lying in the wagon on a soiled blanket, amid a jumble of supplies and sawmill equipment. Noises outside indicated that Billie Colfax was already up and starting the fire.

"Oh . . . Gawd . . ."

Zelig shook his head, trying to clear it. He hated this dry, arid land they were in, with the threat of the Forty-Mile Desert lying just ahead of them. Hated the trail, stretching before them for miles. Hated Billie, always criticizing him for something, calling him stupid or mocking him.

He lay listening to the morning camp sounds, trying to force himself to get up. From nearby came a child's high-pitched shout, the rattle of an iron skillet, a woman's voice.

That girl, he thought. That Emerald. She must be making breakfast for her husband, for Ben Coult.

He could still picture her the way she had been the night of the faro game, standing in the lamplight, her dress ripped. He cursed himself, thinking how close he had come to winning her. He could have had her, permanently, whenever he wanted, *however* he wanted.

Damn.

Well, he thought, just because a gal was married didn't mean nothing. A little married gal could be just as much fun as any other—if not more. Because she would know what it was all about. She would appreciate what he had to offer. And if she didn't, well, that didn't matter, either.

For the dozenth time, he thought of the way the folds of the canvas tent had molded about the two bodies, moving unmistakably. He licked his lips, enjoying the fantasy. He wished he could have lifted up that canvas, flung Ben Coult off the girl, and enjoyed her himself.

He had been about to do just that, too, when he had felt Matt Arbuthnot's arm on his. And Saul Rigney had been on the other side, both of them just looking at him.

He had been too drunk to fight. But some other time, he told himself, he would. If it weren't for that damned husband of hers, sticking to her like a leech . . .

Zelig's mouth tasted foul, and he leaned over and spat onto the dirty blanket. Then, on impulse, he got to his hands and knees and crawled toward the back of the wagon. He lifted up the framework of a saw and pulled aside one of the wagon floorboards. This revealed the dark hole of the false floor.

He thrust in his hand and touched the amazingly heavy, bricklike object wrapped in cloth.

It was gold. Nine amazing, wonderful bars of it.

Never in his life had Zelig imagined that he would come to have such good fortune. As a boy, he had been stupid Zelig, unable to learn his letters, beaten repeatedly by his father, until he had run away from home at age thirteen. Beaten again and sodomized by a drifter who had picked him up on the Natchez Trace. Growing bigger over the years, and stronger, until no one beat him ever again.

Well, he was not so stupid now. He had hooked up with Billie—who as a youth of eighteen had really been a preacher once—and he and Billie were going to be kings in California! They would finance their own sawmills. They would buy into the shipping business and ship their lumber out. They would own boats that traveled to the Sandwich Islands or to Mexico or around the Horn.

But those were Billie's plans. Zelig himself, once they reached California, planned to gorge on whiskey and beef. He would buy into the biggest card games he could find; he would win the keno lottery a dozen times. He would buy a fancy horse with a silver-tooled Mexican saddle and a sexy, big-busted Mexican girl to go along with it. . . .

His hand touched the cloth-wrapped brick, then moved caressingly on to the next.

So heavy, he thought. So rich. He wondered what Billie would say if he knew that he was handling the gold. To Billie, the gold was only a means to certain ends. Billie would never want to run his hands over it, Zelig was sure. Billie never daydreamed. He planned.

Zelig fondled a third bar. They would be rich, he thought. Richer than he could even imagine. And no one would ever suspect that here were the two men who had robbed the Chicago bank. Already, in Zelig's mind, the circumstances of that day in Chicago were fading. He had forgotten the sight of the gushing blood, remembering only the moment when Billie had thrust the bricks toward him. . . .

Impulsively, Zelig took the third bar out of the hole, into the muted light of the wagon. He wanted to see the gold, to rub his fingers over the dulled, burnished glory of it, to smell it, to buff it up until it shone.

He unwrapped the bar. But instead of gold, there was a block of wood.

Wood! Zelig stared at it, his heart thudding. His mouth fell open. The bar was wooden!

Someone had stolen the gold and substituted wood!

Frantic now, Zelig grabbed two more bars, pulled them out, threw off their greasy cloth wrappers. To his relief, these were gold, still gold.

Zelig crouched in the wagon, sweating. What had happened? They had been so careful to keep the wagon guarded at all times. And until the dog had died a few weeks back from drinking alkali water, Blackie had been there, too, ready to growl low in his throat at any intruder.

Yes, someone had always been nearby, save for the night when both he and Billie had played faro. They had been starved for whiskey, and had left the wagon unattended. Anyone could have gotten in it.

Anyone, including Billie himself.

Zelig let out a roar. Then he backed out of the wagon and went to find Billie.

Chapter Thirty-five

✽❧ ❧✾

T HEY were nearing the Forty-Mile Desert, the
most dreaded segment of the California Trail.

There would be no grass, very little water, nothing
but burning sun and hot sands. In places, the oxen
would have to pull in knee-deep sand. They were sure
to lose some of them.

Never in her life had Emerald experienced such
heat. Even here at the Sink, heat bathed them as if
from an opened oven door. The temperature was high
—100 to 110 degrees, Mace estimated—yet the air
was dry. Perspiration did not sit on the body as it did
in muggy Baton Rouge, but evaporated right away.

Emerald craved immense amounts of water. She
drank water by the cupful, as much as she could get,
and as often. It seemed as if she could never get
enough. Her most vivid fantasy was of a tall glass of
lemonade, beaded on the sides with moisture, frag-
ments of lemon pulp floating in it.

The heat frayed their nerves. Martha Rigney
snapped at Saul, and shrieked at Martin, whom she
had never forgiven for participating in the faro game.
Katje whined and complained over having to pick

dried grass for the animals. Even Trude was irritable.

And Zelig York and Billie Colfax had an enormous fight. Over what, nobody knew. But the two men had nearly beaten each other to death. Ben Coult and Pa VandeBusch had pulled them apart just as Zelig was trying to claw Billie's left eye out.

"He did it—thought to fool me, did he? Was gonna cheat me, was he?" Zelig had shouted.

Mace Bridgeman told the story of a previous wagon train, when one man had tried to kill his partner for the crime of twirling his long mustache, and another man shot his brother because he couldn't stand the sound of his voice.

They made plans for the desert crossing. They would start early the following morning, and keep going into the night, taking the trip in one long pull. They would stop only a few times, and then only enough to rest the oxen.

All day, they made preparations. Every water container in the wagon was filled to the brim. This time Emerald felt no qualms about filling chamber pots. And, she told herself wryly, she would even be happy to drink from one if she had to.

They gathered all the grass they could find and stuffed it into gunnysacks, blankets, and old mattress ticking. They even piled grass into the interior of the wagons. Emerald had baked as many biscuits as she could, to eat cold. She had cooked pan bread, and prepared dried meat and cold rice.

At last it grew too dark to cut any more grass. Emerald felt Ben's hand on her arm.

"Set up the tent, will you? We have to get some sleep."

She looked at him. His face was leathery, honed

down nearly to bone, yet his eyes still held a fanatic desire for her.

She tried to pull away from him.

"I said, put up the tent, Emerald. We've a long desert to cross, and I would like to go to bed now."

"Very well," Emerald said evenly. "If you say so."

Ben pressed his lips together, and she knew what kind of mood was coming on him. He would be angry, sarcastic, and take her brutally in the darkness of the tent.

But just then they heard a shout, and turned to see Martha Rigney running toward them, her apron and dark skirts flapping about her legs.

"Ben! Ben Coult! You've got to come! Martin— It's Martin! He's got terrible belly pains, just terrible. Oh, please, you've got to come!" Worry was naked on her face.

Emerald looked at Ben. All at once, he was a doctor again, impersonal in his authority. "Get my bags."

She ran to the wagon and found the worn double saddlebags that contained his surgical tools and medical pharmacopoeia. Her heart was sinking.

Severe belly pains! Just as they were about to cross the most dreaded stretch of desert? It was not good. And, for all that Martin had gambled for her, too, Emerald could not hate him.

She hurried with the bags back to Ben, and offered her help.

"I doubt if we'll need you," Ben said. "His mother can take care of anything necessary." He left with Martha. From the Rigneys' wagon on the far side of the camp, Emerald could hear Martin groaning in agony.

Dysentery? Or something even more terrible? As Emerald began setting up the two sleeping tents, she heard more groans. Then Martin's voice, half-screaming. *"Ma. Ma, oh, it hurts. Ma!"*

Emerald pushed her hair back from her face with hands gone suddenly cold, wanting to stop up her ears. Darkness had fallen, but the air was no cooler.

She put Timmie and Susannah to bed in one of the tents, reassuring Timmie that Martin had a belly-ache but would be all right in the morning.

Timmie looked at her sharply but did not contradict her statement.

"Go to sleep," she whispered. "We have a long day tomorrow. And the desert won't be easy."

"Em," Susannah asked. "Are we really going to walk forty miles all at one time?"

"If that's how far it is, then that's how far we'll walk." She kissed both of them and closed the flap of their tent.

She had saved some milk for Cal, and she fed it to him now, sitting on the campstool in the darkness to hold him in the crook of her arm. He drank lustily from the makeshift bottle, making cozy, sucking noises.

He was a good baby, she thought. He cried loudly when he was hungry, but fussed little otherwise. Cal —for California. It would be a shame if anything happened to him. A baby born on the trail to California and named after that faraway land should live long enough to reach it. He should survive to grow up there and become a man among those fertile valleys. . . .

Please, God, she prayed, holding the baby tightly. *Please* . . .

Ben did not come back, and she could hear anxious voices coming from the Rigney wagon. Several times, Martin cried out, his voice pathetic.

At last Emerald tucked Cal into his basket and

crawled into the tent with him. She stripped down to her petticoat and tried to find a comfortable position on the blanket. It was so hot. . . .

She said another prayer for Martin and finally drifted off to sleep. She dreamed she was trudging across the Forty-Mile Desert, her feet sinking into the sand so deeply that she could not pull them out. She tugged and strained, trying to take a step, for just ahead of her was an enormous long table, loaded down with a Baton Rouge feast—a huge, pink roast of beef, lobster salad, pink slices of ham, fruit salad, pecan pie. . . .

She felt something touch her shoulder. If she could only pull her feet out of the sand, she could go over to the laden table and drink great pitchers of tart, cool lemonade. . . .

The touch on her arm became an actual pinch.

"Hey, miss! Don't do that! You shut up, hear?"

A hand clamped suddenly over her mouth, its palm smelling of sweat and dirt.

Emerald came abruptly, sickeningly awake.

She struggled, trying to scream. But the big fleshy palm blocked off most of her air. She could smell the body odor of the man, foul, sour, reeking of dried sweat and some sicky-sweet smell that she couldn't identify. He was behind her, pressing into her.

"Hey, now, Miss Emerald, quiet down or I'm goin' to have to hurt you, and I wouldn't want to do that." The whisper came again, accompanied by another blast of the sweetish stench.

She struggled against the hand, trying to bite it.

"I said, quit that!" The voice was louder now, and suddenly she realized to whom it belonged. Zelig York was here in her tent!

What could he want? But of course she knew what

he wanted. He had fought for her the night of the faro game, and had been disappointed. He had brooded over it, waiting until Ben was occupied elsewhere. And now he was here, to take her at last.

Emerald arched her body, trying to escape the iron-strong arms. But he was behind her, legs and arms clamped around her so that she could not move.

"Where is it? Come on, girl, where is it?" He took his hand away from her mouth.

"Where is what?"

"Now, listen here. I ain't been drinking nothing, only medicine, and I mean what I say. You're goin' to answer me polite-like. Hear? Because if you don't tell me what I want to know, I'm goin' to kill that there little milch cow of your'n. What do you think of that?"

Kill Bossie? Through her fear, Emerald felt bewildered. Why would anyone want to harm the little milk cow? Then she remembered. Bossie was the baby's hold on life. Without milk, Cal would die.

"You—you wouldn't do that," she whispered. "Not even you."

"I might." Zelig cautiously loosened his grip on her. "Yes, I just might if you don't do what I say. If you tell anyone, even Billie, that I been here—"

"I—I won't tell. Be careful of the baby," she added. "He's in the basket behind you."

"Damn kid." Zelig belched, emitting more of the foul, sweetish odor. Medicine, he had said he had been drinking. Wyatt Thatcher's medicine, she thought. She forced back a swell of nausea as he began shaking her again.

"I said, tell me where it is!"

"Where *what* is? I—I tell you I don't know—"

"The gold bar, what else? You were skulkin' about

in the shadows the night we played faro, you was. You coulda been anywheres about the camp, and none of us woulda been the wiser."

"But I don't understand——"

"The gold bar, you little bitch. Don't play the fool with me. You know where it is because you took it and you put in that there block of wood. Yes, you had the chance, and you knew we had it, and you——"

Gold! Emerald's mind began to move rapidly. Gold! So that was what Zelig and Billie kept hidden in their wagon. That was why they always took such frantic care of their wagon, why they rarely left it unguarded, why they worried so much during river crossings, why they had been the only ones to trade at Fort Hall for fresh oxen.

"But so help me, I'm gonna find it," Zelig went on, his words slurred. "See, Billie thinks it was *me* took it. And he says I'm lyin' when I say I didn't. He's told me I got to get it back any way I can——"

Emerald stared at the dim outline of Zelig in the darkness. The two had stolen the gold, she was sure. So that was why they were going West. . . .

She found her voice. "Why, Zelig, I didn't even know you were carrying gold. So how could I have taken it? And where would I have put it?"

"Here. In Ben Coult's wagon. Maybe you're in league with him. He's your husband, ain't he?"

"But I——that's ridiculous! I hate Ben. I never wanted to marry him!"

"He's still your husband, ain't he? And you're gonna tell me where that gold bar is." He twisted her arm painfully, yanking it behind her back.

"But I can't—— I don't know!"

By the time Ben got back to the tent, Emerald had

controlled her revulsion and shock, and was lying very quietly, dry-eyed. She was shivering, though the air was very hot and close.

When she heard Ben come into the tent, she shut her eyes and forced herself to breathe regularly. Perhaps he would think she was asleep.

Ben took off his clothes wearily.

"The boy's resting now," he said. "I think there's some inflammation in his bowels. I purged him and bled him and sponged him, and I gave him opium. I think he'll be better in the morning. Anyway, we'll have to hope so. I did all I could."

She stirred, thinking of poor Martin.

"What's the matter with you?" Ben asked. "You'd think I had the plague the way you shrink away from me."

"It—it's nothing," she whispered. Zelig had warned her to say nothing of his visit, or of the missing gold, or he would kill Bossie. He might, he implied, even kill Timmie or Susannah if the mood struck him. It was all up to her.

"Well, you don't have to worry," Ben said. "I'm tired, so roll over and go to sleep. Your services are not required tonight."

Emerald did turn away, too numbed even to take offense at Ben's sarcasm.

Emerald was awakened at dawn by noises outside the tent.

"Edgar! Oh, Edgar!" It was Susanna's voice, full of hysteria.

"Oh, the doggie—"

Ben was still asleep. Emerald struggled up, pulled on her dress, and crawled out of the tent. Just outside, to her right in the dry grass, lay Edgar. He was dead.

He had, it appeared, been strangled with a piece of white rag. His little body, the fur dusty and matted, looked very pathetic.

Timmie was inconsolable. "Who, Em, who? Who could have done this!" he raged. "If I ever get my hands on 'em, I'll kill 'em, that's what! I'll get a gun, and I'll shoot 'em dead!"

Emerald stared down at the dog's body, fighting a surge of nausea. She knew Zelig had done this as a warning to her. A warning that Bossie or one of the children would be next if she did not keep her mouth shut.

"Timmie," she said. "I—I don't know why this should have happened. But it did. We'll just have to bury him now. Perhaps he—he didn't suffer much."

Timmie's eyes were a pure, hard blue. "Of course he suffered. He was strangled! Wouldn't you have suffered, Em? If I ever catch that murderer—"

"Well, we haven't time to think of that now," she said, hating herself. "We must start across the desert. If you want to bury Edgar, you'll have to do it right away. There's a shovel in the wagon. And you'll have to put"—she faltered—"rocks on him so the wild animals won't get him."

Timmie looked at her. "The ground's too hard for digging. I'll have to put him in a tree, the way the Indians do."

"A tree? I—I suppose you must. . . ."

She went to build the fire, trying not to look at the dog's stiff corpse. Ben came out of the tent. He examined the dog, frowning. "Who did this?"

"How would I know?" Emerald snapped. "It's been a long trip, and the heat is driving people half-mad. Edgar barked sometimes. Who knows what someone might do? I—I just don't know."

Ben pursed his lips and got to his feet. "Well, at least we won't have to spare food or water for the mutt any longer. See that the body is disposed of, and let's get the wagon ready. It's going to be quite a pull."

"Timmie wants to see that the dog gets a decent burial."

"Burial? For an animal?"

"Yes, for an animal! If the boy wants it, he's going to have it. He's lost his parents; he's suffered the amputation of his foot; he's endured a capture by the Indians. If he wants to bury his dog, it's going to be done. And we're all going to stay here until it is!"

Ben looked at her. "Very well, but tell him to hurry." He left to see to the oxen, dismissing the whole matter.

The funeral, such as it was, was brief. Timmie found a cottonwood, one of those hardy Western trees that grow anywhere there is a drop of water, and carried Edgar's corpse to it, wrapped in a blanket. Emerald did not have the heart to begrudge him the blanket.

Timmie scrambled awkwardly up into the crotch of the young tree. She handed the blanketed bundle up to him.

"Edgar'll stay here, up in this tree, and nothing'll get him." Timmie said. "He'll be like the Indians, nothing but a pile of white old bones after a while."

"Yes. Yes, he—he will."

Between them, they found a few words to say. Susannah added a small prayer of her own, while Emerald blinked back hot tears.

On the way back to the wagon, they met Zelig. Emerald stared at the ground stonily, fighting her revulsion. But she said nothing.

Two hours later, they were on the desert. They

had dreaded this stretch of the trail, talking about it in whispers at the night campfires. And now Emerald could see why. For the sun blistered their skin, and alkali dust stung their faces and sifted beneath their goggles to sting their eyes.

Some of the land looked grayish-green with sage-brush, mesquite, and bitter brush. But there were also dried alkali flats, stretched blinding white in the sun. The harsh wind filled the air with a white dust, and they choked and gagged on it. Their mouths were dry and parched, though they might have had a drink only a few minutes previously.

Heat shimmered in mirages—cities, battlements, cathedrals, fountains. Once Timmie rode up on Windy, grabbed Emerald's arm, and shook it.

"Look, Em! Look over there!" He pointed feverishly. "A big lake full of water! Em—"

"No. Timmie. It isn't a lake. Mace told us about mirages, don't you remember?"

"Yes, but—" The boy hesitated, then licked his lips. Then he flicked the reins and began to walk Windy again, his back slumping.

The sun rose further, until it hung heavily in the sky directly above them. The parched oxen began to lag. It was time for the noon rest, and they knew it.

But Mace had made it clear to the emigrants that they must keep pushing on, and let the weakest animals drop. Dried white skulls and bones scattered along the way proved that other wagon trains, passing before them, had done similarly.

They watched as first one beast, then another, collapsed in the yoke. One of Ben's oxen dropped, and he had to remove the corpse from the yoke and put another animal in its place. The Rigneys lost an ox, too.

But to Emerald's relief, Bossie seemed strong enough. Emerald walked as close to her as she could, stopping to feed her a big bundle of grass and give her one of the precious chamber pots of water. As the cow drank, Emerald could hear the oxen bellowing dispiritedly.

Shortly after noon, they passed a human corpse. It was half-mummified and half-skeleton, dried up from the desert winds, and Emerald shrank from it in sick horror. It appeared to be the body of a man about thirty, tall and cadaverously thin, coated now with layers of the alkali dust so that the body seemed more like a rock formation than a corpse. Two crossed sticks were laid over the body, and a sign was lettered on a piece of wood: *Jess Stooker, born Battle Creek, died this spot 1846.*

Had he a wife? Children? Someone to mourn him? And where was Battle Creek? Emerald stumbled on.

Timmie rode by her again, breathless with excitement. "Em! Did you see that? That man? He was all dead and dried up, and he—"

"Hush! Susannah went ahead to walk with Trude, and I don't want you saying a word of this to her. Perhaps she didn't see him. Let's hope so."

They passed many dead oxen. Some looked fresh, while others were years old and nothing but bleached bones now. They passed rusting wagon shafts and rims, bags of putrid bacon, farm tools, abandoned boxes and clothing. They saw a whole wagon, wheels and all, the tattered canvas top hanging in shreds. They passed the skeleton of a child about Susannah's age, the bones scattered about as if by coyotes.

They began to abandon some of their own goods. Ben made Emerald go through the wagon and lighten it as best she could. She threw out clothes, an iron plow, a trunk, a half-empty barrel of flour.

Reluctantly she added most of the books to the pile, saving only her sketchbook and Mr. Poe's book, the one Timmie loved. She had read all of the books dozens of times now, and when they reached California, she vowed, she would get new ones somehow.

If the oxen flagged and couldn't pull the wagon, they would die here in this sagebrush and alkali desert, all of them. Then they wouldn't need books at all. . . .

The sun moved across the sky. At last it began to sink. They paused just long enough to gulp cold biscuits and dried meat, washed down with warm, foul-tasting water. Emerald was so thirsty that she didn't care how vile the water was. She could have drunk quarts of it; she could have poured it all over her body and gloried in the feel of it against her parched skin.

But already Ben was prodding her. They had to get started again, he said. There were hot springs ahead. Mace Bridgeman and Pieert VandeBusch had ridden on ahead to dam them up so that the water would be cool enough for the oxen to drink.

When they started again, it was as if they had never stopped. At first Emerald's mind had kept returning to Zelig, but now she looked only at the ground, with its clumps of sagebrush, its hummocks of sand, or at the cloud of dust raised by the other wagons.

Ahead of them were the VandeBusches, second in line. All of that family was walking, save Geertrud, who held Cal in the wagon with her. Their riding horses had all died, save for Pieert's, and they had had to abandon much equipment, including Trude's beloved tulip bulbs.

First in line was the Rigney wagon, with Martin riding in it. At the rest stop. Emerald had seen him, big-eyed and pale from his bloodletting. It was clear that he was still in discomfort, but he was trying not to say anything. He had dysentery, she heard him insisting to his mother. It would go away.

They continued to walk. Susannah grew tired, and Emerald put her into the wagon. Timmie, too, was riding in the wagon now, for Windy was tired. Timmie had watered his horse and fed him as much grass as Emerald would allow. But Windy could no longer carry a rider.

Another ox collapsed. Ben cursed and stopped the team while he cut away the corpse. At this point, Emerald could only be thankful that they had the spare Wylie oxen. She and Ben were in far better shape than the other emigrants. Wyatt Thatcher had only two oxen left.

After dark, it got easier. The sky at first was a soft gray, pricked by only a few stars and a pale moon. Then, as the gray darkened to black, the stars began to come out and soon spread across the sky like a wash of luminous paint. They stopped, rested the oxen, gulped more biscuits and rice, and swallowed a bit of the precious water.

By the time they reached the hot springs, Emerald was walking mindlessly, without thought. The purpose of it all—to reach water, to get to California—no longer mattered. Now there was only the effort of lifting one foot and putting it down again, of occasionally lifting her hand to wipe dust from her forehead.

Mace Bridgeman was at the hot springs, tired and dusty. The frantic oxen were led to drink at the dammed-up spring. And, in spite of herself, Emerald found herself edging closer to the spot where Mace sat on his horse watching the animals drink.

He looked up, and his eyes met hers. *Mace,* she wanted to cry out. *Oh, Mace . . .*

He came over to her and dismounted "Emerald? Are you getting along all right? You're not too tired, are you?"

"I'm fine. I'm thirsty, of course. We all are."

"Yes." He was smiling at her as if there was a great deal more he would like to say to her.

"We've lost two oxen," she told him. She felt awkward. She wanted to fling herself into his arms, but instead she was talking politely to him, as if he were a stranger.

Just as she was trying to think of something else to say, Ben Coult came over. He was scowling, and he touched her arm possessively.

"Emerald. Come with me, I must tell you something."

Reluctantly she turned to go with Ben. She felt like raging. She wanted to be with Mace. To share her day with him, to be in his arms.

But Ben did not seem to notice her agitation. He seemed upset himself, his features contorted.

"The boy died," he said shortly. "Martin."

"What? Died!"

"Yes, he died in the wagon. He has been dead for some hours, I think. When they stopped the wagon, his mother went in to give him some water and found him."

"But—he said he felt fine! He was only eighteen years old!" Her voice was high and angry, denying.

"Stop it," Ben said. "The last thing we need now is female hysteria. The boy died because he was fated to die. Don't you think I did all I could? It's as I told you. A doctor can do little. People expect miracles. They expect the doctor to heal everyone. But he can't. He can't."

Ben turned and walked toward the milling oxen. Emerald stared after him.

Chapter Thirty-six

✨❦❦✨

T HEY buried Martin Rigney by the light of an oil lamp.

They had decided to have the burial right away, by the hot springs, for there would be no point in carrying his body any farther. Here, at least, he would rest by a recognizable landmark, instead of along a stretch of indistinguishable, barren, hideous land.

Emerald stood beside the others. The dark sky overhead was lit by a yellow-white moon. Her knees were trembling with exhaustion, and her thoughts seemed to skitter about, first on one thing, then another.

But for a turn of the cards, she thought, Martin might have been her husband. And now he was dead. Would he be lonely here after they had left, with only insects and lizards for company? And, perhaps later, another wagon train to stop briefly before moving on?

Pa VandeBusch's voice droned on, reading something from Geertrud's black Bible. Oddly, no one had asked Billie Colfax to read the services. Emerald did not quite know why. Perhaps they were now feeling ashamed of the farce of a wedding into which they had forced her. All the emigrants kept their eyes lowered to the hard, dry earth.

Martha Rigney stood rigid, her big hands twisted in her cotton apron, her eyes swollen. Saul was beside her. Grief and weariness grooved his face like seams in wood. Thirteen-year-old Bob Rigney glared at the blanket-wrapped body of his brother as if he would like to hit someone.

Trude was weeping. And at the back of the group stood Mace, looking not at the body but at the stars, as if he saw something there that no one else could see.

Now Pa VandeBusch and some of the other men began to gather rocks to heap on Martin's body, for the ground was unsuitable for digging. Young Bob had lettered a crude sign: *Martin Rigney, age 18, died here.*

There was the sound of rock striking other rocks or, worse, striking softness. Trude cried out, but Martha Rigney stood rigidly, watching all of it.

Emerald felt Ben pull her arm. "Come on," he said. "It's over, and we've got to get moving again."

"I—I can't go yet. I have to be alone. Please." She broke away from him.

"Emerald—"

But she fled, lifting her skirts and running away from the circle cast by the oil lamp, away from the small group of emigrants, the shadows of the wagons.

She stopped at last, breathless, and sank to her knees. She cried out once, a dry sob. Then she simply crouched there, hands to her face.

Margaret, she thought. And Orrin, and Edgar, and Martin—all of them . . .

She heard boots crunching on dry sand and pebbles. She stiffened.

"Emerald? Is it you?"

Mace! She jumped to her feet.

He walked toward her, his hat off and his teeth and eyes gleaming in the light from the moon. "For God's sake, what are you doing, you little idiot? Do you want to get lost out here on the desert? Don't you know that we've got to get started again?"

He took her arm, turning her about forcibly. She resisted. "Oh, yes, that's right!" she cried. "Let's bury Martin, mourn him for five minutes or maybe ten, and then be on our way again! Let's leave him lying here on the ground to—to dry up like the other bodies we saw!"

"Emerald. Darling, you know we have to do it. Do you want all of us to die? With no one surviving to read the Bible over us?"

"No. I—" Emerald felt her bile rising, hot and uncontrollable. She jerked away from Mace and, turning, was sick.

She felt his arm supporting her as she vomited. At last she was finished. She stood swaying, wanting to weep from humiliation.

But Mace was still holding her, and she knew that without him she would have fallen to the ground.

"Are you all right, darling?"

"I—I think so."

"Then take this and wipe out your mouth. It's filthy, but it's better than nothing." From a pocket Mace produced a large bandana, one that she had often seen about his neck, or pulled up about his mouth and nose.

"Wipe," he ordered.

She obeyed meekly. The handkerchief smelt of desert and of Mace. "Thank you," she said.

"There. Now we'd better get back. Your husband is no doubt wondering where you are."

"My husband."

"Yes. Had you forgotten him?" Mace laughed bitterly, then took her back to the wagons.

They trudged on. As before, Emerald walked close to the little milch cow, determined not to let the animal out of her sight. It began to seem as if the stop at the hot springs had never happened, as if Martin had never died, as if Mace's arm about her had been an illusion. Beside her, Bossie seemed to go slower and slower.

Emerald felt as if her feet did not belong to her. Any minute now she would trip and fall flat, over one of the ox skulls, over a hummock or rock. And once she fell, she would never be able to get up again.

"Emerald, quit lagging!" Ben shouted. He cracked the whip in her direction as if she were another ox.

She looked at him, too tired to reply.

"I said, keep going, Emerald! You're not falling down on me now. And you're not riding in the wagon, no matter how tired you get."

"I'm not asking to ride in the wagon."

"You'd better not." Again Ben snapped the whip. In the moonlight, Emerald could see blood drying black on the backs of the oxen.

"They're bleeding," she whispered through dry lips.

"It can't be helped. We've got to go on. They know it, and I know it. If you don't relish the sight, Emerald, you don't have to look."

"A-all right." She felt numb. She struggled on ahead, pulling the little cow by the tether about her neck. But still the sound of the whip followed her, and she realized that she was hearing not one lash, but many. All of the emigrants were lashing their beasts.

She walked to the VandeBusch wagon to see how Cal was. She found Trude and Katje walking together,

Trude half-supporting her sister. Trude, too, looked tired, her hair totally hidden by her sunbonnet, her face drawn.

Geertrud sat inside the wagon. The baby was asleep against her breast, his head jogging with the motion of the wagon.

"How's the baby?" Emerald asked.

Geertrud pushed a lank strand of hair out of her face. "He cried a bit, but he's fine now. What about the milch cow? Is she getting along?"

"Yes. I—I fed and watered her. But I think she's getting weaker."

"I was afraid of that. I don't know what we'll do if she dies."

The two women looked at each other, and then Emerald turned away. She knew Geertrud was trying to tell her that Cal might die.

She continued to walk, reaching out to pat the cow's roughened coat. Bossie was moving more slowly than before, she noticed in dismay, and sweat was lathered on her back. She rolled her eyes.

"Are you thirsty?" Emerald whispered. "I'll get you some water."

She went to the wagon, found one of the filled buckets, and set it down before the cow. She watched the animal drink.

"What are you doing, you damn little fool?" Ben strode up behind her and snatched the bucket away from the cow. "We need that water!"

"Well, Bossie needs it, too!" Emerald shouted. She reached for the bucket, and they faced each other over it, neither of them letting go.

"I tell you, you're not going to take our precious water and waste it on that cow of yours! She's on her last legs, anyway. She's been lagging!"

"She hasn't been lagging! She's doing fine. All she needs is a drink of water, and she'll be all right."

"Emerald, we need our water for the strong animals, the ones that can pull the wagon. The weak ones are expendable. That cow's going to die, and you know it."

"No! No, she isn't! She can't!"

"Whether you want to admit it or not, dear wife, she is. She's going to keel over any minute now, and if you give her that water, she'll die with a pail of water in her, water we can ill spare."

"*I* can spare it. I—I won't drink any more water myself. I'll give Bossie mine. It's the baby I'm worried about. If Bossie dies, then Cal won't have any more milk to drink. How will we feed him?"

"We won't."

"What? But we have to!"

Ben's face darkened. "Do you think that I like this any better than you do? Do you think that I enjoy knowing that a baby I delivered is probably going to die? Well I don't. I hate it. But I can't stop it from happening!"

"But—"

"Margaret Wylie was a fool to come on the trail in her condition. She knew what she was up against, or she should have. If you want to blame anyone, Emerald, blame her."

"But Margaret didn't *know*. None of us did."

"Oh, hell! Just get out of here, will you, Emerald? There's hard pulling ahead. Let the cow alone. If she's going to live, she'll live. If she's not, she'll die. But without my water in her."

"*Your* water?"

"Yes, my water. Just as you are *my* wife, Emerald, my possession." He was glaring at her, face contorted.

432

That violent Ben was always very near, she thought.

"That's right, you're mine, do you hear me?" he shouted. "And you'll take orders from me. And I say no water for that cow, do you hear?"

She slapped him, despite her exhaustion and fear, with such force that her fingers stung.

"What— You bitch! How dare you—"

He lunged for her, totally the other Ben now. She shrank back from him.

"I—I don't care what you say or do to me, Ben Coult," she blurted. "I'm going to water that cow. And if you don't let me, I—I'll find a way to kill you. I— Sooner or later, I'll get my chance. I didn't think I was the sort of person who could kill. But when it comes to a baby—well, I am. I think I could."

"You little bitch—you're crazy!" He stared at her.

"Maybe." She tightened her fist around the bucket handle and took it away from him, not even amazed that he would let her take it. She was stronger than he was, she thought dazedly. Stronger and more determined.

She set the bucket down and watched as Bossie drank loudly, thirstily.

"I'll make you sorry for this," Ben said.

She gave him an icy look. "I've no doubt you will. But I'm not going to worry about it now."

Several miles beyond the springs, they reached a stretch of sand where the oxen sank knee-deep. Emerald knew she would never forget this part of the journey, the constant, bone-wrenching struggle, the shouts of the men, the weak bellows of the failing oxen, the squeal of strained wagon wheels.

She watered Bossie again and tugged at the rope whenever the cow began to drag along too slowly. She talked to the animal. "Come on, Bossie. You can make it. If I can, you've got to do it, too. Just a few more steps—"

But Bossie only looked at her, her brown eyes liquid and suffering. Emerald knew that if they did not stop and rest soon, it would be all over for her.

But at some point, she looked up and realized that the sky was washed pale gray. It was almost dawn. They reached a downgrade, and the sand became less deep.

As the sun rose, they saw cottonwoods like a green necklace along the river ahead.

"Bossie! Oh, Bossie, look," Emerald whispered. "You mustn't give up now. Look, water's ahead!"

The animal pricked up her ears. She could smell the water.

"Good, Bossie! You must keep going on now. You have to."

They reached the Truckee River at last, incredibly wet and tree-shaded and flowing and beautiful. She felt that her prayers had been answered.

They were safe; they could rest. They could fatten the oxen, bathe in the flowing water, wash clothes, cook real food again. Heaven, Emerald thought, was a river lined with cottonwoods.

She milked Bossie, and with the meager trickle, fed Cal. Then she put him in his basket and joined the others in sleep.

No one bothered to put up tents or to crawl into wagons. They all simply collapsed where they were. Ben and some of the other men slept in a grove of cottonwoods. Timmie and Susannah curled up together under the wagon, like puppies. Emerald found a spot by a large mesquite bush. She closed her eyes and tumbled instantly into sleep.

Her sleep was disturbed by chaotic and frightening visions of Wolf Dreamer. She heard Indian chanting, the tantalizing notes of the Indian flute. She felt herself rising, swooping in the air like a bird.

When Emerald awoke, her dress was wet with perspiration. She stirred and tried to stretch, her muscles stiff and painful from the long walk.

Then she heard a sharp clink, and a scraping sound, as if something were being moved along the ground.

She sat up. The sun had inched past noon, and the camp lay silent. Baby Cal slept in his basket, his small mouth puckered.

There was another scraping sound. Emerald turned quickly and saw that Ben's wagon moved slightly, as if someone were walking inside it.

She got to her feet and crept toward the wagon. She pulled aside the flap and looked in. Zelig York crouched over a barrel of flour. He was stirring through the flour with a stick, sending up puffs of white.

"I told you we don't have your gold!" Emerald snapped. "Would you please get out of that wagon?"

Zelig raised startled eyes. For an instant he reminded Emerald of a huge brown rat. His small eyes were crusted with red, his skin black from sun.

"I ain't gettin' out until I find what I come for."

"But I don't have your gold. And I wouldn't want it, anyway. I've told you that!"

Zelig scowled. "Girl, you don't realize. I got to find that gold bar or Billie's goin' to get nasty. You ain't never seen him that way, have you? Well, it ain't nice. Now, someone in this here wagon train took our gold, and we mean to find out who. And when we do——"

"Go and look for it somewhere else, will you? I haven't got it. And I—I hate the sight of you."

435

"Oh, you do, eh? Well, I like the sight of you. All purty you are in that tight dress with them boosums of yours stickin' out. Yes, you're a purty thing to look at."

Zelig tossed the lid of the flour barrel crashing into the interior of the wagon and began to climb toward the front. Emerald inched away. She had been a fool to defy him.

He climbed out of the wagon, and Emerald picked up her skirts and began to back away from him, stumbling on the dry, uneven ground.

"I—I'll tell Mace Bridgeman about you. . . ."

"Will you now? I'd like to see that." Zelig grinned triumphantly. She saw that he was making no attempt to lower his voice. Why didn't he care who heard him?

"Well, Zelig? Did you find it?" A voice came from behind her. Emerald turned to see Billie Colfax, tall, long-nosed, round-shouldered, sauntering toward her casually.

"Nope," Zelig said. "Emerald, here, says she didn't take it and don't know where it is."

"Maybe it's in one of the other wagons, then."

"Oh, it's really true," Emerald said. "I don't have any idea where that gold bar is. I—I've never even seen one. I—"

"Quiet!"

"What?"

"I said be quiet, bitch, or I'll use this on you." Billie held a rifle up nonchalantly. He was also wearing a pair of pistols.

"You're no preacher at all, are you, Billie Colfax?" she accused. "No real preacher would threaten a woman with a gun! And no real minister would be carrying bars of gold across the desert!"

The cold, pale eyes looked at her. "Oh, I'm real enough. But that was a long time ago, when I was only eighteen. Things have changed since then."

Emerald thought how Margaret, in Council Bluffs, had been so relieved to have a man of God along.

"Well," she said furiously, "I think it's a shame that a man like you should be conducting weddings and funerals when you have no right to do so. And I think—"

"Quiet, I said. I don't like you; I don't like any women. All I want is my gold. I earned it, and I intend to find out where it went to. And when I do—" The big, pale hand tightened on his rifle.

Emerald faced him recklessly. "I don't think you're going to do anything! Mace Bridgeman won't let you! He'll teach you a lesson you won't forget."

Billie smiled. "I don't think he'll teach me any lesson at all."

"What—what do you mean?"

Billie gestured toward the river, where the emigrants still sprawled in sleep beneath the cottonwoods. Emerald stared, narrowing her eyes. Something didn't look quite right.

Then she realized that all their hands were tied behind their backs, their feet bound with heavy, greasy rope. Bandanas or shirts gagged their mouths. Ben. Pieert VandeBusch. Mace. Pa. All of them, she saw, all the men were there.

"Why, you've tied them up!"

"Yes. And I mean to see who's taken my gold." Billie's right hand caressed the barrel of his rifle.

Chapter Thirty-seven

❧❧

"EMERALD? What do you think is going to happen? What—what are they going to do with us?"

Katje's face was gray with alkali dust and fear. There was a red mark on her cheek from where she had been sleeping. She tugged anxiously at Emerald's sleeve, blinking in the hot sun.

"I don't know, Katje. I'm not sure," Emerald whispered back.

It was ten minutes later, and all the women and children of the wagon train had been aroused from their exhausted sleep and herded together into a group. Only Bob Rigney—at thirteen Emerald still thought of him as a child—had been tied up with the men, whom Zelig guarded about one hundred feet away, under the cottonwoods. Billie was searching the wagons, throwing food and blankets onto the ground, ripping open barrels, prying up wagon beds.

"Found it yet?" Zelig called. The barrel-chested man was obviously enjoying his role as guard. He swaggered about, once kicking Mace contemptuously in the ribs. As Mace's eyes narrowed at him, Zelig laughed.

Emerald tried to take slow, even breaths, to fight back her rising panic. She had to stay calm. Timmie and Susannah needed her, and the others did, too. They were a frightened, demoralized group, jerked bewildered out of their sleep. The brief nap had not rested them; it would take several days before most of them would feel strong again.

Emerald looked at them, one by one, assessing them. Trude sat with her arms clasped about her knees. Her dress was stained with dust, dirt, and perspiration. Her blond hair hung in strings; the round, pretty face only looked weary now.

Martha Rigney sat near Trude, her face glazed with shock, her eyes oddly blank. She had had to leave her son's body in the desert and stumble on. For the first time, Emerald found herself wishing that Martha could be her old, blustering, moralizing self. Anything, she thought with sudden pity, would be better than this strange, silent, staring woman.

"I want to go back to sleep. And it's too hot out here in the sun. I'm thirsty. . . ." Katje was whining like a little girl.

"Katje, don't carry on so," Geertrud said. "If you must talk, then why don't you pray? Perhaps God will hear us." Geertrud crawled awkwardly toward her daughter and patted her hand. Geertrud was more tired and sick than any of them, Emerald thought, but her spirit seemed calm.

Susannah sat playing with Cal, cooing to him as if he were a doll.

"Em!" Timmie, who had been squirming restlessly, nudged Emerald. "Em, what's going on, anyway? Why is that dumb old Zelig walking around with a gun and pointing it at us? If I had a rifle—" He pantomimed shooting, and started to get to his feet.

440

"Timmie! Hush!" Emerald grabbed him and forced him back down again. "Timmie, you've got to sit here and do exactly as Zelig York says. It will be better for all of us. Once he finds it, I'm sure he'll let us go."

"Finds what, Em?" Timmie persisted. "What's he looking for, anyway? Why's he making such a mess of the wagons?"

"It's gold, Timmie."

"Gold?"

All of the women looked at Emerald with shock.

"Gold, wow! But who'd have any gold?" Timmie asked excitedly.

"Zelig York and Billie Colfax were carrying some gold bricks in their wagon. And now Zelig says one of them is missing. They think one of us has taken it and is hiding it somewhere."

"Gold—gold bricks!" Timmie was obviously enthralled by this idea.

But Trude's face had hardened. "Where did they get this gold?" she asked sharply. "I heard something on the boat when we were coming up the river to Council Bluffs. Something about a bank robbery in Chicago. It had been in the papers, and there was a man on the boat who'd been in Chicago at the time. He said nine bars of gold were taken. And a man was killed."

Emerald looked, startled, at Trude, and the two girls' eyes met.

"This man said some other things, too," Trude went on, keeping her voice low. "He—he said that one of the bank employees was shot in the belly; it was a terrible wound. And a woman was—molested. In the vault."

Emerald thought of Zelig, of his hands violating her

body. Of Billie's chill gray eyes. Yes, she thought Trude was probably right.

Katje began to cry in huge, gulping sobs.

Timmie's face reddened, and he clenched his fists "Maybe Zelig, maybe he's the one that killed Edgar Maybe he's the damned dog-murderer!"

"Timmie, your language. Even if Zelig did kill you dog, there's nothing we can do about it right now We'll just have to sit here until—"

"I think he's the murderer! I think he killed Edgar! I'd like to shoot him," raged Timmie. "I'd like to crawl back to Ben's wagon and get out a pistol and some bullets and—"

"Timmie." Emerald put her hand on the boy's shoulder. "Timmie, you can't do anything like that—not now, at least. You're only a boy, and they have rifles and pistols. No, we must—we must just wait here for now. Once they find that gold bar, I'm sure it will be all right."

Emerald doubted her own words of reassurance, yet she did not know what else to do.

Slow minutes passed. The sun, directly overhead, beat down on them. Cal started to fuss. Geertrud picked him up and rocked him back and forth. He nuzzled her shoulder restlessly.

"This baby will need his milk soon," Geertrud said.

"Perhaps they'll let me milk Bossie," Emerald said doubtfully. "I'm certain they wouldn't deny food to a baby."

Zelig strutted among the prone men, prodding Wyatt Thatcher with his boot, poking Ben Coult with the barrel of his rifle, laughing to himself.

As Zelig's rifle prodded him, Emerald saw her husband shudder away from the weapon, his eyes sick with fear. An ugly ripple ran through Emerald. Ben had courage enough, she thought, when he had no one to face but his wife. But when it came to real trouble . . .

Zelig laughed at Ben's discomfort. He sauntered over and nudged Mace's chin with the rifle barrel.

"Say, guide man and fancy artist! How do you like the fix you're in now? You and them fancy animal pictures of your'n—how'd you like it if I were to take up that big leather folder of your'n and dump out all your paintin's, eh? Spread 'em all out in the sand for the ants and snakes to look at, eh?"

Mace, who was bound and gagged more tightly than the others, strained away from the tree as if trying to break his bonds by sheer physical force. Muffled sounds came from behind the gag.

"Cursing at me, are you, Bridgeman?" The barrel-chested man laughed.

Mace jerked his head with defiance.

"Shut up, you damned guide, you." Zelig said. "I'm the one's got the rifle now. And if we find you were the one took the gold, you'll be in a bit of trouble, you will."

He poked the rifle into Mace's face for emphasis. Mace's eyes were hard gray stones, glaring back in hatred. He did not cry out, but Emerald felt fear slithering down her spine like a thick-backed rattlesnake.

An hour of agonized waiting went by. Billie had nearly finished searching the wagons. They could see and hear him as he labored, cursing under his breath, throwing objects savagely onto the ground, overturning barrels, kicking wagon wheels, shaking feathers out of mattress tickings. But at last he walked up to Zelig and said something in a low, angry voice.

Zelig looked stricken. "Hey, listen." His voice rose

protestingly. *"I* didn't take it. I told you that. Wh
would I do that to you, to my old buddy Billie? Lister
you know me better'n that."

"Perhaps I don't know you at all." Billie looke
coldly at Zelig, who seemed to shrink under his look
Emerald sensed the man's fright. Why, it was' Billi
who had killed the man in the bank, not Zelig, sh
realized suddenly. That was why Zelig feared Billi
so.

"But listen," Zelig gabbled, spittle flying from hi
mouth, "that brick's got to be here somewhere! Where
else could it be? No one would be dumb enough to
leave it in the desert, would they? How could the
ever find it again? No, it's got to be here."

"Then you tell me where."

Zelig forced a laugh, his face white and perspiring
"But Billie, how would—how would I know? You
looked, didn't you? You did the searchin', not me. Listen, you can't think I did it. Why would I lie to my
partner?"

"Someone has it. Someone in this wagon train."

"But—but not me, Billie. Not me!"

"Then you think of a way to get it back, Zelig. Because I worked and planned too hard to let it go now.
We had nine bars, and I want nine bars. Do you hear
me?"

The big bearded man seemed to shrink beneath
Billie's look. If it were not for the situation they were
in, Emerald thought, Zelig's terror would have been
laughable.

"But—but Billie, we—" Zelig paused. He seemed
to be thinking very fast, casting about for an idea.
"We can make 'em tell us. That's it! We'll make 'em
tell. We got 'em here, don't we? Right under our

noses. We got the men all tied up nice, and the women."

Zelig and Billie looked at each other. And suddenly the bravado flowed back into Zelig and he started to laugh. His Adam's apple worked convulsively.

"All right! All right, now!" Zelig shouted. "You people just think you're so damned smart, don't you?" He was looking at Mace as he said this. "Well, I got something to tell you. You ain't smart at all. Not one bit. 'Cause I got an idea that's going to make someone tell us where that there gold brick is."

He walked closer to the gathered women, his rifle raised and pointed toward them. His eyes were gleaming.

"Take off your clothes, pretty ones. That's right. All of you women, take 'em off. Strip. There's nobody to see you but us, now, is there? Well, we'll see how much your men like it. Because sooner or later, one of you's goin' to talk."

The women all looked at each other. For a long moment no one moved or said anything. Katje put her face in her hands.

"You wouldn't do such a vile thing!" Emerald jumped to her feet and faced Zelig, staring into the small, gleaming eyes.

Zelig's mouth twisted. "Wouldn't I? You just watch, honey, and you'll see what I'll do and what I won't. I think this is gonna work. That there new husband of yours—he's not going to sit still and watch what's goin' to happen to you, I'll wager. You all got men there under the trees, don't you? One of 'em will tell, soon enough. Now, strip. Hurry it up."

Emerald drew a deep breath.

"I told you what to do. Now, you better do it if you know what's good for you."

So he did mean it. The roof of Emerald's mouth turned dry as shoe leather. The women all looked at her, depending on her to tell them what to do.

"No," Emerald said quietly. "We won't take off our clothes. We won't do any such thing."

"What?" Zelig looked puzzled. He came closer to her and pointed the rifle directly at her. It gleamed dully.

"I said, we won't do it." Quick mental pictures raced through Emerald's mind. Katje raped. Susannah naked. Geertrud forced into sexual indignities. Zelig, she was sure, would think of horrors she herself could not even imagine.

"You'll do it quick enough," Zelig shouted. "This gun says you will. And you'd better be quick, girl, or I'll think of something special just for you. I been achin' for you a long time. Now I'm goin' to be satisfied. How do you like that, eh?"

Emerald tried to stifle her panic. She glanced quickly at the men and saw that Mace was looking at her. His eyes glittered, every muscle tensed.

If only she could run to him! If only she could throw herself into his arms! Mace's eyes met and held hers, and Emerald felt as if he had touched her, as if he had kissed her.

"Well?" Zelig said.

"Please," she said. "Some of us are ill. And there are young children among us, innocent children. I beg of you—" She faltered. Pleading was not going to help them.

Then, abruptly, an idea came to her. "Zelig," she said urgently, "neither you nor Billie has been able to find the gold. But you didn't pack our wagons. We did, we women. Maybe you should let us look. We'll find that gold brick fast enough. We know where to look!"

Zelig made a noise in his throat, and Emerald sensed his disappointment. He wanted to sport with them.

"Zelig? What do you have to lose?" she said. "You said yourself that you couldn't find the gold."

The barrel-chested man hesitated, his eyes gleaming at her with desire. "All right, then, little pretty. And afterward . . ."

Afterward. Emerald swallowed nausea. But she forced herself not to think of that now. For now there was too much to do. . . .

She issued instructions to the women, her voice ringing with an authority she didn't really feel.

"It's going to be a treasure hunt." She tried to make it seem fun for Timmie and Susannah. "Only this time the treasure is real. Real gold!"

They crowded about her, silent and obedient, their eyes anxious. Even Martha Rigney was depending on her, Emerald saw with amazement.

"We all know that each wagon has its secret hiding places," she went on. "Money sewn in pockets or hidden under floorboards. We women packed the wagons, most of them, and we know them inside and out. I imagine we'll do a better job of searching than any man could. *Because we've got to.*"

She did not have to say more. They all knew what she meant. Geertrud was biting her lower lip, and Trude's face was carefully expressionless.

The search began. There were nine of them—five women and four children, including the baby. Leaving Cal still in his basket, they fanned out among the wagons and began to work. As she walked toward Ben Coult's wagon, Emerald fought a feeling of unreality.

447

All of this for a bar of gold, she thought, which no one could spend here, or drink, or eat. And what would happen to them when they did find the gold?

She climbed into Ben's wagon. She hesitated for a minute, looking about her at the stacks of food and goods, now knocked askew by Billie. Barrels, farming tools, Ben's medical saddlebags. Where should she start?

She drew a deep breath and reached for the saddlebags, pulling them open and thrusting her hand inside. No gold here, nothing but vials and surgical knives carefully arranged in a case. Her hand closed over a small, sharp knife. She heard a noise behind her.

Zelig, his mouth grinning in its nest of beard, was climbing inside the wagon.

"Hey, little girlie. I said look for gold, not mess with knives. You want to play with knives, I can oblige. I been carryin' one most of my life."

"I—I'm sorry," she croaked desperately. "I didn't mean—I was only looking at it. . . ."

"Looking at it, yeah."

Emerald's knees felt soft, barely able to hold her up. She had ruined everything! Now Zelig would follow her about as she searched, would not let her get away with anything.

While he stood behind her, whistling a dry tune, Emerald searched the rest of the wagon. Grimly, relentlessly, she dumped everything out of the wagon and onto the ground. The wagon had a false floor meant for the storage of tools and supplies. She would have to get into that false floor and test its sides to be sure there was no hiding place that Billie might have missed.

It was a hot, heavy job. Perspiration poured down

her sides, soaking her dress. Longingly she thought of water, of the Truckee flowing nearby, its waters so tantalizingly cool. Her mouth was dry, but she knew she couldn't stop for a drink.

The moments ticked on. The women continued to work. Trude, Timmie, and Susannah tore apart the Arbuthnot wagons. A hundred feet away, Billie paced among the tied-up men, his rifle aimed in their faces.

Beneath the floor of the wagon bed, Emerald did find another false wall, and she pried it apart with a chisel. Inside, she found a pouch wrapped in oilcloth. She pulled it open with shaking fingers. It held silver coins and bills, Ben's savings. And there was a small miniature painting, framed in gold leaf, wrapped in tissue paper, of a dark-haired girl with large, brown eyes. Ben's wife?

Zelig shoved her aside and grabbed the pouch of money. The miniature fell to the ground, and Zelig kicked it aside.

"This may not be exactly the kind of gold we're lookin' for," he laughed, "but I ain't choosy. Money is money, ain't it?" He poured out all the coins and bills and deposited them in his own pocket.

"Em! Em, have you found anything yet?" It was Timmie, slipping past Zelig to tug at her sleeve. The boy's hair was rumpled, and a smudge of white flour clung to his cheek.

"No. Have you?"

"Nope. Red Arbuthnot, he had some money. And a couple of rings and a brooch. That's all. Billie took 'em." Timmie's voice was matter-of-fact. "They had some pockets sewed on the inside of the canvas," he added. "There wasn't anything much in 'em, though. I guess they didn't have the gold."

"Well . . ." Emerald stifled her stab of disappointment. "We must keep looking, Timmie. Look under the wagon. Look everywhere! Pretend we're playing a game, Timmie, and that it's pirate's treasure we're looking for!"

Timmie's eyes sparkled, and Emerald knew that she had said the right thing. She watched him hurry off and was glad that he didn't sense just how deadly serious this game was.

She explored every corner of the false floor, then began to go through all the supplies. She knelt on the ground outside the wagon and rummaged through blankets, quilts, barrels, pots, pans.

"Ain't you found anything yet?" Zelig demanded.

"No, but we will. If it's here, we'll find it."

"You'd better." He licked his lips, and Emerald turned away from him in disgust.

At last she had to admit that Ben's wagon held no gold. She turned toward where Trude was working.

"Nothing here," the blond girl called. Smears of grease from the tar bucket that hung at the rear of the wagon stained Trude's skirt.

On impulse, Emerald began to walk down the dry, sagebrush-covered slope where the men were tied. Billie lounged alertly near them, his rifle cocked and ready, as if he were only waiting for someone to move.

"Hey, girl!" Zelig shouted as she left. "What are you goin' down there for?"

"I only want to talk to them. You'll have to take the gags out of their mouths."

"Talk? What for?"

"So I can ask them where the gold is," she said sarcastically. "That's the reason for all of this, isn't it?"

She stood waiting as Zelig walked down and untied the gags, while Billie watched. Red Arbuthnot was first. Almost as soon as the cloth was jerked away,

Red spat on the ground and released a stream of obscenities, his light-blue eyes snapping.

"You bastards! Jumping us like a pair of coyotes! You let us go or I swear I'm goin'—"

"You're goin' to do what, old man? You ain't doin' nothing, or I'm going to kill you right now. Hear that?" Like a rattler moving, Billie suddenly stood in front of Red, jamming the rifle barrel almost in his teeth. Red gulped, swallowed, and fell abruptly silent.

When the gag was taken from Mace's face, Emerald wanted to cry out, for his lower lip was swollen and bloody, his cheek gashed. He must have fought hard before being tied.

"Mace, your lip! Are you all right? Are you—"

But he shook his head, warning her to be quiet.

"Oh, he isn't hurt much," Billie said. "I hit him with a gun butt, is all. Now, go on, girl. Ask your questions. And tell them what's going to happen to you if we don't find that gold bar."

"All right." Quickly Emerald told them, making her words blunt and to the point. Most of the men, she saw, already understood the situation. But young Bob Rigney looked shocked. And Ben Coult squirmed in his ropes and would not look at her. She knew that he didn't really care what happened to her. He would risk nothing to help her.

When she had finished, Mace said, "Any man who knows where that gold brick is had better speak up now. Anyone who has it and is keeping quiet is more of a fool than I'd thought. Corpses don't have much fun spending money. Think on it."

They thought, and stirred restlessly. Pieert Vande-Busch muttered to himself, his face slick with perspiration. But no one said anything. There was only the sound of the water in the river, flowing over rocks near the banks, and the noises coming from the wagons as Trude and the other women continued their search.

"Emerald . . ."

The whisper was so low that Emerald could hardly hear it. But Mace was looking at her, his eyes gray and clear.

"Emerald, I—"

"Bridgeman! Enough blabbing, or you'll get this gun between your teeth."

"No, thanks, I wouldn't relish it," Mace said lightly.

"You wouldn't attract the ladies none without them pretty front teeth of your'n." Zelig gave a loud cackle.

Mace laughed low in his throat. It was a hard, angry sound. The muscles of his forearms were corded against the greasy rope that tied him, and Emerald knew that if he hadn't been tied up, he would have killed Zelig.

"No, I guess I wouldn't, at that," was all he said, however.

Emerald, after giving Mace one last, desperate look, stumbled back up the bare slope to the wagons.

Where was the gold brick? And what were they going to do if they couldn't find it?

Chapter Thirty-eight

❧ ❧

WOLF Dreamer was thirsty. His horse had died in the worst of the desert land, just before he reached the hot springs. Now he staggered along on foot, moving toward the horizon, where, he knew, the river waited.

His arm still festered and throbbed. His body felt overheated, like a strip of meat drying to jerky in the sun.

Long ago he had stopped wondering why he was doing this. If there was blood lust in him, he no longer felt it. He no longer thought of Green-eyed Woman. He did not dream anymore; he did not consciously think of anything.

He walked, nothing more. One foot, then another.

The sun had been up two hours. At his feet he could see the corpse of an ox, desiccated in the sun.

Wolf Dreamer paused, sniffing the dry wind with his finely carved, sensitive nostrils. Was that the dank smell of water?

He trudged a few paces farther. Yes, he decided. He was nearing the river. He could picture it in his mind, the clear water flowing and eddying, lapping at green banks. He let the picture of it merge and grow and fill his thoughts.

The river. He would keep going until he reached the river. Beyond that, he would no longer think.

Another hour had passed, a tense time spent searching the remaining wagons. To Emerald's intense relief, Geertrud had been given permission to feed Cal. The baby fed avidly, but Geertrud's hand, holding the makeshift bottle, trembled.

Billie had not objected when Emerald began to search his own wagon. He had only looked at Zelig. Billie Colfax trusted no one.

The sun seared their shoulders and necks. Zelig was never far from Emerald; he watched her constantly. But she carried on with her work as best she could, trying to ignore him. Zelig, she told herself, was a problem she would face later.

Twice Zelig had dragged all the women into the central area between the wagons and searched them for weapons, running his hands with obvious zest over their thighs and buttocks and breasts. Even Susannah had received this treatment. If he caught any of them hiding a gun or a knife, he said, he would shoot her.

The women had all glanced at each other, and Emerald's and Trude's eyes had again met.

They continued to root through the wagons with increasing desperation, covering ground they had already searched.

"Emerald," Trude whispered. "I wonder if it's even here."

"It's got to be here."

"But where? Where? Suppose it's been buried along the trail somewhere? Suppose we never find it."

"We've got to keep looking, that's all."

Emerald resumed her work with shaking hands. Zelig was growing impatient. Each time she came near him, his eyes seemed to fasten on her more lustfully. Eventually he intended to have his way, she feared.

As if to feed her worries, Zelig's complaints about their progress grew louder and more frequent. "Well, girl? I thought you said you women knew every inch and cranny of these here wagons. Don't look like it to me."

"We—we do. We'll find it. All we need is time."

"Yeah? More time. Well, it seems to me we ain't got all that much time."

"Please," she begged desperately. "We'll locate it. I promise we will."

She stood staring at the wagons in bafflement. They were grouped askew, wherever they had been when their drivers had finally unyoked the teams. As far as she knew, they had covered every inch of them, inside and out. They had peered in every piece of equipment, in every barrel and trunk and box. They had looked under wagon beds and in secret compartments and pockets.

But they had found nothing.

Trude climbed out of Ben's wagon, pushing her sunbonnet back, her eyes weary. "I haven't found anything," she told Emerald in a low voice. "I don't know how many times I've been over the wagons, all of them. It just isn't there. I guess you were wrong."

"I haven't found anything, either," Emerald admitted. Her body sagged with disappointment. They had done their best, yet their efforts had been fruitless. Perhaps Trude was right, and the thief had hidden the gold brick along the trail, marking it and hoping to return for it later. If so, they would never find it.

Trude wiped her hand nervously on her frayed

cotton dress, and Emerald again noticed her tar-stained skirt. "The tar buckets," she said. "We haven't looked in them. At least I haven't. Have you?"

"Tar buckets? But I— Who would—"

They stared at each other. Then they ran toward the rear of Ben's wagon. Because the oil was so precious and could not be replaced, Emerald grabbed an empty pail and poured the oil into it.

To her disappointment, the thick, viscous unpleasant-looking liquid revealed nothing.

"The other wagons," Trude said. "Hurry!"

They found the gold bar in Wyatt Thatcher's wagon. As Emerald tipped out the oil, the bar fell into her pail, still wrapped in cloth but coated now with thick oil.

Emerald stared down at the black, ugly, greasy rectangle for which a man had been killed, for which they had all been held at riflepoint these hours. How ugly it was, she thought. And what would happen now to Wyatt? To all of them?

Two hours later, the brassy, glittering sun hung over the tops of the cottonwoods. Emerald, now tied to a tree near Mace, felt as if they had been here by the Truckee for a lifetime now, instead of only a few short hours.

So much had happened. First had come the terrible moment when Zelig and Billie had turned to Wyatt Thatcher. The little bandy-legged man had squirmed in fright, his skin pale and covered with sweat.

"I—I didn't mean no harm," he insisted. "I woulda told you about it, honest I would."

Why, they demanded, had he done it? Who did he think he was? And what had he intended to do with the gold?

"I—I don't know. . . ." Wyatt was like a child caught robbing candy. His cockiness had evaporated, leaving only a scrawny, frightened little man. "I just found it, is all. So I hid it."

"Just found it, eh?" Zelig had roared, saliva flying from his mouth. "Lookin' in our wagon, were you? And how'd you know we was carrying gold, anyway?"

"I knew you had *something*. The way you was guardin' that there wagon, like you had the crown jewels in it or somethin'. And then I got to thinking. See, I'd heard about that robbery in Chicago, and read the papers about it, too. The gold bullion that was taken. And I waited my chance, and I thought, Well, why not? They left Chicago awful sudden, didn't they? And they never wrote no letters, not even when they got the chance. So, I thought, why not give it a try? And after I'd got rid of the dog—"

"Our dog? You got rid of Blackie?" Billie's eyes turned colder.

"I— The mutt was goin' to drink the alkali water, anyway. I saw him, and I just didn't stop him, is all. I wouldn't kill no animal, not a dog. I'm not that kind of man. But I—I needed the money," Wyatt pleaded. "A man has to eat, don't he? I figured you wouldn't miss just one bar. You had nine of 'em, see—I'd read that in the paper—so I figured you wouldn't even know the diffcrence." He went on, "I'm aimin' to set me up a gambling house somewheres in California, maybe in San Francisco, with a little faro, some keno and blackjack, a respectable place, you know. But I didn't have no capital—"

Billie kicked Wyatt in the mouth. Wyatt, tied hand and foot, fell back, his body convulsed. Teeth flew out in white bits, and blood ran from his mouth.

"Oh, please," Emerald cried. "The man is helpless! You can't hurt him like that—"

"Shut up," Billie said.

"If I were free—" Mace began, struggling again, his face savage.

"But you ain't free, are you, now?" Zelig swung his rifle at Mace. "You're trussed up like a chicken, you are, the great trail guide and mountain man Mace Bridgeman. And surrounded by a lot of chickens and pansies, all of 'em, who couldn't fight back even if they tried. Wonder how you're goin' to feel by tomorrow, eh? Still tied up and all? When the sun comes up again and you ain't had nothin' to eat or drink?"

Mace and Emerald looked at each other. His face had whitened, and Emerald knew her own must have done the same.

She should have known. Zelig and Billie planned to tie them all up and leave. They would take whatever supplies and animals they wanted.

The others were stunned, but Emerald found her voice. "You—you wouldn't dare do such a thing! It's monstrous. Why, we'd all starve to death."

"It's not starvation that will take us, Emerald," Mace said bitterly. "It's thirst. And that will kill us damned fast."

Emerald looked at the river, flowing so close to them, beautiful and shaded through the trees. "Thirst! But—but what about Cal? Who will feed him? And who will untie us?"

Mace was silent.

Zelig threw back his head and laughed again. "Maybe the Injuns, who knows? They might find you. Or maybe another wagon train might happen by," he jeered. "Then we wouldn't have you on our consciences, would we?"

"I don't think our deaths would disturb your conscience in the least!" Emerald snapped. A dulled, helpless anger filled her.

We're going to die, she thought. The desert will kill us. And Zelig and Billie will go on to California, to spend their gold and do as they please.

"The baby," she said. "If Cal doesn't get his milk, he'll die."

"We'll leave him the milch cow," Zelig said roughly.

"But what good is the cow if we're all tied up and we can't—"

"Don't beg, Emerald." Mace's words were low and hard. "They plan to kill us, and you're not going to change their minds. So don't try."

"But—"

"I said, be still. Let them go about their business." *And don't provoke them,* she knew he meant. *Or you'll only make our situation worse.*

She forced herself to remain silent. It was the hardest thing she had ever done, to stand there and watch as the women and children were tied to the thinnertrunked trees or to wagon wheels. Katje wept steadily, her face reddened and ugly. Geertrud was white, and Martha Rigney submitted numbly.

The men, for the most part, were silent. Ben Coult did not once look Emerald's way. *Coward!* she wanted to scream at him. But what did it matter now? They would all be dead soon enough.

Timmie Wylie was the only one who showed any fight. The instant Zelig came near him, the boy began to struggle. He kicked Zelig with his wooden foot, and the big man yelped with pain.

"Hey! What are you doing, you little bastard? You lie still or I'll shoot you right here and now!"

"No, you damn bastard yourself! You damn stupid

dog-killing bastard!" But the resistance went out of Timmie, and Zelig tied him tightly.

Susannah was next. Tied up, she looked small and white and frightened, far too fragile for the greasy, thick hemp that bound her. Contemptuously, Zelig shoved Cal's wicker basket with his foot, pushing the baby closer to Susannah. Cal wailed.

Emerald swallowed hard. She was the only one left untied.

"Well," Zelig said, "just one thing I ain't done yet. One thing I mean to do before we leave."

He looked at Emerald.

The blood left her face, and she swayed. Any minute now she would collapse. She looked at Mace and saw his tightly pressed lips, the anguish of his expression. Were his lips moving? *Darling. Darling.*

"I said, come on, girl, or I'll rip that dress off'n you right now. How would you like that?"

Emerald heard Zelig, but the words no longer made any sense to her. They were only noise, rough noise. She heard Trude whisper behind her. "You'll have to go with him, Emerald. Don't fight it. Just close your eyes, and it will be over in no time."

Emerald stared blankly at the blond girl. She had hated Trude once, had blamed her for taking Mace. How long ago that all seemed now.

"I said, come on, dammit!" Zelig jerked her arm.

Chapter Thirty-nine

❧☙

AN hour later, Zelig brought her back and tied her to a small cottonwood. Then he and Billie left.

"Emerald," Mace whispered, "talk to me. Are you all right? When I saw him take you away—"

"Yes. I'm all right."

"Are you sure?"

"Yes." She said it bleakly. She felt the ropes cutting into her wrists and hung her head. She felt so ashamed, so dirty. All of them knew what had happened to her! She wished she could die.

Mace's voice hammered at her, harsh, savage. "Then stop looking so woebegone, dammit! You were taken by force. So? It's happened to women before; it'll happen again. You're strong. You'll survive it."

She raised her head and looked at him. "How can you say that? How can you *possibly*—"

"I said, stop looking so shamed. You did nothing wrong. You did what you had to." His voice was angry. She twisted in her ropes, feeling as if he had dashed icy water over her.

"But I—"

Mace's chin lifted. His lips were dry and cracked,

461

but his mouth was a grim, straight line. "Are you going to waste time feeling sorry for yourself, Emerald Regan, or are we going to spend some time thinking how to get out of this?"

"I'm not feeling sorry for myself!"

"Then act like it. Put your mind to thinking. We don't have long."

Emerald glanced at Cal. She knew what he meant. Cal had been whimpering for some time now. He was tired and wet and hungry. Soon he would begin crying in earnest. It would be torture to lie here, bound hand and foot, and listen to the baby cry.

She began struggling against the ropes that tied her wrists behind her back. The hemp dug into her wrists. Her knuckles scraped against the rough tree bark. Zelig had tied her too tightly, and already her fingers felt numb.

Zelig and Billie had been gone nearly half an hour. They had taken a coffle of six horses with them, and saddlebags laden with food and water, as much as they could carry. Mace's portfolio lay now in the sand where they had tossed it. Unencumbered by wagons, they would be able to cross the Sierras quickly.

Good riddance, Emerald thought savagely. She hoped their horses all broke their legs. She hoped they got lost in the mountains, or were snowed in like the Donners. She hoped they both died—of thirst.

She shook her head, trying to erase the pictures that tormented her. Zelig, lunging at her, shoving her into the shallows and using her there. She shivered with disgust. But at least she had managed, after his lust was spent, to scoop up a handful of sweet water and gulp it down.

Zelig, watching her, had laughed. With a quick motion he had adjusted his trousers. "That's right, girl. Drink your fill. You'll need it!"

She had turned from him. "Could I carry some water back to the others?"

"Hell, no. What for?"

"But they're thirsty. They—"

"Just shut up. What do they matter?" Zelig had hesitated, then added regretfully, "For two cents, I'd take you along with me. A woman like you—damned shame to leave you out for the buzzards. A shame and a waste."

But he had said nothing more about it. And Emerald, wading out of the water with her dress wet and clinging to her body, had barely listened to him, anyway. Go with Zelig? She wouldn't even think of such a thing. She didn't want to be the only one spared. If Mace were to die, if Timmie and Susannah and Cal were to die, then she didn't want to live, either.

But now Zelig and Billie were gone, and the emigrants waited to die.

"Em," Susannah croaked. "I'm thirsty."

"We all are, Susie. But you'll just have to wait a bit, until—until we can think how to get ourselves out of these ropes."

"I don't think we can get out." The child squirmed, looking smaller and more fragile than ever inside the thick, fat rope that bound her.

"Hush, Susie," Timmie said in his big-brother way. "We'll think of something. You'll see."

"Of course," Emerald said. But she knew no one would come to free them. The land was empty. There was only the sun, the sagebrush, the river. And if Zelig had tied the others as tightly as he had her, there was no chance any of them could get loose.

They had certainly been trying, all of them, ever since the two men had disappeared in a cloud of whitish dust. Even Ben Coult had emerged from his lethargy to strain at the greasy ropes that bound him.

"Pull, dammit," Mace told them. "Pull for your lives. Perhaps one of the ropes has been frayed. Or you can find something sharp to rub it against. If an animal can chew its own hind leg off and escape a beaver trap, we humans ought to be able to manage, too."

On and on Mace's voice went, encouraging, ordering, exhorting, scolding. And frantically Emerald tried. She strained and rubbed until her wrists were raw and bloody. The others, too, were doing the same thing. Trude's face was white and perspiring with effort. Even Wyatt, blood running in gouts down his chin, worked frantically.

But still the ropes held, the knots like welded iron.

"Rub!" Mace shouted. "Rub against the tree bark! Sooner or later it'll fray!"

Time passed. The sun began to sink, a red, molten ball at the edge of the horizon. Katje was crying again. And Martha Rigney grunted softly as she labored, the ugly, rawboned face focused inward in concentration.

Cal, in his basket, cried furiously, his face red. His fists and feet jerked. His wail was an insistent scream of hunger and thirst.

"Em," Susannah said. "Cal is hungry. He wants his milk."

Emerald swallowed. "I—I know, honey."

The little girl's voice rose. "But who's going to feed him, Em? Who's going to milk Bossie?"

"Nobody, unless we get loose." Mace's words were flat. He seemed to look at the child as if for the first time. "You look like a little sparrow, Susannah," he said thoughtfully. "So little—your wrists look like bird bones. Can you wriggle loose, child?"

"I—I don't think so."

"Twist about," he ordered. "See if you can slide the rope up and down your wrist. See if you can make it slip off."

There was a long, tense silence while Susannah did as she was bid, her mouth set. Once she cried out from pain. Emerald thought of the little girl she had first seen in Saint Louis, clinging to her mother's leg. How long ago that had been. And now Susannah was five, and facing death.

The little girl struggled, and Cal screamed.

Emerald wished she could stop up her ears. *Please,* she prayed raggedly. *Please, help us— Help all of us—*

Wolf Dreamer reached the river to the north of the emigrants, as he had planned.

He drank his fill and bathed, soaking his festering wound in the healing water. Then he filled his water bladder and walked along the riverbank toward the wagon train.

A magpie squawked raucously. Insects clattered in the dry air. The sun was sinking.

Soon, Wolf Dreamer thought, he would find the white men he had followed for so long. He would lie in wait until dawn. Then he would attack and do what had to be done. He would move fast, and he would count many *coup*. Perhaps he would take hostages, and perhaps he would not.

A picture of Green-eyed Woman came to him, and his excitement began to intensify. His gut sang like a quivering flute. He felt as he always did on the hunt, when the quarry has been sighted. Tight. Breathless. Waiting.

And then he saw the two men in a boiling cloud of whitish dust. Wolf Dreamer moved behind a cotton-wood, instinctively pulling his old rifle out of its beaded deerskin cover and getting out his powder horn and balls. There were two men, he saw, leading four more horses behind them. The horses were all loaded heavily.

The men slowed. They seemed to be arguing about something. One of them, the big, barrel-chested one, was gesturing to the other. The second man, taller, thinner, scowled.

The horses slowed to a walk, as the men still argued. The bearded one, it appeared, wanted to go back to the wagon train. What had he left behind? Wolf Dreamer wondered. His favorite rifle?

Wolf Dreamer lifted his own weapon, assessing the six horses. The animals looked like fine ones, a bit worn down, perhaps, but a good rest would remedy that. And he needed a mount.

He stuffed in a charge of powder, putting extra balls into his mouth. He could fire and reload his rifle at full gallop, carrying the balls in his mouth and spitting them into the muzzle. His aim was good, too. He had practiced often.

He aimed the rifle at the big-chested, bearded one, who was still gesturing at his companion. He pulled the trigger and had the satisfaction of seeing the big man fall backward on the saddle.

Now you won't be going back to camp, Wolf Dreamer thought. The big man hung in the saddle for a moment. Then, like a doll, he fell. His ankle was caught and held in a stirrup, and his horse dragged him for a number of feet, already dead.

As soon as Wolf Dreamer fired, the other rider wheeled and raised his rifle. Wolf Dreamer pulled himself farther into the shadow of the cottonwood. One more, he exulted. One more white man.

Quickly he reloaded the ancient gun. He raised it and fired.

The other man fired back.

Wolf Dreamer did not see if his own ball had reached the mark, for an enormous pressure exploded in his belly, cutting like a hundred hunting knives.

He looked down and saw the red gushing out, the purple-white of entrails. And then, just before the blackness came and took him, he realized that all his dreams had been for one reason only. And Green-eyed Woman was but a part of that purpose, a means to that end. He had dreamed his own death. He had sought his own oblivion.

The darkness closed over his eyes like a thick buffalo hide.

"I—I can't get the ropes loose!" Susannah wept. "Oh, Em, I can't! It hurts me so."

"But you've got to try. You must."

"I am trying, I *am,* and I can't—"

Suddenly the expression of effort on Susannah's face changed to astonished surprise. "My hand's loose," she said wonderingly. She brought it around in front of her and stared at it.

"Get the other one loose, Susannah," Mace said.

The little girl twisted, her shoulders moving awkwardly. Long seconds passed. They were all waiting.

"I can't."

"Yes, you can. You've got to. You're the only one who's been able to get free. You must keep trying."

"I *am* trying! I am!"

467

Such a small girl, Emerald thought. A child who could not yet button her dress evenly. And now she was being expected to manage knots tied by a strong man, knots meant to hold.

"Harder, Susannah," Mace said. "Harder!"

"I *am*. I— Oh!" The child's eyes filled with tears. They overflowed and ran down her cheeks. "Em, I'm so tired. I can't try anymore. I can't."

"All right, Susie." Emerald tried to keep her voice calm and reassuring. "Why don't you stop and rest for a minute, then? We have plenty of time. We aren't in such a big hurry as that."

They waited while Susannah's narrow little body slumped down in the ropes, her free hand wiping perspiration off her forehead.

"Make your wrist slippery, Susie," Mace said suddenly. "Spit on it."

Susannah looked up. Obediently, she brought her hand to her mouth and spit.

"That's it," Mace said. "Rub it on your other wrist. Rub—"

Susannah rubbed. For a moment her eyes lit up with a brief, rare smile and she said, "It isn't nice to spit. Ma told me."

In spite of her anxiety, Emerald managed a smile. "In this case, I think you can spit and remain a lady."

The little girl didn't answer. Her face was twisted with effort. Then, slowly, uncertainly, she brought her left hand out. "I did it! Em, I did it!"

"Good," Mace said. "Now I want you to slip loose and go into Ben's wagon and see if you can find one of his doctor's knives. Then come back and give it to me. Carry it carefully. Hold the point downward, and don't trip."

Susannah ran skipping off toward Ben's wagon.

"God was with us," Geertrud said, her voice catching. "He was near. I'm sure of it."

Within half an hour, all of them were freed, and Emerald fell into Mace's arms.

"Darling . . . darling . . ." She wept convulsively.

"Emerald, it's over now. We're all alive. Thanks to your courage, and Susannah's." He stroked her hair, her cheeks and temples, infinitely tenderly.

"A-alive," she wept. "But—"

"Hush, little green eyes. Don't talk about that now. To me, Emerald, you'll always be shining and sweet and new, and nothing can ever change that. Not the Forty-Mile Desert and especially not Zelig York or Ben Coult. I love you, Emerald. I always will."

Dusk settled, fragrant with water smells, with the scent of sage and dried grasses. Emerald and Mace sat together on the riverbank, his arm about her. She clung to him, delighting in his clean, wonderful, masculine scent. She felt as if she could not get enough of looking at him, touching him, kissing him.

They had found Bossie and fed Cal. They had drunk long, sweet drafts of river water. They had attended to Wyatt Thatcher's severe lip gash and broken teeth, and to other minor injuries. They had bathed in the river, all of them. Now Trude, humming, was preparing a meal from the remaining supplies not taken by Zelig and Billie.

It was like a miracle, Emerald thought, and somehow a new spirit united the emigrants. Matt Arbuthnot talked quietly with his father and brother, arms about them. Pieert and Wyatt Thatcher helped Timmie gather wood. Martha Rigney even seemed different now, softer. She had smiled tentatively at Emerald. Only Ben did not share this new spirit. He avoided

Emerald, deliberately ignoring her. He had not spoken to her since they had been untied.

"Emerald——" Mace ran a fingertip over the contours of her cheek, touching her tenderly, possessively. A few feet away from them, the water lapped. "Emerald, if you knew how I've wanted this, longed for this. To sit here with you——"

She thought of Ben, and reluctantly pulled back from him. "But—my husband. Ben. I shouldn't be here with you, Mace. I haven't any right."

"Emerald, *he* hasn't any right, and I think he knows it now. Your marriage to him wasn't legal. You signed no papers. And your ceremony was performed by a felon, a thief and murderer. How could that possibly be lawful, either in the eyes of God or of man?"

"But——"

"Are you afraid of him, darling? Don't be. I guarantee you he'll give no trouble now. And as soon as we get back to civilization, Emerald, he'll have no power over you, because I'm going to marry you—for real."

"Marry me?" she repeated stupidly.

Mace fondled her curls, still damp and tousled from the river. His laugh was a low, easy chuckle in his throat. "Yes, darling. Marry you. I think I've always loved you, ever since that moment I saw you in the river at Council Bluffs looking so beautiful and fiery and innocent and angry. Oh, I knew then that you were the woman for me. And I spent nearly two thousand miles trying to escape that inevitability. I tried to fight it—God, how I fought it. All the way along the trail, and even with——"

"—with Trude," she finished for him. But now she felt no anger for the other girl. She felt only pity, for

Trude did not have Mace's real love, and never would.

"But—" She hesitated, then stammered out the words. "I thought you said you weren't the marrying kind. You said you didn't want a wife!"

He threw back his head and laughed. "God knows, I said I didn't want one." He reached for her and enfolded her in his arms. "Darling, it won't be very easy for you—I'm a wanderer, and my work will always be very important to me. But we can try, can't we? I —I've got to spend my life with you, Emerald. No matter what it costs. I never want to suffer another moment like the one when I came back and found you married. Or had to watch Zelig York taking you away—"

For an instant Mace's eyes shone with the old fierceness. Then, slowly, he relaxed and kissed her.

"Yes." Emerald sighed, nestling in his arms. "Oh, yes."

They continued to sit by the river, listening to the sounds it made, feeling easy with each other. Later, Emerald knew, there would be time to think ahead to the future. What would become of the Wylie children? Timmie might grow up to become a rancher, or per- haps even governor of the new territory. Susannah would become one of the new, strong women the country would need. Or maybe—Emerald smiled to herself—she would become governor. What of little Cal? Of Trude and all the others?

Maybe she and Mace would settle by the azure- blue lake in the Sierras Mace had once spoken of, the lake twenty miles long and as beautiful as a piece of sky.

Much struggle lay ahead, she knew. They must fight to make it across the jagged Sierra peaks before the snows set in. They must find Timmie and Susannah's uncle—if he existed. But the Wylie children would always have a place in her heart. And in her home, wherever it might be.

Yes, the journey ahead would be hard. But somehow that didn't seem important at this moment. For now there was only the Truckee, splashing over stones, shaded by rustling trees, a haven after the desert.

She was with Mace. It was enough.